The Kicking the Bucket List

Cathy lives in Bath with her husband and three cats. In her spare time she is happiest digging, planting or reading in the garden or on a walk with friends in the local country-side – usually ending in a pub. For more about Cathy, you can find her on Twitter, Facebook and on her website.

@CathyHopkins1
/cathy.hopkins
www.cathyhopkins.com/

The Kicking the Bucket List

the

CATHY HOPKINS

HARPER

Harper
An imprint of HarperCollins*Publishers*
The News Building,
1 London Bridge Street,
London SE1 9GF

A Paperback Original 2017
1

www.harpercollins.co.uk

A catalogue record for this book
is available from the British Library

ISBN: 978-0-00-820067-1

Set in Birka by Palimpsest Book Production Limited,
Falkirk, Stirlingshire

Printed and bound in Great Britain by
Clays Ltd, St Ives plc

MIX
Paper from
responsible sources
FSC™ C007454

For Mum

1

Tuesday 1 September

The offices of Wilson Richardson solicitors were on the first floor in a block on the main road through Chiswick in London. The carpeted stairs smelt musty and I noted that the reception area on the first floor was in need of a lick of paint. Rose, my neat, petite sister, was already there, not a hair of her dark bob out of place and still dressed in black though it was almost eight weeks since Mum had died. I'd decided against funereal clothes and, it being a warm September day, had dressed in grey trousers and a pale green kaftan top. We were spared the awkwardness of our meeting because we barely had time to greet each other or sit before we were ushered into Mr Richardson's office by a receptionist with blonde hair pulled back severely from her forehead. My youngest sister, Fleur, used to call the style the Dagenham facelift, back in the days when we were still speaking to each other.

A tall, bald man with glasses was seated behind a heavy oak desk. 'Mr Richardson,' he said.

'I'm Rose and this is Dee. You may have her written down in your papers as Daisy,' said Rose.

'I am here and can speak for myself,' I said.

Rose sighed. 'Go ahead then. I was only being helpful. Your two names can be confusing for people.'

I focused on Mr Richardson. 'I'm Daisy, Dee. Most people call me Dee but my mother liked to call me Daisy.'

'As I said,' said Rose.

Well this is a great start, I thought, as the solicitor gestured to three chairs that had been placed opposite the desk for the reading of Mum's will. 'Please, have a seat,' he said.

'My sister Fleur will be with us shortly,' said Rose as she sat down.

'She's always late. She'll be late for her own funeral,' I said, then half coughed and cursed myself.

As we waited, I felt as if I was back at school and had been called in to see the headmaster. I wanted to get the reading over with and get home. Rose's left foot was twitching so I reckoned she was feeling the same. She was the most in-control person I had ever known, but that foot gave her away; it always had, as if she wanted to be up, out and anywhere else. Out and away from me, away from Fleur, I imagined.

I don't know about her life at all any more, I thought as Rose checked her watch. *I wonder if she's happy. How are she and Hugh getting on? What will she do with her share of the inheritance, and does she need it as badly as I do? Probably not.*

We already knew that Mum would have left us equal shares of her money; she'd told us all years ago. The house in Hampstead, where we grew up, had belonged to Dad's parents back in the 1950s and Mum and Dad had inherited it when they died. Victorian, four bedroomed and near the Heath, it had accumulated in value over the years. Mum did shabby chic before it was trendy, and the house had an old-fashioned charm about it, with original features, fireplaces and wooden floors so, despite being in need of modernization (the estate agent's word for falling down) and the ancient plumbing and life-endangering electrics, it still went for just over two million when Mum sold it and moved to a retirement village. My share would be more than enough to sort out my finances, have a good pension pot and some to help my daughter, Lucy if she needed it. *No substitute for having Mum here, though*, I thought as a wave of grief at her loss, still so raw, hit me.

We didn't have to wait long. Five minutes later, the receptionist ushered Fleur in. Her skin was brown and her hair a sun-kissed blonde as if she'd been away. She had also decided against black and was dressed in a crepe summer dress with tiny coral and cream flowers and red kitten heels that looked like they cost a bomb. I tucked my scuffed M&S loafers under my chair as Mr Richardson indicated that Fleur should take the empty seat.

'Traffic was awful . . . ' she began but didn't continue when Rose sighed heavily to express her disapproval. Part of Rose's anal personality was that she was obsessively punctual and disapproved of anyone who wasn't on time. Fleur must have realized that we'd heard it all before, even if it was a long time ago. She took a seat with a brief nod to me.

Mr Richardson cleared his throat and picked up some papers from his desk. 'So let's get on, shall we? Your late mother, Iris Parker, instructed me to invite you all here today. She left her will, which I'll get to, but she asked that I read a letter to you first. Shall I go ahead?'

Rose glanced at Fleur and me. 'Letter? When was it written?' she asked. She was clearly put out that she didn't know about this. *Hah*, I thought, *good*. Though I hadn't known about it either.

'April of this year,' Mr Richardson replied.

'Three months before she died,' Rose commented.

Mr Richardson nodded. 'That would be about right. Shall I begin?'

'Please,' said Rose. *Answering for all of us*, I thought. *Nothing ever changes.*

Mr Richardson began to read.

'"My dearest girls, for girls are what you will always be to me.

'"I'm writing a few things I want you to know when I am gone.

'"First of all, remember me but don't be sad. I've grown weary of late and am ready to go and be with your father, who I am sure will be waiting for me. Remember me but think of me with you as I used to be when I was in better health and let those memories bring you comfort.

'"Secondly, don't feel guilty about my last chapter. It's a waste of time. I tried to tell you all but you were all so wrapped up in it that I don't think you heard. Guilt is an indulgence and – like anger – it eats away at you. Let it go. Hear what I have to say next and take it in. I was happy to go to the retirement village. I made good friends there, had good care and maintained my independence, which was important to me. Much as I love you, I think we'd have driven each other mad if I'd come to live with any of you. We're all grown women and each have our own way of doing things. To sell the family home and move was my choice. Mine. I'd outgrown that lovely old house in Hampstead. It was way too much for me to manage. I wanted to simplify my life and my responsibilities and had felt that way for some years. So despite all your thoughts about my best interests and where you thought I should have been, let it go. I was where I wanted to be.

"'Daisy, you especially. What would I have done in Cornwall? I don't know anyone down there, apart from you. It would have been like living in a foreign country for me, and I'd have missed my dear Jean and never have met Martha, who has become such a good friend these last few years. It turned out for the best.

"'As I write this, I don't know when I'll go or which of you will be with me, if any of you so I wanted to say, so all of you can hear this and take it in, that most of us can't choose the time or circumstances of our passing. Don't feel bad if you don't make it to my side. I have a lifetime of memories with each of you, as you do of me. Remember and cherish those and don't cling on to my final weeks or months. They are only part of my journey. Remember the whole. I've had a good and full life. Let me go. Just as with birth, none of us can predict how the end will be. Remember, Daisy, you had your plans for a home birth with Lucy. You had the birthing pool, your CD of that god-awful music with dolphins squeaking in the background (heaven knows how that was supposed to relax you) and your aromatherapy oils, and Andy was supposed to be there to support you and rub your back. Hah. Remember? Then you had to have a Caesarean in a hospital and not a dolphin in sight. Rose, you'd planned it all too, practical as ever, and booked into that lovely private hospital – and what happened? You gave birth in the back of a taxi. I wonder if the driver ever recovered."'

I glanced at Rose. This was the perfect moment for us to acknowledge each other and our past with some affection, but she kept her eyes on Mr Richardson, her back and posture stiff.

'"Whatever got us down here when we were born,"' Mr Richardson continued reading, '"will get us out; but, like with birth, it might not be the smooth transition or perfect time we have planned or hoped for. I believe some force or power will be there to guide me out just as it guided me in. So don't worry if you're not with me, or stress over the circumstances if it appeared to be a bumpy exit. When it's my time, it will be my time.

'"Remember I love you and am proud of you all, my dear independent, individual flowers. Be proud of who you are and what you've achieved and don't compare yourself to each other. Each flower has its own beauty. Know that and be who you are. Be yourself.

'"And so, I know you will have come expecting to hear my will. As I always said, whatever I had will be divided equally. No arguments. I know Fleur that you're comfortably off but circumstances in life can change. The rich become poor, the poor become rich. And Daisy, you never know, an agent might discover your wonderful paintings, sign you up and make you a fortune. And Rose, you and Hugh have your jobs and your family and might not feel you need the inheritance that I will leave, but it is yours by right. Long before your father died, we had agreed. Everything we have will be divided equally between you, a third each. But not until a year after my death."'

'A year?' I gasped.

Mr Richardson looked up. 'Do you need a moment?'

'Did you say a year?' I asked. 'From now?'

Mr Richardson nodded. 'Yes.'

I groaned inwardly. Unlike Rose and Fleur, I was struggling to make ends meet, work teaching art was sparse where I lived and the sales of my paintings had decreased, mainly due to the fact that I'd felt uninspired of late.

'Shall I continue?' asked Mr Richardson.

Rose gave a curt nod.

'Please,' we chorused.

Mr Richardson went back to the letter.

'"In that year, I have something I want you all to do. A condition of my will. I've thought about this long and hard and am acting in your best interests, although you might not believe me at first."' Mr Richardson looked up at us. I stole another glance at my sisters. Rose's expression was tight, Fleur's curious. Mr Richardson rustled the papers on his desk, then began to read again.

'"Dear ones, my friends, Martha and Jean, and I all know we are in our last chapters. We talk about it a lot. What we've done with our lives, what we believe about death. Some of the elderly people here at the village talk about bucket lists – what they would have liked to have done if they'd had the time, or what they managed to do before they had to come and live here. I've had a happy and full life. I got to do everything I wanted. I had no need of a bucket list. I've had many experiences, known joy, love, as well as sadness, which is part of life; but I do have one regret and that is that you, my girls, are no longer in contact with each other and that I, your mother, didn't do more to remedy that. Don't think I don't know that your visits to me were separate by design so that you didn't have to see each other, and not, as you all claimed it was, because of geography or just life taking over. I might be in my late eighties but I'm not daft. At first, I didn't know how to get you back together again. I know how stubborn you all are, but then, talking things over with Jean and Martha, a plan began to hatch in my brain. A kicking the bucket list! A bucket list is something you do while you still have time. A kicking the bucket list is for when you don't. I may not have much time left, but you three do. So I have devised a list that I want you to follow. I've made this request a condition of my will so that I'll hopefully achieve with my death what I didn't manage in life, and that is to get you all back together. And how is this going to be achieved? Well, first of all, I'm going to ask that, for the next year, you spend one weekend every other month with each other."'

Beside me, Rose had clenched her fists. Fleur looked over at me and raised an eyebrow.

"'I'm going to ask that some of the weekends are spent at each other's houses – so dust off your spare rooms, I know each of you has the space now; but not just to visit each other, no, that would be far too boring. Sitting opposite each other drinking tea? No. I have organized a quest of sorts. I'll tell you more about it later, but I want you to have shared experiences. Don't worry, it's all organized, and Mr Richardson will explain what I want you to do. With this plan, I can rest in peace, knowing that I have done all I can. There won't be tasks like climbing Machu Picchu, learning how to line dance, etc. Oh no, mine will be much more fun, but maybe not in the way that you'd imagine. Just pencil in the second weekend of every other month and follow the instructions that you'll be given. If any one of you fails to take part, no one gets their inheritance, so every second month, Mr Richardson will ask for your signatures saying you've all done as I asked.

'"Oh, I wish I could see your faces now. How are you going to refuse the last wish of your dead mother? I thought the 'I shall rest in peace knowing I have done all I can to bring you back together' bit is particularly good. Yes, I suppose it is blackmail of sorts. Not something I would normally adhere to, but I'll be gone by the time you hear this letter, and won't be around to hear you complain."'

Fleur burst out laughing and Rose shook her head, as though she couldn't quite believe what she was hearing. I could. I could easily believe it, and imagined Mum's eyes twinkling with mischief as she wrote the letter.

'"In the meantime, I'd like you to try talking to God or whatever power you believe in,"' Mr Richardson went on. '"I've read that meditation is listening to God and prayer is talking, so have a word. Talk to the wall if you prefer, like Shirley Valentine did. You don't have to believe or do it every day, just now and then, when you feel like it or if something's troubling you. I think it puts you in touch with what's going on inside of you and that's never a bad thing. In the hustle and bustle of life, we can often ignore what our hearts are telling us and I've found it makes me feel better so see where it takes you. If you don't, I'll come back and haunt you. Only joking Daisy. Don't worry.

'"Rose, Daisy, Fleur – all I care about is your well-being, and that you're happy in your lives. What mother doesn't want that for her children? I hope that this condition and my kicking the bucket list will go some way to helping you attain that. Goodbye my darling girls, God bless. With love as always, Mum. Deceased. Dead. Departed."'

I let out a deep breath. 'Holy shit.'

'Exactly,' Fleur agreed, then chuckled. 'The sly old fox.'

Rose looked as if she'd sucked a lemon.

2

Tuesday 1 September

I stared out of the window and tried to absorb what we'd just heard while Mr Richardson went to make copies of Mum's will and letter for us.

Rose and Fleur occupied themselves on their mobile phones. The atmosphere was uncomfortable, the air thick with unspoken resentment. *No change there*, I thought. Rose, Fleur and I had hardly spoken in three years, not since a row that had driven us all apart. The argument had been about what we all thought was best for Mum when it became obvious that she needed care after her stroke. Before that, I'd been on reasonable terms with both my sisters, though we weren't exactly close. It had been over thirty years since we'd lived together as children, then teens. We had drifted in and out of each other's lives in our twenties and thirties, then slowly grown further apart in our forties. Fleur was often abroad and Rose occupied with her job and family. We got on well enough when we did see each other, falling back into old roles and familiar teasing when we met up at Christmas, for big birthdays or family gatherings, but that was all.

For the last three Christmases, we'd made our visits to Mum separately.

When Mum had moved to the retirement village, Rose had suggested that we spread time with her over the festive period, so that Mum had three visits to look forward to instead of one. The arrangement suited me because the train companies often did engineering works over Christmas, making travel difficult from where I lived in the south west, but it also meant that I didn't see my sisters – not that either complained. Years ago, Rose had commented that, 'I wasn't really in her life any more.' It had stung. I had thought differently – that we were family, sisters, and always would be, despite time apart, but I knew what she meant. I wasn't involved in the ordinary everyday events that made up a life. What she said had hurt all the same, but then Rose had always been able to do that to me. She'd been dismissing me since we were little – not including me in her gang when we were in junior school, shooing me away in our teens when her friends were over. I was always too young, not cool or clever enough to be in with her crowd.

All of us were worried about Mum. Even though she'd made a good recovery from the stroke, apart from a weakness down one side of her body and difficulty walking sometimes, her doctors warned that it might happen again. Rose, Fleur and I agreed on one thing. We wanted the best for her last chapter in life. Rose had a demanding job in publishing, a husband, her children, still at school then, and no spare room. Fleur was living in California at the time and there was no way Mum was going to uproot that far. I'd been the obvious choice to take care of her. I'd lived alone since my daughter Lucy had flown the nest almost six years ago. She'd gone first to live with her aunt on her father Andy's side, in London, then later with her boyfriend to live in Australia near Andy, so I had her old room on the first floor that could be used.

'Dee, you could go and live with Mum and take care of her,' Fleur had suggested.

'You can work from anywhere,' said Rose. 'There's loads of room in the old house for you to paint.'

'But my life is in Cornwall. I don't want to uproot any more than Mum does, and if I let go of my house, I'm unlikely to ever find such a place to rent again. My landlady will find a new tenant, and when Mum does pass, the family home will have to be sold and I'll be homeless.'

'Don't be overdramatic,' said Rose.

'It's OK for you two. You have your own homes. I don't own mine.'

'And whose fault is that?' asked Rose.

I'd chosen to ignore her jibe. 'What would I do with Max and Misty?'

'Mum's allergic to cats,' said Rose, 'so if she came to live with you, you'd have to put them in a rescue home.'

'Forget it. I can't – won't – abandon them. I can't believe you can even suggest that. And what about Lucy when she comes home?'

'She only visits every couple of years,' said Fleur. 'There'd be room at Mum's.'

'Summer Lane is her UK home as well as mine.'

'You're being selfish and uncaring,' said Rose.

'I am?'

'And putting your cats before Mum,' added Fleur.

I was outraged. 'I do what I can. Neither of you have ever appreciated the distance I have to travel to visit, never mind the cost. Door to door can take seven hours, and that's if the buses, ferry and train run smoothly, which more often than not, they don't.'

'Oh stop moaning,' said Rose.

'It's all right for you, Rose. You live less than an hour away in Highgate.'

'I don't though,' said Fleur. 'I live in California, yet I still manage to get to see Mum.'

'You let her down more times than you turn up, though,' said Rose. 'Don't you know she marks the date in her calendar when you say you're coming? She likes to anticipate a visit, gets food in, bakes for you, then you cancel and turn up out of the blue with your expensive presents to make up for your absence.'

'Fuck you, Rose. I *like* to spoil her. What's wrong with that? Stop trying to make me feel guilty. I do what I can,' said Fleur.

'Yes, but you have property in London so it's not a big deal to visit when you're in town,' I said.

'Dee, you're the best option,' said Rose.

'I am not. Stop trying to control me and take over my life. Both of you are being insensitive to my situation and to suggest I give up my home is the last straw. And anyway, it's up to Mum. We should ask her what she wants.'

While we'd sulked and seethed at each other, Mum did her research online then went ahead with her own plans. The three of us, smarting from our wounds, withdrew from one another. We visited Mum separately. It was easy enough to do without dragging her into our quarrels, and actually it was nice to have time alone with her when I did visit. I could fantasize that I was an only child. Mum'd reassured me that she was fine about not coming to live with me, or me coming to live with her – she understood and not to feel bad about it, but of course I felt dreadful. I felt I'd let her down when she needed me.

*

Mr Richardson reappeared and handed each of us an envelope. 'It's all in there. Do feel free to call if you have any questions.'

'Thank you, we will. In the meantime, I have to dash,' said Rose as she put away her phone and got up.

Fleur and I left soon after and went our separate ways. I didn't mind. Mum might have made plans to get us back together but I couldn't see it happening, not in a million years.

As I headed for the train station, I decided that after we'd done whatever Mum had requested, I'd have nothing to do with either of my sisters. I had a feeling that they felt the same.

3

Wednesday 2 September, morning

I picked up my bag from where I'd left it when I got home last night and pulled out the envelope that Mr Richardson had given me. As I put it on the bedside cabinet to read again later, I remembered Mum's request that I talk to God.

I sat on the bed and looked up at the ceiling. 'OK Mum, no time like the present so here goes. Dear God, my mother's suggested that I talk to you. I know, it's been a while – that's because I'm not convinced that there's anyone listening and, if there is, speaks English. How does it work? Do you have a Google Translate system on your cosmic exchange for incoming prayers? Er . . . ' *Why am I talking to the ceiling?* I wondered as I noticed a damp patch in the left corner above the door. *If God is omnipresent then I could just as well talk to the floor.* I looked down and there, as clear as daylight, was a message from God, spelt out in cat hairs and toast crumbs. It said, Dee McDonald, your carpet needs hoovering. 'So . . . God . . . I'd be interested to hear what you have to say about wasps and why they exist. And why is there so much trouble and hatred in the world? What do you have to say about that?'

No reply. Just the ticking of the clock by the bed and, in the distance, the sound of an occasional passerby going about their business outside. In the dressing-table mirror I could see a slim woman propped up against a pile of teal blue velvet cushions on a cast-iron bed, a silver grey cat sleeping by her side. Me, dressed in jeans and a pale blue top, chestnut-coloured shoulder-length hair loosely tied back. My roots needed doing. I made a mental note to get some wash-in-colour on my next visit to Boots.

I jumped at the sound of the phone ringing, got up and went to answer.

'Is that Daisy McDonald?' A man's voice. Not one I knew.

'It is,' I replied, adopting the same solemn tone.

'William Harris here. My mother, Eleanor Harris, was your landlady.'

'Was?'

'Yes. I'm sorry to be the bearer of bad news but am calling to inform you that she passed away last week.'

I sank back on to the bed and listened to the rest of what he had to say, whilst at the same time trying to quell my rising panic. Letter in the post to me, confirming it all. *Oh god, I know what that means. He'll want me out,* I thought as I made myself focus.

When he'd finished, I put the phone down. Mrs Harris had been elderly so it was a call I'd been expecting and dreading for a few years. Hard to take in now that it had actually happened. I didn't know her well, but it was a blow all the same. We'd met when I first came to the south-west just over twenty-eight years ago, fresh out of art college, my head full of dreams of a studio by the sea. She came to my first exhibition in the Clock Tower down by the bay and liked my paintings. When she heard I was looking for somewhere permanent to live, she'd offered me a house at the back of the village. I could hardly believe my luck when I saw it, especially as the rent she asked for was ridiculously low considering the size of the place and the location. It was a mid-terrace with three floors, a loft up top with great light where I used to do my paintings, two bedrooms on the first floor with an ancient but adequate bathroom, a kitchen, living room, loo on the ground floor, and at the back was a wrought-iron veranda that led to a small neglected garden that I'd brought back to life over the years, planting roses, lavender and wild geraniums.

Mrs Harris said that all she wanted was a good tenant, a caretaker. She wasn't bothered about getting the best price, as long as the house was looked after. It had belonged to her parents and was still full of their dark mahogany furniture, faded velvet curtains and threadbare rugs. She'd grown up there, so wanted it to go to the right person, someone who was going to stay in the area; not a holiday let, which would mean never knowing how long anyone was going to stay or who they were. The house, though smaller, reminded me of my old family home so I felt like I belonged there from the start. It worked well. I rarely saw her because she lived in Truro and visited once a year, when she'd come in June and nod appreciatively at my roses and the fact I hadn't tried to change the décor. I paid my rent into her account on time, kept up with repairs, and filled the house with books, artefacts from my travels and friends' paintings, giving it a cosy, bohemian and lived-in feel. It was my home. Mrs Harris's death would mean the end of our arrangement.

Wednesday 2 September, afternoon

'Dear God, me again,' I said, as I hacked down shrubs in the back garden as if it might solve my problems. 'Sorry we got cut off this morning. Life took over, I'm sure you understand, being omniscient and all. Anyway. Home. I might not have one for much longer. Can you help? Or should one not put in personal requests?'

As if in response, the phone rang. I ran in to the kitchen to answer. 'Hello.'

'Is that Dee McDonald?' A man's voice again. Well spoken. Not William Harris.

'It is.'

'Michael Harris here.'

Ah, the elder brother, I thought. I'd met him once briefly, years ago, when he was passing through on his way to visit his mother. He was about my age, a handsome, solid-looking man, and very sure of himself in that way the privileged and privately educated often are.

'Sorry to spring this on you, but I'm just round the corner and I . . . I believe my brother called.'

'He did. I'm sorry for your loss.'

'Thank you. I . . . Would it be convenient to drop by?' *Christ! He and his brother don't waste any time,* I thought as I caught sight of myself in the hall mirror. I was wearing my gardening clothes, had no make-up on and looked flushed from the exertion of weeding. I brushed back strands of hair from my face with my free hand, then rubbed away a smudge of earth from my forehead.

'I won't stay long,' he continued. 'But I'd like to speak with you rather urgently.'

I hesitated for a moment, then decided: best get it over with. 'Sure, just give me five minutes.'

I raced to the cloakroom, splashed my face, applied a slick of lipstick and smoothed my hair. *Why the effort?* I asked myself. I'd given up on men a long time ago, but old habits die hard, and from what I remembered of my brief encounter with Michael Harris, I'd felt intimidated by him.

On the dot of five minutes, he knocked on the door. He was still attractive: eyes the colour of polished conkers, a full head of sandy hair flecked with grey. He looked a kind man, the type who could be relied on, probably due to his tall stature and broad shoulders. He'd put on a bit of weight around his middle, which I felt gratified to see. It made him look more approachable.

'I expect you're calling about the house,' I said as I let him in and ushered him into the front room.

He nodded as he looked around, appraising the place. 'I'm on my way to Truro. Funeral arrangements and so on.'

'Of course. I'm so sorry . . . my condolences. I . . . '

He nodded again briefly and I got the impression that he didn't want to talk about the death of his mother. 'I'm sorry not to have given you more notice, but my brother called me to say he'd spoken to you earlier and as I was driving this way I . . . ' He had the decency to look faintly embarrassed. 'I wanted to call in. I know it's been your home for so long but—'

'I can pay the rent if you give me your details. I've never missed it.'

'I know. It's not that. I . . . that is my brother and I, now that our mother has passed, well, we'll be putting the house up for sale. I know William has put it all in a letter but I felt that was rather formal in the circumstances which is why I thought I'd take the opportunity to speak to you in person.'

'Circumstances?'

'You having been here so long.'

My stomach constricted. This was my worst nightmare, but I did my best not to let my reaction show on my face. *Of course, they want their inheritance. The house must be worth at least five hundred thousand. Can't blame them, though he doesn't look short of money*, I thought as I took in the navy cashmere pullover, well-cut chinos and brown leather brogues. Michael Harris had a gloss about him that said he lived well. He smelt expensive, too: Chanel for Monsieur. I recognized the scent, woody with a hint of citrus. It had been Dad's favourite. Mum had kept a half-used bottle of it for years after he'd died. The familiar fragrance always stirred up sadness – as if Dad was there for a moment, but of course, like the cologne, the scent of him soon evaporated into nothing, leaving me with a sense of emptiness at his absence in my life and a longing for something or someone to fill it.

'I wanted to let you know that we'll give you first option on the sale,' he continued, 'that's the least we can do.'

I laughed and Michael looked at me quizzically. It struck me that if Mum hadn't made the condition that delayed my inheritance for a year, I'd have been in a position to buy the house immediately. However, I didn't want to tell him about Mum nor the will, not until I'd had a chance to talk things over with my friend Anna.

'I am sorry,' he said again.

'I'll have to go over my finances. Can I get back to you?'

He looked surprised. 'Of course, er . . . in the meantime, we need to have the house valued – estate agents. Only fair to you and us. We'd want three valuations.'

'That would be sensible. Just let me know when they want to come.'

He glanced, disapprovingly, I thought, around the living-room artefacts. There were rather a lot of them and most of them had a story – a memento from a holiday or a gift from a friend. His glance rested for a second on the bronze Greek statue with an oversized penis on the mantelpiece. Anna had given it to me five years ago after a date had gone disastrously wrong and I had told her I was giving up on men. Anna brought the statue to make me laugh. And it did.

'Satyr with penis rectus, a classic example of the ithy-phallic. Some say it was Dionysus, others that he was one of the wood satyrs said to have been a companion,' said Michael. 'In contrast to the sleek beauty of so many Greek statues, its vulgarity conveys a strong image, don't you think?'

Stuck-up prick, I thought, then almost got the giggles when I realized how apt that was in the circumstances. 'Also known as the wahey, look what I've got,' I blurted. I don't know what made me say it, but he had sounded so pompous.

He didn't laugh or ask to look around any further, and I was glad to see him to the door.

'I'll be in touch to arrange valuations,' he said after he'd taken my email address and I his. He made his way through the small front garden and out to his car, a black Jaguar which was parked opposite, outside Anna's cottage. Before he got in, he turned back to take another look at the house, but saw me still standing on the doorstep. 'Er . . . good to have met you again.'

Yeah sure, I thought. *You just want me out and your money in the bank.* 'And you,' I said and gave him my most charming smile. *With knobs on. Greek ithyphallic ones.*

*

I went through to the kitchen, sank into a chair and blinked away tears. This wasn't my home any more, it belonged to the Harris brothers. My ginger cat, Max, stared at me from his place on the windowsill. An image of the Buddha looked down at me from one of the many postcards and photos I'd pinned to a notice board next to the cooker. He was half smiling, eyes closed, his expression serene. *Smug bastard*, I thought. *I don't suppose you had to pay rent for your spot under the banyan tree.*

A montage of my life was pinned up on the board: my daughter, Lucy, as a toddler in a red bathing suit, paddling in the sea in Goa, again at nine years old dressed as Charlie Chaplin for a fancy dress party, a wedding photo with Andy, my first husband and Lucy's father – the twenty-four-year-old me at our wedding wearing a crown of cream rosebuds. Another photo showed Nick, handsome, adventurous, the free spirit. Everyone had adored him, but neither family life nor commitment were for him – at least not with me. Halfway down the board was a photo with someone cut out – that would have been John, my last partner. We were together for six years until I had an epiphany at a dinner party. He was a well-regarded local artist and was rattling on in his usual superior manner and it was like the blinkers came off and I saw him for what he really was – a pompous bore who had sponged off me all the time we were together. I later found out that he'd never been faithful. Back then I took the prize in the 'Love Is Blind' contest. I'd had a symbolic cutting up of all his photos, then I'd burnt them with Anna's help. I'd felt like an old witch as I watched his self-satisfied face shrivel and disappear into flames then ashes.

Further down the board, there was a photo showing my cats, Max and Misty, wearing Santa hats; lots of photos of Mum over the years, some in fancy dress – she loved to dress up for any occasion. She wore reindeer jumpers at Christmas, dressed as a fairy princess on birthdays, the Easter bunny in spring and, one Halloween, she put a sheet over her head and pretended to be a ghost. I was only six and screamed the place down. My dear mad mother. Other photos showed friends at barbecues, dinner parties over the years. Most of the photos were taken at No. 3 Summer Lane: my home, my safe place, through good times and bad.

It isn't just the house I love, I thought as I gazed out of the window, *it's the whole area and the people in it*. I knew everyone, was friends with most of them. I couldn't go out to the postbox without meeting someone for a chat and a catch-up. We were a community who supported each other through all weathers.

I fell in love with the Rame peninsula the first time I came to attend a music festival up on the cliffs. It's a hidden gem just over the River Tamar on the other side of Plymouth. There are the twin villages of Kingsand and Cawsand, both picture perfect, with narrow lanes lined with cottages painted pink, blue and ochre, leading down to the three beaches in the bays, all easy to get to for holiday-makers wanting an ice cream, pub or pasty to follow. On the other side of the peninsula is wild, unspoilt coastline with beaches that are harder to reach without a long climb down a winding cliff path. At a third point is Cremyll, where the small passenger ferry docks. It's a wonderful way to enter the area, the boat chugging in through the yachts moored on the Plymouth side, to see the stately home of Mount Edgcumbe up on the hill with lawns in front stretching down to the sea.

'Dear God,' I said. 'I need five hundred thousand pounds and I need it fast.' I turned to Max. 'Where am I going to find money like that in the next few weeks or months? I can't wait a year until I've fulfilled Mum's requests whatever they may be.' Max blinked and turned away. God was probably bored with requests like that too.

At least I had the presence of mind to ask Michael Harris for time, I told myself. I'd learnt the 'can I get back to you?' trick years ago from Rose though, being the people-pleaser I am, usually forgot to put it into practice. I didn't need to go over my finances at all. I knew exactly what I had – four hundred pounds in the bank. I had a part-time job teaching art at the local secondary school and I ran workshops in the evenings in the winter months. Both jobs paid a pittance. I earned enough to pay my bills and, with the occasional painting I sold, have some sort of a life. Though in recent months, I'd had no new ideas or inspiration to do my own work. I had no pension plan or savings either; like so many of my generation, we thought we'd never get old. Of course, I'd get my inheritance in a year if my sisters agreed to go along with it but would the brothers Harris wait? Somehow I thought not.

4

Wednesday 2 September, late afternoon

'Genius,' said Anna when she'd finished reading Mum's letter. 'Have you any idea of what you'll have to do?'

We were sitting in her kitchen and catching up over a pot of Earl Grey tea. Like me, Anna had been out gardening and was dressed in an old T-shirt and jeans, her short dark hair tucked away under a blue and white polka dot hair band. I'd known her since art college and been friends ever since. She shared my love of Cornwall and when the cottage opposite came up for sale ten years ago, at the same time she was separating from her husband, she didn't waste any time buying it with her divorce settlement. Her proximity was one of the many reasons I didn't want to move. I couldn't imagine life without her. We even had keys to each other's house so we could drop in on each other anytime.

I shook my head. 'None. Just that we have to meet some man that Mum hired as a PA to organize it all. He'll give us our instructions at the beginning of every other month.'

'Starting when?' she asked as she cut a slice of her home-baked lemon drizzle cake, put it on a plate then handed it to me.

'Next month. October. Mr Richardson will let us know where to be, when and what with, then this mystery man will take over.'

'Exciting.'

'God only knows what she's devised for us all.'

'I can just imagine her glee when she was thinking this up. How's it going to be funded?'

'All taken care of from funds from the sale of the family house.'

'So while you thought your mother was living a quiet life and letting you get on with yours, she was busy scheming up a "kicking the bucket list" for her wayward daughters.'

'With the help of her friends, Martha and Jean. Fleur's already called them to see if she could get anything out of them, but neither will spill the beans.'

'How are you feeling about it?'

'Mixed. It was a shock to all of us. Curious to discover what Mum's planned, but mainly still sad. I miss her so much and can't bear that I'll never see her or hear her voice again.'

Anna looked wistful. 'That never goes away.'

'And I feel bad I didn't get up to see her more often.'

'You went every six weeks. She understood – distance, money.'

'Rose dropped in twice a week.'

'Well she could, couldn't she? She lives in London. Don't beat yourself up about it. Guilt is a waste of energy.' Anna glanced back at the letter. 'Have you been talking to God as she requested?'

I smiled. 'A couple of attempts. I asked where I was going to get the money to buy the house but I reckon if there is a God, he'd think I have more than many and should be grateful.'

'Possibly but remember that quote from Matthew in the Bible? The one about not worrying about your life? "Look at the birds of the air, that they do not sow, or reap nor gather into barns, and yet your heavenly Father feeds them. Are you not worth much more than they?"'

'That's exactly the sort of thing Mum would have come out with. She was always sending me happy quotes in her last few months. She had one for every occasion, as for your Bible lines, if you lived with two cats and saw what they brought in, that would be the end of the "look at the birds of the air" theory, because they're not in the air, they're lying dead on my kitchen floor with their heads chewed off.'

'Cynic,' said Anna. 'Do you think your sisters will try talking to God?'

'Fat chance. Rose is an atheist and Fleur thinks she *is* God.'

Anna laughed.

'Mum hated me saying anything critical about either of my sisters. She refused to acknowledge that we'd fallen out or that we only spoke to each other if completely necessary. She always chatted away about Fleur and Rose as if nothing had changed between us, and gave me their latest news and what was happening with Rose and her writers in the publishing world, how Fleur's property portfolio was going. I'd nod and listen and imagined that Rose and Fleur did the same.'

Anna pointed at the letter. 'She might not have acknowledged it to you but clearly she was more than aware how things were with you and your sisters hence this brilliant plan to get you back together. She'd obviously been doing a lot of thinking and scheming in her last months.'

I nodded. 'Her letter reflected a lot of what was going on in her head before she died. She was death obsessed. On my last visit to her, she said she was researching what she could about the next stage of the journey. Where we go when we die, what life's been all about, that sort of thing. She said she wasn't afraid and was convinced that there's something after life, something good.'

'We'll probably have the same curiosity when we're in our late eighties. When I was in India in my twenties, I asked a guru if there was an afterlife. "Only one way to know for sure," he replied. "Die and find out."'

'Sounds like good advice. Mum was never what I'd call a religious person in a church going sense but she was spiritual. On her shelf, she had a wide range of books – the Bible, The Tibetan Book of the Dead, Bhagavad-Gita, Richards Dawkins, *There is No God*, all Elizabeth Kubler Ross's."

'She was always open-minded, wasn't she?'

'She was, right up to the end. She had great attitude and embraced death's inevitability with the same enthusiasm she did every other part of her life. Last time I went to see her, it was like listening to someone who was making holiday plans, checking out the reviews of the destination before they set off. She said it would be like an adventure, like going to the airport, aware she was off somewhere, just not knowing where.'

'Knowing that she wasn't afraid must give you some solace.'

Tears welled up in my eyes. 'Sometimes. Some days I think I can handle it; other days I can hardly breathe and don't want to see anyone or do anything.'

'Of course there will still be times like that. It's only been a couple of months since she died. Grief is like standing on the edge of the ocean. Some days, the water laps around your feet; you know it's there, it's manageable. Other days, from nowhere, it blasts in like a tsunami and knocks you right over. They say it takes two years to even feel normal again.'

'I can't imagine ever feeling normal again.'

'You will, although you'll probably always feel her loss. I know I do of my parents.'

'A day doesn't go by when I don't think of her. I catch myself thinking, oh I must tell Mum that, or see a programme in the TV guide that I think she'd like, or hear an interview on Radio Four and think I must give her a ring – then I remember, I can't. I miss that she's not there to talk things over with – like now, the fact that I might lose my home and so have no place to curl up and hide away on the tsunami days when I miss her most. She'd have been so reassuring. She always had such good solid advice to give. I miss that and her kindness and care.

Mainly, though, I'm in awe at Mum having thought up her plan for us and never saying a word. I need the money, yes, but it's not just that, in fact, even thinking about that seems mercenary. I mainly want to do this list of hers because it will give me some extended contact, in the sense that she's gone but left this legacy, mad though it may be.'

'And you will get your inheritance in the end.'

'Not necessarily. There's no guarantee that one of my sisters won't refuse to take part or back out at some stage. In devising her plan, Mum's made me completely dependent on the two people I'd choose not to need anything from. That's the bit I'm not happy about, and I'm pretty sure they feel the same.'

'Clever old bird,' said Anna. 'She was right. How could any of you refuse to carry out her last wish? You never know, it could be an adventure.'

'With Rose and Fleur? I doubt it. More like one long argument. Rose can be quite contrary when the mood takes her and Fleur isn't always easy either. If it was with you, it would be different. But the bottom line is that it was Mum's last wish. This condition mattered to her and so it matters to me. I want to do it for her.'

Anna reached out and squeezed my hand. I felt a rush of affection for her. It had been her who'd picked me up the day that Rose's husband, Hugh had called to tell me that Mum had died of a massive heart attack. I never knew anything could hit so hard and went to pieces, numb with shock and disbelief. Not that death was new to me, of course it wasn't – aunts, uncles, cousins, friends had all gone over the years. My father had died when I was aged six and though too young to really understand at the time, I mourned for him and what could have been rather than what was. With other deaths, I felt for their family and close ones rather than how it affected me. It all depended on what the person had meant. Mum was not only my mother, but one of my favourite people on the planet and with her passing, I felt that my heart had broken. Well meaning friends called, brought cards and flowers, those that had known her offering condolence or advice. But what could they say? In the days immediately after her death, I felt full of cut glass and it hurt like hell.

Anna had nursed me like a child, bringing food, dealing with post and emails.

Some mornings I'd wake up, feel normal for a brief moment, then remember Mum had gone for ever and weep. It was so final. I'd never see her dear and familiar face again, see the kindness and concern in her eyes, hear her voice, her laughter, have her there to turn to.

Anna had understood. 'The loss of a parent is immense and the pain you feel at their passing is exactly equal to what they meant to you,' she told me. 'If you loved someone deeply, you will suffer deeply. Don't deny it, suppress it or feel you should get over it; *feel* it and know it is evidence of how much you loved her.'

On the bad days, I would lock myself away and pore over photograph albums just for a glimpse of Mum, something to hold on to. I wore an old cardigan of hers that she'd left behind after one visit and inhaled deeply to try and catch the scent of her. I called her mobile to hear her voice and the message she'd recorded that she'd thought was so hilarious. 'Hello. Iris Parker here, I'm avoiding someone I don't like. Leave me a message and if I don't call back, you'll know it's you.' I found and read everything I could about life after death in the hope that somewhere she continued and that, although her body had gone, her consciousness and spirit lived on. But mostly I was aware that the phone no longer rang. She'd gone somewhere I couldn't follow and she wasn't coming back.

5

Friday 4 September

I was in the front garden, enjoying the sun on my bare arms and face when Anna appeared at the gate. She was wearing a peacock blue vintage halter-neck dress, a chunky green glass necklace and her hair was glossy from blow-drying.

'Why are you all dressed up?' I asked.

'Lunch with Ian.'

'Shows off your figure.'

Anna did a twirl. 'Ta. So. Have you spoken to either of the Harris brothers?'

'I have. I decided not to put it off and emailed Michael Harris first thing this morning to say that I won't be able to buy the house for at least a year. I told him that Mum had died and that I'm going to have to wait for my inheritance to come through. He must have passed it on to his brother William because he got straight back. As I expected, they aren't prepared to wait that long and are sending the estate agents in the next few days.'

'Wow, they don't waste any time. You'd have thought they'd have understood, seeing as they're in the same position, having just lost their own mother.'

I shrugged. 'Yes, but they don't know me or owe me anything. I'm just a tenant in their late mother's house. Why should they wait any longer?'

'Out of the kindness of their hearts and because you've been here so long. What difference would a year make? Did you tell them about the kicking the bucket list?'

'No way. It wouldn't have helped.'

'Want me to help you clear up for the estate agents?'

I sighed. 'I suppose.'

'It's not over yet Dee. Houses don't always sell straight off. First of all, it can take weeks for the agents to do the photos and copy for the brochure, then it has to be approved and so on. And we're going into the autumn. It's September. Everyone knows the housing market is best in the spring. See if you can talk them into waiting until next year. Appeal to their business sense. Who wants to buy in the winter down here? You've got a good argument, especially being where we are. Everything looks better in the spring – your garden, the area. If they're prepared to wait a while, it might buy you some more time.'

'Worth a try I guess, though – as we both know – September and October are fabulous months down here, especially if there's an Indian summer.'

A mischievous expression crossed Anna's face. 'I've had another idea. *Don't* clear up for the estate agents, nor any viewing you get when it goes on the market. If you can put people off for a year, you'll be in a position to buy again.'

'But how? This house is lovely and the area is so picturesque. What could possibly put people off?'

'Ghosts. Tell them it's haunted. By your mother or, even better, by theirs!'

I laughed. 'Good idea.'

'Or casually mention a problem with the sewage and flooding. We're near enough to the sea to make people worried.'

'And we could get the lads from the pub to come over and smoke in the living room. Nothing smells worse than the smell of stale cigarette smoke—'

'Yeah. Make it smell like an old pub. But best of all,' Anna pointed to herself, 'tell people about the noisy neighbours. I'll turn up the CD player with some obnoxious music and you can sigh in a long-suffering kind of way and say, yes, I've tried everything but that woman over the road won't turn it down. She's very difficult, I think she has mental problems. She has four kids too, they're just as bad, the eldest has a drum kit and the youngest is teething, poor thing, cries all night.'

'Ever thought of writing, Anna? You've got a good imagination and you're right, the options are endless.'

'Ian and I could pretend we're drunk and make a racket when you've someone booked in for a viewing.'

I sighed again. 'It's a good plan, Anna, but you know I'll never do it. It would feel dishonest.'

'Oh, forget that. It's your home. You have to fight for it. You're too nice, that's always been your problem. Don't let people walk all over you. Don't be such a wimp.'

'OK. Maybe.'

'Maybe? I know you won't.' Anna regarded me for a while. 'It'll be all right, Dee.'

'Will it?'

'Course. As I said, it's not over yet.'

Thursday 10 September

I popped into the local shop for milk and cat food. My days are filled with glamorous events such as this. Sometimes I go a bit mad and buy a tub of organic rhubarb yoghurt, the kind with probiotics. No stopping me when I'm in a wild mood.

While waiting to be served, I listened to customers discussing the good weather we were having, then I spied the display of scratch cards next to the till. Waste of money, I normally think. I'm not a gambler, but there was one for five pounds that had a prize of five hundred thousand pounds. It seemed to be calling to me in the same way that Häagen-Dazs Salted Caramel ice cream sometimes does. *Buy me, buy me.* I could hear it, clear as day. *Someone has to win*, I thought as I found a fiver in my purse and asked for the card.

'Fancy your chances then, do you?' muttered Mrs Rowley, as she handed me the card.

'I do,' I replied. 'You've got to think positively don't you agree?'

Mrs Rowley grimaced. 'Not necessarily. I want to punch people who are too cheerful, especially first thing in the morning.' She was a miserable old sod, but popular in the village because she made the rest of us look like a happy bunch. 'Let me know if you win and you can buy a round in the Bell and Anchor.'

'I will,' I said and turned to go. I glanced at the queue behind me, all of whom had been listening. There were no secrets in this village, and normally I didn't mind my neighbours knowing what I'd bought or not, but who was first in line after me? Michael blooming Harris, who had an amused look on his face. *Damn. He'll think I'm desperate and he wouldn't be far wrong*, I thought as I shoved the scratch card into my bag. 'Not for me,' I said. 'For my friend.'

'Friend? That's good of you.'

'That's me. Lady Bountiful. Anyway, back again so soon?'

He nodded. 'I'm meeting with the estate agents later today. I always like to meet them face to face, know exactly who I'm dealing with.' He had a very direct gaze, which I found disconcerting, and . . . was I imagining it or was there a charge of electricity between us? No, couldn't be. Must be the prunes I had with my porridge this morning. I hated him. He was going to take my home and, besides, men like him went for thirty-year-old blondes with breasts that point north, perfect nails, and who have done fancy cooking courses in the south of France. They don't look at middle-aged women like me with a body on the slow journey south.

Michael Harris only stood out because there was a shortage of decent men in the village. The only single men around my age were Ned and Jack who pretty well lived in the pub, Arthur who smelt of stale biscuits, Joss and Paul, who spent most of their time smoking weed and, anyway, were too young for me, and Harry, who was a bit of a worry and liked to hang out in the cemetery and flash his bits when anyone went past. Ian was the only decent single man, but Anna had bagged him and had been seeing him for the last year. Luckily he wasn't my type, so we hadn't had to deploy hairdryers at dawn over him. Michael Harris stood out purely because of statistics. I dismissed the thought of him being attractive before it could take root and make me feel inadequate.

'Just let me know when you want them to come,' I said as I left.

6

When I got home, I went into the kitchen, sat at the table and got out my scratch card. 'OK God, you're omnipresent – or, as they'd say in the *Godfather* movies, you're connected – so now's your chance to show what you can do and save my bacon.' I scratched the card. Amazing! I'd won! Hallelujah. Two quid. All my troubles were over.

The phone rang, disturbing my reverie of what to do with my winnings. It was Fleur.

'Not good news I'm afraid,' she said. 'Rose called earlier. She says she won't be party to Mum's condition and is going to contest it.'

My heart sank. 'Can she do that?'

'She can but she won't win. I've already spoken to a lawyer friend of mine. He said if she doesn't have a valid reason to not meet the conditions of Mum's will, she won't get any inheritance.'

I groaned. 'And neither will you or I. We all have to sign. If she doesn't go along with it, that means no inheritance for any of us. She's so selfish. She must know what her decision would mean for me.'

'I know. I'm sorry Dee.'

*

I tried to call Rose but got the answering service. I felt so angry, I went straight over to Anna's with a bottle of Pinot Grigio and the intention of getting very drunk.

'Why did Rose call Fleur and not you?' she asked on hearing the latest.

'No idea.' I found wine glasses in Anna's cupboards and poured us both a large drink. 'Maybe it was because she knows it wouldn't be the end of the world to Fleur if she didn't get her inheritance either. Fleur has her own money and so does Rose. Rose probably knew I'd give her a harder time for not taking part.'

'They'd seriously let an inheritance like that go?'

'Maybe, if it didn't fit in with their plans.' I knew that finances were hard for Anna too, and the thought of my two sisters waving goodbye to a life-changing sum was hard to take in.

Anna looked at me sympathetically. 'I am sorry, Dee. Do they know how much you need the money?'

'Fleur does now. I filled her in when she called about Rose.'

'Get her to tell Rose.'

'Rose won't care. She only cares about herself and her family, and with both she and Hugh being high earners, I guess she can afford to say no. Either that or the thought of spending time with Fleur and me is so abhorrent to her.'

'But you're sisters. They can't be that unfeeling.'

I took a gulp of wine. 'What I feel or need doesn't matter to either of them.'

'Want me to make voodoo dolls of them both and stick pins in?'

'Yes. No. We haven't even begun Mum's tasks and we're already at war with each other.'

'You're going to have to call her Dee. Call her up and tell her how much it means to you.'

'You mean beg. No. Never. You know what she can be like – what both of them can be like.'

Anna nodded. 'You mean the funeral?'

'And the reception. If we couldn't be supportive of each other at times like that, it's not going to happen now.'

*

It was back in July. I'd stood outside the open doors of the chapel in the blazing sunshine, Anna by my side, and watched the swarm of people go in and settle into their places. Some had been familiar, the last surviving friends of Mum's; some family, distant relatives that I hadn't seen for years. Rose, with Hugh and their two children, Simon and Laura, went in. I remember thinking that Simon would be in his third year at university; Laura, tall like her father, and stunning, in her first year. They'd grown so much since I'd last seen them. Rose was the petite one of my sisters, taking after Mum at five foot three. Hugh had put on weight and, with his thinning silver hair and rotund chest and belly, resembled a plump pigeon. Rose had got thinner and looked strained, but she was immaculate as always in a black dress as well cut as her hair. They didn't see me on their way in.

Anna nudged me when she saw Rose. 'Have you spoken to her lately?'

I shook my head. 'She called a couple of times to talk over funeral arrangements and rub in how she was having to organize it all. Mum wrote out what she wanted years ago, even the hymns and prayers, though she wouldn't reveal what. She'd said she wanted it to be a surprise and that she might get Jean to sing "Ave Maria", which she would do magnificently out of tune, and Martha could throw away her walking stick and do some interpretive modern dance, like Marina Abramović, the Yugoslavian performance artist who likes to fling herself at walls in her birthday suit. "That would make the vicar sit up," she said.

'And that wasn't all. She said she might have "Ding Dong, The Witch Is Dead" and an entourage of male strippers to carry her in.'

Anna laughed again, causing an old gentlemen to frown at us on his way inside. 'I loved your mother.'

'Despite her jokes, I am sure it will all be dignified and appropriate. Although eccentric at times, Mum had class and knew how to behave in public.'

'Unlike us,' said Anna, as the elderly man found a pew but turned and continued to stare.

'When Rose called, she didn't ask about my life at all. You'd have thought after so long she'd have had some interest.'

'And did you ask about hers?'

'I suppose not.'

'Then you can't be too pissed off at her.'

I gave her arm a gentle pinch. 'She made me feel crap for not sending Lucy the airfare to come from Australia, but she couldn't have come even if I'd had the money – or maybe she could have but not for long enough to merit the cost of such a journey. Lucy likes to stay for weeks when she comes, have a proper stay. She's got that planned for next year, after we've both had time to save up. I'll send her what I can towards her fare. I always do. It's OK for Rose, she and Hugh earn loads between them.'

'You don't have to defend yourself or Lucy to me, Dee.'

'I know. Sorry. Guess we'd better go in.'

We went inside and took our places behind Rose and her family who were on the front pew. None of them turned around.

Fleur hovered at the back of the chapel when she arrived, but was soon ushered up to the end of our bench. Even in the tense atmosphere of the crematorium, people couldn't help but turn to look at her. Like the rest of us, she was in black, a knee length A-line dress and cowboy boots.

'Very rock chick,' Anna commented.

'That's Fleur,' I replied. She looked great, ten years younger than her forty-six years, like she'd been cracked fresh out of a polystyrene pack that morning, her body and legs toned and tanned, blonde hair just past her shoulders, beautifully cut and highlighted and her skin glowing – which was surprising, considering the amount she'd drunk and smoked in her life.

Glancing around, Fleur spotted me and we nodded, polite. Fleur stared at Anna, though. She too stood out in a crowd, but more because of the fuchsia-pink highlights she'd had put in last week. Today her funeral black dress was accessorized with ruby red lace-up boots and a pink pashmina.

It had been strange to see Fleur and Rose for the first time in three years, so familiar and yet so removed from my life now. Both of them looked like Mum and had her blue eyes and fine features, though Fleur was a couple of inches taller than Rose. I took after Dad, with the same honey-brown eyes and height.

'Do I look like Morticia Addams?' I whispered to Anna. I was wearing a long black dress and kimono-style black devoré jacket. I'd thought it looked appropriate but, next to my sisters, I wondered whether it was more fitting for a Goth party than a funeral.

'From the movie? No. More like Lurch,' Anna whispered back. 'Stop worrying. You look fine.'

Anna was an only child and never fully got my feelings of inadequacy when faced with Rose or Fleur. They'd both had their place in our family clearly defined. Rose, the eldest, the brains; Fleur, the youngest, and with her perfect heart-shaped face, the beauty. When we were young, Rose was the quiet, studious one – secretive, even. Fleur was an open book, bouncing off the walls with energy and crazy ideas. When Mum talked about me, she'd smile and say, ah Daisy, my middle child; well she's different, she's the dreamer. I certainly felt like I was dreaming that day. Saying a final goodbye to Mum didn't feel possible or real.

'A good turn-out,' Anna whispered as she looked around. 'There must be well over a hundred people here, and it's standing room only at the back.'

'I don't know who they all are. A lot of Mum's friends have already died,' I replied.

'Good,' said Anna, 'then she'll have someone she knows to show her round when she gets to the other side.'

'Maybe,' I replied. I was glad that I'd talked about death with Mum and knew that she didn't fear it. She was always a positive soul, endlessly curious, her nose often in a book and – in latter years – her laptop. She was very computer savvy, Queen of the Silver Surfers, forever googling, ordering on line, booking weekends away in foreign resorts or spas until she was no longer able to travel. Every autumn, she'd signed up to learn a new skill. Over the years, she'd done life drawing, learnt Italian, flower arranging, Indian cookery, tango, yoga, meditation, to name a few. When she wasn't doing one of her courses, she played piano, painted watercolours, created a wonderful garden and home to entertain her large circle of friends and pursue her many interests. I wished that I was like her in that way, but I knew I'd felt jaded of late, disappointed in some aspects of life which had made me cynical and, at times, rather sad.

Music began to play, *Adagio* by Albinoni. The hum of conversation faded and everyone stood as the pallbearers began to make their way up the aisle carrying Mum's coffin. It was covered in masses of white roses and gypsophila, her favourites. It was the most poignant sight I'd ever seen and, with it, the finality of her death hit me hard. My knees buckled and Anna put her arm around me, steadying me.

The vicar took his place at the front and signed that we should all sit down. As I looked at the closed coffin, I felt wracked with grief that I couldn't see the dear being that was in there for just one more moment. I wished that I'd been with Mum at the end, been able to hold her hand one last time. I told myself again that there was no way I could have made it, but it gave me little solace. *Too late*, I thought, as an avalanche of emotions engulfed me: guilt, loss, sadness, anger but also, somewhere in there, relief that Mum wouldn't have to suffer years of decline and incapacity. She'd been frail the last time I saw her, struggling to see as well as walk. 'Old age isn't for sissies,' she'd said.

Rose had asked if I wanted to do a reading but I'd said no. I didn't think I could have kept it together. Clearly Rose and Fleur felt the same, because it was Hugh who got up and read 'Miracles' by Walt Whitman, in his confident public schoolboy's voice, followed by Martha, the friend Mum had made in the retirement village.

'Who's she?' Anna whispered as she walked to the front with the help of an expensive-looking walking stick. Although elderly, she was a tall, striking woman, impeccably turned out, her hair dyed a subtle ash blonde, her nails a not-so-subtle red.

'That's Martha.'

'She's fabulous. Looks like she might whack anyone who got in her way with that stick.'

I didn't know much about her, apart from the fact she'd been a Bluebell Girl in Paris when she was younger, then married a consultant and lived in the Far East until her return to England ten years ago to be nearer her son and daughter.

Martha read 'A Song of Living' by Amelia Burr then, finally, Mum's oldest friend and neighbour, Jean, got up and read 'Do Not Stand at My Grave and Weep' by Mary Elizabeth Frye. I'd known Jean all my life; she was like a sister to Mum. I was moved to see the effort it took her to walk up to the front then talk about Mum in her familiar

Scottish accent. An image of her as a young woman in tennis whites popped into my mind. Mum was mad about tennis too, and she played most weekends with Jean and her late husband Roy, whilst Rose, Fleur and I sat on benches by the courts and stuffed ourselves with cucumber sandwiches and lemonade. I'd always liked Jean. She was full of life, shared Mum's sense of humour, but was smart too. As well as bringing up her family, she'd studied gardening, ran a very successful landscape design business and written and sold many books on all aspects of the subject long before it became fashionable. Now here she was, an old lady with white hair, slightly bent with age.

After the reading, she went on to speak fondly about Mum, her sunny outlook, her love of her daughters, and for a few moments she brought Mum's image, sharp and bright, into the chapel. A memory from when I was little flashed into my mind as Jean spoke of Mum's lifelong love of pranks. If ever Rose, Fleur or I went out of a room to get something, Mum and Jean thought it hilarious to hide behind the curtains or sofa, so we'd return to an empty room and wonder where everyone had gone. They were still doing it when we were teens, much to our embarrassment.

And then it was over. *Twenty minutes and time's up. Twenty minutes to sum up a life, then she's out and the next one's in. That can't be it, can it?* I'd thought. *Eighty-seven years of a full and well-lived life ends with a few readings, a bit of music, a eulogy and a couple of lines from the vicar.*

Doors at the back were opened and sunlight streamed back in. As the ushers motioned us to leave, a track began to play over the loudspeakers. 'Wish Me Luck (As You Wave Me Goodbye.)' Typical Mum. She would have wanted to leave us laughing, and it was that reminder of her sense of humour that brought the tears.

*

The gathering after the funeral was held at an old pub near Hampstead Heath where Rose had booked an upstairs room.

'Weird to have a party where the guest of honour is missing,' said Anna as we walked into the bar area, where a buffet had been laid out and which was already full of people drinking, talking, catching up.

'True, and Mum did like a party. She'd have liked this, to have seen all her nearest and dearest in one place,' I said. I wasn't in the mood for making idle chatter, though: my sole aim there was to find Rose and Fleur. I knew that they would have been grieving as I had, and hoped that we could be some comfort to each other.

Rose was on autopilot on the other side of the room by a window, organizing, greeting, making sure people had drinks. I glimpsed Fleur over at the bar on her own, her back turned. I tried to make my way over but was waylaid by various people offering condolences and sandwiches for which I had no appetite.

After a short while, I saw Rose go out in the corridor.

'I'm going to go and find Rose,' I said to Anna.

'Good. I'll wait here,' she replied, and she plonked herself down next to an old dear who looked like she didn't know a soul.

I found Rose alone in the kitchen area. 'Rose, can we talk?'

She barely looked at me. 'Not the time or place,' she said, then proceeded to issue an order to a waitress. I felt gutted by her response.

I went back into the main room and looked for Fleur at the bar, but she'd disappeared so I went back to Anna.

'Any luck?' she asked.

I shook my head. 'Rose is too busy and I think Fleur may have gone. She never was one for family gatherings, unless she was the centre of attention.'

Anna squeezed my arm. 'Don't take it personally. Funerals are odd events. Nobody is ever quite themself.'

I wasn't so sure. Rose and Fleur had acted exactly true to form as far as I'd seen. Not wanting to hang around any further, I'd looked for Rose to say goodbye and explain that I had a train to catch. She had been occupied serving tea to guests and seemed indifferent to me leaving before the gathering had dispersed. I'd left feeling hollow and sad that I'd found no solace with my sisters. *You can choose your friends, but not your family. Who needs sisters? Not me*, I'd thought as Anna and I headed for the station.

*

Anna poured more wine. 'I know the funeral was hard for you Dee but it was difficult for all of you. Whatever your mum has planned for the next year is bound to be very different.'

'True but maybe Rose has got the right idea,' I said. 'Why put yourself through it?'

'Stop being so negative. Only the other day you were telling me that you wanted to follow your mum's wishes so that you'd have extended contact with her. I can't believe you'd give up so easily.'

'I'm not the one giving up, Rose is.'

'You are too if you don't at least try and persuade her to participate.'

'Rose can be stubborn and unmovable if she makes up her mind about something.'

'So can you.'

'You're supposed to be my friend.'

'I am and if I can't tell you to snap out of this defeatist mood and try and get Rose on board, who can?'

'You don't know her like I do. If she's decided not to do Mum's list then there's little I can do to persuade her.'

'You're being pathetic,' said Anna.

'And you're being horrible.'

'No I'm not. I'm telling you the truth. Call her when you get home.'

'Maybe.'

'Call her. Don't be such a wimp.'

'I hate you. You're mean.'

'I hate you more. Now. Would you like another glass of wine to go with your misery?'

7

Saturday 12 September

The agent from Scott Frank came just after breakfast. A young man with rosy cheeks, dressed in a sharp suit. 'This will be an easy sell,' he said after he'd been around the house leaving a trail of strong aftershave. 'We'll have a buyer in weeks.'

'Are you certain? I thought this was a slow time for the property market,' I said.

'Oh no. I already have a waiting list of buyers in London looking for properties down here, especially ones as charming as this.'

*

Taylor and Knight came just before lunch. A middle-aged blonde woman in a navy trouser suit and silver jewellery. 'It will get snapped up,' she said, then sighed, 'you've made it lovely. I'd buy it myself if I could.'

*

'This won't be on the market long,' said the man from Chatham and Reeves who'd arrived early afternoon. He had an old-fashioned manner about him, was dressed in a tweed jacket and corduroy trousers and smelt slightly of burnt sausages. 'Character, original features and the garden is established, perfect country-cottage style. Just what our buyers are looking for in locations like this.'

Noooooooooooooooooo, I thought.

*

Michael telephoned late afternoon. 'Just to let you know that I'm going with Chatham and Reeves. They want to send a photographer round the day after tomorrow if that's all right?'

'I have no choice, have I?'

There was a silence on the other end of the phone. 'I am sorry, Dee, but I hope you understand.'

'I understand perfectly,' I said as I looked at my Greek statue, which was still resplendent on the fireplace. A vision of where I could shove it came to mind as I hung up the phone.

*

Anna came over immediately on hearing my news.

'You can stay in my spare room if the house sells quickly,' she said.

I was touched by her offer, but I knew she used her spare room to store the vintage clothing she put up for sale on the Internet, and to make the jewellery she sold. Her daughters also slept there when they visited, which was often, plus she had a constant stream of visitors. I'd cramp her style if I lived there with her. 'Thanks, Anna, but you use that room,' I replied, 'and much as I love you, we might drive each other mad if we lived together. I don't want to run that risk. I'll find a room in the village when the time comes: that's my best option.'

'But not yet,' said Anna. 'House sales take months, and that's if there's a buyer straight away. Come on Dee, buck up, you're acting like a victim. You *do* have a choice. We always have a choice.'

'Stop being so positive. It's annoying.'

'Now you're talking like Mrs Rowley in the shop,' said Anna. 'You know I'm right. You have to fight. Don't just roll over and accept what's happening like you have no say in it. Fight to get Rose on board. Fight to keep your house.'

'OK. How?'

Anna looked blank. 'I don't know. I'm just full of lines from self-help books that I've read over the years. They never covered specifics. You know the kind – *Feel the Fear and Do It Anyway. How To Stop Worrying and Start Living. Kick Your Crutch and Walk Free.* Those kind of books.'

If nothing else, Anna always made me laugh.

*

'Dear God, grant me the serenity to accept the things I cannot change, the *courage to change the things I can,* and the wisdom to know the difference,' I said to the ceiling when Anna had gone. *She was right*, I thought. *I have to fight for my home. If I can just keep any prospective buyers at bay for a year, I will get my inheritance, be able to stay here and all will be well. In the meantime . . .* My thoughts were interrupted by the sound of a text coming through. I looked at my mobile but didn't recognize the number. It read: 'Winner or loser? Hero or victim? Your choice.' *Must be from Anna*, I thought. *She forgot to take her mobile out and is using Ian's to tell me to call Rose. Well, that's me told and she's right, I do have to snap out of feeling defeated and fight, so OK, Anna, message received and I choose to be a winner.*

I took a deep breath, went into the hall and called Rose's number. Hugh picked up.

'Dee. Oh yes, er . . . Rose can't come to the phone at the moment.'

My stomach tensed. Just as I thought she would, she was shutting me out. 'I guess you know all about the condition of the will?' I asked.

'I do,' said Hugh.

'So why doesn't she want to go ahead with it?'

I heard Hugh sigh. 'She'll have to tell you that herself,' he said. He was never one to get involved in family squabbles. 'I'll see if I can get her to come to the phone.'

The line went quiet and I really wanted to hang up. I was too old for this lark, but Anna's words kept echoing: you have a choice, don't just roll over. A few minutes later, Rose came on to the line. 'Dee. How can I help?'

She sounded so official. 'This is Dee, Rose, not one of your staff. And I think you know how you can help. You can do what Mum asked us to. Her last wish.' I might not have been in touch with Rose for years, but I knew what mattered to her. She was always the good daughter, never disobedient, always seeking Mum or Dad's approval.

'Plus you need the money,' said Rose.

'I do, but regardless of that, it was still Mum's last wish that we get together and do whatever she's programmed. She'd thought this out, Rose. I think the least we can do is go along with what she wanted. What if she's still watching us from somewhere? What if there is an afterlife and she can see that you intend to disregard her wish and not hear how much she regretted us not talking.'

'Oh for God's sake, Dee, there is no such thing as a ghost or an afterlife. You live, you die. Mum's gone.'

OK, I thought, *I knew that might not work. Time to try another tactic.*

'You're probably right,' I said. 'But part of her will live on with her kicking the bucket list. We know from the letter that she put time and thought into it. If we don't do it, we'll never know what was really on her mind these last months. I knew she'd been thinking a lot about death. You probably knew that, too – all those books in her room. I want to do it, for her but also for me, because in a way it will help me hang on to her a little longer, like she will still be there, telling me what to do every other month.'

Rose was quiet.

Enough said, I told myself, *don't push her.*

'I suppose there's nothing to lose if we at least see what she wanted,' said Rose finally.

'Exactly,' I agreed. 'Step at a time.'

'I might drop out if she's dreamed up something completely insane. You know what she was like.'

'Your prerogative, but I think we owe it to her to at least give it a chance.'

'Let me think about it,' said Rose. 'I'll get back to you.'

I sighed. Blooming Rose. She'd not changed. She never agreed to anything easily, it was always: let me think about it. She'd played the 'I'll get back to you' tactic perfectly, like she always had: taking control and leaving me hanging, at her mercy and wondering what she'd do.

Rose

Saturday 12 September.

'What did you say to Dee?' Hugh asked after I'd put down the phone.

'That I'd think about it.'

'Fleur?'

'Fleur's in.'

'I think you should do it, Rose. It might be just what you need.'

'I probably will . . . just . . . I still feel so angry with them both.'

'Over the funeral?'

'They're both so selfish, always have been and now they expect me to turn the page on the fact that neither of them offered to help and just carry on like it never happened. Someone had to settle the bill, see the last people off, book taxis for the out-of-towners.'

'It was their mother's funeral. They probably didn't even think.'

'Exactly. They never think and they're not the only ones

who lost a mother. Fleur didn't even say goodbye at the wake. I know. I should let go but I can't. Not at the moment.'

'To be expected when you're going through what you are. It's one of the stages. Denial, anger, depression, acceptance, something like that.'

'Well I'm stuck in the anger stage.'

'The funeral was back in July,' said Hugh. 'You can't keep carrying this. You have to let it go.'

'I know and I know it's not really about them but anger is an emotion I can deal with at present so I'm sticking with it.'

Hugh smiled. 'Anyway, it was probably easier that you did it yourself. I've often heard you say that neither Fleur or Dee are great organizers.'

'Stop being reasonable and nice. I want to rage about something and they happen to be in range.'

'Fine. Rage away,' said Hugh.

I had wanted to speak to both of my sisters at the funeral before they left but it had been full on from six in the morning, then Dee'd picked the worst possible time to try and talk to me. She probably took it the wrong way, prickly as always. She was always oversensitive. And Fleur just disappeared, probably wrapped up in her grief like she was the only one who existed. I meant to make it right at the will reading then but got a call I couldn't ignore. I had to go and it's all been crazy since then. Life takes over, appointments, people to see, plans to make.

'So much for sisters,' I said.

Hugh came over and gave me a bear hug. 'You have me, Rose, you always have me.'

That much was true. I had Hugh. Neither Fleur nor Dee

had partners. I was being mean and not thinking straight. I'd call Dee and let her know I'd do the programme. Of course I would, but not today; tomorrow, I'd call her tomorrow.

8

Saturday 3 October

Two envelopes arrived in the morning post.

Train tickets to Somerset from Mr Richardson, with an address and instruction to pack a case for Friday and Saturday, 9 and 10 October, and to meet our list organizer, Daniel Scott, on Saturday morning at nine a.m.

I looked up the address and sighed with relief. Greyshott Manor Hotel and Spa just outside Taunton. *Dear Mum. She'd arranged a weekend of pampering*, I thought. *Why did I ever doubt her? What a sweetheart. And sensible. If Fleur, Rose and I could relax in each other's company, maybe we could begin to mend some bridges.*

The other envelope contained an official looking letter:

Dear Ms McDonald,

Regarding the matter of my late mother's house, as you know, I have given the estate agent the go-ahead to start marketing. If there is any change in your circumstances and you find yourself in a position to proceed, please let me know as soon as possible. I respect that you were a good tenant for my mother for many years, so you have until the end of the month to give me your decision,

Regards,

Michael Harris

At least he was proposing to give me more time. Maybe a miracle would happen. I texted him back: *I will be in touch after this weekend.* ☺ If I was right about the kind of man he was, the smiley would annoy him. *Good*, I thought.

Friday 9 October

I had an easy train journey, read a book and arrived at the hotel early Friday evening. It looked lovely. An old manor house set in acres of parkland.

Inside was a wide reception hall with oak floors, wood-panelled walls, tasteful antiques and the scent of lavender beeswax polish in the air. I was shown to the first floor by a well-spoken young woman with a ponytail called Felicity, who was eager to let me know all about the facilities of the hotel. When I saw the beautiful room with heavy drapes and king-size bed with velvet and brocade cushions, and the enormous bunch of country garden flowers, I felt myself tearing up at the idea of Mum having arranged such a treat for us. I hadn't had a spa weekend in years, and was really looking forward to whatever treatments Mum had planned.

'Have my sisters arrived?' I asked. 'Rose Edwards and Fleur Parker?'

'Ms Edwards has arrived. I believe she's having supper

in her room,' said Felicity. 'And Ms Parker called this afternoon to say that she would be checking in later and didn't require dinner.'

Fine, if that's how you want to play it, I thought after Felicity had left me alone. I was glad to have some time to enjoy where I was. I ran a bath in the marble bathroom, poured in all the Molton Brown white sandalwood products from the shelves, then lay in it for half an hour, inhaling the woody scent and feeling utterly spoilt. After my bath, I put on the enormous fluffy white courtesy robe, ordered a chicken Caesar salad and a half-bottle of Sancerre. *Bliss*, I thought as I sank back into the plump cushions on the bed. *All I need now is a handsome hunk with a thing about older women to share it all with. Maybe not. I'd feel self-conscious after so long. Maybe a long-sighted hunk? And can I really be bothered? It's been a long time, years, since I've had a lover. I'm not sure I remember what goes where any more.* I flicked on the telly. A romantic comedy was starting. *Before Sunset.*

If a man was with me, I thought, *the channel would be changed and football put on. The duvet would be nicked in the night; I'd be kept awake by his snoring. No thanks. Sometimes it's good to be single. I can watch what I want, sleep spread-eagled across the bed with no one to consider and no one to try and please.*

Fleur

Friday 9 October, 11 a.m.

I called Rose's house to suggest we drive down to the hotel together. I thought it would be a good chance to re-establish contact, find out how she's doing. No one home. Left a message. Am packed and ready and looking forward to the weekend. Perhaps we could all have supper together this evening, break the ice, start things on a positive note.

1 p.m.: Texted Rose's mobile. No answer.

5 p.m.: Tried Rose's landline again. Still no one home. Might as well set off.

6 p.m.: Rose replied to my text. She's already at the hotel. The mean cow. It clearly didn't even occur to her that we could drive together. That's how much she wants my company. So much for a cosy pre-programme supper – no way that's going to happen now. Let it go, Fleur, let it go. Oh well, I don't have to be there until the morning so I'll get there in my own time when I'm good and ready and I'll go straight to my room. Bugger the pair of them.

Dee

Saturday 10 October

Rose and Fleur were already in the lobby, seated at a low table, when I came down in the morning. Rose was dressed in her preppy casual look – jeans, a white shirt and pearls; Fleur, in pale pink cashmere and white jeans, looked as feminine as ever. I was in grey leggings and a loose T-shirt. We were at a spa, after all, and here to relax: who cared what we looked like? Not me. I'd had a good night's sleep, a delicious room-service breakfast of scrambled eggs, smoked salmon and soda bread, and felt in a positive mood, looking forward to whatever Mum had planned for us. Maybe an aromatherapy massage? A facial? Reflexology?

'I've already googled him,' said Fleur, looking at her phone.

'Who?' I asked.

'Daniel Scott,' she replied and held up her phone screen for Rose and me. It showed a man with silver grey hair and smiling eyes, possibly in his fifties.

The photo looked like a professional PR shot but the man in it looked interesting. *Damn,* I thought. *And I look like a bag lady.* I was just wondering whether to run upstairs and change when the real-life Daniel appeared. He clocked immediately that Fleur had his face on her phone.

'Been checking me out?' His eyes twinkled. So did Fleur's. Not mine, though, when he glanced at me. I felt myself sag inside. I felt sixteen again. Sixteen and I'd met a boy I liked, then along would come my younger sister and I'd become invisible. Game over. A memory from that time came to mind. I'd had a crush on a boy called Jimmy Nash and had gone to a local sport's club with Fleur to watch him play football. The pitch was full of boys; as soon as they spotted Fleur, I'd watched with dismay as a ripple of male nostrils, Jim's included, rose and fell like a Mexican wave in recognition of the scent of fresh and beautiful bait. My sister. She always had that effect on men.

'Of course,' said Fleur. 'We want to know what we're in for.' She flicked a lock of hair and gave him a cheeky smile.

'Good for you,' said Daniel as he pulled up a chair to sit with us. 'Always best to do your research.'

'Exactly,' said Fleur. When he turned away, she looked over at me and raised an eyebrow. She wanted us to be teens checking out the talent again, but I didn't feel like playing along. Decades on, it would still be game over.

Rose looked less impressed. 'I agree too. Who are you and what qualifies you for this job?'

Daniel appeared unfazed by her hostile tone. 'Why don't we go into the library area, then I can answer all your questions,' he replied, then turned to me. 'And you must be Daisy.'

'Dee. Only my mother called me Daisy.' I smiled at him. I wanted him to know that – unlike Rose – I was friendly; a friendly, saggy bag lady.

He led us into a snug room at the back of the hotel. It smelt of a peat fire, had old leather gentlemen's armchairs and walls lined with books, the kind of place you could curl up and spend hours reading. Rose, Fleur and I sat around a coffee table in front of the fireplace.

Daniel closed the double doors and came to sit with us. 'We shan't be disturbed in here. So. Allow me to introduce myself. I'm Daniel Scott and—'

'How do you – or rather did you – know our mother?' asked Rose.

'Rose, I take it,' said Daniel, then looked at Fleur, 'and you must be Fleur.'

Fleur nodded. 'Yes. Sorry, how rude of us,' she gave Rose an accusing look. 'Rose, Daisy . . . Dee, and Fleur. Daughters of Iris.'

'She named us all after flowers,' I said, then cursed myself for saying something so obvious.

'Iris did tell me. I think that's charming. Now, I know you must be wondering what you're in for. It must be strange to be in your situation and wondering who the hell I am. Your mother got in touch with me last year to ask if I would meet with you all when the time came . . . '

As he spoke, I had a chance to appraise him properly. He looked fit, not rugby fit, more yoga fit, lean and long limbed, and he had an elegance about him as he sat back in his chair, at ease with us and with the world. A man with nothing to prove. White hair slightly longer than in his PR photo, a pale blue linen shirt, jeans, three rubber bracelets on his right wrist, orange, yellow and green – the kind that say you support a charity, a woven-thread Indian bracelet on the other wrist. His face showed his age and was slightly craggy, lived in, but not in a weary way; he had laughter lines around blue eyes that looked intelligent. He also looked amused by what was happening. *But is that by us or by the situation he's in with us?* I wondered. *Whichever*, I decided, *Daniel Scott is a very attractive and charismatic man.*

'So you met our mother?' asked Rose.

'I did,' said Daniel. 'On several occasions. She came to one of the meditation centres I oversee. She studied with the swami at the centre for many months about eight years ago and then again in her last year.'

'Swami Muktanand. I remember her telling me about him,' I said.

Daniel nodded. 'That's right. She was a true seeker, your mother, very open minded. We kept in touch.'

'Did you visit her at the home?' asked Fleur.

'I did.'

'Did she contact you or you her?' asked Rose.

'She contacted me.'

'When?'

'March or April this year – yes, late March I think it was. She said she'd been thinking a lot about her life, what she'd achieved and what she hadn't.' He stopped for a moment and regarded us all, each in turn. 'She cared deeply that you should all be happy in your lives, and she regretted that you are no longer close.'

'Yes, yes, we know all this. We've had the letter,' said Rose.

'Rose, no need to be abrupt,' said Fleur. 'Let the man speak.'

'I just want to get on with it, whatever it is,' said Rose.

Daniel nodded. 'I understand. I also understand that this must be unusual for you all – not what you expected.'

'You can say that again,' said Rose.

Daniel gave her a brief nod. 'I'll do my best not to waste your time. In short, she devised a list of activities for the year. She did it with her friends, Jean and Martha,' he looked at Rose again, 'but I expect you know that much. She asked that I bring it to life, like an events manager – that's my part. No more. I'm not here to comment or prove anything to you or to advise, merely to put her programme in place. Whatever else happens is strictly between you and your late mother.'

'So what's first?' asked Rose.

Daniel reached into his briefcase and pulled out an Apple MacBook Air, which he placed on the table in front of us. 'A recording from your mother.'

There was an audible gasp from all of us. 'What! From Mum?' I asked, 'I mean with Mum in it?'

Daniel smiled and nodded. He really did have a nice smile. I smiled back.

'That's wonderful,' I said.

Rose let out a breath. 'Let's hear what she has to say first.'

'I think it's wonderful too,' said Fleur. 'We never thought we'd hear her voice again.'

'It's not just her, Martha and Jean have taken part too,' said Daniel. 'Shall I turn it on?'

'Please,' said Rose, as if giving a command to a waiter.

I wished she'd lighten up a bit. *Don't shoot the messenger*, I thought.

'OK. Here we go. Don't shoot the messenger,' said Daniel as he pressed his keyboard and found a folder.

'I was just thinking that,' I said and laughed.

Fleur rolled her eyes. 'Yeah sure.'

'I *was*.'

Any further conversation was cut short when an image of Mum appeared on the laptop. My eyes welled up with tears at the sight of her. A little bird, she'd become so frail in her last year, her white hair tied up in some sort of red polka-dot turban. She was sitting on a sofa in her living room at the bungalow at the retirement village, and by her side were Jean and Martha. Three little birds. They were all grinning like kids who were bursting with a secret to tell.

'Is it on?' Mum said to someone off screen. Daniel, I assumed. 'Yes. Right.' She turned, looked directly into the camera and beamed at us. I couldn't help but beam back. I was so pleased to see her. 'Hello dollies,' she said, using her old term of endearment. 'Met Daniel have you? Don't shoot the messenger, especially you Rose. Don't give him a hard time. He's only doing his job.'

I glanced at Daniel and our eyes met. Twinkle. Acknowledgement. Nice. *Take that Fleur*, I thought as I turned back to the screen. I looked closer and saw that the three of them had knotted their scarves on top of their heads, like housewives from the 1950s. Mum had a mop in her hand, Jean had a duster, and Martha a can of furniture polish. They held their items up near their faces in the manner of women in post-Second World War advertisements, then they all did a cheesy smile.

I laughed. Fleur gave me a look as if to say, what the . . . ?

'So, our outfits,' said Mum as she looked back to the camera. 'I'll get to that in a moment. By now, you'll have had my letter from Mr Richardson and know that I want you to follow my list for a year. Oh, I do hope you're all there and one of you isn't being awkward. It might seem a bit odd, but I am doing this for you, really I am.'

'We want to pass on a wee bit of what we've learnt in our lives,' said Jean.

'Our very *long* lives,' Mum added.

'Yes, true,' said Martha. 'We're all in our eighties now. None of us knows who will go first, but one knows that it's inevitable that it might be soon. As the saying goes, nothing more certain than death, nothing more uncertain than the hour.'

'Wuhooooo,' said Jean, and lifted her hands up into the air as if mimicking a spirit rising.

'Cheerful,' said Mum.

'I know, that's me,' said Martha with a smile, 'but it's a fact. Anyway, as you probably know from Iris, we've all been reading up about the afterlife and what's next—'

To her side, Jean slashed at her neck with the tips of her fingers, acting out having her throat cut, then she shut her eyes, let her head loll to one side and stuck her tongue out.

Fleur and I burst out laughing, and even Daniel chuckled. Jean was always mucking about when we were growing up. It was good to see she hadn't changed in her later years.

'But I felt more concerned about this life,' Mum interrupted. 'I want no regrets when I go, and my major regret is you three not getting on. And I wonder if you're all happy with the choices you've made. I know the world news is grim at the moment, it breaks my heart to hear what man is doing to man, and I worry how my girls are going to survive through it all, the anger and hatred you see every time you turn on the TV. That's partly why I want you to follow my list. Sometimes you have to work hard to rise above the sorrows of the day, with what's happening to you as individuals, but also what's happening on a grander scale in the world at large. What I propose in the programme we have devised is my true legacy – not the money, though you will get that later, but ultimately it can't buy what I want for you.'

'It can pay the heating and health bills, though, so we're not knocking it,' said Jean.

'Happiness doesn't come from possessions or the material. One has to go deeper,' added Martha.

I glanced over at Fleur and wondered how she felt about what they were saying. Her face gave nothing away. Rose's left foot was twitching as it always did when she was uncomfortable.

'I'm leaving this list so that you can explore, to a small degree, where happiness lies. To go forward with hope in your heart. Hah. If I was in better voice, I'd cue to a song right now.'

'Dance on through the din, dance on through the pain—' Jean sang blissfully out of tune.

Martha crossed her eyes and pulled a horrified face.

'Wrong lyrics, Jean,' said Mum. 'But you know what we're saying. Listen to songs that lift your heart, be with people who inspire you, go to places where you feel peace, cherish the ones you love.'

'Indeed. Choice not chance determines destiny,' said Martha. 'And if you're in a good frame of mind, if you're happy, then it is easier to react to whatever life throws at you.'

'So choose happiness when you can,' continued Mum, 'and I hope the methods we've arranged for you to look at in the coming months will go some way to help you do that.'

'I've known you all your lives,' said Jean, 'since you were wee girls. What we want to say to you is: don't waste your time with arguments, don't miss out on the friendship of sisterhood because of petty disagreements or distance or whatever it is you tell yourselves to keep you all apart. I remember you when you were close when you were younger, even if you don't. Give yourselves a chance to be close again.'

Mum nodded. 'And follow your dreams. Make time for them.'

'Do any of you have dreams, goals, things you'd still like to do?' asked Jean. 'Regrets about things you never did or said? Make time while you still have your health and move-ment. You don't appreciate it until it's gone. To have a healthy body means that you are free. Don't underestimate that freedom.'

All three of them nodded at that. I thought about my dream – to be a successful and respected artist. I'd started out with such enthusiasm, but in recent years settled for just getting by.

'The list looks at some of the different approaches to finding happiness,' said Martha. 'Of course, that happiness can be random, just comes across you some days out of the blue—'

'Days of grace,' Jean interrupted. 'That's what I used to call those times.'

'But there are times when one needs a helping hand,' Martha continued.

'Yes,' said Mum. 'Like Rose: you work so hard, but I wonder if you ever get to enjoy the lifestyle you've worked to create. Kick back, baby girl, don't always feel you have to be in charge. Enjoy time with Hugh and your children and let some of your feelings out before they make you ill. You know the saying – disease is really dis-ease. Learn to be at ease, Rose. And you Dee, you keep so much of what you're feeling inside. You were always the peacemaker, but at what price? You've hidden away much of your true potential. Be the expressive soul you were meant to be. Bugger what the others think. Fleur, you took flight so early into a bad marriage and to live abroad. But where are your friends now? I rarely hear you speak of them.' She looked at Martha and Jean with such tenderness. 'Friends are priceless; as everything else slips away and no longer seems to matter, your friendships will. Cherish them, nurture them. You three have sisters, find the friendship you had with them again.'

'No pressure then,' said Fleur.

'Shh,' whispered Rose. I noticed her eyes were shiny, wet with tears, which was unlike Rose who, as Mum had said, was so in control of her emotions as well as everything else.

'So. Cleaning,' Mum continued from the screen. She brandished the mop. 'That's what this first weekend is about. Don't worry, you don't have to do any. It's about giving the insides a clean, and we thought three different methods would be a good start to kick off with. The three approaches are: the emotional, the physical and the spiritual. First you will be starting with a session with a counsellor to get you all talking to each other. Clean out what you've all been holding back.' She brandished her mop.

Rose and Fleur groaned.

'No, don't groan,' said Mum.

I laughed nervously. *This is spooky*, I thought, *like she's here in the room.*

'You've got a lot to say to each other. You've all been bottling it up inside. Get it out, get rid, you'll feel better for it,' Mum continued.

'Session two is colonic irrigation,' said Jean.

'*What?*' gasped Rose.

'Martha's idea,' said Mum with a chuckle. 'Clear the crap. Great for the skin apparently.'

'And lastly, tomorrow,' said Martha, 'a meditation session to clear out the negative thoughts, or at least go beyond them to find some peace inside. I found it very helpful when I was younger and living in India.'

'Me too. But not in India,' said Mum. 'I know, this is probably not what you expected, but none of the weekends will be. We've tried to make it a varied programme with a few surprises. And the reason we want you to explore the different ways to be happy is simply because we wish you happiness. So. That's it, I think.' She looked at her friends. 'Anything to add?' They both shook their heads so Mum turned back to the camera. 'OK. Good. Excellent. See you in a couple of months.'

The three of them went back into their 1950s ad pose, held it for a moment, then the screen went blank.

Daniel turned to Rose, Fleur and me, then handed us each a sheet of paper. 'Your schedule for this weekend is on there, as well as my mobile number. Please call if you have any further questions. Oh and I must mention that, as well as the weekends, Iris asked me to send you the occasional message—'

'From you or her?' asked Rose.

'From her. You should have already got one – about being a winner not a loser?'

'I wondered who that was from,' said Fleur.

'I thought it was from Anna,' I said.

'Rose?' asked Daniel.

'I got it. How many will there be? What are they about?'

'I'm afraid I'm not at liberty to disclose that. Iris wanted them to be a surprise.'

Rose let out a heavy sigh. 'I hate surprises.'

'I don't,' said Fleur. 'I love them.' She looked at Daniel flirtatiously but it was hard to read his reaction.

'If you could confirm I have the right email addresses too, please. Apart from that, your first session today is at eleven,' Daniel continued. 'Second is at two this afternoon. The evening is for relaxation and leisure, and tomorrow the meditation session starts at ten.' He stood. 'I know it's a lot to take in, so I'll give you some privacy to talk about the recording. Have a nice day and I'll see you tomorrow morning – and may I say how much I am looking forward to working with you on your mother's last wishes.' He picked up his laptop and briefcase and gave us a slight bow. 'Until later.'

*

'And may I say how much I am looking forward to working with you,' said Fleur in a perfect impression of Daniel's south London accent after the door had closed behind him. She'd always been a good mimic, another talent to add to her already long list.

'I take it you didn't like him?' I asked.

Fleur gave me a look to say, isn't that obvious? 'Too silky smooth. I bet you do, though. He's just your type.'

'He is not. Why do you say that?'

'I know you. He's Mr Touchy-Feely.' She went into her Daniel impression again. 'I'm an emotionally intelligent man. Oh, I understand, let me give you some privacy, I am *so* sympathetic. Your type.'

'You were the one flirting with him.'

'It's always good to keep in practice but, seriously, not interested.'

'Sounds like the lady doth protest too much.'

'No, really. I mean, did you see those rubber wristbands? So pretentious. You don't even have to believe in the cause because your bracelet says it for you. They say I support charities. I support meaningful causes. Right on, brother, and all that.'

'What's wrong with that?'

'I think the people that really do something don't flaunt

it. They just do it, quietly, *sans* bracelet, *sans* advertisement to the world that says they are one of the good guys.'

I didn't tell her that up until a month ago I'd worn two bracelets from charities I supported. 'No more than wearing a pink ribbon for breast cancer awareness or a poppy on Remembrance Day.'

'Oh knock it off you two,' said Rose. 'What does it matter if he wears bracelets? As Mum said, don't shoot the messenger.'

'What did you think of him, Rose?' I asked.

'It doesn't really matter what I think, does it? We're doing this for Mum, though I did think he was a bit full of himself. Smug. Probably because he knows what we're in for.'

'Your type?' asked Fleur.

Rose gave her a withering look by way of reply.

'And what about Mum's programme of events?' I asked.

'Ridiculous. Colonic irrigation as a way to explore happiness? Seriously?' said Rose. 'I think perhaps Mum was on some weird medication when she thought this up, because frankly it's bordering on insane. I mean, come on, a dead woman sends her three daughters to have colonic irrigation as one of the conditions of her will. It's mad.'

Fleur laughed. 'I agree, it does sound a bit bonkers when you put it like that. I thought we'd be doing happy things, seeing as it's supposed to be an exploration of how to be happy.'

'Like what?' I asked.

'What makes anyone happy? Looking at flowers. Skipping in sunlit fields. Eating cupcakes. Drinking champagne. Buying shoes.'

Rose looked at her as if she was deranged. 'Buying shoes?'

'Oh, I don't know, but having a colonic would definitely not be top of my "how to be happy" list.'

'Maybe she's punishing us for not seeing each other?' I suggested.

Fleur suddenly burst out laughing.

Rose turned to her. 'Why is that funny?'

'I've just realized the inference. Why she's done it. Mum was saying we're full of shit.'

Fair point, I thought.

'In that case, our mother might have been eighty-seven but she was surprisingly immature,' said Rose. 'I suppose she thought it was funny too.'

'She probably did,' I said.

'Don't worry,' said Fleur. 'I've had colonics. They're not so bad. Your skin will glow and your eyes will sparkle. Doesn't hurt. Might even do us some good.'

'And this is supposed to bring us together how?' asked Rose.

'I can see the sense of it, sort of,' I said. 'A clear-out is always a good thing. Like clearing the leaves out of drains, get rid of the rubbish and you get to the clear water underneath.'

Rose raised her eyes to the ceiling. 'Typical of you to say something like that. Did you hear it at one of your New Age workshops down in Cornwall?'

'No, but I do tell my art students that when they feel that their work isn't going well. In any creative venture, you always have to clear the gunk first. Don't you tell your writers that?'

'No. I tell them to rewrite.'

'Same thing, sort of.'

But I'd lost Rose's attention. As far as she was concerned, she was the only one whose opinion mattered when it came to being creative. She glanced at her watch. 'There are so many other things I could be doing with this weekend. I'm going to my room. I'll see you for the first session at eleven.'

With that, she turned and walked off.

Fleur sighed and took the paper from me. 'Ah. Happy days,' she said as she glanced at it, then left the room and took off in the direction of the bar.

9

Saturday 10 October

At 11 a.m., the three of us trooped back to the library for the first session, where our counsellor was already waiting. She looked to be in her sixties, a large woman with silver hair past her shoulders, chunky amber jewellery, layered clothes the colours of autumn: ochre, brown and orange, and a pair of wide, comfy shoes, the kind bought by older people with bunions. Fleur would probably comment later on her bosom and need for a good bra – an over-shoulder boulder-holder, she used to call them.

The counsellor introduced herself as Beverly. She spoke with an American accent, East Coast – possibly a New Yorker. 'I met your mother on several occasions when she came and stayed here in her younger days,' she said.

'Our mother actually came here?' asked Rose.

Beverly nodded. 'She did. She attended a few of the workshops I ran over the years. She contacted me earlier in the year and told me she was putting together a list of activities for you and asked if I would meet with you as part if it. I suggest that we begin by introducing ourselves. Would one of you like to start?'

'We're sisters,' said Rose. 'We grew up in the same house. We don't need any introduction.'

Beverly regarded her for a few seconds. She had a very direct gaze. 'I do this with all my clients, even the married ones. We so often think we know each other, but actually there's always something new we can learn. Rose, why don't you go first? Tell us a little about yourself.'

Ha-ha. Take that Rose, I thought.

Rose gave a tight smile and, without looking at Fleur or me, began to speak. 'My name's Rose Edwards. I live in Highgate, London. I'm fifty-one years old. Two children. One husband. I work in publishing.'

'Speak to Fleur and Dee, Rose.'

Rose turned in her seat. 'What do you want to know?' she asked through gritted teeth.

'How do you feel about being here, Rose?' asked Beverly.

The look Rose gave Beverly almost made me laugh. I knew it so well. Her 'I won't be bossed around and you watch your step missie' face. Beverly reflected it right back. *This could be fun*, I thought as I settled in my chair as Rose continued. 'I *feel* frustrated. I don't want to be here. I have better things to do with my time.'

'Good,' said Beverly. If Rose was expecting an argument, she wasn't going to get one. 'Now you Daisy.'

I turned to look at Fleur and Rose. 'Mum was the only one who called me Daisy. I'm Dee McDonald. Forty-nine. Divorced, presently single. One daughter, doing well, and thanks to both of you for asking about her. OK, we might have fallen out but she's still your niece.'

'Mum always let us know how she's doing. Anyway, we're in touch on Facebook,' said Fleur.

'You are?' Ouch. That was news to me and hurt. Lucy hadn't accepted me as her Facebook friend, but then ours had never been an easy relationship and we'd often been at war with each other when she was growing up. We weren't close like Mum and I had been, though I hadn't given up hope that one day we might be. Lucy was wilful and stubborn as a child, ran wild in her teenage years, and her opinions often clashed with mine. As soon as she left school at eighteen, she was out the door and went to get a job in London and live with her aunt, Andy's sister. She'd lasted less than a year there, then went to live in Byron Bay in Australia, near her father, who she adored and who could do no wrong. We Skyped regularly, but letting me see her Facebook page was a no-no as far as she was concerned.

'Yes. She often messages me,' said Fleur. *Turn the knife, why don't you Fleur?* I thought.

'Let Dee speak,' said Beverly. 'How do you feel about being here Dee?'

'I was feeling great, but now I feel insulted that my sister Rose feels she has better things to do with her time than be here with Fleur and me. I think the least we can do is try to approach things with a positive attitude.' What I didn't say was that I was gutted that Lucy and Fleur were friends on Facebook and I'd been left out. It felt too familiar, reminiscent of times with Fleur and Rose when I'd been excluded from their various groups of friends.

Rose rolled her eyes.

'Good,' said Beverly. *Good? Is she mad?* I wondered. *You*

could cut the atmosphere in here with a knife. 'And lastly, Fleur.'

'Fleur Parker. Youngest. Married twice. Presently single. Nicest of the three.' She grinned at Beverly.

'Don't hide your feelings behind jokes and charm, Fleur. How do you feel about being here?'

'Actually I feel good,' she replied, and turned to look at Rose and me. 'I think the stupid standoff has gone on long enough and it's time to make up. We've just lost our mother. It's a time to be with family.'

If it's not too late, I thought.

'We were never close,' said Rose.

'Yes we were. We *were*. I remember loads of good times with both of you. You have a selective memory, Rose. I've missed you both.'

I was surprised to hear this. Fleur had always been so independent, and never appeared to need anyone, except in her thirties when she'd gone through a bad patch with alcohol. She used to call in the early hours of the morning when she'd been drinking to bemoan about some relationship or other, but mainly to berate me for not being there for her, as if she was the only one who ever had problems. Rose had had many years of the same phone calls, and both of us had grown weary of them and taken to putting the answering machine on after ten in the evening.

'I do have a selective memory,' said Rose. 'And that is why we're not close – because I remember what you can be like.'

Beverly nodded. 'Fleur's turn, Rose.'

'People change,' said Fleur, 'conquer demons.'

'Do they?' Rose replied.

'Not you apparently,' said Fleur.

'Meaning?'

'You haven't changed at all. Still judging, sitting on your high and mighty throne with no compassion.'

Ooh, that's harsh, I thought, though had to agree. Rose could be heartless.

'OK, good,' said Beverly. 'We've broken the ice a little. Now I want each of you to use three words to describe your sisters. Positive words. This time we'll start with you, Fleur. Three words about Rose.'

Fleur looked at Rose then back at Beverly. '*Three?*'

Rose looked indignant at the insinuation that three positive words were going to be hard to find. I thought it was just Fleur trying to be funny and have a dig at the same time.

Beverly nodded. 'Three.'

Fleur hesitated. 'Can Dee go first?'

'Can you, Dee?' asked Beverly.

Rose sighed heavily, looked at her watch, crossed her arms and legs and the left foot began to twitch.

'OK,' I said, and looked at Rose. If I was to be honest, I'd say uptight, anal and patronizing for her, and self-obsessed, impatient and frivolous for Fleur, but I'd been in therapy and knew how to play the game. They get you to start positive then bring out the knives later. 'OK. Rose. Hard-working. Conscientious. Focused.'

'Conscientious and focused are almost the same, can you give us another word?' asked Beverly.

I looked at Rose again. 'Stylish. She always looks immaculate.' Rose shifted in her seat but didn't look displeased.

'Good,' said Beverly. 'And for Fleur.'

'Beautiful. Light-hearted. A free spirit,' I said. Free spirit meaning she does exactly what she pleases, but Beverly wouldn't know that and what I'd said seemed to have worked. The atmosphere had lightened a tad.

'Fleur, your three words for Rose,' said Beverly.

Fleur had a mischievous look. 'Five foot three.'

I couldn't help but laugh. Rose rolled her eyes again.

'I get the feeling you're not taking this seriously, Fleur?'

Fleur gave her a 'duh' look. Beverly gave it back to her just as she had returned Rose's look earlier. 'I *am* taking it seriously,' said Fleur. 'Doesn't mean we can't tease each other. That's all it was.' She shrugged, then turned back to Rose and appraised her. Rose looked bored and turned to look out of the window. 'Capable, organized, efficient.'

Rose turned back. 'That makes me sound like a bank clerk.'

Fleur raised an eyebrow as if to say, *And your point is?* 'She's a great mother too,' she continued, 'and highly intelligent.' Rose visibly relaxed a little. She'd prided herself on her high IQ and top grades all through school and university. 'Bossy as hell. Hah. There are another three good words for her.'

'Positive Fleur, keep it positive for now,' warned Beverly.

'OK. Um . . . great cook. She does a mean Sunday lunch, or rather did. I haven't been invited for over three years and, yes, I am doing fine thank you very much, thanks for asking.'

Typical of Fleur. Making up her own rules as usual, I thought as I counted her words to describe Rose. *A lot more than three.* I glanced at Beverly. I suppose she saw people like us every day in her line of work. I wondered if she ever got sick of it, listening to people moaning on and having a go at each other. Her expression gave nothing away.

'OK, now Rose, three words for Dee.'

Rose glanced at me. 'New Age hippie.'

'Is that said in a positive way?' Beverly asked.

'And I am not a hippie,' I objected.

'You went to art college,' said Fleur. 'You drink herbal tea, wear Eastern-style clothes.'

This time it was my turn to roll my eyes. 'That does not make me a hippie. And I rarely drink herbal tea these days – that was a phase, not that you'd know.'

'Let Rose speak,' said Beverly.

'It wasn't meant in a negative way,' said Rose. 'I meant she's idealistic, romantic, child of God, you know, Woodstock and all that. Creative. Talented. There.'

'And Fleur, what would you say about Dee?' asked Beverly.

Fleur pouted. 'Rose nicked my words. *I* was going to say creative, talented.' I almost laughed again. Half a day in each other's company and we'd reverted back to being nine-year-olds; Fleur sulking because someone had used something of hers. I remembered endless tantrums if anyone dared to touch anything that belonged to her, and God forbid if either of us ever tried to borrow any of her clothes.

'I'm sure you can think of some others, Fleur.'

Fleur looked at me. 'Er . . . happy. Yes, you're a happy person Dee, sunny, or you were . . . Er . . . '

Yes, I was, I thought. I felt flattered she'd used the word happy to describe me, but also sad that I didn't think it applied any more. I wondered if Beverly would ask us to use three words to describe ourselves. Mine for me would be: wrinkly, disappointed, broke.

Fleur looked over at Rose. 'I know two good words for Dee. Animal-lover.'

Rose laughed but it came out as a snort. Beverly looked at her quizzically.

'Family joke,' said Rose. She looked annoyingly pleased.

'Not a joke shared by me,' I said. I knew they were referring to Max and Misty and probably saw me as a mad old cat lady.

'OK, let's stay focused,' said Beverly. 'Now we're going to say what you don't like. Dee. Why don't you go first again, and remember to speak to them, not to me.'

Old insecurities threatened to surface. 'Neither of you ever got me or where I was coming from. We made our choices and went our separate ways. And you know nothing about my life.' I took a deep breath and blinked away tears. I didn't want to break down and feel exposed or vulnerable in front of them, in case they went in for the kill as they sometimes did when we were young. 'You could both be cruel.'

Rose scoffed. 'Like when?'

A memory from when I was fifteen flashed into my mind. 'Stuart Robinson.'

Fleur laughed. She remembered too.

'Who was Stuart Robinson?' asked Rose.

'Dee had an almighty crush on him,' said Fleur. 'You must remember, Rose. Our April Fool? It was only a joke, Dee. A bit of fun.'

I took another deep breath. He was more than a crush. I'd loved him with a love that was true, but he'd hardly noticed me. I turned to Beverly. 'One Saturday morning, I was woken from a deep sleep by these two. "Stuart's at the front door and wants to see you," said Fleur. They seemed pleased for me and as excited as I was. I begged, "Don't let him leave, make him a coffee." I leapt out of bed, got dressed, splashed my face and made it down the stairs in record time. Stuart at our house. Come to see me. I was a teenage girl. Over the moon. I got downstairs. No Stuart. Just Fleur and Rose. "April Fool," cried Fleur. And there, Beverly, you have just one example of how mean my sisters could be.'

Beverly nodded. 'OK. Good, but if you can, just give me the three words for Rose and Fleur for now,' she said.

I felt a flicker of anger deep inside.

'Rose. Controlling. Cold. Stubborn.'

Rose bristled. 'If anyone's stubborn, it's you.'

'Please let each person speak without interruption or comment,' said Beverly. 'You'll get a chance to express your views later. Please continue Dee. Your words about Fleur.'

'Self-obsessed. Unreliable. Frivolous.'

'Unreliable? You can talk.'

'Rose. Your words about Dee and Fleur.'

Rose sighed. 'Dee. Irresponsible. Dreamer. Gives up too easily – er, that's more than three but you know what I mean. Fleur, selfish, shallow, also irresponsible.'

Well this is going well, I thought, as Fleur and I both crossed our legs and arms at the same time.

As the session went on, Rose clammed up completely. She'd said her piece.

Fleur's phone beeped that she had a text message. She got it from her bag and was about to read it.

'Turn your phone off, Fleur,' said Beverly. 'This is uninterrupted time with your sisters.'

Fleur did as she was told but looked shocked. It was

probably years since anyone had told her what to do. By the way a vein was throbbing on the left of her forehead, I could see she was holding in a curt reply. As Rose's foot was her giveaway, the vein in Fleur's temple was hers.

Watching both of them, the foot and the vein, I felt the air go out of me like a deflated balloon. *We're all still holding in what we really feel*, I thought. *And probably a good thing*. Fleur's temple vein only ever showed when she was angry.

'Would you like to talk about what's kept you apart?' Beverly asked.

'No,' snapped Rose. 'It would be raking over old ground.'

'Fleur?' asked Beverly.

Fleur shook her head. 'I think we ought to move forward.'

'Dee?'

'No point if the others don't want to,' I replied. I wanted to break something. *It would have been more therapeutic if Mum had organized a plate-smashing session*, I thought, as I became aware that I was grinding my teeth, which was my giveaway for when I'd had enough.

'A good start,' Beverly said when our time was up. 'You can't expect it all to be resolved in one session, but at least you all got a chance to say something, and from these small beginnings come great advances.'

What planet is she on? I wondered as I headed for my room. I had a headache and needed some space.

Five minutes later, a text via Daniel from Mum arrived. 'Often what you find annoying in a person is a reflection of yourself.'

'Much as I loved you Mum,' I said, 'you could be a right smartarse sometimes.'

10

Saturday 10 October, 2 p.m.

In the afternoon, we made our way to a modern spa in a building to the left of the hotel. A bright young thing with spiky blonde hair bounced out to greet us. 'Hi. Michelle's my name, colonics my game,' she said in a New Zealand accent, without pausing for breath, 'if we ate all the right things we'd feel a lot better and not need colonics but I know how it is, busy busy lives, but we must have our five a day and try to eat food without preservatives, but no matter, because today will leave you feeling like you've been on a three-day detox and that's fantastic.'

I didn't dare look at either of my sisters in case I started laughing. I had to admire Rose's self-control too, because what she didn't know about eating right wasn't worth knowing. I knew from visits to her house before our fall-out that she bought organic food from one of the posh home delivery services. Not that she ever cooked any of it. That task was left to the live-in au pair, who had always cooked the children's supper before they'd left to go to university.

As I remembered, Rose and Hugh rarely got home before eight in the evening.

I knew all about eating the right foods too. I've long been a fan of organic food and a balanced diet and know that it's true – eat rubbish, you will feel like rubbish; eat good, fresh nutritious food and you feel more focused and energetic.

'So, remember girls,' said Michelle. 'I know this programme you're on is about finding happiness. Eat right and you will be – happy, that is. In other words, you are what you eat.'

I saw Rose flinch. She hated being called a girl, especially by someone half her age. Fleur burst out laughing.

Michelle gave her a quizzical look. 'Did I say something funny?'

'Family joke,' said Fleur and looked at me as if to say, come on, Dee, remember? 'You are what you eat. School?'

I remembered and burst out laughing too. *Hah, take that Rose. The dynamic has shifted and now it's Fleur and me against you.* Rose had a face like thunder.

'Wasn't funny then, isn't funny now,' she said.

'Are you gunna tell me what's going on?' asked Michelle.

Rose shook her head. 'My sisters are retarded. So. Michelle. Colonic. Shall I go first and we can leave these two adolescents to their silly sniggering?' She walked off then turned back. 'You know, Mum was right. You are full of shit.'

That only made Fleur and me laugh more.

It had been over thirty years ago. Fleur was twelve, in her first year, and the school had put on a series of lectures with the exact same message about making the right food choices. Bright posters showing fruit and vegetables with the slogan 'You Are What You Eat' were all over the classrooms and corridors of the school that Rose, Fleur and I attended. The idea of eating right was as popular back then as it is today.

'Bring in examples of healthy produce for a classroom display,' said Mrs Madison, our form teacher.

Mary Riley put fruit on her head, 'Oo, I've gone bananas,' she joked.

Anna Fairchild held melons to her chests, and her best friend, Claire, put runner beans round her neck and declared, 'I'm a human bean.'

Susan Wilson, being more daring, waved a courgette in front of her crotch and, to anyone who went by, said, 'Hello darlin', fancy a bit of this?'

We were all a bit giddy and sex-obsessed back then.

Fleur, being Fleur, had to take it further. She drew a human-looking penis with arms, legs, hairstyle and face remarkably like Rose's, and in case anyone missed the likeness, she wrote Rose's name under the drawing, along with the slogan, 'You Are What You Eat'. She stuck it up next to one of the posters of fruit and got a public shaming in assembly as well as a week of detention. She didn't care. She was school hero and a clown.

Rose was furious and didn't speak to her for a month. The cartoon was Fleur's revenge. She was jealous. She fancied a boy that Rose had been seeing, but she was too young for him and, though easily the prettiest of us all, she was flat-chested with the figure of a boy while Rose had curves and breasts. Curiously, it's Rose who's thin now and Fleur who's got the curves.

Was that the beginning of the distance between Fleur and Rose? I wondered as Rose and Michelle disappeared into a treatment room. *Could it have dated back so early? Maybe. Rose prided herself on her reputation as the model pupil, a little Miss Perfect, and Fleur had struck right to the heart of that. With her prank, Fleur had also shown she wasn't to be trusted when it came to boys.*

'Tea?' Fleur suggested, and strode off towards the library without waiting for a reply. I followed her in, intending to stay a short while then escape to my room to mull over the session with Beverly.

'Rose used to torment us terribly,' said Fleur as the waiter brought us Earl Grey tea in silver pots. 'Remember that time she tied us to a tree in the park?'

'I do. She'd told us it was a game. She was the sheriff—'

'Of course. She always had to be top dog.'

'She told us we were naughty cowboys—'

'Then she disappeared and left us there while she went home for supper.'

'I couldn't have been more than seven; you'd have been about four. I guess Rose was jealous when we came along and usurped her role as only child, getting Mum and Dad's sole attention.'

'We were close once, weren't we Dee?'

I nodded vaguely. *When we were very young*, I thought, *but then we grew to be teenagers, which brought its own hurdles with hormones and boys.*

'Remember, we used to tell each other all our secrets back then – who we'd kissed, who'd tried what,' Fleur continued.

'I do.' I remembered her telling me about her early explorations, but I never had as many conquests to report, so would play up my fumbling experiences with the few boys who had showed an interest so that it sounded as if I was as popular as her. As Fleur got older and had boys falling over themselves to get near to her, she advanced to the 'did you go above the waist or below?' confessions. I still tried to join in, but she was way ahead of me and my role became that of listener.

'Rose never joined in, did she?'

'Not after the cartoon incident. I think that's when she became more private and self-contained. She kept her secrets about boys and what she did with them to herself.'

'Do you remember her diary? Hidden and locked.'

'Did you try and get in?'

'Course. Didn't manage it though.'

'She's a typical Scorpio, secretive and with a sting in the tail if anyone crossed her.'

Fleur looked at me quizzically. 'Do you still believe in all that stuff?'

'I think it has something to offer.'

'I'm Leo. What are they like?'

I laughed. 'Can be show-offs who like to entertain and be the centre of attention.'

'*Moi?* Never. And you're—?'

'Pisces. According to the Zodiac books, the romantic dreamer.'

'Maybe there is something to it then,' said Fleur as she nibbled on one of the home-baked biscuits we'd been brought. 'All seems a long time ago, doesn't it? Hey, remember when we found Mum's sanitary towels? You must have been about six. Not knowing what they were, we'd used them as doctor's masks in a dressing-up game.'

'Vaguely.'

'You must remember. We were having a great old time

and burst in on Mum who was entertaining the vicar in the kitchen. Mum roared with laughter but the vicar didn't know where to put himself.'

A long time ago, I noted, aware that Fleur's recollections were from when we were very young, with no recent ones to share. As we laughed over the vicar incident, I suddenly felt overwhelmingly sad about the years in which she'd been lost to me.

*

Back in my room for a quick break, I called Anna and told her about the session with Beverly. 'I'm not sure Mum's scheme is going to bring us any closer.'

'What you resist, persists,' she said. 'Give it time.'

'Wise words,' I said.

'That's me. Embrace the experience.'

'It's a colonic next.'

'Ah . . . well, enjoy.'

After I'd hung up, I thought about what Mum had said about wanting us to be happy. Fleur had described me as a happy person. What happened to that girl/woman? Daisy, the easy one? The happy one? The peacekeeper? *If Mum's list of tasks will help me get back to her, then great, I'll do it. And if part of the programme means clearing the crap, I'll do that too*. As I went down to have my treatment, I wondered what Mum had lined up next – a vajazzle maybe, to complete the front and back.

*

Half an hour later, I lay on a couch in a clinically white room with a rubber tube inserted into my back passage while lukewarm water *avec les herbes* flushed in and out of my colon. *All part of life's rich tapestry*, I thought as the tune of 'The Hokey Cokey' ran through my mind, accompanied by the words '*les herbes* go in, *les herbes* go out, in out, in out, shake it all about; knees bent, arms stretched, rah, rah, rah.'

For some odd reason, lying there with a strange object inserted into one of my orifices made me think back over my relationships. With my husband Andy, I'd married my best friend, so sex was never erotic or dangerous, it was comfortable and familiar. We were young and, despite thinking we knew it all, we really didn't. Once, after reading some article in a magazine about how to spice up your sex life, I suggested experimenting, maybe trying role-playing or dressing up. I'd imagined doctors and nurses, or me as a French housemaid sort of thing. That evening, Andy came to bed naked apart from a plastic Viking helmet complete with horns that he'd found in our dressing-up box for parties. Sadly, our role-playing turned into the weary eunuch and the frigid nun. But he could make me laugh like no one else and, for a while, I had no need for passion. John, my last partner, was different. He did like to experiment sexually – sadly with other women as well as me. And with Nick, the man in between Andy and John, the sex was exciting and passionate. It was with him that I'd discovered that sex could feel sacred, a communion of spirits. He told me that he felt the same but he wasn't ready to settle down. Back then, the fashionable attitude was to be cool and undemanding when it came to love. Needy and clingy were dirty words. My friends and I told each other that if you loved someone, you had to give them their freedom, let them go and if they kept coming back, then it was meant to be, if not, it wasn't. Nick and I parted tearfully but I let him go and didn't pursue him. I waited to see when he'd return. I felt sure we were meant to be. That was the last time I saw him. I heard that he married a Brazilian girl six months later, which taught me a major lesson in life – when a man says he doesn't want to settle down, he means: not with you pal. I went to my favourite book at the time, *The Prophet* by Kahlil Gibran and read, 'For even as love crowns you, so he shall crucify you, Even as he is for your growth so he is for your pruning.' Nick cut back the flower of love I felt for him and left the branch bare.

There had been a few lovers since John, a couple of disasters, a few maybes, no one special. My last disaster came to mind. It was with Martin Mitchell. Not really my type – too swarthy, with Mick Jagger lips and full of himself, but I knew he liked me. He lived in London, was divorced, and had a holiday home up on the cliffs. He'd asked me out several times when he was down in Cornwall. I refused over several summers, but his attention was flattering and, in the end, he wore me down. For lack of anyone else and a fear of becoming an old maid, I agreed to go out for dinner. Watching him eat was like watching a cow chewing cud and I should have quit then, but after two bottles of wine on our third date, we went back to his house and fumbled our way to his bed. Much to his embarrassment, he couldn't get an erection. I tried to reassure him it was all right and, as the wine wore off, was already regretting being there. But no. He had to show his worth.

'There are other ways to pleasure you,' he'd insisted, and not wanting to hurt his feelings or make him feel like a failure, I stayed. I knew how fragile the male sexual ego was. *It will be my good deed for the week*, I thought, *then I'll be out of here*.

'This should do the trick,' he said romantically as he nosedived under the sheets, where he stayed for the next half-hour suckling and breathing air up my lady parts.

I counted cracks in the ceiling as he continued his task with enthusiasm, and did a bit of appreciative moaning so as not to seem like a spoilsport, but it felt like a slug was doing aerobics between my legs. *The sooner we get this over with*, I thought, *the sooner I can go home to a cup of tea and a good book.*

When he finally detached himself, we heard a *fft fft fft* sound. He'd been going at it so long, air had got trapped inside me and of course had to get out some way or other. I couldn't stop it rippling out. *So much for all the pelvic floor work I've done over the years*, I thought. The air had been breathed in, the air was coming out, no stopping it.

We could have laughed about it – sex can be a funny business, after all – but he came up from the sheets looking dismayed and said, 'I've been fantasizing about you for years. I finally get close to you and what do you do? You fart in my face.'

I was indignant. 'It was *not* a fart. It didn't come from the intestines so no gas or odour.'

But the moment for shared amusement had been ruined.

He sent me a text the following week. *Got some Viagra. Ready 2 give it another go?*

I texted back. *Friends staying. Sorry.*

He didn't pursue it and I decided to give up on men after him.

'It was like he was blowing up a balloon,' I told Anna, 'I'm surprised I didn't float off out of the window and into space. I could have made the news. A strange object was seen orbiting the planet last night. Was it a bird? Was it a plane? No, it was Dee McDonald after a session with Blubber Lips Mitchell.'

Anna thought it was hilarious, hence her gift of the Greek satyr and the message not to give up.

'Wind up the Watford Gap,' she said. 'There's a word for that.'

'A word?'

'There is. "Queef" – the fanny fart.'

'So you've experienced it?'

She shook her head. 'No, but queef is a useful word to know when playing Scrabble.'

That was five years ago. I hadn't had a lover since.

*

When I came out of the session, neither Fleur nor Rose were to be seen. I looked to see if either of them had texted me to suggest supper together, but there were no messages. My room, bed and a bath beckoned, and I succumbed to the luxury awaiting me. It was only day one on Mum's plan and I had reconnected a little with Fleur, so that was progress of sorts. I ordered room service and sank back into the sumptuous cushions on my bed.

11

Sunday 11 October, 10 a.m.

The scent of joss sticks drifted out of the conference room at the back of the hotel where our meditation session was to be held. Daniel was there, sitting at the feet of an elderly Indian man who was seated on a chair covered in a white sheet. Both of them were wearing white kurtas and loose white trousers.

'Guru gear,' whispered Fleur, as Daniel nodded at us and indicated that we should find a place. There were already about twenty other people in the room, seated on yoga mats that had been placed on the floor, so we went to take our places at the back. Rose sat cross-legged with ease. I knew from Mum that Rose attended yoga classes regularly, the kind where you do it in a hot room. Bikram yoga. Anna calls it Biryani yoga, after the time we went to the village hall to give it a try. We couldn't do the postures so snuck out the back and went for a curry instead.

As we waited for the session to begin, I sat with my knees up in front of me and Fleur did the same. I looked around at the other people. Some were sitting with their eyes closed, others like us, just waiting. No one spoke and the atmosphere felt very peaceful.

After a few more people arrived and settled, Daniel stood and introduced the Indian man as Swami Muktanand. He looked like Father Christmas, with smiley eyes, a white beard and a serene face. It was hard not to smile back at him.

'Welcome my dear friends and brothers and sisters. I am *so* pleased to meet you,' said the swami. 'First today, listening short time to me. Second, practising meditation. The word meditation means concentration. What differs in the various methods of meditation is what you concentrate on. Some use a mantra or music or sound, some meditate on candle or an image, some turn inside and focus within on breath. Today we will do very easy method to help release negative thoughts and feelings. Sit comfortably. OK. Everyone ready? We begin. Breathe in, hold for three, one two three, exhale. Imagine when you breathe in that you are inhaling energy, purity, goodness. When you breathe out, you are letting go of any anger, hatred, fear, bad feeling. OK? Simple. Focus on breath. If thoughts wander, no worry, imagine you are mountain, still and ancient, thoughts are birds flying by overhead, let them go. If thoughts wander, no worry, bring them back to breath. It is your anchor to present moment.'

'I can do the ancient bit,' Fleur whispered. 'I feel creaky sitting like this.'

'Shh,' Rose whispered back. As in any class, she was taking it all seriously, sitting straight backed, the model pupil. Fleur, also reverting to type, pulled a face at her.

'The breath is point of concentration. OK, now we begin proper fantastic. Close eyes. Focus,' said the swami. 'Breathe in, hold one . . . two . . . three . . . good, breathe out.'

We dutifully did as we were told, and for the first five minutes I did manage to concentrate. Breathe in, hold . . . breathe out.

I like what the swami said, I thought, *the breath is an anchor to the present.*

Focus. Don't think.

Breathe in, hold . . . exhale. Breathe in energy, breathe out anxiety, anger, fear. Woah, that's going to be a long breath out. I'm going to be here for weeks.

Breathe in, good, hold one two three, let go of my anger, fear and sadness. There's a lot of that, Mum dying, missing Lucy, worry about my home, exhale.

Breathe in, hold . . . let go of my disappointment, worry, negativity.

I wonder how everyone else is doing?

I felt like I might be huffing a little too loudly on the out breath and wondered if that was right? I took a peek. Everyone was sitting with their eyes closed, even Fleur. I glanced over at Daniel. He looked very peaceful, not like he was exorcizing years of negativity.

Close your eyes, I told myself.

I closed my eyes but the image of Daniel stayed.

He has a nice nose. Straight. Noble. I wonder if he's single.

I opened my eyes again and tried to see if he had a ring on his finger but couldn't see from my vantage point.

Close your eyes Dee, I told myself again.

I've done meditation before when I was in India and at

home. I ought to be good at this. I've chanted Om and Nam-myoho-renge-kyo with the best of them.

I wonder where Daniel lives.

Why am I thinking about him? Focus.

Breathe in, hold . . . let go of sadness and worry. Mum suddenly came to mind and, with her image, a wave of grief. *Breathe.* I didn't want to cry in a room full of people, *exhale, exhale, exhale.*

I need a wee. I wonder if I could sneak out and get back without disturbing anyone. Probably not. I must go beyond it. Beyond my thoughts, beyond wanting to wee.

My bum hurts.

I shifted my position.

Fuck. I've got pins and needles. Oo. Agony.

I shifted again. *Phew, that's better.*

I wonder how Rose and Fleur are getting on. No. Doesn't matter. Focus.

Rose looked so smug that she could sit cross-legged. I bet she could go the whole way and do the lotus position if she wanted. I used to be able to. I must get fitter. Go back to Pilates.

God, I'm thinking a lot.

I am a mountain, my thoughts are birds. Fly away, fly away birds. Actually what kind of birds? Pigeons pooping? Crows cawing? Chickens clucking? Ducks flying in formation? Or swans? Seagulls? Vultures? They can be violent. I wonder if the swami has accounted for the fact that there are different kinds of birds and some can be a hell of a lot more distracting than others. Mustn't complicate things. I am a mountain of serenity. Breathe in, hold . . . exhale. Oops, here comes a flock of sparrows, hundreds of them. Christ, my meditation has turned into Hitchcock's The Birds. *Get out the gun. Shoot the fuckers, that will sort them. Oh dear. That's not very peace and love, Dee. Oh hell, I am going mad. Breathe in, hold . . .*

I wonder how long we've been doing this? Feels like ages.

Breathe in, exhale, hold . . . No, it's the other way round. Breathe in, hold . . . exhale. Breathe in, hold . . . exhale. Yep, getting the hang of it now.

'And now you may open your eyes,' said the swami. I did as he instructed and he smiled beatifically at us all from the front. 'Good, no?'

Exactly. No, I thought. Clearly I am bonkers.

*

As we filed out into the corridor, I whispered to Fleur, 'How was it for you?'

'I dozed off, I'm afraid,' she said.

I didn't get a chance to ask Rose. She was halfway down the stairs on the way to get her room key.

*

Half an hour later when I went to check out, the receptionist told me that both of my sisters had gone. No goodbye, no offer to drop me at the station. *Meanies*, I thought. Rose would go back to her family, secure life, mortgage paid off, Fleur to her glamorous flat in Knightsbridge. Neither had the worries that I had, yet neither even thought to ask how I was getting home.

And breathe in, hold . . . exhale, I told myself as I saw Daniel approaching.

'How did you find the session?' he asked.

'Good. Relaxing.' I felt that I blushed a little. I was never a good liar and, standing so close to him, looking into his eyes, I felt the pull of chemistry.

'Excellent. You can practise at home too.'

'I will.'

'Are you heading there now?'

I nodded. 'Back to Plymouth.'

'Train?'

I nodded.

'Me too. Have your sisters gone?'

I nodded again. I had turned into one of those nodding toy dogs that people put in their cars. Perhaps I could tell him it was another type of meditation – you put your head down, then up, then down then up. *Shut up, Dee, try and act like you're a sane human being*, I told myself. 'Fleur and Rose both drove here,' I said. 'Separately.'

He looked in the direction of the door. 'You strike me as being very different women.'

'I guess we are, always were.'

'Striking looking too.'

'Fleur was always a beauty and Rose has always had great style.'

He smiled. 'I meant all of you.'

I squirmed. *He's just being kind*, I thought, then blushed when I saw that he was staring at me. 'Middle child,' he said.

'Meaning?'

'Eclipsed by the other two, you don't see your own beauty.' I was about to protest when he pointed at himself. 'Middle child too. I get it. I have an older brother who's made a fortune. In worldly terms, he's a great success. Younger brother who excelled at sports. And then there was me.' He pulled a face. 'I never felt I could compete with their achievements. I was the one at home with my books, always looking for answers.' I smiled in recognition. 'Anyway. Enough of that. How are you getting to the station?'

'Cab.'

'Want to share?'

'Sure. What about the swami? Or does he beam himself back to wherever he's come from, like in *Star Trek*?'

Daniel laughed. 'I wouldn't put it past him. No. He's staying at the centre in Bristol tonight. I arranged a driver for him.'

'Centre?'

'Yes, there are meditation centres all over the country. I can tell you all about them on our ride to the station.'

Suddenly the weekend looked a whole lot brighter – a cab journey with a new and attractive man, and not a sister in sight to cramp my style.

12

Rose

Sunday 11 October, evening

It was only when I was on the motorway, halfway back to London, that I realized I could have offered Dee a lift to the station. Fleur had her car. Maybe she gave her a lift. Hope so. Oh fuck it, there are taxis. Dee's a grown woman. One weekend down, five more to go, and if they are anything like the last two days, God help us. I know Mum meant well, but Christ Almighty, colonics? I gave the therapist fifty quid to forget the whole idea and keep her mouth shut. I've a ton of manuscripts to get through without having a rubber tube shoved up my jacksie in the pursuit of happiness. And the meditation session? Fat chance of me finding peace within with everything that's going on in my head at the moment. I came out of it feeling agitated and annoyed that I couldn't do it. Truth be told, I'd like a bit of peace of mind. I bet Fleur and Dee hate me for taking off in a hurry and for not hanging out with them more, but what do they know of my life? Maybe they'd understand if I told them. But I don't want to talk to them about what's going on, or anyone else apart from Hugh for that matter – and no, not even God, Mum.

Fleur

Sunday 11 October, evening

Truth be told, I'm lonely. I am. Coming back to my dark, empty flat, I don't think I have ever felt more so. Boo-hoo. Poor me. Think I'll have a glass of wine.

I was pleased to get the chance to reconnect with my sisters – well, Dee anyway. Rose can be a bitch. Dee was always a sweetie. We did have a bit of a laugh yesterday reminiscing about the old days. My sisters. Who else knows me inside out? Have known me since birth? OK, we can wind each other up something rotten, but don't all siblings do that? I've enjoyed seeing them again and hope they'll become part of my life again. I do. Even Rose.

Mum's death hit me hard. Hit us all hard. While she was alive, wherever she was, was my true home to go back to, even in the retirement village, my port in a storm and all that. I have nowhere else like that in my life now. No one else. No husband, no boyfriend, no great network of friends, partly due to travelling and living in different countries. Made a bit of a mess of things really. Boo. I'm feeling sorry for myself. Why not? Self-obsessed, Rose said I was. Cow. Probably true though.

It's so lovely that Mum left her list for us, caring from beyond the grave. Seeing the recording of her yesterday morning – woo, it was like she hadn't really gone. Not really. And five more to go. Hah. How many parents attempt something like that? She was a rare gem. I'll look forward to seeing her familiar face every other month and hearing what she's thought up. It's a precious legacy she's left us, if a little off beam. That's probably where I get it from. Fleur Crazy Parker, that's me. But where has she gone? I keep asking myself, over and over. And Dad? Where did he go? Why didn't they get just one phone call to say, hey I've landed on the other side. I'm fine.

People look at me and imagine that I have it all, and yes, I have money, the fancy car, my portfolio of properties, a new flat in Knightsbridge, but no one to share it all with. Yes, I know a ton of people, but there's a difference between acquaintances and true friends. I long for someone to be there on a Friday night, at the end of the week, to pour me a glass of wine, ask how my day went. Someone who really knows and accepts me. It's not easy meeting men at my age, and without a circle of friends to introduce me to their single friends, how am I going to meet anyone? I tried Internet dating for a nanosecond. Too depressing. Arabella, my neighbour, tells me that you're supposed to treat it like a job, put in the hours, but I'm not that desperate. Or am I? I used to be able to pull men with a glance. Not so sure I can any more.

Really I just want someone who is there for me, who loves me. Mum was that person, but she's gone, leaving a great fat empty hole. But seeing Rose and Dee again, I see Mum in them, in gestures, mannerisms, in phrases we all use without realizing; they are such a part of us. Rose has Mum's petite slim shape and her bird-like eyes, taking it all in. Dee has her nose and her wide, smiling mouth. They ought to give them back. Ha-ha. Old joke, Fleur. Dee's looking good, but I think the dark hair needs a change. She dyes it. I can tell. Highlights and a good cut, that's what she needs. Three inches off to bring it to her shoulders. Would take years off her. After a certain age, a woman needs a softer hair colour. Blonde, honey, fudge. Opinionated. *Moi?* Never. Hah. Dee and Rose missed that word when asked to describe me.

But Rose and Dee are family. My family. All that I have left, apart from distant cousins I hardly know and never will. That stupid fall-out. We let it go on too long. While Mum was here, I felt connected to my sisters in a way. I always knew where they were, how they were, what they were doing. Mum always told me their latest news, so it didn't actually matter too much that we didn't speak in person. I knew they were there somewhere in the background. So yes, Mum's mad programme to teach us the way of happiness. I could do with a bit of that, and companionship, so I'm in for the duration, whatever she has planned, colonics and all. Bring it on.

Dee

Sunday 11 October, late evening

As soon as I got back to Kingsand, I headed over to Anna's to tell her the latest. I could see her bedroom light was on at the front of her house, and knew she'd probably be up reading as she did most nights, probably with a cup of cocoa. Anna and I pride ourselves on being the last of the great ravers and sometimes go really wild and read past midnight.

I had a key to her house so I let myself in and headed up the stairs.

'Only me,' I called.

She didn't reply, but I heard a strange muffled sound coming from her bedroom. Something sounded wrong. I opened her door and gasped. 'Anna! What happened?' I said as I ran over to the bed.

Anna was in her nightdress and had been gagged and tied to the bed. She was moving her head as though trying to say something, so I quickly undid the gag.

'Who did this to you? Are you all right?' I began to undo the ties holding her to her bed. 'Are you hurt? Are they still in the house?'

Anna's shoulders were heaving and a strange noise came from her throat, a strangulated cry. It took me a few seconds to realize that she was laughing.

'Jesus, Anna. What's going on? What's so funny?'

Anna sat up. 'Ian. He's been reading *Fifty Shades of Grey* and thought we should try and spice up our sex life.'

'Oh, for heaven's sake. So where is he?'

'In the bathroom. He went in there to get some massage oil. He'll be back in a sec.'

'*No.* God. Sorry. I . . . I just came to tell you how the weekend went. I'll go . . . '

As I headed for the door, I heard the toilet flush across the corridor and a moment later, Ian appeared. 'Oh. Company,' he said when he saw me. He didn't seem fazed at all by the fact he was stark naked.

'Woah! Just leaving. Sorry for the intrusion,' I mumbled as I averted my eyes. 'See you later. Oh god. Sorry, sorry.'

Ian and Anna cracked up laughing. 'You can stay if you like. I think the moment here might have gone,' called Anna.

'No no, not at all. As you were. Sorry. Carry on,' I called back as I hotfooted it down the stairs. 'Coffee tomorrow?'

'Absolutely,' Anna called back. 'I'll come to you.'

Well, she's a dark horse, I thought as I crossed the road and let myself into my house, where I went straight to the fridge, found a bottle of white wine and poured myself a large glass.

Monday 12 October, 11 a.m

'So tell me more about this Daniel character,' Anna asked after I'd filled her in on my weekend. She'd come over for breakfast, so I'd made us scrambled eggs on toast and a pot of tea.

I shrugged. 'Not a lot to tell.' I was glad I'd had the night to sleep on it. I'd been on a high when I went running into Anna's the previous night, but in the harsh light of the day, I was seeing things more clearly. I'd got on with Daniel. He'd listened as well as talked and laughed easily too. I liked that. He asked about my art, my life, Lucy, and it was only on the train home that I realized I still knew very little about him, apart from the fact that he had two brothers, lived in London, organized events for Swami Muktanand as well as worked as an executive behind the Heaven on Earth centres that taught meditation. He was currently single.

'So you shared a cab and then went for a drink?'

'We both had over half an hour to wait.'

Anna raised an eyebrow. 'Fate. It's like *Brief Encounter*.'

'Oh stop it. In *Brief Encounter*, Celia Johnson's character was married. I'm not married and neither is he.'

'Ah, so you established that much.'

'I did, but I bet he has a lot of women after him.'

'So? No reason he wouldn't pick you. You look great. You *are* great.'

'Thanks for the vote of confidence but . . . I don't want to get involved with anyone. I'm quite happy on my own. I just can't go there again – all that wondering if he'll call. Can I trust him? Worrying about taking my clothes off in front of a stranger. The years it takes to get to the comfy silences. Anyway, there's bound to be something wrong with him. If men aren't unfaithful, they're alcoholic, sportaholic, workaholic or just plain dull.'

Anna put down her fork and stopped eating. 'Oh Dee. It's not like you to be so negative about men. You've talked yourself out of anything happening before you've even got to know him. And what about my Ian? He's none of those "holic" types.'

'Sexaholic,' I said and she laughed. I didn't comment on her saying that I was negative. The truth of it was that I didn't want to get hurt or disappointed and it was easier to just stay away from men and any involvement. John had done a lot of damage when I was with him; he'd slowly worn away my confidence with his criticism, then later lack of interest in me sexually. I did therapy for a while after we'd split up and, of course, the therapist said that I had to own my part in the breakdown of our relationship.

When I did, I learnt that, deep down, part of me felt that men don't stay around. Maybe this had come from Dad dying so young, and so I attracted men to me who would fulfil that belief. After one session, when I came out feeling miserable, I decided that therapy was like picking at scabs, and that in order to move forward, I had to stop poking away at my past and any hurt therein and leave it to heal. The session with Beverly hadn't done much to change my mind either. Leaving the past in the past had worked well since I'd stopped therapy. I had my cats. I had my work. I had Anna and, until recently, I had my home. It was enough, and I'd chosen not to think too deeply about my choices.

'I like that Ian wants to keep things interesting,' said Anna, bringing me back to the present.

'How did it go last night in the room of sin after I'd left?'

Anna laughed. 'He tried something rather ambitious for a man who's due to have knee surgery next week. He got himself into an awkward position, cricked his neck, his back locked so he couldn't move, so it was abandon bed, find the Deep Heat in the medicine box, then a cup of tea, that healer of all ills.'

'Fifty Shades of Earl Grey, the hot alternative for the over-fifties. Probably not what he had in mind.'

'Exactly, and the only penetration was that of the ointment for sore muscles.'

I cracked up laughing. 'Sexy. God, we're like a pair of teenagers.'

'And why shouldn't we be?' said Anna. 'I might be fifty but I still feel like a nineteen-year-old inside sometimes. Just because we are middle-aged, why do people assume that we've suddenly become boring old farts and stopped having fun?'

'Possibly because of the back injuries? But Mum used to say the same thing even in her eighties – that she still felt young inside and, just because her body had grown old, why should she stop having a laugh sometimes? "It doesn't all have to be doom, death and dentures," she used to say.'

'She was a wise old bird, your mother. I agree. Let's say no to dribbling and dementia.'

We were both quiet for a moment. 'I'm sorry about walking in on you last night. I hope I didn't ruin things.'

'You didn't. It was funny. Ian and I laugh a lot. And I wish you could have seen your face! Don't worry. Ian'll recover. And you know, Dee, I am sure there's someone out there for you too, and it might just be this Daniel. He sounds interesting.'

I grimaced. 'Well, no hurry. I'll see him again in December. I tried to grill him about what was coming next on Mum's list, but he wouldn't give any of it away, apart from to say that some of it would be fun.'

'Some?' Anna raised an eyebrow.

'In the meantime, I have more pressing things on my mind like, where am I going to live?'

'How's that going?'

'Three viewings booked in over the next few weeks already. The estate agent said things are a bit slow, but the people he's sending round are all very keen. Michael will be very happy about that.'

'Talking of which, he was in the pub on Saturday night when you were in London. He and Ian got talking at the bar so, of course, I had to go over and meet him. Actually he seems like a nice man. He asked about you. Seemed interested.'

'Only in how soon I can vacate his house.'

'No. When he realized I knew you, he asked about your paintings. He said his mother had one of them.'

'Really?'

'Yes. He didn't talk about the house at all. Ian found out a bit about him. Divorced apparently. His wife left him for her tennis coach.'

'And your point is?'

She shrugged. 'Michael. Daniel. Men are a bit like buses. You wait for ages then two come along at once. Options, my dear.'

'Anna, stop it. Not that I am remotely interested, but I am pretty sure I am not Michael's type.'

'Who knows what his type is? I'm just saying keep your options open. I know. I have a plan. Have an affair with Michael. Marry him. Arrange for him to have an accident on the stairs one night – they are steep in your house – then . . . problem solved. The house is yours.'

'I really do think you ought to write a novel with your overactive imagination.'

'I could, couldn't I? We've had *Girl with the Dragon Tattoo*, *Gone Girl*, *Girl on a Train*. I could write about you, the quiet girl who no one suspected. I could call it *Girl in a Thermal Vest*.'

I bristled. I was wearing a thermal vest. How did she know? 'Sorry, but I don't think I will be having an affair with Michael – or arranging his murder.'

'Sometimes you can be really boring, you know that? So tell me more about your weekend. You've had counselling, a colonic and a meditation session. What's next on the *Eat Pray Love* tour?'

'More like the Weep, Wail, Whine tour. I thought I was going mad in the meditation. I think I may be seriously disturbed.'

'I could have told you that. It's why I love you,' said Anna. 'Spending time with you makes me feel sane.'

'Cheek. You can talk, with your murder plans, you mad old witch.'

'Talking of witches, how did you get on with Fleur and Rose?'

'A slight thawing with Fleur but Rose was as uptight as ever. Then they both took off with no goodbyes.'

'Ah, but that was a good thing. It meant you got to spend some time with Daniel.'

'I am not interested in him beyond his role in this programme of Mum's. End of.'

'OK. Message received. What's his surname so I can google him?'

'End of, Anna.'

'Killjoy.'

When she'd gone, I felt sad. I looked at Misty who was sitting on the windowsill. 'Will I ever have sex again? What do you think, puss? Any hope?'

Her body started to convulse and, seconds later, she threw up a fur ball.

13

Dee

Thursday 15 October, morning

I woke feeling full of energy and better than I had in weeks, despite the fact that the estate agents were bringing potential buyers around. I called Anna to ask if I could go around to her house while they were looking at mine.

'Call you back in a sec,' she said. 'Someone's at the door.'

The phone rang a minute later. *Anna calling back*, I thought as I picked up. 'Allo,' I said in a fake French accent. 'Dee McDonald, femme fatale and murderer here.' At the other end, I heard either a suppressed laugh or a cough. It didn't sound like Anna. 'Anna, *Anna*, is that you?'

'Er . . . no. Michael Harris here.'

'No! *Shit*. I mean, not shit that it's you, though . . . Oh hell. Never mind. I thought it was Anna. Private joke.' *Get yourself together Dee*, I told myself. I took a deep breath. 'Can I help you?'

'I just wanted to touch base. You know there's a viewing this morning?'

'I do.'

'And . . . I wondered if maybe I could buy you a drink. Talk things over. I'm aware of how disruptive this must be for you.' *And how's a drink supposed to help?* I thought. 'Are you busy today?'

'I . . . '

'I could pick you up at one?'

'I . . . ' I was so surprised at his invite that I couldn't think of an excuse fast enough. 'One?'

'Great. I'll see you then.'

'I . . . '

Too late. He'd hung up.

*

Michael drove us out to the Whitsand Bay Hotel out near Portwrinkle. It was a perfect autumn afternoon, with the sun sparkling on the water along the coast, and I felt rather glamorous sitting back in the leather interior as we drove along the winding cliff road. The hotel was one of Mum's favourite locations when she was in the area. With its grey castellated walls, it had the look of an old Scottish castle. At the back of the hotel were terraced lawns leading down to a small beach, and the view of the coastline was one of the best in the area.

Michael parked the car and we found a table at the back. *I could get to like this*, I thought, when Michael went in to get drinks. With John, it was always me who went for the drinks, idiot that I was. I thought I was acting for equal rights and he'd like me for not being the kind of woman who expected a man to do everything for her but, as the years went on, it became clear that he expected me to do everything for him. *Not thinking about him*, I told myself. *I am going to enjoy the moment.*

'You smell like my father,' I said when Michael reappeared and placed a gin and tonic in front of me.

He looked bemused. 'Is that a good or bad thing?'

'Oh. Good. Chanel?'

Michael nodded. 'Is your father still alive?'

I shook my head. 'He died when I was six.'

'Oh, I'm sorry. And I was sorry to hear about your mother. Were you close?'

'Very. This was one of her favourite spots,' I pointed at my glass, 'and one of her favourite drinks. We shared many sitting just here over the years.' I blinked away sudden tears. 'And you? Were you close to your mother?'

Michael looked out to sea. 'Less so in latter years. I wish I'd got down this way more often.'

I nodded. 'I wish I'd got up to London more often. Mum used to come down here a lot when she was younger, but not so much in her later years. She loved travelling and loved this part of the world.'

The silence that followed felt awkward. Grief is such a private thing and I hardly knew Michael. Clearly he felt the same because he changed the subject. 'So what's Dee short for?' he asked. 'Deirdre. Desdemona?'

'Daisy.'

'Daisy? So why Dee?'

'School friends called me Dee and it stuck, plus I guess it was a way of trying to establish myself as an individual, not one of the flower girls. See, my mother's name was Iris, my sisters are Fleur and Rose. I was Daisy. By calling myself Dee, it was a way of separating myself, being independent.'

'You wanted to separate yourself?'

'Yes. No. Oh I don't know. It's complicated. You know. Families.' I laughed, aware I was making no sense. 'Do you get on with your brother?'

Michael grimaced. 'We're very different. How about you and your sisters?'

'Not so much any more. We did once but . . . people drift apart and you don't hear so much from them. They move on to a different phase that doesn't include you and that's the way it is and you have to let them go and accept a different kind of relationship – fond but not so close.'

Michael nodded. 'Sad but true. I know all about the shifting sands of life.' He looked wistful and I got the sense that he'd been lonely of late.

'Unless you have a cat or dog. They don't drift away as long as there's food on offer, especially dogs.'

Michael laughed. 'I never drift away when there's food on offer . . . Just saying.'

'I'll remember that.'

'Actually, I was thinking about getting a dog. You're right. They do make good companions.' He studied me for a few moments 'Your name, Daisy, it's nice.'

I shrugged. 'Exactly. Nice. Daisies are ordinary. Roses are beautiful, delicate. Fleur sounds so feminine, French, chic. My sisters are extraordinary, as was my mother, but *Daisy*? It's not special at all. I think I'd have liked Desdemona better. Maybe I'd have turned out more exotic.'

'You wanted to be exotic?'

'When I was younger, a teenager. What teen doesn't want to be different? Arrogant of me, do you think?'

'I didn't say that, and I would never describe you as ordinary.'

Silence again. Had he just paid me a compliment? Or did he mean, I wasn't ordinary, I was odd. I wish I'd kept my mouth shut.

Michael looked out at the coast to our left. 'What's the church in the distance?' He pointed to a tiny dot that could be seen on top of a hill far away.

'That's Rame Head. The church is a ruin; nothing left except the shell now. Imagine how it must have been in the old days, though, with villagers walking for miles over the fields then up the hill. A sacred place with just sky and sea around it, never changed through all the centuries. It's another of my favourite spots in the area. You can see out to sea in both directions, for miles. Better than here even.'

'Maybe you could show me on the way back?'

'It's a bit of a hike up there.'

Michael laughed. 'Are you saying I couldn't do it?'

'No. No, course not,' I said.

'I don't mind a hike,' he said and patted his stomach. 'Do me good.'

It seemed churlish to refuse so, after we'd finished our drinks, we drove back along the coast to the car park at the foot of the hill at Rame. Michael strode out confidently across the field, then climbed the many narrow wooden steps carved into the hill to the top. I chased after him and we were both puffing by the time we reached the top.

'I see what you mean about it being a hike,' he said as

he took in the panoramic view of sea and sky. 'But worth it.'

We had a quick look inside the church, but there was nothing to see but damp bricks and the remains of a fire and a few empty beer cans where someone had probably had a late-night picnic. We went back out and round to the front where there was a concrete terrace. It was the best place to take in the stunning view of coast stretching away on both sides. I sat a short distance away from him and this time the silence wasn't awkward. There was something about the place that was calming and, by the time we got up, fifteen minutes or so later, I felt more comfortable with him.

'I love this area,' I said as we headed off down the hill again, Michael going first.

'I can see why,' he called back without turning around. 'Cornwall does seem to have its own magic.'

'That's why I don't want to leave.' It was out before I could stop myself and I heard Michael sigh.

'I know, and I'm sorry, but selling the house doesn't necessarily mean you have to leave Cornwall.'

'Doesn't it? Then where am I going to go?'

Michael gestured hopelessly as he continued his way down the steps. 'There are other houses.'

'Rents are high and most are short-term lets now for holidaymakers.'

'I believe what makes a house a home is who lives there, what they put into a place. You've made that house what it is. You could do it again.'

I resisted a sudden urge to push him down the hill. 'So where's your home then?'

He still didn't turn around. 'It was in Putney but I recently separated and got divorced. I'm in temporary accommodation, so I do understand about having to leave a familiar place, but I tell myself, home is where my books are, my things.' I heard him sigh again.

'Is this what you brought me out here to say? To remind me that I should be looking for another house?'

'No. Not at all. You must really see me as the big bad wolf. No. I . . . I just wanted to clear the air. Acknowledge what's happening. There's no reason why we can't be—'

'What? Friends?'

'Maybe. Why not?'

I stuck my tongue out at his back just at the moment he stopped and turned around.

'Pth, pth,' I spluttered. 'Swallowed a fly.'

He raised an eyebrow and turned away again. I could see he hadn't bought my fly routine and I cursed myself. He'd been making an effort to be nice and I'd rebuked him.

Neither of us spoke as we drove back to Kingsand. There had been a moment up at Rame when we were at ease with each other, and if I hadn't acted like a petulant teenager, maybe we could have been friends. He was good company and I'd like to have found out more about him. If we'd become friends, he might have agreed to delay the sale of his house. Too late.

Curious how the word silence can cover such completely different atmospheres, I thought as I tried the swami's technique. Breathe in, hold . . . ah fuck it.

Friday 16 October

A couple were due to come round with the estate agent and, despite Anna's plans to put them off with voodoo spells and bad smells, my natural house pride had taken over and I had cleaned, polished and swept. The house looked immaculate.

I let them in and went up to the top floor out of the way, but where I could hear the couple commenting as they went around. 'Bit dated,' said the man. 'And there's *no* bidet,' said the woman on reaching the bathroom.

Who has a bidet in this day and age? I thought as I remembered a time when I was about five and I'd visited a neighbour with my mother and my sisters. The house had a bidet. Not being any the wiser, I thought it was for little people and, being one myself, I'd used it then pressed the handle. I couldn't work out why it didn't flush but instead shot water up my bottom. After the shock, I'd wrapped what I'd done carefully in loo paper and put it in the pedal bin next to the sink. Thinking I was being helpful, when I got back downstairs, I'd whispered a warning to Rose. She burst out laughing and told Mum and her friend. Oh how they hooted. Dee pooed in the bidet. How hilarious. When they'd finished sniggering, Mum told me to go back up the stairs, take the parcel of tissue out of the pedal bin and put it down the proper loo. Fleur was too young to understand what had gone on, but had caught the gist of what had happened. She called me Poo-Pee, a name that stuck for weeks. She only stopped when I threatened to cut the hair off all her dolls. That shut her up. Not one of them saw or cared how humiliated I was.

The house viewing only took ten minutes. The couple didn't even bother to look on the top floor. Not the one for them. Good.

Saturday 17 October

I didn't sleep well last night so I decided to go for a nap in the afternoon and to do it properly, in bed, no clothes, eye-mask to keep out the autumn sun that was shining through the curtains.

Bliss, I thought as I snuggled under the duvet. I was deep asleep when I was woken by the sound of someone in my room. I pulled off my mask to see a couple and two kids at the bottom of my bed staring at me.

'Waargh,' I cried. 'Who the hell are you?'

'Waargh!' cried the little girl with them. 'It's a ghost bandit.'

'A naked one,' said the little boy. He looked very pleased about that.

Mr Bentley, the estate agent, appeared from the hall behind them. *Of course, he has keys*, I thought.

'Oh dear. Didn't you get my text message?' he asked.

'No, I didn't,' I said as I pulled my duvet up to my neck.

'I'm so sorry,' he said. He didn't look sorry at all. He looked like he was about to have a sniggering fit, and so did the couple he was with.

'Er . . . well, we'll go then,' said Mr Bentley. 'Let you carry on sleeping.'

'Thank you.'

The group trooped out, apart from the little boy, who

looked about ten. He pointed at the curtains and then at my mask by the bed. 'Are you a vampire?' he asked.

'I am, and I particularly like little boys.'

He was out of the door in an instant. But that's it. I am never napping in the afternoon again.

Monday 19 October

I spent the morning cleaning but the third lot of viewers didn't turn up.

'Changed their minds and are going to look in Padstow instead,' the estate agent told me.

'Good plan,' I said. 'It's lovely there.'

With a bit of luck, I'll be able to stay for the winter, I thought as the agent took off to show another house.

14

Dee

Saturday 5 December

A bleak month. The winter of our discontent or, as Fleur used to say while practising the latest dance moves as a teen – the winter of our disco tent. *Time for an overdue prayer to God*, I thought, *so that Mum doesn't come and haunt me.*

'Dear God. The snow has come early, the weather Siberian, with gale-force winds and hail. My heating's broken, the central locking has gone on my car and the windows won't open or shut, the roof in the bathroom's leaking, the blind in my bedroom has snapped and Max had a problem with his bladder and had to have three nights in the animal hospital. I think I paid for an extra wing with what it cost. But then you know that, being Mr Know-It-All omniscient being. I am broke. And cold. And miserable. Woah, woah, we're all doomed. You could hire me out as Cassandra the Prophetess of Disaster, guaranteed to bring catastrophe in her wake and ruin any party. Please send money along the cosmic portal (if there is one), Amen. Thanks.'

The reason I was broke was because the only bit of extra income I got from my evening classes with the oldies had been spent sprucing up my house for my sisters. On Mum's programme, the location for weekend number two on the kicking the bucket list was No. 3, Summer Lane. Luckily, it was still my home. Viewings dried up in late November and the only person who was interested still had to sell their house so, thanks to a chain, so far there had been no sale.

I had no idea what weekend two entailed. Daniel wouldn't say when he phoned to check that I had space for my sisters to stay, but he added, 'All will be revealed when I arrive.'

In preparation for Fleur and Rose, I had been over to Plymouth and bought scented candles and soaps, Molton Brown bath gels, new pillows (my old ones for the spare beds were lumpy and bumpy and I had no doubt Rose only slept on the finest Siberian goose down), new towels (old ones were hard with age and wear), organic nibbles for Rose, Belgian chocolates for Fleur, fresh flowers from M&S, two bottles of good wine.

'Why are you bothering?' asked Anna when she popped in to find me baking what I remembered was Rose's favourite cake, Fleur's too. Apple and blueberry. I'd even got organic flour to appease Rose.

'I want everything to be nice for them.' I showed Mum's latest text to Anna. It said: 'Kindness is the key to a happy life.'

'A little kindness goes a long way.'

'It does. Mum really was a sly old fox sending me a message like that just before they arrive.'

'It must be lovely getting these messages from Iris, reminders of her.'

'It is,' I agreed. 'Although slightly peculiar to be getting messages from the beyond.'

'Better than having to go to a séance,' said Anna.

Saturday 12 December

By Saturday morning, the house smelt lovely and looked warm and welcoming. As I made a few last-minute tweaks, I wondered about Anna's comment. Why did I feel the need to make such an effort for two people who hardly figured in my life? *Kindness, kindness*, I reminded myself, though I had to admit that I hadn't been doing the preparations with good grace or out of kindness at all, more like fear that Rose and Fleur would find my standard of living wanting. I'd agonized over whether to put the Christmas decorations up or not. I usually did around the twelfth. I decided against. Rose might be critical. From what I remember, her trees were always statements of money and elegance; one colour – silver or gold – not both. My approach was throw it all on, the more tinsel the better, and I'd had a fake tree for the last few years because I felt bad about seeing all the real ones thrown out with the rubbish on 6 January. It seemed like a waste to me, but that might have been seen as me being New Age or old hippie again. No doubt Rose would find a fake tree and a ton of tinsel tacky, so I decided to delay the bauble-bling mania until they'd gone.

*

They both arrived just before ten o'clock, having made an early start and driven by car together.

Progress of a sort, I thought. Mum would have been pleased that they travelled together.

I showed them to their rooms, Rose on the first floor, Fleur up top in my studio. As they got settled in, I noticed that Rose had brought her own pillows.

'You don't mind, do you?' she asked as she stripped the two new ones I'd bought off the bed. 'I sleep so much better on my own, don't you?'

'I . . . ' *Kindness, kindness*, I told myself. 'Of course not. I hope you'll be comfy on the mattress.'

'Meaning?'

'Meaning nothing. Just, I hope you'll be comfy on the mattress. As you said, you sleep better on your own pillows, the same probably goes for your own mattress, but obviously you can't transport that.'

'I just want to be able to sleep, especially after that drive. I'm exhausted and we haven't even started yet. Why do you have to live so far away?'

'I live here because I like it. I'll travel to London when one of the weekends is at yours. I've left towels on the chair, or did you bring your own?'

'Dee, if you're pissed off with me because I brought my own pillows, just say.'

I took a deep breath. 'I'm not. Really.'

'Really?'

'Really. As you say, nothing like the comforts of your own home.'

'And what's *that* supposed to mean?'

'Nothing. God Rose, nothing.'

'I knew it. I knew I shouldn't have brought my own pillows. I've offended you. But really, I find it hard enough sleeping as it is, never mind in a strange bed. Loads of people I know take their own pillows when travelling.'

'It's fine. Really. Come down when you're ready and I'll make some tea.' I made an effort to smile. *And I can use the pillows I bought to put over your face in the night*, I thought as I went downstairs to the kitchen, where my eyes went straight to a photo of Mum on the board. 'And you can stop looking at me like that for a start.'

'Who are you talking to?' asked Fleur, coming in behind me a few moments later.

'No one,' I said.

'But I heard you, just now, as I was coming down the stairs. Don't tell me you've started talking to yourself?'

'No. I was . . . talking to God,' I lied. 'Remember Mum asked us to in her letter.'

'Oh yes, that.'

'Do you do it?'

'Keep forgetting. What do you say to him, her or it?'

'Oh you know, any old thing. Chat, ask questions, sometimes pray.'

'For what?'

Patience, I thought as I put the kettle on. 'World peace,' I said.

Fleur burst out laughing. 'Good luck with that. Actually,

I was thinking about it the other day. If there is a God, it can't be easy being omnipresent. Like in the beginning, it was probably amazing, experiencing everything, everywhere, all brand new and shiny, but now there's TV, satellite TV and catch-up TV, plus Netflix and so many others, which means that God, if there is one, having to be at one with everything, must have to experience movies, shows, YouTube clips over and over and over again. Enough to drive anyone bonkers. Like arghhh, another episode of *Top Gear* again and again in every language. No wonder God has gone mad and abandoned planet earth. It's down to over-exposure of TV programmes and movies and anything in cyberspace.'

I laughed. 'That's deep, and a philosophy I can't say I've heard before.'

'I can do deep,' said Fleur, as she poked around in my cupboards and found a packet of Hobnobs which she opened.

Rose came down to join us and at first there was an awkward silence.

Fleur offered her a biscuit. 'Hobnob?'

Rose waved her away like she was an irritating fly. It felt as if it might be a long weekend. It had been years since they had been in my home, in my kitchen, in my world, and even longer since we'd been comfy cosy together – if we ever had been.

'Look, I really want you both to be comfortable, so please help yourself to anything in the fridge. Come and go as you please. Just be at home.'

Both nodded, then started looking at the photos on my board and asking about various people on it. 'Oh how's Marie? You still friends?' 'Ever hear from Andy?'

I answered, 'Yes to Marie – she lives in the next village – and no to Andy, though I hear his news through Lucy.'

'Hey,' said Fleur, after she'd scrutinized the board. 'Everyone in your world is up there, but not one of us.'

I cursed that I hadn't noticed that before they came. I used to have pictures of us there, lots of them, but seeing their faces staring down at me as I ate my muesli every morning was more than I could bear after our big blow up over where Mum should live, and, one by one, I'd removed them.

'I'll find one and put it up,' I said. 'Do you have photos of us at your place?'

'Actually, I do,' Fleur replied. I could tell from the way she said it that she was put out. Rose didn't answer so I took that as a no. Luckily there was a knock on the door and any further discussion of photos was ended as Daniel arrived. He was laden with bags and boxes, which he put in the corner of the kitchen.

I'd made an effort with my appearance as well as the house, and had put on a little make-up and my best (and only, courtesy of the Oxfam shop) jade green cashmere sweater with good jeans, not the ones that were baggy round the knees. I'd tried to tell myself it wasn't for his benefit but I knew that it was. He'd been on my mind a lot since October, and when he'd telephoned to check the sleeping arrangements, I'd felt like a girl, nervous and excited.

My small kitchen felt crowded with everyone in there, but it was the only place we could all sit around a table for the recording. Fleur and Rose seemed to fill the room with their presence and perfume (Annick Goutal for Rose, Acqua di Parma for Fleur. I'd seen the bottles in their bedrooms), and with Daniel in the mix too, it felt rather overwhelming. Seeing him again was a jolt, he was better looking than I remembered and, being in such close proximity on my own territory, I had the sensation of having drunk a double espresso.

'Just got here?' I asked.

He shook his head. 'I arrived last night. Stayed at the Bell and Anchor.'

'Wise decision,' said Fleur. 'It is a long way from civilization. The drive took us for ever.'

'Surprisingly for a long way from civilization, we do have electricity and even Wi-Fi,' I said.

'Sorry, Dee. I didn't mean to offend, but you have to admit it's a long way.'

This coming from Fleur, who has travelled the world and been more long distances than anyone, I thought. I decided to let it go, plus I didn't want to appear petulant in front of Daniel. I wished he'd let me know he'd stayed last night. I could have gone to meet him, but supposed he wanted to keep his distance and didn't want me, or any of us for that matter, asking too many questions about what Mum had in store for us. I felt disappointed. *If he was attracted to me, surely he'd have sought out the opportunity to see me without my sisters*, I thought, *so he clearly isn't. He's been hired to do a job and we're the clients.*

I made tea, got out the cake tin and offered them all a piece. 'Home baked. Apple and blueberry.'

'Has it got sugar in it?' asked Rose.

'A little.'

'Not for me then. I don't do sugar any more. Have you got an oatcake? Organic if you have.'

'I do actually, but what about you Fleur?'

'Maybe later,' she said. 'I'm watching the old figure too.'

Rose looked indignant. 'I'm not watching my figure.' She wrinkled her nose in disgust. 'It's sugar. Everyone knows it's the enemy.'

I burst out laughing. 'Come on, Rose, chill out a bit. One piece of cake isn't going to kill you. This used to be your favourite cake. This whole sugar thing, it's like anything – do it in moderation.'

'I'll have a piece,' said Daniel, and helped himself. 'Looks delicious.'

'Thanks. I used my mum's recipe. I made it specially.'

Rose sighed. 'And now you're doing the guilt trip.'

'I am not.'

'Yes, you are. You made it *specially*.'

'I don't do guilt trips, that's your department.' It was out before I could stop myself. Rose ignored it.

Fleur laughed. 'Oh well, Mum, we've got off to a good beginning.' She turned to Daniel. 'OK, messenger from the dead. Turn on your laptop and let's see what's next on the agenda.'

Daniel shook his head. 'Messenger from the dead? Makes it sound like we're in some kind of horror movie.'

Fleur looked over at Rose and me and raised an eyebrow. Even Daniel laughed. 'You girls.'

I was about to comment that Rose didn't like being called a girl, but I bit my lip again because I am kind, kind, and anyway, if it bugs her that much, she can tell him herself, but she was busy shooing away Max who had wound himself around her ankles. Hah. As I remembered, she wasn't mad about cats. With a bit of luck, he'd do his party trick and pee on her shoes to mark his territory.

Daniel got out his laptop and switched it on. Rose and

Fleur sat at the table as I finished making tea. *How can something so familiar be so weird at the same time?* I wondered as we waited for Mum to pop up and join us in our strange version of Happy Families, the cast being three living, one dead.

There they were again. Mum, Martha and Jean, smiling from the screen. I felt a lump come into my throat. I glanced at Fleur and Rose; both of them had glistening eyes too. *At least that's one thing we all have in common*, I thought. *We all loved our mother.*

'*What* are they wearing?' Fleur asked.

'Looks like keep-fit clothes,' I replied. Mum had a pink bandana round her head, Martha and Jean were in baseball caps, Jean with hers turned backwards. The sight of them made me smile.

'Hello dollies,' said Mum. 'I bet you're wondering what's the old bat cooked up this time on the "how to be happy" programme? Well, this weekend is simple. Day one a bit of physical exercise. Day two, you're going to get creative.'

Rose groaned. 'It's like being back at school.'

'Research shows that regular exercise can help reduce cancer, heart disease and stroke,' Martha continued.

'Aye, and depression,' added Jean. 'The best prescription for the blues is to get out and get some fresh air in your lungs. It can work wonders for the black dog in the corner.'

'So, basically today will be just a taster,' said Mum. 'Anyone knows that to benefit from exercise, you have to do it regularly, and it's important to do something you enjoy or else you won't do it.'

'I did t'ai chi and still do what I can,' said Martha. 'Jean does a bit of Pilates—'

'Mainly because I can do that lying down,' said Jean.

'And I still try to do a bit of yoga,' said Mum. She looked upwards and stuck out her tongue as far as it would go. 'That's the lion pose. I can still do that one. But for you, start today with a hike and have a think about what exercise you'd like to do as part of your lifestyle. I know, Rose, that you do yoga too, but what about you, Daisy and Fleur? Are you moving about enough? I chose to do this weekend down with you, Daisy, because it's nice to accompany a walk with some lovely scenery, and it doesn't get better than down your way, plus I've no way of knowing what month this weekend will fall in.'

'Depends on when you kick the bucket,' said Martha.

'Exactly,' Mum agreed. 'Could be the middle of summer or the middle of winter, but the chances of it being a nice day in the middle of December are more likely in Cornwall. Remember that Christmas I was down with you, Daisy? Many years ago. We walked after lunch and the sun was shining down on us. Kingsand to Mount Edgcumbe.' I nodded. I did remember. Mum loved that walk. 'So that's the first part. Do that walk. Breathe in the air. Enjoy the scenery, then a bit of lunch maybe in the pub at Cremyll and back to Kingsand, where Daniel will have organized an exercise class.'

This time it was Fleur who groaned. 'Exercise class? What's she trying to do? Kill us?'

'It's important to do something that's fun so that you stick to it,' said Jean, 'so we thought a bit of Zumba.'

'But first a hike to get one's lungs and heart going,' said Martha. 'Blow the cobwebs away.'

'In fact, if you can, you could jog the last half-hour. Not race, just jog,' said Mum.

'I haven't brought the right footwear,' said Fleur, looking at her powder-blue suede boots with kitten heels. They matched her sweater and eyes perfectly.

'And the Zumba to get you moving and dancing,' said Jean.

'Really, girls, take it seriously,' said Mum. 'Old age comes round too soon. Preserve your mobility as long as you can.'

'And no excuses like you haven't brought the right shoes, so we've ordered some for you – and fitness clothes,' said Jean.

I looked at Fleur. 'Spooky,' I said.

'No. Just Mum knowing what I'm like,' said Fleur.

'Tomorrow we've divided into three sections, and are going to look at different ways to express your feelings,' said Mum.

'We had a good long chat about what we'd enjoyed over the years, and being creative scored highly,' said Jean.

'So first a painting class,' said Mum. 'I know – easy for you Daisy, but tomorrow I want you to paint for fun, not to sell your work, and Fleur and Rose, just give it a go.'

'After art will be a singing class,' said Martha. She took a deep breath and let rip an impressive high note. 'You might be amazed at how that can make one feel. I've been in a choir for as long as I can remember, and singing with others, the union of voices in harmony, can bring pure joy.'

'She hasn't heard us sing,' I commented.

'True,' said Fleur.

'Shh,' said Rose.

'Followed by a writing exercise,' said Mum. 'Remember when you all used to keep diaries when you were teenagers? Have you still got them? I think they're a great idea. A private place to let out all your secret thoughts and feelings. I remember you used to keep yours locked, Rose. Well, no one will have to read what you write tomorrow if you don't want them to. Daniel will explain it all to you.'

Martha looked at her watch. 'Time for tea, ladies.'

'Is it?' asked Mum and looked at hers. 'So it is. OK. See you next time.'

The screen went blank and, though I'd felt the room was crowded earlier, now it seemed empty. Mum had been there with us and now she was gone.

'Is that it?' I asked.

Daniel appeared to be sending a text and, a moment later, three mobiles pinged.

I reached into my bag for my phone at the same time Fleur and Rose found theirs. Fleur and I laughed when we saw the message, and even Rose smiled as we read the text from Mum. 'There are few hours in life more agreeable than the hour dedicated to the ceremony known as afternoon tea.' Henry James (1843–1916).

'Martha was a stickler for tea at four,' said Daniel, 'and that day when we were recording, it was four o'clock.'

'Mum liked her routines too,' I said. 'Morning tea at eight a.m., coffee at eleven.'

'G and T, slice of lime not lemon at six,' said Fleur. 'Remember she used to call it a sundowner?'

'I do,' said Rose.

'I could do with one now,' said Fleur.

'In the *morning?*' asked Rose.

Fleur gave her a bored look.

'So, any questions?' asked Daniel.

'Are you going to join us on the hike?' asked Fleur.

'I'd love to, but I'm only PA on this journey, not participant,' he said, then handed us a bag and box each. 'Trainers, fleeces for the walk. I trust I got the right sizes.'

I took my items and looked away from him. If I wasn't careful, I'd go into perky mode. Men I fancied had that effect. I knew the signs – like suddenly the world seemed to buzz and be brighter and full of possibilities. I felt alive. I didn't want Fleur or Rose to see it happen. They'd tease the hell out of me, so instead I went into my 'I am so not interested in Daniel' act. So cool. Who was I fooling? And anyway, it was a waste of time. He didn't fancy me. Fleur was watching me carefully. I looked straight back at her. 'You ready for this?' I knew she hated exercising, or used to.

'Sure,' she said. 'Bring it on.'

'What was the plan if it was pouring with rain?' I asked Daniel as we put on our trainers, fleeces and scarves.

Daniel smiled. 'She told me to find a gym and take you all there for a session on the running machine.' He handed me three twenty-pound notes. 'For your pub lunches, from the fund.'

'Right, come on Dee, lead the way,' said Fleur. 'Compared to the first weekend with its colonics, this will be a walk in the park.'

'Arf arf,' I said, falling back into the familiar language of our childhood when someone made a joke.

Rose was already out the door, so we went to join her, then waved goodbye to Daniel, who headed off down towards the bay and Bell and Anchor. We took the route through the narrow lanes, past a small square with three-storey houses on the right and the Golden Sun pub on the left, then up towards the field to cross into the park and to get to Cremyll.

Luckily, the sky was blue and, though cold, it was dry. We climbed over the stile at the top of the village, and on to the path that crossed the sloped field leading to the woods. Rose marched ahead like she was on a mission.

'What's the hurry?' Fleur called after her.

Rose turned back. 'If we're to get the most out of it, we need to speed up, as Martha said – get the heart and lungs going.'

'Or we could amble and have a catch-up,' said Fleur.

'Or a bit of both,' I added.

'Thanks, but I'm going to walk on,' Rose called back, and set off again at a pace.

Fleur smiled. 'And there you have us,' she said. 'Rose forging ahead busy busy, me a lazy arse always looking for the easy way out, and you somewhere in the middle.'

We hurried to keep up with Rose. 'Maybe. But I agree with Fleur, Rose. There are no rules to this.'

'Fine,' said Rose as we caught up with her. 'You do it your way and I'll do it mine.'

'Do you ever chill out, Rose?' Fleur asked.

'Course I do. Actually, this is a treat for me – to get out in the country in the fresh air. Being in the city, I'm either at home, on the tube, in a taxi or at work, so I don't mind this a bit. Also, I'm a naturally active person.'

'I think you also need to take time to stand and stare, to take in the scenery,' I said as Rose forged ahead again. I got the feeling that she wanted to be alone. Fleur and I let her go and fell into a comfortable pace of our own. I'd done the walk hundreds of times since I'd lived in the area, but the landscape never failed to lift my spirits. Down below, to our right, we could see the village of Kingsand, with its painted cottages, nestling in the bay. To our left and up the hill were fields, and straight in front were the woods leading to Mount Edgcumbe Park.

'The sea will be on our right for the whole walk,' I said as I indicated the view and coastline.

Fleur stopped and looked around. 'It's beautiful. I can see why you like this area so much, Dee. I'd forgotten how lovely it was.'

'That's why I don't want to leave,' I said, and I filled her in on what was happening with the house.

'The market probably won't pick up until the spring now,' she said.

'That's what the estate agent said.'

Fleur knew a lot about property. It was how she'd made her money. Although flaky and unreliable on many levels, she had a good business head on her shoulders, and had got on the property ladder early after her first divorce had left her with a tidy sum. She'd bought two houses in London, done them up, sold them, and carried on that way for the best part of twenty years until now she had a handsome portfolio, her own management company, as well as a house in California and flat in Knightsbridge. She'd managed things well, so that someone else ran the office and did what she called the boring stuff, leaving her free to come and go as she pleased.

She hadn't been so lucky when it came to men. Her first husband was a control freak who'd left her for a younger and more malleable woman; her second was an alcoholic playboy, Harvey, who almost destroyed her. She'd got into drugs, mainly cocaine, and drink. It was during those years that Rose and I had got the late-night phone calls, when she was out of her head and neither of us could reason with her. Dark days for her and for us. She spent time in the Priory drying out, getting clean, then she'd go back to Harvey like he was an addiction too, and the whole sad process would start again. Mum didn't know the half of it, and Rose and I did our best to keep it that way. In the end, Harvey left her for a rich heiress and went to live in Miami. Fleur went to pieces and back to the Priory. Finally she did clean up, her nostrils were still intact, and she'd been single – as far as I knew – for the best part of eight years.

'I'd lend you the money to buy your house if I had it in cash,' said Fleur. 'I know you're good for it with our inheritance coming at the end of Mum's list, but everything I've got is tied up in my properties or in bonds, and I doubt I could lay my hands on the amount you need without having to sell something.'

'Oh, you mustn't do that. I'll see what the New Year brings . . . but thank you, that's so kind. Even if you did have it to lend me, though, I wouldn't want to borrow it, in case I couldn't repay you.' I looked ahead at Rose. 'Until this year is over, nothing is guaranteed. We're only on weekend two.'

I was touched by her offer, but then Fleur had been more than generous since she'd become wealthy. At Christmas and birthdays before our fall-out, she'd sent me lavish presents: gorgeous jewellery, French perfumes, cashmere gloves and scarves. They were lovely presents to receive but I'd found it hard to know what to get her in return. On my low income, I often felt indebted, and that my presents were inadequate. She could buy what she wanted and had it all.

'What could possibly stop us?' asked Fleur. 'I'm in for the duration of this. I'm loving having this extended time with Mum, even if it is on a recording, and I think Rose is committed for the same reason. But seriously, Dee, if it looks like you might lose your home, let me know and I'll see if there's anything I can do. If the worst comes to the worst, I could see if I could buy your house as an investment and you could pay me rent.'

I gave her arm a squeeze. I knew she meant well, but having my younger sister as my landlady wasn't an option that I'd choose. I'd feel obliged to her. *Hopefully it won't come to that*, I thought as we reached the woods. 'So what about you? How's the love life?'

She laughed. 'What love life? Been there, done that. I find men either boring or they want too much or want to control me. I like being my own boss, no one telling me what to do, how to dress or behave.'

'So, no men at all?'

'I didn't say that, just no one special.' She looked wistful for a moment. 'Truth be told, I don't know what I want any more. All that romanticism about finding The One seems to have faded away in the light of experience.'

'I know what you mean.'

'But what about you? Any interesting men in the area lurking up on the cliffs?'

I shook my head. 'Either too young, too stoned, too needy or too old.'

'What about the chap who owns your house?' asked Fleur.

'Precisely. He owns my house, therefore has the potential to make me homeless. Not a great starting point for any relationship, is it?'

'OK, then what about Daniel for you? He's a handsome man,' Fleur persisted.

I shrugged and wondered whether to confide just how attractive I found him. Past experience of Fleur not being trustworthy won, so I hesitated then said, 'He is, but I want more than handsome . . . I'd have to get to know him better. We know hardly anything about him.'

'So why don't you do that? Find out who he is. Go for it. I think he's just your type.'

'Not really, no more than yours. Are you really not interested? As you say, he is a handsome man.' I wanted to be doubly sure that I wasn't going to have to compete with her, because I knew there would be no contest.

She shook her head. 'All yours. You know me, I go for the bad boys, the ones with an edge and sense of danger. He seems to be a nice man. I'd get bored.'

'Hey! What does that say about me then?'

'No. Sorry! I didn't mean you're boring. He's just not my type, but I could see him being yours. Look, I don't know what I want. Sometimes I think it would be nice to meet someone, but I know I choose badly.'

'So why not go for Daniel if you want a change from the bad boys?'

'Give it up, Dee. I don't feel the chemistry. And if it ain't there, it ain't there.'

I was reassured and relaxed into enjoying our walk. It felt good to be strolling along, catching up on our lost years. Fleur seemed to have calmed down since I'd last spent time with her, and was listening as well as talking. In previous years, she was a classic case of, 'OK, enough about me. What about you? What do you think about me?' I began to feel that maybe Mum's grand plan wasn't such a bad one after all. If only Rose would thaw a little. I could see her in the distance. She'd turned and was jogging back to us.

'Here comes Miss Goody Two-Shoes,' said Fleur.

'Oh yes, we're supposed to jog the last bit. Come on. Be fun. Last one to the pub has to get the first round in.'

*

'So how's it going for you so far?' I asked Rose. We were in the pub at Cremyll, where Fleur and I were tucking into a ploughman's lunch with a glass of wine. Rose had gone for grilled salmon, salad and water.

'How's what going for me?' asked Rose, as she cut up a piece of tomato.

'The quest. Weekend two.'

Rose pulled a face. 'Different. At least no more sessions with Beverly.'

'I'm enjoying it,' said Fleur. 'Sea, sky, my sisters' company.'

Rose ignored her. 'Dee, about your situation. I called Hugh on the walk this morning. How long ago did you move to Cornwall?'

'Oh. About twenty-eight years ago.'

'What year exactly?'

'What does it matter?'

'It might. Hugh said he thinks you might have an assured tenancy on your property.'

'Meaning?'

'That you're a sitting tenant. This chap who wants to boot you out, can't.'

'Seriously?'

'Hell, I should have thought of that!' said Fleur. 'Where's my brain? Of course. You've been there so long, you must have rights.'

'Would you like me to look into it?' Rose asked.

'Or I could,' said Fleur. 'I know more about property than you do, Rose.'

'It doesn't matter who knows what, or who's the expert, the thing is, it's worth looking into,' said Rose. 'And I am sure I know just as much about property as you do, Fleur – or at least Hugh does.'

Fleur looked put out. 'Why do you always do that, Rose?'

'Do what?'

'Dismiss me like I haven't got a brain. I've made my living from doing property.'

'But you didn't bring up the assured tenancy. I did,' said Rose.

'Look, it doesn't matter who brought it up,' I said. 'Rose, I'm grateful, and I'll look into it.'

'But will you?'

'What do you mean by that?' This time, it was me who felt put out. I wasn't sure if I wanted either of them taking over my affairs.

'You know what you're like. *Mañana, mañana*. Tomorrow, then it doesn't get done.'

'That's not fair. You don't know me at all. How can you say that?'

Rose sighed. 'Because here you are at forty-nine and you don't even own your own property. If you add up what you've wasted in rent, you've probably paid more than enough for a deposit on your own place.'

'But I had my own place, or as good as, and the rent was low thanks to Mrs Harris.'

'You must have always known your landlady was going to die sometime. Why didn't you have a back-up plan?'

'I don't think that's any of your business.'

'So why don't you have savings?'

'I don't have to defend my position to you. Maybe I don't put the same value on possessions as you. There are more important things in life.'

'I think we should change the subject,' said Fleur. 'Dee's right. It's her business, not ours.'

'Yes and I am an adult, Rose. Not one of your children to be told what to do or what I should have done. Stop trying to control me.'

'I wasn't. I was trying to help. Don't be so prickly.'

The cheek of her! I thought. 'I don't need your help.'

'Don't you?'

'No. Back off, Rose. I'll look into it. If it's true that I have rights as a sitting tenant, then I'm sure I can find out just as well as you could.'

Rose gave a curt nod. 'I was only trying to help.'

'Take over, more like. Let me do it.'

'Make sure you do then. You might find you're in a stronger position than you thought. You have rights, and this Michael Harris chap can't get rid of you quite so easily.'

'I don't want to fight him, go to court or anything.'

'Just find out, will you? See what your options are.'

I saluted her. 'Yes, sir.'

Rose sighed. 'You don't have to be like that. I'm just looking out for you.'

'Well you don't need to, and you're being prickly now.'

Fleur popped a bit of cheese into her mouth. 'Well, this is going well isn't it?'

Fleur

Saturday 12 December, 2 p.m.

God, it was good to get out in the fresh air, blow some cobwebs away; I wish Rose would lighten up, though. She came down hard on Dee in the pub. Rose probably means well, but I could feel Dee squirming. Rose always was such a control freak, always telling us what we should be doing. I hate that word, 'should'. OK, Dee could have got herself more sorted property-wise, but being down here, seeing how she lives, I get it. She's created a real home. I like being there; it reminds me of our old house back in Hampstead. I miss that place, God, I do. Although I hadn't lived there for years, it was where I grew up and I still felt it was my real home, a place to return to that was safe and familiar, then *pff*, it was gone, sold, and then *pff*, Mum gone too. I feel anchorless, lost at sea. What's left? Uptight Rose and, well, there's still Dee. I reckon we could be friends again. I hope so anyway.

Dee

Saturday 12 December, 2.30 p.m.

'I feel more like a snooze than a dance class,' said Fleur as we headed into the village hall for Zumba.

Looking around, I saw there were about fifteen people plus Rose, Fleur and me.

'I'm looking forward to it. I like dance.'

'Me too, after a few drinks. Can we go to the back? In case I can't keep up.'

'Good idea,' I replied, since the other women in the group looked years younger than us and very fit.

Our teacher was a young, slim, dark girl called Phoebe. She was Mike and Bet at the pub's daughter, so I knew her well. She waved hi to me.

After a few minutes, the music started up. A heady Egyptian track and soon we were gyrating with the rest of them. It felt good. After five minutes, it became Latin, at which Fleur was a natural. *This is going to be good*, I thought as I glanced over at Rose, who hadn't quite got the steps but was giving it her all nonetheless.

After twenty minutes, I began to feel like I needed an oxygen tank, and I could see that Fleur was struggling to keep up too. Rose's attempts were hilarious, like watching an ironing board try to dance, but she was still giving it her best, determined as ever to get the hang of it.

The track changed to African music and Phoebe directed us into what felt like aerobics. 'Knees up, thump down, turn, turn again, jump, jump, jump, arms up in the air.'

It felt like someone had pressed fast forward, and we were off at an alarming rate.

'Stomp stomp, turn. Knee up, now the other one, arms up. Shout, Zumba.'

The rhythm was fast, and most of the class seemed to know the moves perfectly. Fleur, Rose and I looked like a special-needs outing, going left when the others went right, right when they went left, forward when they went back and back when they went forward.

At least we're at the back so no one can see us, I thought as I paused for a moment to catch my breath. Fleur went forward into someone who was turning and almost knocked them flying.

'And turn!' called Phoebe, and she ran to the back of the class as all the participants turned to face her. Suddenly we were on the front row.

'ZumBA,' called Phoebe.

'ZumBA,' the class called back.

As we were now in full view of the class, Fleur, Rose and I went into overdrive to keep up. *The pride of the flower girls lives on*, I thought, as I battled to overcome my lack of fitness. And up, and down, and to the side two steps, and forward two steps. We were with it, as if someone had given us a shot of adrenalin.

My heart was thumping in my chest and my knees felt like they were going to give way. *Please, please ask everyone to turn again*, I prayed, and finally Phoebe called, 'And turn,' and thankfully we were the back row again.

Fleur leaned against the wall. 'I'm going to die.'

I stopped, panting for breath. 'Me too.'

Rose was still giving it her all, but wasn't quite in time with the others, and soon she too gave up and sagged against the wall next to Fleur.

We staggered through the rest of the class and, at last, we were finished.

'Happiness is that blooming class being over,' said Fleur as we limped out.

'Ow, my back,' Rose groaned, as we made our way home along the lanes.

'My knees,' said Fleur.

'My hips,' I added.

'But we did it,' said Rose.

'Yeah, we rocked it or Zumba'd it, or whatever the saying is,' said Fleur. 'There's life in the old girls yet.'

'Hey, less of the old,' said Rose, but she was smiling.

'What we need now is a large glass of wine,' I suggested.

'Zumba to that,' said Fleur. 'You in, Rose?'

'Lead the way. We've earned it.'

Saturday 12 December

The evening started smoothly enough, with a fire burning in the grate in the front room, a fig and cassis candle filling the house with its soft fragrance. Fleur was sprawled with a glass of wine – and Misty on her lap – on the sofa watching trash TV. Every now and again, I'd hear her groan. 'I can't move. My muscles have seized up.' Rose was tappety-tap on her laptop upstairs, while I was in the kitchen making roast chicken the way Mum used to. I liked having a full house and I enjoyed cooking, and I felt that we'd all relaxed a fraction with each other since the Zumba challenge.

I was just basting roast potatoes when Rose appeared in the kitchen with Tupperware boxes full of what looked like her supper.

'Now don't go off on one,' she said as she found a plate and cutlery, 'but I've brought my own food.'

'I can see that, and I wasn't about to go off on one, but I've cooked for all of us. Why didn't you say something before? And if you can't eat certain things, you could have let me know.'

Rose sat down at the table. 'I'm not doing gluten or dairy at the moment. I just find it easier to take my own food with me than cause problems.'

'Why? Are you on some health kick or something?'

'No. Yes. Sort of. Just cutting out a few things. You know, eat well, stay young and all that.'

'It wouldn't have been a problem. I've done weeks of no gluten and of no dairy and I'm cooking chicken that has neither of what you're trying to avoid.'

'Look, I didn't want to be a nuisance. I was trying to make things easier.'

'But you're my guest. Rose, why don't you ever let anyone do anything for you? It must be exhausting sorting out the world and everyone in it, like you did before with your call to Hugh about the house – not that I'm not grateful, but don't you ever want to just let it all go and have someone look after you for a change. Cook you a meal? Bake you a cake?'

For a brief moment, Rose looked as though she might cry, but then she took a deep breath. 'Just leave it, will you? I . . . Just leave it.'

'Fine,' I said. I got a bottle of Chablis out of the fridge. 'But you're going to have a glass of wine, aren't you?'

Rose hesitated. 'No thanks.'

I was about to say that I'd bought it specially, but remembered what she'd said before when I said I'd baked the cake specially.

'Of course, alcohol is pretty well pure sugar, and we all know that's the enemy.'

'Oh, don't be like that. I never was a big drinker, so I hardly bother any more.'

I took a deep breath. Breathe in, hold . . . exhale. Why

was it Rose could make me so irritable? I became a different person when she was around. Defensive, quick to snap. I didn't want to be that person. *Kind, kind, must be kind*, I reminded myself. 'Look sorry. Fine. You're on a special diet. Can't be weight. You certainly don't need to lose any.'

'I . . . Look sorry, Dee, do you mind if we don't go into it? It's just . . . too boring.'

'I don't mind listening. I'd like to know more about how you are.'

Rose sighed. 'OK. I *am* on a health kick – to help get through the menopause, stop the hot flushes and all that, so no sugar or wheat, but I don't want to talk about it. It's dull when people go on about it.'

'Fine,' I said.

'Is that fine as in fine, or fine as in f for fucked up, i for irritated, n for neurotic and e for exhausted?'

I laughed. Rose being funny, that was rare. 'Probably the latter.'

'Aren't we all?' said Rose.

'All the more reason to have a drink.'

'Actually, fuck it, you don't happen to have a gin and tonic, do you?'

'I do. Want one?'

She nodded and for a moment looked vulnerable. 'Make it a double.'

As I fixed Rose's drink, I glanced over at her. She was putting her food on her plate, a furrow of concentration on her forehead. I felt a wave of affection for her. My anal elder sister. I realized I had no idea what her life was like, what she thought about, what was really going on. *No matter*, I thought as I sliced lemon, then put the glass in front of her. *For now, we're all here, as Mum wanted us to be. Rose has always been a private person. Perhaps it's me who has to change and accept that she is who she is.*

15

Rose

Sunday 13 December, 10.30 a.m.

The art exercise
Daniel had arranged for a teacher to come to Dee's house
with materials. I could see that Dee was put out, probably
because she taught art and knew the woman, Moon, from
the village. She was an odd-looking creature, like a wizened
old fairy with long grey dreadlocks, in crushed velvet
clothes, Dr. Martens boots and a massive ruby pendant on
a chain. She'd have been good on a book cover for the
fantasy children's market. Dee spent ages explaining to her
why we were doing the exercise, which I didn't think was
necessary. No apologies, no excuses, that's my motto.

'Paint whatever you like,' said Moon after she'd handed
out paper, a palette, brushes and paints. 'Feelings, a mood,
a moment. You can do it in landscape, portrait or abstract.'

Well that's clear then, I thought. 'Aren't you going to show
us some technique?' I asked.

The fairy crone shook her head. 'Not today, my lover.' She spoke in a Cornish accent. 'Today is about freedom of expression. Slash it on, dab it on, flick it on. Whatever you feel.'

I am not your lover, I thought. I also wondered how much she was being paid to come and basically do nothing, but I kept my mouth shut and tried to appear willing. I'm a rational person and, although I had better things to be doing with my weekend, I'd worked out – six weekends, twelve days. My part of the inheritance divided by twelve meant each day of the kicking the bucket list earned me a lot of money to give to Simon and Laura, so if today's task meant putting up with Griselda the wrinkly weirdo, then so be it.

Fleur used Dee's studio. Dee worked in her bedroom and I sat at the kitchen table. Moon sat in the front room smoking roll-ups and making strange, unidentifiable sounds. 'She likes to do dolphin chants,' Dee explained when she came down for water for her jar.

I can't paint. Never could. I chose to do an autumn scene but the result was unrecognizable as anything. All that came out was a red and orange blodge. It looked like an open wound, seeping and oozing.

*

After an hour, Moon reappeared and told us all to bring our work into the kitchen so we could appraise each other's masterpieces.

'And what inspired this?' asked Moon when she saw my attempt. Personally, I'd have said it like 'and what inspired *this*?' Or '*what* inspired this!?'

'I wanted it to be a fusion of colour,' I said. 'Inspired by the autumn.'

Moon seemed happy with that. I could always bullshit my way out of a mess. 'It's wonderful, Rose,' said Moon. 'Completely uninhibited.' Clearly she was pretty good at bullshit herself.

Surprisingly, Dee's painting wasn't much better.

'Not my best,' she said as we looked at her creation. It was a grey descending mass of what could have been a bird but looked like a nightmare scene from a horror movie. *I wonder what goes on in her head behind the serene face she shows the world?* I thought as I studied her and then the painting.

Fleur had painted four flowers that didn't resemble any particular type. They were the kind of flowers a child would draw. 'They're meant to be Mum and us,' she told us.

'Wonderful,' said Moon. 'I love the simplicity of it. You've really captured the essence . . . of a feeling.' *Oh, do go on Moon*, I thought. *Tell us more.* But she didn't. Clearly Fleur's work of genius had left her speechless.

Yeah, nice sentiment and that, I thought about Fleur's flowers, *but . . . I wouldn't hang it on my wall.*

'Yes, well done,' said Dee. 'I'm touched that you wanted to paint us but . . . is that all you did in the time?' She picked up the painting and turned it over before Fleur could stop her.

Fleur looked sheepish as Dee examined the work on the back of the flower painting. I went over to have a look. It was covered in scribbles of cartoons. They were mainly of us. One showing Fleur as a Disney princess on a throne, another showing me as an alien with a huge gun. Fleur had written 'Rose, mutant ninja turtle' underneath it, and one of Dee as a hippie dancing in a field of flowers. She'd made her cross-eyed.

'I thought the flower paintings were a bit out of character,' said Dee.

Hah, you've caught out Fleur, I thought.

'I was just messing,' she said.

'Juvenile. Some things never change,' I said as I placed the paper back on the table, flower side up.

Sunday 13 December, 1.30 p.m.

The singing exercise
Curiously the ancient fairy turned out to be the singing teacher as well.

'A woman of many talents,' said Dee, though I got the feeling that Moon wasn't her favourite person in the village.

She got us all standing in Dee's front room. She had a long Aborigine pipe with her and blew several deep, resounding notes on it. 'I want you to mimic the sound,' she said. 'Feel it deep within, right down in your solar plexus, then let it out as you exhale, hold it and let the sound vibrations reverberate through you. *Hompherrrrrrrrrrrrrrrrrrrrrrrrrrrh*. Sound is sacred and can heal as well as bring joy.'

Is that right? I thought. I could see that Fleur and Dee were having a hard time keeping a straight face.

Moon blew another note and looked to me. 'Go on Rose, feel it.' I made a sound that came out as a squeak. 'No, no, Rose. Feel it in your stomach. Inhale. Exhale. Let it out.'

She demonstrated and let out a deep sound that was quite frightening. '*Hompu-errrrrrrrrrrrrh*,' I tried again. Another squeak.

Moon encouraged Fleur to have a go. She was completely off key but gave it her best. It sounded as if she was about to throw up. *If sound can heal, it can also hurt*, I thought as I suppressed the urge to cover my ears.

Dee was next. Hers was more of a croak. *At least we're all unique*, I thought.

'It reminds me of when we were little and trying to see who could do the loudest burp,' said Fleur. 'Remember?'

Dee and I both looked out of the window as if we'd seen something really interesting happening out there.

'Now. All together,' said Moon, and she started with her magnificent burp. '*Homph-errrrrrrrrrh*.'

If you can't beat them, join them, I thought. I let rip. '*Hooo-errrrrrrh*.'

Dee and Fleur joined in. It was a cacophony. We were all completely out of tune and sounded as if someone was being strangled. Even Moon looked defeated. *But hey Mum, this is what you wanted*, I thought as I took a deep breath.

'Next we're going to open and heal the chakras,' said Moon, and instructed us to lie on the floor. She lit a joss stick then placed crystals along the middle line of each of our bodies from the middle of the forehead to the groin.

'Each chakra has a different vibration and sound,' explained Moon. 'For each one, I will lead and you will follow. Starting with the third eye,' she went into a high-pitched humming.

By the time we reached the fourth chakra, Dee and Fleur were convulsed with laughter and, try as I might to keep it together, I couldn't help but laugh too.

'Maybe Mum planned this because she knew we're all tone deaf,' said Fleur.

I thought Mum had planned this because she knew we'd have to laugh and, in the end, we did, even Moon.

'At least this session has got us to agree on something,' said Fleur after Moon had gone, 'and that is that we shan't be auditioning for *The Choir* any time soon.'

I had to agree. Being creative is not my bag, whether it be art, music or writing. Although I work in a creative field, with authors, I have always known my place. I can appreciate and recognize true talent. I can advise and edit. I will always be Salieri and someone else Amadeus.

Sunday 13 December, 4 p.m.

The writing exercise
'Just let out your feelings,' said Arthur, our tutor for the afternoon and, Dee told us, Moon's partner. He too favoured long grey dreadlocks and wore a grey kaftan top over jeans. *The* Lord of the Rings *look – and expressing your feelings – must be popular in this neck of the woods*, I thought. *Where did Mum find these people, or had she left it all up to Daniel? And how much is she paying them?*

'Write what's happening in your life,' Arthur instructed us as he handed out paper and pens. 'Your thoughts, your feelings, hopes, fears, whatever comes out. Don't try to write the perfect piece. Don't edit, criticize or repress yourself. At the end, you can rip up what you've written, burn it or keep it. Your choice.'

This I can do, I thought as I took my papers, retreated to my room and wrote:

I found out that I had cancer the day of the reading of Mum's will. I didn't tell Dee or Fleur, partly because we'd hardly seen each other for years, but mainly because we were all struggling with having just lost Mum. They didn't need to know what I was going through on top of all that. There were enough emotions flying around as it was: grief, anger, guilt, without adding shock at my news into the mix – plus, back then, I didn't know the prognosis. I wanted to find out what I was in for before I started telling people. There are many types of cancer, some with a better outlook than others.

I told Hugh, of course, and Simon and Laura know now, and my friend Kate, but no one else. No one at work, I don't want them treating me differently or thinking I can't do my job. Treating me as Rose who has cancer. Poor thing. Such a shame. No. I don't want that. I'm still the same person inside, course I am. I may have to tell people in time though. It depends on how I respond to treatment, but what will I say? Just popping out to the hospital. No, not to visit a friend . . .

Doctor Campbell texted just as I was coming out of the reading of Mum's will so I had to dash off. Crap timing. I could see it pissed Fleur or Dee off big time that I didn't hang around, but the text said urgent and I'm sure they'd have done the same in the circumstances.

It started with a lump in my breast. I didn't consciously

ignore it but I didn't do anything about it in the beginning. As always, I was busy. More urgent things to do than spend hours sitting in some clinic waiting to be seen, and I didn't think it was anything to worry about. I'd had a cyst a few years before. No big deal. That's what I thought when I found the lump. No big deal, another cyst, but some months later I noticed a few more lumps in my armpit. A few alarm bells rang and, this time, I made an appointment to see my doctor. She arranged a mammogram, ultrasound and biopsy of the lump whilst reassuring me that, as I'd thought, it could well be a cyst again, but best to get it checked. Standard procedure. I went to see her, fully expecting to hear that everything was fine. Not this time. I got to the surgery and waited to hear, nothing to worry about; I even remember thinking they could save time and put my results in the post. But when I got in to see my doctor, she didn't say everything was fine. She said the C word. High grade. Not only that but the biopsy had showed that the lymph nodes were also cancerous. Everything seemed to go into a blur after that. My doctor was mouthing words at me: further scans and tests. I didn't take it in. Not then. Was sure there had been a mistake. They'd got my results mixed up with someone else's. Happens all the time. Sadly not, the doctor told me. Anyway, Mum's programme to find happiness became the last thing on my list of priorities. How to tell Hugh, Simon and Laura? That was all I could think about. And what was I in for?

When I told Hugh, we decided to wait until things were clearer to tell Simon and Laura. I didn't want to worry them if I didn't have to. Course we spent hours looking up treatments, outcomes, etc., on the Net; researching, trying to gain a modicum of control. I was good at that normally, but it felt like things were moving at a pace beyond my ability to stop them. The doctor had a course of tests and treatments mapped out in record time. I had a CT scan of my chest, abdomen, pelvis, as well as a bone scan. It wasn't looking good. They found several malignant deposits in my liver, as well as extensive bony metastases in my spine and ribs. Result – metastatic breast cancer, stage 1V. High grade. Hah. I used to pride myself on getting those. Incurable. I was still sure there was some mistake. I felt fine. They had to be wrong, but then the oncology consultant showed Hugh and me the scans and there was no denying it. 'In the early stages, this type of cancer is often asymptomatic, which is possibly why you feel it can't be true,' I was told.

I felt so angry. Why me? Why now? I didn't have time for this. And guilty. Could it have been prevented if I'd gone sooner? Why didn't I go earlier? Idiot. When I'd first felt the lump? Because like everyone else on the goddamn planet, I didn't think it would happen to me. Cancer happens to other people, not me. Wrong.

Fleur left a message, wanted to talk about Mum's will, and I sent an email back saying I wouldn't be joining her and Dee in working through Mum's list, but I wasn't thinking straight. I felt crazy that day. Then Dee called a few days – or was it a week – later? Pleading with me to follow Mum's wishes. She must have thought me such a selfish bitch. I knew she needed the money. She probably thinks we're rolling in it to have even considered for a moment letting Mum's inheritance go. Not the case – we're comfortably off but not rich; and I'm not a fool, I won't forgo the inheritance just because I have cancer. Hell no. I'll do it for Simon and Laura's sake. A sum like the amount I'm due to inherit will get them on the property ladder. So maybe my diagnosis wasn't crap timing. Maybe it was perfect timing, and I can sail off into the sunset knowing my family will be cared for. I have to think of my children's future and what I will leave behind if things don't go well. Seems ironic, Mum telling me in the letter read out at Mr Richardson's to chill out before I get ill. Too late, Mum. But as Hugh pointed out once we'd calmed down a little, maybe Mum's programme will be just what I need. A distraction. A look at happiness as dictated by three wise old birds. Why not? Messages from Mum. I have a message of my own for her and that is hey, I might be coming to join you sooner than you think.

But maybe I'll learn something that I can pass on to my kids as well as the money. Maybe not, if mad Moon and her strange pipe are anything to go by. To me, happiness just descends sometimes for no reason. You can't manufacture it. Not really, but I guess there are some things one can do – meditate, exercise, eat right. Acupuncture is supposed to help with the after-effects of chemotherapy if/when I get to that stage. I'll give it all a go. A nutritionist put me on this stricter-than-strict diet. Why not? I'll try anything, but I could see that I offended Dee by not eating the food she'd prepared. I could tell her what's happening to me but no. Not yet, if ever. She'll just have to think what she thinks and that I'm an almighty pain in the ass. I can deal with that, would rather deal with that than have her pity me.

Actually she's a sweetheart. Always was. Bit of a dreamer, bit idealistic. I shouldn't take my problems out on her. Or Fleur. I could have told Fleur on the way down here. We were in the car for four hours together, but actually it was good to hear her prattling on about her life. I could feel things were normal for a while and it was good to hear about something else besides the C word and all that it involves. So I will tell them when I have to, not before. Dr Campbell said that the drug treatment can cause hot flushes and sweats, especially if I haven't been through the menopause yet, which I haven't. If I have an off-day I can tell them it's that.

The first stage of treatment is hormone therapy for three months. It might block the cancer cells. Might. But only if the type of cancer I have is what they call hormone receptor positive. Tamoxifen is my drug of choice. We won't know if it will work until I've tried it. 'On the plus side,' (*now there's a joke*, I thought) said the oncologist, 'the treatment has few side effects apart from bringing on an early menopause. And you won't lose your hair.' Well hurray for that. So bring it on. She didn't dwell on the negative side – that being, the cancer I have is incurable because it has spread to my organs, so really, all they can do is buy me time.

It was hard telling Hugh, Simon and Laura. I tried my best not to cry in front of them. I learnt fast that this thing is not just about me. They suffer too. I see the way they look at me, such sadness in their eyes and, last week, when he thought I was asleep, I heard Hugh in the bathroom, sobbing his heart out. Hugh, who never cries. That hurt more than anything. I did consider telling Dee and

Fleur, but they can't fix this and I don't want my illness to define me. All Fleur and Dee could do is be sad about it, and seeing more people be miserable, that's not going to help. I want to stay in control, and I know it's selfish but I want to use my 'Mum' weekends as an escape from thinking about what's coming. Mad as her kicking the bucket list is, it's my best chance, apart from at work, at having some time when I can just be me. Rose. Not Rose with cancer.

The irony is it's now my kicking the bucket list too. So, my choices are a) to have Dee and Fleur's pity for the remaining months, or b) have them think I am an uptight asshole. I choose option b) and to carry on as normally as I can for as long as I can. Uptight asshole I can do. Cancer victim, no thanks, I'll pass. Mum asked that I talk to God. A tall order to ask of someone who doesn't believe, but if I did talk to him, I'd have two words to say, and those are, fuck you.

16

Dee

Sunday 13 December, evening

The events of Sunday evening changed everything.

Fleur and Rose had been gone half an hour when the phone rang. Daniel. He was still at the Bell and Anchor. Had my sisters gone? Yes. Would I meet him for a drink? Yes.

'What's it about?' I asked.

'Tell you when you get here.'

I got changed, put on a bit of make-up, not too much in case he thought I'd tried too hard, a spray of Mitsouko perfume, and set out to meet him. *What on earth does he want?* I wondered. My mind went into overdrive as I walked down the lanes to the pub. *Was there something on the list just for me? Did he want to discuss an upcoming session for future months?* I didn't really care. I was feeling very positive after the weekend and that I was making progress with both sisters, getting to know them again. I'd been touched by their offers of help about my housing situation. Not that I'd want to take either of them up. I valued my independence and didn't want to ruin things by feeling beholden to either of them in any way, but it was nice to feel that they were both there for me in their separate ways.

Daniel was by the bar nursing a pint of beer when I walked through the doors and smiled in greeting. He looked the part of a local in a navy fisherman's sweater and jeans. I felt a surge of . . . what? Attraction? Anxiety? Anticipation? All three?

'So how can I help?' I asked when I joined him.

'First a drink. Wine? Something soft?'

'Wine. White. Dry. Thanks.' I needed a glass to relax.

As he ordered, I quickly glanced around the pub to see who was in there. A few locals who nodded hello, but no sign of Ian, Anna, or – worst still – Michael Harris.

We took our drinks and found a corner near the fire. I was waiting for him to say something but he was unusually quiet.

Eventually I asked, 'Are we here to discuss Mum's programme?'

He shook his head. 'I can't discuss the list or your sisters with you.'

'Oh. OK. No problem. So what is it then? How come you're still here?'

'I've never been to the Rame peninsula before, and I took the opportunity to have a look around the area. It was getting late by the time I got back here, so I decided to stay down another night.'

'Ah. So this is social?'

'It is. Sort of. I wanted to see you again. I enjoyed our

time together last time so . . . ' He reached over, took my hand and looked directly into my eyes. 'Look, I'm just going to come out and say this. I felt attracted to you the first time we met, felt a connection, and I might be wrong but I think you felt it too.'

Cue me to say something. He was looking at me, waiting. But I was aghast. Things like this didn't happen to me, and to come out with what I'd been feeling, as he had, and to admit that the attraction was mutual, would expose me, leave me open to getting hurt again. I knew nothing about him and I wasn't sure I was ready to let down the walls I'd built so carefully to protect myself.

'I know it might seem full on,' said Daniel, 'but I'm old enough to recognize something – someone special – when it happens.' Cue me again, but my brain appeared to have gone into meltdown; too much was going on inside – a rush of adrenalin, attraction, elation, fear. He stroked my hand with his thumb then let go and sat back. 'I'm rushing you. I apologize. Let's talk about something else. Tell me about your work, your painting.'

Now *that* I could talk about, and I was grateful for the change of subject whilst I processed what was happening. A stunningly good-looking man with denim blue eyes was sitting in front of me, telling me he thought I might be someone special. *Anna would say go for it. What have you got to lose, you idiot? Am I mad to hesitate?* I wondered as I filled him in on my work at the school and the night classes.

'So the painting session today was a bit old hat for you?' he asked.

'I thought we weren't supposed to discuss the programme?'

He laughed. 'Rules are for breaking.'

'Actually the session was surprisingly good. The painting I did wasn't, but it got me started on something. An idea for a series of work. Birds.'

'Birds?'

I nodded. 'It began with something your swami said in our meditation session. He said not to be troubled by thoughts but to see them as birds flying overhead and let them go.'

'And you are the mountain below, still, serene.'

'Yes, that was it, but I got to thinking that there are many kinds of birds. Small ones, large ones, the gentle and the cruel.'

Daniel laughed. 'You're right there. There are beautiful birds and ridiculous ones too. Well that's ruined that visualization for my meditation then. I'm going to be seeing vultures, seagulls . . . pigeons, oh no . . . all that bird shit. Dee, what have you done to my peace of mind?' He looked at me directly as he said the last part. I looked away, unsure of what to do with the rush of heat he was causing inside me.

'Oh! Sorry. Think about clouds passing over then, that should work.'

'It's OK, you have a creative brain. I like that. But these birds gave you an idea for your paintings?'

'They did. I thought I'd paint different kinds in different atmospheres to reflect different states of mind. Swans on a river, beautiful, peaceful, the exhilaration of a murmuration of starlings, the comedy and riot of colour of parrots, that wonderful look of disdain that owls can give you. I don't know yet, I need to sleep on it, but I feel inspired.

Buzzing, in fact. To take the bird analogy further, like an egg about to hatch.'

Daniel laughed again. 'You should paint that too.'

'I did a painting of a menacing dark flock today, just as an experiment, and it unlocked something and now my head is full of colours and images that I could develop. I was just jotting ideas down when you called.'

Daniel leaned over and squeezed my hand. 'You light up when you talk about something you're passionate about.'

I blushed. He appeared to be genuinely interested and impressed by what I was saying. It had been a long time since I'd had such rapt attention from a man. When I was with John, he was the artist with a growing international reputation. I was completely in his shadow. When he spoke about art, everyone listened, captivated by his knowledge and use of language. If I was with him and spoke about my work, I could see it was like an interruption, distracting from the great man, so I stopped talking, kept my ideas to myself and grew more and more silent.

'So if you were a bird, what would you be?' Daniel asked.

'God, I don't know. Let me think. What about you?'

'You must tell me that.'

'I don't know you well enough.'

'Not yet.'

I liked the way he said that and the way he smiled.

'My ex-boyfriend would have been a peacock,' I said.

'Was that good or bad?'

'Good in the beginning but bad in the end.'

'Vain?'

'That's what peacocks are known for, isn't it? Maybe I'll do a painting inspired by him. That would be fun.'

'What about your sisters?'

I felt a rush of excitement. 'Actually, yes. I could let the birds be inspired by people, all sorts of people, not just John and my sisters. What a great idea. So let me think. Rose. Something hard working – a busy bee bird, but that's too ordinary. I'd need something striking and stronger for her. I know, a peregrine falcon. I'm told they've been spotted up on the cliffs at Whitsand Bay, though I haven't seen any yet. And Fleur, something exotic and colourful like . . . a bird of paradise. Perfect. One that likes to preen.' I sat back and met his gaze. Neither of us looked away. His eyes were tender and smiling, completely focused on me. Something deep inside of me responded and I smiled back, my eyes not leaving his. *Oo*, I thought as I felt a jolt of electricity. *Haven't felt this for a while.*

'Sounds good to me,' he said. Suddenly he sat back, looked at his watch then pulled his mobile out. 'Mustn't forget. Time to send the next text from Iris.' He started laughing as he texted and, a moment later, my phone pinged that I had a message.

'Do these go out to all of us?'

He nodded. 'They do.'

I got my phone out of my coat pocket, looked at my message then back at Daniel. He was looking smug.

'Are you sure you didn't make this up and it's from you and not from Mum at all?'

'Scout's honour. I have a list from her and the times within the programme to send them. That one was scheduled for end of weekend two, Sunday evening, which it is.'

The text read: 'If you believe that something fantastic is about to manifest in your life, it probably will.'

Daniel took my hand, looked into my eyes again, then let his gaze slowly slide down to my mouth. It felt utterly erotic. *And we haven't even touched each other yet*, I thought. He didn't say anything for a few moments and neither did I, but there was no doubt in my mind what was happening. Chemistry with a capital C.

'I believe it,' he said finally. 'Question is, do you?'

I did. *I do*, I thought, but I wasn't ready to let him know. The feeling between us was strong, seductive, but part of me felt terrified. A message from Mum. *Very timely*, I thought as we got up to leave. *Maybe it's time to trust again and follow my heart.*

Monday 14 December, 8 a.m.

Up, showered and shaved, so I am smooth as a baby's bottom apart from where the razor slipped and I nicked myself just below my knee. *Bugger.* I stuck a bit of tissue on the cut. *Mmm, sexy*, I thought as I caught sight of my leg in the mirror and made a note to book in for regular waxing.

Before I got dressed, I pulled out all the drawers looking for the Jo Malone Pomegranate Noir body lotion that Fleur had sent me years ago. I'd kept it for special occasions. I found it shoved behind my underwear in the second drawer down, and when I took off the lid saw that it had gone hard with age. That's how many special occasions there had been in the last few years. I made another mental note to use any such gift in future. Such a waste. I went to the wardrobe and pulled out some of the gifts I'd already bought for friends for Christmas. I found the coconut bath lotion I had bought Anna. *I'll have to get her another present*, I thought as I applied it liberally.

Back to the underwear drawer. *What a sorry sight*, I thought as I sifted through a pile of off-white comfy knickers. I was sure I still had a sliver of lace in there somewhere. *Why haven't I got a thong?* I asked myself. *Because they're like wearing dental floss*, came back the answer. I guess it's easy to tell the state of a woman's love life by her underwear drawer, and mine was saying, action in the bedroom department, nil. *Why am I taking such care? Why am I feeling so edgy and hyper? Because Daniel is coming back at ten for coffee before he goes to get his train, that's why. He might fancy a bit of coconut tart with it. That's me. The coconut tart. I think I might have overdone it with the bath lotion.* After our drink in the pub last night, he'd walked me back to the house and we'd stood on my doorway just looking at each other, holding hands, grinning like idiots.

A memory of Fleur from when we were teenagers flashed into my mind. She was getting dressed before going on a date, dressed in an itsy-bitsy bra and pants set, emerald green and black lace, and was busy with the body lotion. I'd asked why all the effort? 'Dyb dyb dyb, dob dob dob. Girl Guide's motto. Be prepared and do your best,' she'd replied with a wicked grin.

Good motto, I thought as I found an unused pair of black lace low rise. *Where have these come from?* I wondered as I unwrapped them and put them on. *Some friend must have bought them for me one birthday, probably Anna and I'd forgotten about them.* I looked in the mirror. Oh dear. I hadn't taken my clothes off in front of a man in a very long time. Not since Blubber Lips, in fact. *Oh, please don't let Daniel be like him*, I prayed. Actually I wasn't in bad shape, slightly crepey around the neck and the knees and boobs could do with some tightening up, but still slim, thanks to Mum and Dad's lean genes. *Is it too early for candlelight? Maybe I should close all the curtains? God, I'm so nervous. Relax. Breathe, hold . . . exhale. And Daniel might not even want to have sex. He might think me a brazen hussy for even considering it. We hardly know each other.* But a sweet sharp tingling in my stomach reminded me of the look in his eyes last night. *Dyb dyb dyb, dob dob dob. Be prepared*, said Slut, my inner sex goddess.

*

9.50. Daniel arrived. He looked as agitated as I felt.

10.00. Coffee. The air was charged and the atmosphere thick with desire and anticipation.

10.15. Bed. With Daniel. I know. I am a slut.

10.30. Wow. I *really* am a slut. Daniel's pretty filthy too.

10.40. I remember this.

10.45. Oo, don't remember that. Let's do that again.

11.00. Slight cramp in the left buttock. I don't care.

11.05. If we were in a movie, this would be the 'Have a cigarette whilst we lie in each other's arms moment.' But neither of us smoked. 'I knew it would be good with you,' he said as he brushed a strand of hair behind my ear.

11.10. 'Should we get up?' I asked as I glanced at the clock by the bed.

The look in Daniel's eyes told me otherwise.

11.20. Round two. Slower. Both of us with eyes open, drinking each other in. Nice. Very nice.

Monday 14 December, afternoon

Daniel gone. Bit sore. Knees weak. Thigh muscles shaky from major workout – OK, three major workouts. Heart full. High as a kite.

17

Dee

Monday 4 January

A letter came in the morning post.

Dear Ms McDonald,

I am writing about rather a delicate matter.

As you know, the house at Summer Lane is now on the market for sale. I have discussed this with Michael and we are both aware that it can take months to sell a property. The housing market probably won't pick up until spring and then, even if we do get a buyer, it may take months to exchange and complete. Sales can fall through due to chains, people unable to get a mortgage and so on. There are no guarantees.

Due to this fact, my brother and I both feel that we have no choice but to raise the rent to reflect the current market. My mother was indeed very happy to have you as a tenant and caretaker of her home for the years that she was alive and insisted that your rent stayed the same for that period. However, we now feel that, as it may be months before we secure a buyer and a sale, that we must update the arrangement regarding your monthly payments.

I hope that, having lived there for many years at such a reduced rate, you will feel that this is a reasonable request. I did suggest this to my brother soon after my mother's passing, but he persuaded me to leave things as they were for a while, partly because we initially thought you might have been able to purchase the house for yourself and partly because we know that our mother valued you as a tenant despite the almost negligible income from the low rent.

As the possibility of you buying No. 3, Summer Lane is no longer feasible in the near future, we feel that it is only fair that we make these changes and hope that you will understand our dilemma and that we are not running a charity.

I have spoken with Mr Bentley from Chatham and Reeves and they have advised us that the current rate for a property of that size, in that location, would be around nine hundred pounds per calendar month – perhaps even more in the holiday season. We appreciate that you are a long-term tenant so would be willing to let you have it for seven hundred and fifty per month until we secure a buyer. I am sure you will agree that this is still good value.

Under these circumstances, we will understand if you choose to vacate and find other premises. If this is to be the case and you wish to give notice, we would appreciate if you could let us know of your decision as soon as possible,

Regards,

William Harris

And a Happy New Year to me, I thought, and put my coat on over my pyjamas and headed straight over to Anna's.

She hadn't got dressed either, but let me in and put the kettle on.

'Call Rose or Fleur,' she said after reading the letter. 'They both said they'd help.'

I groaned. 'That's the last thing I want to do. It would confirm to Rose everything she thinks about me – that I live with my head in the clouds, out of touch with reality, and can't cope on an everyday level. I know I was lucky with Mrs Harris for all those years. She was a gift from the gods and I can't really blame William Harris or Michael. As William said, they're not running a charity. And neither are my sisters. I don't want to go running to them. I'm forty-nine. It's pathetic. God, what must Michael and William think? They must feel that I took advantage of an old lady.'

'Of course they don't,' said Anna.

'There was a time when I was earning more and I offered Mrs Harris more rent, almost double, I did, but she refused, insisting she was happy for me to be there, that the house was looked after and loved and that was what mattered to her more than anything.'

'Dee, you don't have to defend yourself to me. I know what the arrangement was. You didn't take advantage but you *were* very lucky to have had someone like that as a landlady. In this day and age especially, when everyone's out to make money from their property, she was rare.'

'They must feel like I was her charity case. Did you read that in the letter? "We are not running a charity." God, I feel terrible.'

'Well don't. You know the truth. What does it matter what they think? It was a blessing to have met Mrs Harris, but the arrangement suited her too. Don't forget that. And now that's changed and you must adapt. That's life. It throws change at us. What about Daniel? Could he help?'

'No! God *no*. I don't want to present myself as a loser to him either. It's still such early days with us.'

'The possibility of losing your home doesn't make you a loser,' said Anna. 'Don't be so down on yourself. Things like this happen all the time to all sorts of people. Life has just dealt you a blow, that's all. We'll get through this.'

I loved the way she said 'we'. She was a good friend.

'What about the advice Rose gave you? Remember? About looking into your rights. That would show the Harris boys, if you came back fighting.'

'You're right, I'll do that straight away. With Christmas, then New Year and . . . seeing Daniel, I haven't followed it up yet. But I will.'

'Let me know what I can do to help,' said Anna. She stood up and began to sing, 'We shall not, we shall not be moved.'

The sight of her singing away in her nightie and slippers made me laugh. She always knew how to cheer me up.

*

Later that day, one of Mum's texts arrived. 'Learn to walk, or better still, dance on shifting sands.'

Once again, the message was spookily appropriate.

*

I spent the afternoon on my computer and the phone to an advisor at the council. I found some enlightening websites and the advisor was more than helpful.

In the evening, I sat down with Anna to reply to William Harris.

When we'd finished, she read it out to me.

'Dear Mr Harris,

Thank you for your letter of 4 January.

I read your proposal with interest, as I am sure you will read my response. Perhaps you and your brother are unaware of the rights of an assured tenant.

It applies if:

- You moved into a privately rented home between 1989 and 1997. I moved into No. 3, Summer Lane in 1991.
- You paid rent to a private landlord.
- Your landlord does not live in the same house.

Other facts you may be interested to read are:

- As an assured tenant, you can challenge rent increases. (I shall look into this further, but for the time being I can inform you that I will not be paying the amount that you suggested.)
- You can get certain repairs done. (In all the time I have lived here, I never contacted your mother once to do repairs. I always paid for them myself, and it was partly this that gave her the peace of mind that her property was well cared for. However, now she is gone, I believe I am within my rights to ask you to fix the roof, guttering, heating and plumbing, which is ancient, external wall, windows and doors

– all of which need doing. I shall have quotes done in the next month and send them on to you.)

• You can pass your tenancy to someone else if you die. (Will do. My daughter.)

In the meantime, I am well aware that you are not a charity and hope that the matter of No. 3, Summer Lane can be tied up in a manner that will suit both of us. I am still happy to buy the property from you when I get the inheritance from my mother, which is likely to be later this year. I will look into whether, as an assured tenant, I can buy it at a reduced rate.

I look forward to hearing back from you on this matter and the repairs,

Regards

Dee McDonald

'OK?' Anna asked.

I groaned. 'Seems harsh in places. Maybe I should soften it a bit. Michael Harris has always been very polite in his dealings with me and William said in his letter, Michael talked him out of trying to raise the rent before now.'

'This is business Dee and I am not going to write love from Dee, sorry sorry, kiss kiss at the end of the letter.'

'I wasn't going to suggest that!'

'We need to be firm here. You have to say what you mean. Grow some balls. Learn to fight for what's important to you.'

I laughed and saluted her. 'Yes sir, sergeant major.'

'Ready to print and post?'

'OK. Ready to print and post.'

I'm dancing on shifting sands, Mum, I thought as I went

to look for a stamp and envelope. Asserting myself was a new sensation for me and although one part of me felt slightly mean despite Anna's pep talk, another part felt good. I'd researched my rights and taken a stand.

Happy New Year, Dee, I told myself. A new, more confident me was emerging. I had a new boyfriend, a new series of paintings to work on and, for the first time in months, a sense of security. *Thank you Anna and thank you Rose for pointing me in the right direction*, I thought, and made a note to text Rose and tell her so.

18

Fleur

Saturday 13 February, 8 a.m.

This weekend is at mine. Family here at last. I've filled the fridge with goodies from the deli down the road. Got some very fine wine. Mira, the cleaner, has been in and cleaned and polished so everything is gleaming. Hah. I bet Rose and Dee won't believe it. I was always the untidy one when we lived at home. I hope they like it. It will be like a sleepover, all of us together. We were definitely getting on better last month.

I wonder what Mum has in store this time? I'm determined this is going to be the best weekend, whatever we have to do. I'm going to try and find out a bit more about Daniel. Not for me, for Dee. I have a sneaky feeling she has a crush on him. I'll get that out of her too. I'll be subtle, of course, encourage her to talk sort of thing. She was always an open book when it came to men. I want to get Rose talking, too – it's about time she told us more about her life and what's going on behind that oh-so-cool and controlled mask of hers. It's going to be great. I can feel it.

Dee

Saturday 13 February, 7 a.m.

'I suggest we arrive separately and not let on to your sisters that we've been seeing each other,' said Daniel as I lay in his arms in his bed.

We'd met up when we could since December. He had work commitments and so did I, but we'd managed a couple of times – once he came to me and once I'd met him in London and gone to his flat in Camden. It was on the ground floor with a small courtyard at the back. He hadn't done much to it since he'd rented it a year ago, apart from putting up a poster of the Buddha in the hall. His clothes were on a hanging rail, other clothes still in boxes or cases. *A man passing through*, I'd thought the first time I was there. Last night was my second visit and we'd had an early Valentine's night tucked up in bed with a bottle of champagne.

'At least not until we've finished Mum's list,' I replied.

'Good. My role is supposed to be completely neutral, and I don't want any undercurrents interfering with your mother's programme.'

'Understood. Our secret.'

'What we have is very special but we have to be cool for now.'

'That will be me.' I was happy to do as he asked. What

I had with him was mine, precious and not to be shared, picked apart or teased about by Rose or Fleur.

Saturday 13 February, 11.30 a.m.

I arrived at Fleur's late due to snow and ice causing traffic delays. Fleur had bought the flat two and a half years ago, so I'd never been there and was intrigued to see where and how she lived now. It was a first-floor apartment in a block on Sloane Street in Knightsbridge. I found the building, where a uniformed porter greeted me. I stamped snow off my boots, thanked him for opening the doors, then made my way through the marbled reception area to the lift and up to Fleur's floor.

She was waiting for me at the door and ushered me in with a welcoming smile.

'Love the boots,' I said as I looked at the kingfisher blue suede knee-highs she was wearing. They matched her long cardigan perfectly. I handed her a bunch of white tulips that I'd bought at a flower stall near the tube. They'd cost a fortune but I didn't want to arrive empty handed.

So far so good, I thought as she led me into an elegant and airy living room with floor-to-ceiling windows that looked out over Knightsbridge. It had been decorated in shades of ivory, taupe and white, with silk curtains and dark wooden floors. She'd had an interior designer do it for her and it looked as if no expense had been spared.

'Gorgeous flowers,' I said as I took in the vast arrangement of white orchids and bamboo on the coffee table. The tulips that I'd brought her looked pathetic next to them.

Daniel was already there, perched on a sofa. He greeted me politely, nothing more. I said, 'Hi,' and turned away.

'I'll show you your room first,' said Fleur and took my bag. I breathed a sigh of relief that she didn't ask where I'd stayed last night, probably assuming I'd been with one of the friends I had in North London. I followed her out into the hall and along a corridor.

'Kitchen,' she said as she opened a door to reveal a magazine-worthy kitchen, which was as immaculate as the living room, with white granite tops, cream painted units and limestone floors. It looked like it had never been used. 'Help yourself to whatever you like.'

She led me on to the back of the flat. 'You're in here,' she said as she opened another door to a large bedroom.

'Wow,' I said. 'I see you've gone for a minimal look throughout.'

'Yes. Do you like it?'

'God yes. Course I do. It's stunning. Makes everywhere look more spacious.' Fleur dumped my bag on a king-size bed covered in a shimmer of pale taupe silk, then opened another door to reveal a white marble and mirrored bath and shower room. 'Wow again,' I said, though I couldn't help but think that, although lovely, the flat looked soulless and unlived in, like an upmarket hotel.

Fleur seemed happy with my reaction. 'Make yourself at home,' she said and disappeared back down the corridor.

'I will,' I called after her, but the atmosphere was as far from my home as it could be. No artifacts or books, just the latest edition of *Vogue* and a single white orchid on the bedside cabinet.

Through the open door, I noticed Rose unpacking in the

room opposite. I went to stand in the hall and looked in to see another room in a similar style to mine, except there was a gold bedspread on the bed and one of the walls looked as if it had been gold-leafed. 'Hi,' I said.

Rose gave me a nod. 'Here we are again,' she said with a shrug of her shoulder. She took off her red sweater to reveal a white silk shirt underneath. 'I'm boiling. I think Fleur keeps the heating on full blast.'

'Very stylish, isn't it?'

Rose wrinkled her nose. 'But like a show house, don't you think? I guess she has a cleaner come in. Fleur could never keep it this immaculate.'

I laughed. 'True.' When we had lived together, Fleur's room had always been a mess of clothes, open drawers, a dressing table piled with nail polish, make-up and perfume, and her shoes left lying where she took them off. 'How have you been since we last met up?' I asked. Rose and I hadn't been in touch much since she'd been down in Cornwall, apart from Christmas cards sent both ways, and I'd sent an email to both sisters in January letting them know that I had my housing situation in hand, and thanking them for their input. I had heard from Fleur in the interim. She'd sent a box of Jo Malone bath oil and lotions, which had arrived a few days before Christmas, and I'd agonized over what to send back. In the end, I'd sent her a pale grey velvet scarf that I'd found in a local shop. It seemed like a poor return, and took me back to the anxiety of many Christmases and birthdays before the fall-out when I didn't know what to buy the woman who had everything.

'Good. Fine. You?' Rose replied.

'Also fine, thanks.' No jokes about being fucked up, inse-cure, neurotic and exhausted this time, I noted. I used to think Rose was like a cactus plant that flowered once a year. When she did open up, it was lovely but rare.

'Guess we'd better go in then.' Rose brushed past me on the way back to the living room.

She's closed up again, I thought as I followed her into the living room, where I took the seat furthest away from Daniel.

After coffee, served in delicate china cups, we were ready to watch Mum's latest instructions. Daniel had put his laptop on a glass dining table and Rose, Fleur and I took our places, ready. I noticed a couple of framed photos on a shelf by the window: a beautiful one of Mum when she was younger, and a second of Rose, Fleur and me, taken in the garden in Hampstead when we were in our twenties. I felt touched it had pride of place in her home.

Daniel pressed the Play button and there was Mum in her room at the retirement village. She was lying on a couch, wearing a green silk kimono and had a blue ostrich feather around her neck. Martha stood at her head and was feeding her grapes. Jean was on her other side, fanning her.

Mum smiled out of the screen and I smiled back, so glad to see her again. 'Hello darlings,' she drawled in a Marlene Dietrich voice. She indicated her friends. 'This is the life hey?'

'Is for you Iris Parker,' said Jean, and smacked Mum on her knees with the fan. 'Why couldn't I be Cleopatra?'

Mum laughed and sat up straight while Martha and Jean took their places beside her, both groaning as they lowered themselves on to the sofa.

Martha laughed. 'Hazard of old age, dears. One can't get up or down without a groan.'

'Well, here we are on weekend three,' said Mum. 'I do hope you're all there and there haven't been problems with the weather or flu bugs. I've told Daniel if that happens, not to worry, and to reschedule for a weekend you can all do. So . . . what's this weekend about?'

Martha picked up a cocktail glass from the small table to the side of the sofa and took a sip. 'It's about indulgence, darlings. I know we put you through it a bit the first two weekends, but that's life – it can't all be cocktails.'

'But sometimes, it can,' added Jean. 'What we want to say this time is that happiness is as much about contrast as anything else. Like that quote from Joyce Grenfell. "Happiness is the sublime moment when you get out of your corsets at night." A relief that something is over or has changed.'

'To warm up when you've been cold, to be somewhere cool when you've been hot,' said Mum, 'to be fed when you're hungry, to be busy after a quiet patch, or to have some down time when you've been busy, etc. If life was all on one level, no contrast, it would be a very dull place indeed.'

'Contrast but balance too,' said Jean. 'In seeking happiness, if you seek the pleasure of life too intently, you lose the meaning. If you seek the meaning too intently, you lose the pleasure. You need to find a balance.'

'Like a glass of wine in either hand,' said Mum.

'Don't be silly, Iris,' said Jean. 'You know what I mean.'

'I do,' said Mum. 'So no walks in the cold this weekend or colonics to look forward to or baring your soul to Beverly.

No, as a contrast – or in Jean's word, as a balance – to the other tasks, this weekend we're going to give you a few treats. Treats for the senses: to see something wonderful, hear something wonderful—'

'To feel amazing, have taste sensations, know the comfort and pleasure of touch and the power of smell,' added Martha.

'Sounds like my kind of weekend,' said Fleur.

'I expect Daniel's there with you,' said Jean, 'and as always he's got the schedule. Today, we just want you to relax, so stay in your dressing gowns if you like. Three therapists will be coming to the flat to give you massages and facials. It will be a day of pampering. For an early supper, Daniel will have arranged for a fabulous meal, cooked by an Ottolenghi chef, to be brought, then this evening a night out at the theatre, and you'll go by taxi. We had to leave what you see up to Daniel, because we don't know what will be on at the time, but it will be ballet or opera. Something marvellous to lift the soul and be a treat for the eyes or the ears.'

'Tomorrow,' Mum continued, 'a day out in Harrods with a make-up session, a hairdresser, then time with a personal shopper—'

'Because the right outfit can change how one feels,' said Martha. 'It really can. I always say, wherever one is, one should never forget one's sense of style.'

'Poser,' said Jean.

Martha gave her a snooty look. 'One has standards and so should the girls.'

'I want each of you to choose a perfume so that we don't leave out the sense of smell,' said Mum. 'Go for the ones you've always worn if you like, I know you all have your favourites, but try a few new ones too. I know Fleur is as happy as a sandboy when in the perfume department surrounded by sumptuous scents.'

'So enjoy,' said Martha. 'You could probably all do with a bit of relaxation time with the busy lives you lead.'

'I told you that the weekends would be varied,' said Mum. 'We wanted to make them so as to include different experiences, because different things appeal to different people and you three are such individuals. Have any of you come across a man called Rudolf Otto?'

We looked at each other and shook our heads.

'He writes about an experience that he calls the numinous, a word meaning to have a sense of elation at the wonder and mystery that is life,' said Jean.

'But what triggers this is never the same for two people,' said Martha. 'For one, a piece of music can inspire the feeling, whilst the same piece can leave another cold. For someone else, it's a walk in the mountains or to witness a sunset and to stop and experience the glory of nature. For another the feeling will be triggered by being in a place of worship like a cathedral or temple. For another, on looking into the eyes of a newborn child. You see? Different things can inspire the numinous, which is why we've tried to include all sorts of sensations and experiences in the programme in the hope that you will find your personal route to it.'

'Can't say I felt very numinous during the colonic,' said Fleur. I laughed but Rose ignored her.

'You must seek and find what evokes this feeling in you, what inspires for you the experience of the soul soaring, of joy,' said Mum. 'But for today, just enjoy. Relax and enjoy.'

They went back to their Cleopatra tableau, with Mum lying back, Jean with the fan and Martha with the grapes.

'Bliss,' said Fleur. 'Especially as it's freezing outside.'

'And a relief that she's not got us doing anything too mad,' said Rose.

'Lying on a sofa with an ostrich feather around your neck and talking from beyond the grave is pretty mad if you ask me,' said Fleur.

'Yes, but that's her,' said Rose. 'She hasn't got *us* doing anything bonkers.'

Fleur turned to me. 'You seem rather subdued this morning, Dee. You all right?'

'Oh yes, fine,' I said. 'Good. Thanks.'

I was anything but fine. All my senses felt heightened, but I was trying my best to look calm. I had found my numinous. Daniel. I was in love. Truly, madly, deeply. I'd been seeing him for almost two months, but this was the first time I'd been with him with my sisters present, and it was hard being so close to him and not being able to touch him or share a look. I could hardly remember how I'd behaved around him before we became lovers, and faking indifference wasn't proving easy. After Nick, I never thought I would feel this way again, but I did and more. In Daniel, I'd found a soul mate. We seemed to fit and it was so easy to be with him. He didn't play games – apart from the tantric ones that he'd introduced me to.

I needed to put Fleur off the scent. 'Oh, I was thinking about work, I guess.'

'Work? Why?'

'Since I last saw you, I've started a new series. Er . . . it's going well, but like anything creative, it has rather taken over.'

Fleur seemed happy with my explanation. I didn't dare look at Daniel in case I gave us away. Fleur would see in a second that something was going on and it was true that my work was going well. Since December, I'd focused on my bird series, and was already some way to having work ready to show in an exhibition. It felt like a dam had burst inside of me and the images had been flooding in. I'd done some small canvases, some larger. One I was particularly proud of was of an eagle flying into and across the canvas, filling it with massive outstretched wings, its beak down, as though it could fly through and out into the room. Daniel was my biggest fan; he'd seen the painting on his visit to me and wanted to buy it. When I said I'd give it to him as a gift, he'd insisted that he paid for it. 'It's how you make your living,' he said, so considerate and understanding that the classes I taught were only a means to an end.

*

Daniel attempted to make his exit once he'd given us our schedules and funds for the weekend. He had his jacket and scarf on, ready to leave, when Fleur decided that she wasn't letting him go so easily.

'So, mystery man,' she said as he headed for the door. 'Don't rush off. Don't you think it's time you told us a bit more about yourself?'

Daniel stopped and turned back, careful not to meet my eyes. 'What do you want to know?'

'Work. Where do you live? Are you attached? Do you have children? We've been meeting with you since last October but know so little about you. I thought, we must appear rude.'

'Not at all, but there's not much to know. I live in North London, work for the swami mainly—'

'Doing what exactly?' asked Fleur.

'Oh, setting up his tour schedules. PA work.'

'Where does he go?' I asked. I thought I'd better say something in case my silence betrayed me, though I already knew a bit about Daniel's work.

'All over the UK. Teaching, visiting hospices.'

'Hospices?' asked Rose.

'Yes. The swami works with the terminally ill.'

'Doing what?' Rose again.

'Helping them to find their peace. For many, it's a relief for someone to address what is happening to them, to address that part of them that isn't ill or dying, to have something to say about the importance of the inner state of mind through their last chapter.'

'Really?' said Rose. 'I guess it's easy to preach when you're not one of them.'

Her tone was sharp, and I thought her comment unkind when she knew so little about what they actually did, though I hadn't known about this aspect of his work either. 'So what does the swami actually do?'

'He teaches them to go within through meditation, to go beyond what's happening on the outside. He helps show them that there is more to them than just a body, that the body is merely a temple for the soul and transitory – a shell, if you like.'

'What if they don't believe in God?' asked Rose.

'That doesn't matter. There is a state of peace inside everyone regardless of belief.'

'Sounds presumptuous of him to me,' said Rose.

'Why?' asked Daniel. He took a seat back at the table.

'Oh, come on. Isn't that obvious? To swan in there with platitudes about peace and telling people how they should be feeling at such a traumatic time of their life.'

'You'd be surprised, Rose. Most people welcome him.'

'Is it like giving the Last Sacrament, like a priest?'

Daniel considered Rose's question. 'Yes and no. Yes, in that the Last Sacrament can bring peace to a believer. And no, in that the swami doesn't belong to any creed. He helps people to find their own inner peace, regardless of whether they have faith or not.'

Rose scoffed. 'I bet some people are about as far from feeling inner peace as they will ever be. I think you're being naïve and idealistic, Daniel.'

'Your prerogative. The swami would never force his teachings on anyone, but many are very receptive to him.'

'Did he help Mum?' asked Fleur.

Daniel nodded. 'I believe so. As you know, she was always interested in meditation, and she visited the centre many times last year before she came to see me about this programme.'

'She never mentioned it,' said Rose.

'But maybe that was because she was planning her kicking the bucket list and didn't want any of us to get wind of it,' said Fleur.

'Maybe, but also maybe she just found the swami easier to talk to than family,' I said. I remembered the books she'd had in her room, and the conversations we'd had about death – or she'd tried to have. Although I'd done my best to listen and talk, I'd found it difficult, and she'd probably seen that. I could understand that a man like the swami wouldn't have shied away, and a debate about death and an afterlife would have been a comfort and a relief to her. Hearing that Daniel was involved made me love him all the more. He was turning out to be the emotionally intelligent and sensitive man I had always been looking for.

'And apart from that, what about you? Children? Partner? Pets?' Fleur persisted. I had to hand it to Daniel. He was the epitome of cool, unlike me, who was beginning to feel panic. I realized I needed to help change the subject.

'No children—' he began.

'What do you think of this programme we're doing?' I asked.

Daniel smiled. 'It's not my place to comment or advise. I think I told you that in the beginning. This is a journey for you and your sisters, not me, so best if I stay out of it.'

'Cop-out,' said Fleur. 'Come on, dish the dirt. Who is the real Daniel?' I took a sharp breath. I couldn't bear for Rose or Fleur to know what was going on. They'd make fun. They'd belittle what we had, but Daniel didn't appear at all fazed. He leant back, as though in no rush to leave, his body language relaxed and open. I prayed that Fleur or Rose didn't notice that I'd tensed up, crossed my legs and my arms. I made an effort to reflect Daniel's ease and uncrossed everything, made myself breathe deeply.

'Not really a cop-out,' said Daniel. 'What I think is irrelevant. It's between you and your late mother. I was instructed purely to organize what needed doing.' He stood up. 'And now I really must be on my way. Your masseuses will be here shortly.'

*

'Dee, so what's going on with you and Daniel?' was the first thing Fleur asked, seconds after he'd closed her front door.

Inwardly I cursed. 'Me and Daniel? Nothing. Don't be stupid.'

Fleur looked at me carefully. 'Hmm. I think you've got the hots for him.'

'Have not.'

'Yes you have. I can tell. You've gone all quiet and . . . coy.'

'I have not.'

'Have.'

'Have I missed something?' asked Rose. 'Has something happened between you?'

'Course not! You were the one asking him the questions.'

'I was trying to find out if he was attached for you,' said Fleur. 'You know you want to know.'

'I already know. He told me he was single when we were down in Somerset, that first weekend,' I said. That much was true.

'That was months ago,' said Fleur. 'He might be gay for all we know.'

Rose began staring at me. 'You do like him though, don't you Dee? You do seem kind of different when he's around.'

I was dying to tell them, but I'd promised Daniel, even though I did feel uncomfortable about lying. 'I like him, yes, but you know it's down to chemistry in the end and, nope, that's just not there, so I can tell you that whatever you sense about how I am today, it's not because of Daniel. Maybe it's because work is going well. My new series.' I filled them in on the bird paintings and, though Rose feigned interest, Fleur's eyes glazed over. It did the trick, though, and got them off my case about fancying Daniel. But Fleur was right, I did feel different when he was around. I was on cloud nine.

'Have you heard any more from your landlady's sons?' asked Rose.

'Yes. I got an email from Michael saying that he looked forward to resuming negotiations later in the year. The house has been taken off the market so they obviously took me seriously about the rights of assured tenants.'

'Excellent result, and you can buy the house when this year is up,' said Fleur.

'I can. I will.'

'Good,' said Rose.

'Good,' I echoed.

*

The masseuses came on the dot of eleven: Cheryl, Katie and Rachel, bright young things with glossy hair, clear skin and eyes. They were carrying massage couches and bags of equipment. They explained our options and Rose opted for a facial and reflexology, Fleur a facial and Swedish massage, and I went for a facial and aromatherapy treatment.

Katie was my therapist and together we went into the bedroom, where I sat on the bed while she set up.

'Shall we start with the massage?' asked Katie.

'Sounds perfect.'

'Take everything off,' said Katie, 'and I'll be back in a moment.' She pulled out a paper shower cap from her bag and handed it to me. 'Put this on.'

After she'd gone, I took my clothes off, put the paper cap on my head and tucked my hair into it. 'Ready,' I called and Katie came back in. She took one look at me and burst out laughing.

I felt indignant. *How rude*, I thought. *OK, so I'm past my prime, but the sight of me naked is not that blooming funny.* 'Why are you laughing?'

Katie looked at my head then at my crotch, and I realized that what she'd given me wasn't for my hair at all. I was wearing a pair of knickers on my head.

I went bright red. 'Oh God, sorry, sorry,' I said as I removed the pants from my head and quickly stepped into them. 'Sorry.'

'No problem,' said Katie, but she kept sniggering all the way through the massage and, in the end, I had to join her. *Mum would have howled with laughter*, I thought as I succumbed to Katie's fingers and the divine scent of rose and neroli. Soon I forgot all about my idiotic mistake and floated off into a state of bliss. *Pure heaven*, I thought, and made a note to tip Katie generously, mainly to keep her mouth shut.

By three o'clock, we were done, and I felt more relaxed than I had been in months. When our masseuses left, we all opted for a snooze, and as I lay back on Fleur's Egyptian cotton sheets in the perfect ivory bedroom, I felt tearful. *Here I am Mum*, I thought, *pampered and pandered to, in*

Fleur's flat with Rose next door. We're all together, just as you wanted, but you're not here. Mum had put so much thought into this list of hers, I wished I could thank her for looking out for me, for us, and for caring so much about our welfare, and I wished I had done more for her whilst she was alive. So much had changed since her death and I no longer felt disappointed and anxious about life. Quite the opposite. Apart from still missing her, I was happy and full of hope for the future and wished that I could have told her that. The massage seemed to have penetrated my wall of coping, and all the grief at having lost Mum came flooding to the surface. I might have seen her face on the recording this morning but, in reality, she had still gone to that place where I could not follow. As I wept, I wondered how Fleur and Rose were doing in their rooms and if the massages had affected them in the same way.

*

Our meal was delivered at six. A mix of salads, which sounded boring but was, as Mum had promised, a taste sensation. Even Rose, with all her dietary requirements, ate every bit.

'Hmm, pomegranate,' said Fleur, 'mango, avocado, smoked bacon; all my favourites.'

I scrutinized her and Rose's faces for signs of grief at missing Mum as I had after the massage. Fleur seemed fine and Rose's expression gave nothing away, apart from looking a bit tired.

'So what do we think so far?' I asked as I watched my sisters relish each mouthful of the dessert, and tried not to think that Rose had turned down my cake but was now happily spooning in the chocolate mousse.

'About what?' Fleur asked.

'Mum's recipes for happiness.'

Fleur licked her spoon. 'This part is pretty good. Dunno. At this moment in time, all is good. What about you?'

I'd never been happier in my life, but that was mainly due to Daniel. 'Unexpected,' I said. 'Changeable. Sometimes I feel happy in the middle of a stressful time, then, like just before, I feel sad at a time when everything is wonderful. I had a wave of missing Mum. What do you think of it all, Rose?'

Rose hesitated a few moments. 'I don't think happiness can be manufactured. I know Mum meant well, apart from the colonic, and I can see what she was trying to do, but happiness is a state of mind, don't you think? It's not necessarily going to happen because you take a walk in a nice location or have a massage. If you're worried about something, then those events will be marred.'

'Are you worried about something?' I asked.

Rose shrugged. 'No. No more than normal. Happy, sad. Good days, bad days. That's life, isn't it? You get on with it. I reckon that overthinking can be an indulgence. I have other things going on in my life. How many people have time out to think about the secret of happiness in the way Mum's asking us to? Don't you think it's indulgent? Like, me, me me. How am I? Am I happy?'

'But that's what marvellous,' I said. 'She has given us something extraordinary, and the times and means to do it. What a legacy.'

Rose was looking at me as if trying to understand what I was saying. Clearly, she didn't feel the same.

'And it's been good reconnecting with you two,' said Fleur. 'I'm liking our time together.'

'But have we reconnected? Really?' said Rose. 'I don't think I truly know about your lives, or you mine.'

'OK. So tell us about yours,' said Fleur.

Rose had appeared to be on the verge of saying something, but clammed up. 'Nothing to tell.'

Fleur sighed. 'I'm sure there is. Tell us about your days, your work.'

'Same ol', same ol',' said Rose.

'So what's that then? What's same ol', same ol' for you?' I asked.

Rose's back had stiffened. 'Too boring. Don't want to talk about it.'

Clearly it was not a day for the cactus to flower.

Fleur turned to me. 'OK, you Dee. You've told us a bit about your work. How's your love life? Any decent men turned up down your way since Christmas?'

I prayed that I wouldn't blush. 'Nope,' I replied. It was the truth. Daniel lived in London.

'Do you care? Would you like to be in a relationship?' Fleur persisted.

'I . . . I guess, if the right one came along.'

'Daniel,' said Fleur. 'Mr Do-Good, talk to the dying, help them find their peace.'

'Oh leave him, Fleur,' I said. 'I think he was sincere.'

'Presumptuous, I thought,' said Rose. 'Who do he and his swami think they are? The angels of death?'

'I'm sure he doesn't think that at all. I think what he said sounded good.' I didn't like hearing Rose and Fleur criticizing Daniel, but didn't want to defend him too much in case they guessed what was going on. *I was right not to tell them about him and me*, I thought. *They're so judgemental and would have got stuck right in with their opinions.*

'You would think that. That's why I thought you'd go for him. You always liked the "let's save the world" types.' She started to sing in a girlie voice, 'Dee's got a cru-ush, Dee's got a cru-ush.'

'Shut up Fleur,' said Rose. 'You might like to discuss every aspect of your life, but you have to learn to respect when other people don't want to.' *That's strong coming from you Miss Opinionated*, I thought, but I was glad she'd said it.

'Oh for God's sake,' said Fleur. 'I was—'

'You were sticking your nose in where it wasn't wanted. We're all adults now, not teenagers sharing secrets,' Rose continued. 'Just because we're sisters, doesn't mean we have to share every sordid detail of our lives. Let us have our privacy.'

Fleur looked hurt and I was shocked. Rose's tone had been harsh.

'Hey, less of the sordid, and she was only asking—' I started.

'Neither of you has changed,' said Fleur as she pushed her chair back and got up. 'I thought you might have, that you, Rose, might have mellowed, but trying to get through to you is like trying to get through a brick wall. And, Dee, I was only teasing and trying to find out a bit about Daniel for you. For *you*!'

She went to her bedroom, slamming the door behind her. I looked over at Rose. She shrugged a shoulder and went back to her mousse.

Saturday 13 February, 7 p.m.

We set off to see a contemporary ballet company at Sadler's Wells.

'It looks so beautiful,' I said as we drove through the snow-covered streets up towards Islington. I felt relaxed from the treatments and cosseted and cosy in the warm taxi, while outside the white-covered buildings and trees of North London looked like a magic land.

Fleur, however, still had the hump with Rose and me and was acting like a petulant teenager, giving monosyllabic replies to whatever we said to her. I half expected her to say, 'Whatever,' or, 'It's not fair. I wish I'd never been born. No one understands me.' I wasn't going to let her spoil the treat. I hadn't been to a ballet in years and was looking forward to it.

Daniel had booked fabulous seats in the royal circle upstairs, and I felt a rush of anticipation when the lights went down and the audience became silent. A spotlight on the stage and three dancers in white appeared, flowing like liquid into each other. The first ten minutes were wonderful to watch, but my eyelids were heavy, *heavy*. I struggled to keep my eyes open. I tried pinching myself but I felt as if I'd been drugged. It was so warm and comfortable in the theatre, plus the fact that I hadn't got much sleep last night at Daniel's that, try as I might, I couldn't stay awake.

I woke up for the interval and I went and bought a glass of wine for Fleur and me and a glass of water for Rose. Mistake. The alcohol only made me sleepier. I didn't remember any of the second half, apart from when I glanced briefly at Rose and Fleur who both had their eyes closed.

ZZzzzzz.

The lights went up. It was over. The audience was applauding. A second call. Rose, Fleur and I joined in with enthusiasm.

When we got up to leave, the woman who was sitting behind us gave us a filthy look. 'Such a waste,' she said loudly to her husband.

'On the contrary,' said Fleur. 'I had a marvellous snooze – so relaxing.'

'Me too,' said the husband with a lascivious grin at Fleur. 'Often do at the theatre.'

He got a whack from his wife on the way up the stairs.

*

In the taxi going back to Fleur's, she was still sulking despite her 'marvellous snooze'. She hardly said a word; nor did Rose, who appeared preoccupied. *We have another day together tomorrow*, I thought. *I don't want it to be like this.* I hated when we weren't speaking when we lived at home, and searched my mind as to what I could do or say to make it better.

As we got out of the taxi and headed for the apartment door, a song from our childhood popped into my head. It was 'Sisters' by Irving Berlin and Fleur had changed the lyrics. I began to sing her version: 'Sisters, sisters, They're like very annoying blisters . . . '

'Shut up Dee,' said Fleur. 'Move on. I have.'

Yeah right, I thought as the porter let us in. I followed her to the lift but I was too tired to pursue it any more. *Tomorrow*, I told myself. *I'll make it right tomorrow.*

19

Dee

Sunday 14 February, 9 a.m.

So much for Fleur's comment yesterday about liking our time together and how we'd reconnected, I thought as I ate a bowl of granola that had been laid out for me in the perfect kitchen. Rose had breakfast in her room and Fleur was still giving us the silent treatment. I remembered when we were younger, she could sulk for days after an argument. Mum said she was like a slow burning casserole when she was pissed off about anything. No point in trying to talk her round, and I wasn't going to let her spoil things. I had a makeover session to look forward to and money to spend. It had been years since I could afford a new outfit. Most of my wardrobe was made up from charity shop finds, something that Anna and I excelled in, though Anna called hers vintage. 'Sounds classier.'

Sunday 14 February, 11.30 a.m.

We took a taxi to the store where our sessions had been booked. I was whisked up to the first floor by a tall, dark stick insect who introduced herself as Kristin.

When we got to a private plush changing room area, she looked me up and down. 'Are you looking for work clothes or casual?'

'Casual.'

'For summer or winter?'

'Oh . . . summer, I think. I tend to wear big old jumpers and jeans in the winter.'

'Evening or day wear?'

'Day.'

'And how would you describe your personal style?'

'Er, comfortable, layered.'

Clearly the wrong answer, because her mouth shrank to resemble a cat's bottom. She continued to assess me. I smiled. She didn't return it. She ordered coffee for me, showed me to an area with a sofa, tables and magazines, then disappeared. Bliss. I didn't care if Kristin didn't approve of my style. I was in heaven.

Twenty minutes, Kristin was back laden with armfuls of clothes. She pointed at a cubicle. 'Strip off and we'll see what works.'

I had to hand it to her, she had my size down perfectly, and although a few things were too garish for my taste (a silk dress with huge red flowers and ferns), she had picked a few things that I liked. I looked at the labels: Sahara, Masai, Grizas, in lovely soft fabrics; they all had a quirkiness about them. I settled for a pale green knee-length tunic with three-quarter sleeves that was cut like a dream and a pair of white linen trousers to go under them. She finished the outfit off with a soft white cotton shawl to be worn pashmina style. 'Layered and comfortable to wear but elegant,' said Kristin.

I looked in the mirror. I looked Joanna Lumley elegant. 'Job done, Kristin,' I said.

Kristin was delighted and packaged up my new clothes in tissue. 'Takes years off you,' she said as I paid up. Cheeky sod.

Sunday 14 February, 1 p.m.

I was directed to the beauty salon where Paris, another tall stick insect, blonde this time, lectured me about the state of my skin. 'You must *must* exfoliate, madam, and always moisturize your neck,' then went on to recommend all sorts of products for 'the older' client. I'd worn the same make-up for the last fifteen years so it was good to get a professional opinion.

'Two rules at your age, it's either eyes or lips, not both, or you look like a drag queen. And less is more.'

'Don't hold back,' I told her, but actually she made me look half decent with soft neutrals around the eyes and a pale rose lipstick.

'Takes years off you,' she said when she'd finished and put my products in a bag. Cheeky sod.

Sunday 14 February, 2.30 p.m.

The hairdressing session proved more of the same, with a lecture about the condition of my hair, the split ends and the colour.

'Oh my God. Have you been doing it yourself? That all-over hair dye is so ageing. Makes you look hard. You need softer colours to make it look natural. Light and shade and I'm going to cut it to your shoulders,' said Hattie, a red-headed stick insect.

Don't any of these girls ever eat? I wondered as I listened to her advice, surrendered to her magic, and emerged two hours later minus three inches of hair, with soft highlights and lowlights and my hair a fabulous glossy honey brown.

'I know,' I said as I left. 'I look years younger.'

'You do,' she replied. Cheeky sod.

Are they all taught to say that in here? I wondered as I looked at my reflection as I crossed the Ladieswear department, but I liked what I saw. Martha was right: a new outfit, good haircut and some new make-up can really boost a mood. I felt like a million dollars.

As I left the brightly lit salon, I saw Fleur come out of the room opposite. She looked the same as always. Beautiful. I was going to chase after her to see if she fancied a coffee but held back: *best leave her to cool off*, I thought as I crossed the floor and took the escalator down to the perfume department. Suddenly I was in ancient Egypt. As I sailed down through golden pillars carved with ancient figures, and into the dark underworld of the ground floor, I found myself transported to another world. On the roof above were representations of the Zodiac shown against a star-studded night sky, in front an enormous gold sculpture of a mummy. Temple after temple opened out before me as I reached the ground floor and took a deep breath as my senses were assaulted by a hundred aromas.

This could be a lovely girlie session, I thought as I searched for my sisters in the crowds, *the only part of the day we could do together*, but I couldn't see either of them anywhere, and Mum hadn't stipulated that we went around as a three-some. The wise old bird probably knew there would be days like this. Rose was never one for girlie outings, so would probably keep this part of the day short and sweet. This morning, she'd said she wouldn't be getting a new scent. 'Annick Goutal for me. Has been for years. I believe when you find a perfume that suits you, you should stick with it.'

I wandered around from counter to counter, trying samples here and there, Miller Harris, Jill Sanders, Sisley, Van Cleef & Arpels, Hermès but, in the end, I also settled for my old favourite, Mitsouko by Guerlain. Daniel had complimented me on it, so I spent my money on all the extras that went with it – soap, bath gel as well as cologne. When I'd paid for my purchases, I went to the counter selling Jean Patou. Mum had worn Joy for most of her life. I sprayed the tester and the air filled with her comforting scent. Jasmine and roses. For a moment, it felt like Mum was there, and my eyes filled with tears. The assistant behind the counter glanced over at me and I turned away to see that Rose had appeared at my side, as if by magic, maybe drawn by the familiar scent.

'They say smell is our most powerful sense,' she said as she inhaled the aroma. She put her arm around me. 'It can bring back a person more fiercely than anything. God, I miss her.'

'Me too. Remember how she used to spray Dad's cologne into the air after he'd gone?'

Rose nodded. 'I do. Evocative stuff.'

We stood for a brief tender, shared moment. No words were needed and, for the first time since Mum's death, I felt some comfort from Rose being there beside me.

She looked at her watch and snapped out of the bubble we were in. 'We're done here, I think. It's beginning to feel more Horrids than Harrods. Too many people for me.' She looked me up and down. 'You look good by the way. Nice, elegant.'

'Thanks.'

'So . . . Next time?'

'Yes. Next time.' She turned and was away, across the floor, then swallowed up by the crowd. 'Keep in touch,' I called after her.

I looked around for Fleur, if only to say goodbye, I didn't want to leave on a sour note, but she was nowhere to be seen. I checked my phone and saw that there was a text from her. *Won't b bck 2night. Stay as long as u like. Post keys thru letterbox when u leave.*

As an expensively dressed lady pushed past me, I suddenly felt alone and out of place in the store. Mum's perfume had brought up such an ache of loss and grief, I wanted to get out and away from the busy crowds browsing, bustling, buying.

I made my way outside into the cold air and called Daniel. 'Fleur's flat is empty for the night, can you meet me there?'

'Give me an hour,' he said. 'You OK?'

'I will be when I see you.'

*

The flat was dark when I got back to Fleur's, so I let myself in, turned on all the lights and went to my room. I put on a shower cap to protect my freshly blow-dried hair, showered with my new scented soap then liberally sprayed perfume, behind my knees and ears. I put on the huge fluffy towelling robe that Fleur had left in the bathroom, got a glass of Sancerre from the fridge then lay back on the sofa. A feeling of emptiness threatened. It should have been a wonderful weekend, no expense spared. Mum had done her best to spoil us thoroughly but I felt hollow inside. I missed her more than ever and I was sad that Fleur had gone off in such a huff. I wondered if she lay here sometimes, in her million-pound immaculate apartment, like a bird in a gilded cage, and felt the same.

Daniel arrived around seven. Once I'd closed the front door, he took off his jacket and we fell on each other with a passion. I was so pleased to see him; one of the things I loved about being with him was that I didn't have to ask if he wanted me, I knew he did.

'You look and smell fantastic,' he said. 'Wallflower,' he teased as he pressed me up against the wall and I started to unbutton his shirt. He stopped me. 'No. I want to see you.' He loosened the belt of my dressing gown, then reached up and slipped it down over my shoulders, caressing each part of exposed skin as he did so, then covered my neck with butterfly kisses. A few moments later, I was naked in front of him. It felt utterly erotic to be like that whilst he was fully clothed. One of the wonderful things since we'd been together was that I didn't feel inhibited in front of him or in any way ashamed of my body. I could see in his eyes the arousal I caused and I could hear it in his voice when he said, 'Turn around.'

I did as he instructed, and he arranged my arms so that they were above my head as he stood behind. He began to follow the outline of my body with his finger-tips. It felt thrilling to be naked in a strange flat with Daniel, who was forbidden somehow, and every one of my senses felt heightened, the feel of the closeness of him behind me, his weight against me, the scent of him, his touch.

Suddenly he stopped. 'Shh.'

'What is it?'

'The lift. Someone's coming.'

I turned around to hear a clunk, then a key in the door. 'Shit. It must be Fleur come back for something.' There was no time to even find my dressing gown, which Daniel had tossed behind a sofa. At the same time, we both looked at the curtains. 'I'll hide behind there. Hopefully she won't be long,' I whispered.

'And I'll say I left something.'

I dashed behind the curtains and, a moment later, I heard someone come into the room.

'Daniel! What are you doing here?' It wasn't Fleur. It was Rose.

'Left my dongle,' said Daniel. 'From this morning.'

I was nervous, close to hysterical, I almost burst out laughing. Dongle.

'I left my overnight bag,' said Rose. 'I didn't want to be carrying it with me in Harrods.'

Phew, I thought. *She won't hang around then.*

'Where's Fleur?' asked Rose.

'I believe she's gone to stay with a friend.'

'So how did you get in?'

Oh shut up Rose, I thought. *And go away.* At that moment, I glanced down from my vantage point. Fuck. The flat looked out on the street below. The street below looked up at the flat and I realized that, with the light behind me, I was completely visible. In the buff. Clearly hiding behind the curtains. I quickly put my hands over my breasts and crotch and prayed that no one would look up. *Rose, please, please, clear off.* I stood barely breathing as I listened. *Please, please don't let anyone see me*, I thought as I noticed a couple of older ladies walking along the pavement down below.

'Dee let me in,' Daniel replied.

'Dee?'

Nooooo, I thought. *Wrong answer.*

'Yes. She came back to collect her things too.'

'Oh. So is she still here? Where is she?'

Arghhhh. This is a nightmare.

'No. Gone. She went to see a friend, I think.'

'So you did see her?'

'Yes. She let me in then went straight out.'

'Oh. But how did you know she'd be here?'

'I didn't. I took a chance that Fleur would be here.'

'Is Dee coming back?'

Oh fuck off Rose, with your questions, fuck off, fuck off, fuck off.

'Oh. Not sure.' I prayed that Daniel was a better liar than I was. I would have gone scarlet and started stuttering.

Oh for God's sake, I thought, as I saw a group of young men on the street down below. *Don't look up, don't look up*, I prayed. They did look up and were soon laughing and pointing. *Yes. Hilarious*, I thought as I shut my eyes. *Absolutely fucking hilarious*.

I heard footsteps. Rose's. 'I'll go and see if her stuff is still here.' Click clack went her heels across the floor.

'You OK?' Daniel whispered, then sniggered.

'No. Get rid of her. Not funny,' I whispered back. There was an agonizing silence. I didn't dare say anything else in case Rose came back in. I barely dared to breathe or move an inch and, down below, my spectators were clearly enjoying the show.

Moments later, I heard Rose's heels again. Click clack. 'Her case is still here and there's stuff in the bathroom, so she must be coming back.'

'Oh, OK.'

'So did you find your dongle?' said Rose.

'Yes. Got it. So I'll be off. Er . . . should I wait for you? We can go out together.'

'No. I'm going to stay a while. Make some phone calls.'

Noooooooooooooo. I took a peek down below. The young men weren't going anywhere in a hurry either. *Please don't let any of them have a phone camera or else this could be all over YouTube tomorrow with the headline: Mystery naked woman hides behind curtains in Knightsbridge.*

'OK. Bye then.'

'Actually Daniel, don't go just yet.' *Noooooooooooo*. 'The dongle. I assume it's the one with Mum's recording?'

'Yes.'

'Could I borrow it?'

Oh God, this is getting worse by the second, I thought. *If he hasn't actually got the dongle on him. How's he going to get out of that?*

'It's my only copy at the moment,' Daniel replied. *Phew.* 'I'll put all the recordings together for you, I promise, so you'll have them on one file.'

'Oh. OK, though I'd prefer it if I could have copies of what we've seen so far if you can arrange that. I'd like to show my husband and children.'

Outside, my audience of young men were still pointing and laughing so, of course, anyone passing on the street also looked up to see what was causing so much amusement. Me. In all my glory. Still as a statue. Getting colder by the minute. *OK, probably not the circumstances you had in mind for prayer, Mum, but dear God, please help. Please. I'm begging you.* I shut my eyes tight and prayed. *A Star Trek moment would do it. Beam me up. Somewhere else. Anywhere else.*

'I'll make that a priority,' said Daniel.

'And um, I wanted to ask about . . . ' Silence. *Oh, please spit it out and go, Rose.*

'About what?' asked Daniel.

'Nothing. Never mind. Not important.'

'You sure?'

'Sure.'

'OK. I'd better be off now then.'

'Yes. Goodbye Daniel. See you in two months.'

I heard footsteps. His. The door closed. The lift clunked down.

I heard rustling sounds as Rose moved around in the room. What if she decides to look at the view? What if she decides to look behind the sofa and finds my discarded dressing gown? *Oh please God, make Rose go home.*

I noticed Daniel leave the building down below. Thankfully, before he turned left, he didn't look up or alert the young men to the fact that he had something to do with the apparition at the window on the first floor.

It was so quiet in the apartment, I could hear Rose breathing. *Will she hear me? What will I say if she does? Oh hi, Rose. Yes, I was just flashing my bits to Sloane Street.*

A phone rang. 'Hugh. Hello darling. Yes, yes I'm fine,' Rose's voice sounded softer than usual. 'I'll be home in a while. I was going to . . . Oh, you've cooked? I'm not really . . . of course. I'll be back as soon as I can get a taxi.'

Oh thank you God, I thought as I heard more movements, then finally the sound of the door closing and the sound of the lift going down.

I waited a few moments, gave my audience the V sign, then came out from behind the curtains. I went to my room, got dressed, then called Daniel to say that it was safe to come back. Needless to say, when he did, the earlier mood had been ruined and we headed out to the nearest bar for a very large glass of wine

20

Rose

Wednesday 17 February

I was in the clinic in West London waiting to see my consultant and get the results of the most recent CT scan to see if the hormone treatment had worked. The scan was to compare the cancer deposits before and after the treatment I'd had for the last three months. If they had shrunk or remained the same size, then good, the treatment would have worked. If the deposits had grown or there were new ones, then not so good, it hadn't worked. The treatment hadn't been so bad, slight nausea and indigestion some days, leg cramps some nights, hot flushes now and then. They'd been a nuisance but all manageable and I hoped I could continue on it.

Here goes, I thought, as Mrs Campbell looked up from her notes. Her face gave nothing away.

'I'm so sorry, Rose, the treatment isn't working as well as we'd hoped. We're going to have to try something else now.'

Isn't working? Hasn't worked. I felt a sinking in the pit of my stomach as I tried to take in the enormity of what she'd told me. 'Something else?'

'There are different regimens that can be used which I'll go into in a minute. We'll be aiming to prolong life and, more importantly, maintain your quality of life. With your particular cancer, you have a choice of two types. Vinorelbine or Capecitabine . . . '

As in my first session with her, I could barely take in what she was saying. One regimen is intravenous, the other a tablet to be taken at home. I can choose. Cycles, weeks on, weeks off. *Thank God, they write it all down and give you the pages to absorb later*, I thought, because my mind was already elsewhere, back at home, wondering how I was going to break this to Hugh.

I left in a daze, armed with papers, the printed summary of what had been discussed, explaining my options, side effects, how the drug is administered. *This cannot be happening*, I thought as I flicked through the pages in the lift. Possible side effects, risk of infection, bowel changes. I stuffed them in my bag. I didn't want to know, not now, not yet. Mrs Campbell had said it would be a gentle chemotherapy, not everyone gets the side effects. *They have to warn you*, I told myself, *even with antibiotics, there's a long list of side effects. They have to let you know the worst-case scenario. It might be all right, the hormone treatment was, but I'm not going to think about this right now. I'll go somewhere quiet and read the notes over. But not now. Not yet. When I've come down a bit.*

Part of me was determined to carry on as normal. Not to let the cancer interfere for as long as I could but, when

I stepped out into the street, I realized that I wasn't ready to face Hugh, my dear love and husband. He'd be devastated, and there was no way to soften the blow. What I needed was a place to go and sit and take in what I'd been told and compose myself before heading home. Or was that what I wanted? If I found a quiet spot, my imagination might run wild, worrying about what I'd just been told, what I had to come, letting fear run riot. I decided – I'm in the west of town. I'll go to the solicitors, keep busy, carry on as normal. Mr Richardson wanted to go over some detail on the will and, as I'd been named as one of the executors, it had to be done sooner or later. *So yes, keep busy*, I told myself. *Put on the busys, as Mum used to say if any of us were stressing over something*. So far, I'd found that was the best way because the minute I was alone or had little to do, my inner demons were sitting there waiting for me with their teeth bared.

*

When I got to the solicitors, Daniel Scott was coming out. He looked surprised to see me.

'Hello.' He jerked a thumb in the direction of Mr Richardson's office. 'Just been in collecting funds for the next stage of the programme. Actually, Rose, as it's to be held at your house in August, would you have a minute later? I need to go over a few details, sleeping arrangements and so on.'

No, I thought. *I'm in no fit state to have a friendly chat.* 'Can we do it on the phone?'

'We could I guess.'

Luckily I was saved by the receptionist. 'Mr Richardson will see you now,' she said, and indicated the door I should go through.

'Sorry, got to go. Give me a ring,' I told Daniel.

I wasn't pleased to see that Daniel was still there when I came out twenty minutes later.

'Time to grab a coffee?' he asked.

I was torn. I should get home. Hugh, Simon and Laura would all want to know what the oncologist had said, a conversation I was dreading. I knew I'd have to keep it together for their sake. No tears. No breaking down in front of them. I had to be strong, stronger than I had ever been in my whole life. I hadn't told Hugh that my appointment with the consultant was this morning because he'd have wanted to come with me and I'd wanted to hear for myself first. If it was bad news, I wanted time to take it in. And it had been bad news, so I was in no mood to spend time with Daniel either, but I didn't want to alert him to the fact that anything was not as it should be in case he let something slip to Fleur or Dee.

'OK, a quick one, I haven't got long,' I said, noting the irony of my words. I wanted to get whatever it was he wanted out of the way. It would save doing it later.

As we left the solicitor's office, I remembered what he'd said about the swami working with the terminally ill. It had intrigued me, and I'd given it some thought, despite my cynical response when he'd told us about it at Fleur's. Daniel had been right when he said that people like me would maybe like to be able to talk about what they are facing. My consultant gave me the facts about what was happening physically. Drugs choice. Treatment schedules.

We didn't discuss how it was affecting me mentally or emotionally, although I had been offered counselling. I'd attended one support group, but it made me ever sadder than I felt when on my own. OK, so sitting listening to other patients' case histories made me realize that I wasn't alone, but watching them break down gave me no solace for my situation. I'd liked the swami. Maybe he could offer something more positive.

We went to a small hotel just off the main road, ordered coffee, and in five minutes Daniel had picked up that something was wrong. So much for my public, 'everything is OK' face.

He reached over and took my hand. 'What's up Rose?'

I brushed his hand away but my eyes brimmed with tears. 'Don't be nice to me. I can't handle it when people are nice to me.'

'OK. Sorry. I didn't mean to intrude, but I can see that something has upset you. Sometimes it helps to talk – that is, if you feel like it. Maybe I can help?'

'No one can help,' I said.

'I got the feeling something was up when I bumped into you at Fleur's that evening back in February.'

I tried to compose myself back to Rose Edwards, professional woman. I don't do overemotional, not in public anyway. We sat in silence for a few moments as a waiter brought us coffee. I took a sip and conveniently ignored the fact that I wasn't supposed to be having coffee at the moment, but hell, what difference was one cup going to make?

'Do Dee and Fleur know what's bothering you?'

'*No.* And they mustn't find out, Daniel. Please, *please*

don't tell them you saw me like this. I'll be fine in a minute. It's nothing.'

'Doesn't look like nothing. Don't worry. I won't mention it to anyone if you don't want. Discretion is my middle name, but it sounds big, whatever it is.'

We sat in silence again. I was battling inside, trying to keep it together, when all I wanted to do was break down and weep.

Daniel broke the silence. 'You know, I've watched you and your sisters when you're together and I see how you are with them. You want to protect them. I see that you care,' he said, then smiled, 'behind the bickering, that is. But I also see behind your public face, that there's someone quite vulnerable. We're all human. We all have our problems to deal with. What are yours? What's the fear, Rose? What's troubling you? You have to tell someone. Can you talk to your friends? Your husband?'

And that did it. I *could* talk to my friends, my family – but not really. I couldn't tell them I was scared, a hundred worries in my mind. What would become of Simon and Laura with no mother? What would become of Hugh? He'd be lonely. What was I going to have to go through? And if I was feeling particularly down, I felt sad and angry at all the things I would miss – Simon and Laura graduating, getting married, meeting my grandchildren. I wanted to live. I had so much to live for. I wanted to cry and rage at the same time, but I wasn't ready to talk about it and Daniel didn't press. He took my hand again and just held it. 'I expect you're trying to protect them too. Am I right?'

I didn't reply.

'Whatever it is, sometimes it helps to talk to someone outside of friends and family.'

'You're not suggesting I go back to Beverly are you? No thanks.'

'No but . . . maybe I could be someone that you don't have to protect or soften your situation for. I'm a good listener.'

Another hour, another day, I might have left, but he'd caught me at the worst possible time. I did need to talk to someone, despite my resistance. *There's the link with Mum,* I thought, *and he does seem to have the measure of Dee and Fleur. It could be like talking to a family friend without the complications. He might understand.* I took a deep breath and told him what had been happening. At first, shock registered on his face, but he listened without interrupting. 'And if I get another of those blooming positive quotes of Mum's about dancing on a shifting carpet,' I said when I'd finished, 'I won't wait for the cancer to get me, I might have to kill myself.'

Daniel laughed at my attempt at humour. 'I can appreciate that in your situation, they might be untimely, but I always think, life isn't made up of what is thrown at you, it's about how you react to it.'

'Is that another of Mum's quotes? Because I can tell you that some of those messages you send make me want to throw up.'

Daniel held his hands up. 'As I said when we first met, don't shoot the messenger. Your mother asked me to send them.'

'I know. Mum said it too, didn't she? Don't shoot the messenger. Not your fault that one of her daughters has cancer.'

'No, but I do believe, Rose, that wherever you are, whoever with, it's the state of mind that you're in that determines if it's a good or a bad time.'

I felt a flicker of annoyance. How could he possibly know what I was going through? I'd made a mistake in opening up to him. I'd done everything I could to be positive. He'd just caught me at a bad time. 'Hah! Easy for you to say. I can't bear it when people come out with platitudes and talk about staying cheerful. You try it if you've just heard your cancer is incurable. I know you mean well but—'

'I've lost two people to cancer in recent years,' he interrupted. 'My mother and my best mate last year. I know it wasn't me going through the hospital treatments, but I was there with him and know what he went through and how he dreaded telling his wife and family because they suffered too.'

'Someone close?'

He nodded. 'Tom. I grew up with him, same street, same school. I learnt a lot from him and, though it may sound lame, he did have moments of true happiness as well as sorrow along the way.'

'So you're saying that sitting in a chair, having chemotherapy and knowing, in my case, that there's no cure, all they can do is maybe prolong my life, that I can be happy? Oh, for God's sake.'

'Yes. Yes I am. Peculiar though it might sound – and forgive me if I appear to be full of shit – but, if you let people in, there can be a lot of love. I'm not saying you'll be happy exactly, but when Tom went, he was at peace. He found his peace. You have to find your peace, Rose.

You're going through a process – shock, denial, guilt, anger, depression – and I'm sure you've experienced some of those, but lastly acceptance. You have to get there. You will get there. You have to find your peace.'

I felt a surge of rage inside me. The cheek of the man, sitting there so smug in his good health with his thread bracelets on his wrist, coming out with his bullshit. 'Well, I'm still in the angry stage. And I might just stay there.'

'Good. Be angry. You have every right to be. You must feel why me? Why now?'

'You bet I do. But it doesn't matter what I feel or think because this thing is happening to me anyway. I feel betrayed by my own body.'

'It's going to happen to all of us sooner or later,' he said. 'Nothing as certain as death, nothing as uncertain as the hour.'

'Didn't Martha say that on one of the recordings?'

'I think she did. It's the truth. In our society, death's a taboo subject, but it's going to happen to us all sooner or later – you've just had an almighty reminder of it.'

'Yes. Death. Coming soon to a cinema near you, Rose Edwards in the lead role.'

'Are you scared?'

'Sometimes but . . . ' Tears came to my eyes again. 'It's telling Hugh and my children I find the hardest. I've always been so strong for them, been there to sort out problems, been the family fixer, always in control of things, but I can't fix this one. I can't make it better.'

'You can make it better,' said Daniel. 'Maybe not the cancer and what that's doing to you, but you can still be in control of your state of mind. Rose, if you can find some peace in this process, it will be a lot easier. Let me help you. Your mother Iris, she was at peace—'

'She was eighty-seven. I'm only just in my fifties. It's not fair.'

'No, it's not fair, but who's to say really what's fair and what's not. Why are some of us born into a free, liberal society with all it has to offer, and others born into poverty and terror? So much in life isn't fair. In working with the swami, I've come to understand the importance of peace of mind. There's a peace inside all of us that is there regardless of external circumstances. We work with many people who are ill or dying to help them find it and stay tuned to it. Believe me, for those who find their peace of mind, it makes it easier.'

'I can't accept that it's happening to me.'

'No one ever does at first. But you're tougher than you think, Rose. And if ever you need someone to talk to, I'm here. I understand. You have my number. I think we were meant to meet today, that it wasn't a coincidence. That's why I hung around waiting for you.'

'And now you sound like some cliché from a romance novel.'

He shrugged. 'I believe in fate. I believe in synchronicity.'

'I don't know what I believe any more.'

The waiter brought more coffee and curiously I found it refreshing to be talking to someone with a different view – someone who wasn't trying to tell me that it was all going to be all right, that miracles happened, and who didn't seem fazed by my anger. Daniel seemed to accept the fact I was angry and going to die and, when he talked about it, he appeared to be offering a ray of hope.

After half an hour, I felt exhausted but ready to go home and face Hugh, Simon and Laura. As I headed back to them, I thought a lot about what Daniel had said. There was more to him than I'd given him credit for, and I was beginning to understand why Mum had been taken with him. The consultants gave the facts, the prognosis and the treatment options – that was their job, to work with the body. I didn't envy them their task, day after day, delivering bad news. At home, my family were tiptoeing around me, treating me with kid gloves, trying to hide their feelings from me as much as I was attempting to hide mine from them. Daniel appeared to understand how it was and he was right. I did have to find some peace in it all. But how?

In the taxi home, my phone beeped that I had two messages. *Sorry about the timing of the following text or am I? D. X*

Then a message from Mum. 'Courage doesn't mean that there's no fear but that you've overcome it.'

I texted Daniel back. *Fuck off.*

He sent back a smiley.

Banter about cancer? Bizarre, I thought as the taxi drew up outside my house but, strangely, it made me smile. I felt grateful to have someone I could tell to fuck off who wouldn't mind. Someone who might understand. And I had his offer of someone to talk to. I might take him up on it. I might not. But I'd liked the fact that he'd talked to me as a normal person and had not been afraid to say what he thought.

21

Dee

Saturday 12 March

I am surrounded by birds. Starlings, blackbirds, eagles, peregrines, penguins. My studio up on the top floor was full of them. Some were in watercolours, a couple (the blackbirds) in charcoals and chalk, one (the swans) in acrylic.

'Best things you've ever done,' said Anna as she looked them over.

'A reflection of all my different states of mind. Bit of a worry?'

Anna laughed. 'Have you put prices on them yet?'

'I'll leave that to you. I can never work out what would be right.'

'I'd be glad to do it,' said Anna. 'And I want the water-colour of the turkey. It reminds me of Ian when he's naked. So. All set for this evening?'

I nodded. Today was my fiftieth birthday and there was

to be a celebration at the Bell and Anchor. Anna had insisted on it. 'We have to mark these occasions,' she'd said, 'and make our memories.'

At first, I'd resisted, but then I thought of Daniel. How long had it been since I'd had a party to remember with a man that I loved there to share it with me? It would be wonderful and I could introduce him to my friends from the different eras of my life, though he'd already met Anna, and Bet the landlady, in the pub. I agreed to a celebration. Anna took over the arrangements and announced that there was also to be a theme. 'Gods and goddesses,' she said. 'There's nothing like fancy dress to put everyone in a good mood, plus it breaks the ice for those who don't know each other.'

Also puts some people off coming, I thought, but I kept my mouth shut; most of my friends were young at heart and up for looking like idiots with little excuse. Anna had sent out invites in plenty of time and, by the week of the party, we were expecting close to eighty people, coming from all over the country, and filling up the local B&Bs, which made their proprietors very happy.

'And you sure you're OK with Michael Harris coming?'

I shrugged. 'Fine. I don't have to talk to him.'

Ian had got friendly with Michael over the last few months, having discovered a shared love of country music and long walks. Anna had been only too happy to encourage the friendship, so that she didn't get dragged out in all weathers to trek over the moors. Apparently Michael had stayed in the area a few times, but I'd only seen him down by the bay in the middle of a howling gale so neither of us had stopped.

I'd invited both my sisters.

'I'll be seeing you in April,' said Rose. 'We'll do something then.'

'Not sure I'll be in the country,' said Fleur.

Only when they'd both made their excuses did I invite Daniel, who accepted. We had it all planned. We were going to go as a couple of Egyptian gods and I'd hired costumes from the fancy-dress shop in Torpoint.

*

By seven o'clock, Daniel's Rameses costume was ready for him, hanging on the back of my bedroom door, and I was dressed as Cleopatra. Anna made my face up in black kohl and gold face paint and, as I looked at my reflection, I felt very glamorous and exotic. Anna was dressed as the Medusa, in a colourful kimono, with rubber snakes and bones in her hair and make-up on her lids, so that when she closed her eyelids, it looked like she had zombie eyes. Quite frightening but very effective.

'What time will Daniel be here?' she asked.

I checked my watch for the umpteenth time. 'I thought he would be here by now. He was supposed to be leaving London around midday. I've tried ringing him but it goes to message.'

'Probably because he's driving,' said Anna. 'Maybe traffic's bad.'

'He was getting the train.'

'Oh. Don't worry, I'm sure he'll get here.'

At seven thirty, we made our way down the lanes to the Bell and Anchor, much to the amusement of anyone who happened to be out. Anna waved cheerily at them.

'We always dress like this on a Saturday night in Cornwall,' she said to a middle-aged walker who had stopped and was staring.

The pub was packed when we arrived and there was a cheer when Anna and I walked in. I scanned the faces for Daniel, but there was no sign of him, and soon I was caught up in the happy atmosphere, greeting old friends, laughing at their costumes and catching up. Marie had come as a Norse goddess, her blonde hair in two plaits which she'd wrapped around her ears. Mary and Marian from London were screen goddesses from the 1920s; a crowd from Derbyshire, who used to live locally, had come as Indian gods and goddesses with blue faces. Ian had come as Elvis, the rock god, and was having a pint with Michael Harris, who'd come as a Roman god in toga and crown of leaves. 'Nice legs,' Anna said as she looked over at him. I nodded to them both and Michael raised his glass and smiled. I smiled back and was glad he didn't appear to be harbouring bad feelings about the house. Maybe we could be friends in time after all. Around the room, I spotted Linda, the hairdresser, as Patti Smith, a rock goddess, Crystal the masseuse as screen goddess, Marilyn Monroe, over at the bar chatting to Mark, the mechanic, who was dressed as a traditional God in long white robes and full beard. A Mayan god (Barry the builder) chatted to Aphrodite (Bet).

Gordon the dentist appeared at my side and gave me a hug. He was in a silk dressing gown and socks.

'And you are?' I asked.

'Sex god,' he said and flashed a pair of Union Jack boxers.

'In your dreams,' said Anna.

Gordon was with Jack the farmer, who was wearing a

furry costume with ears. 'I read the invite the wrong way round and thought it said come as a dog,' he told us.

'Your mum would be happy,' said Anna as she handed me a glass of champagne then indicated the packed room. 'All these gods and you're talking to them all. Still no sign of the love god?'

I shook my head. 'And his phone is still on message. I hope nothing's happened to him.'

Anna gave me a hug. 'He'll be here. Probably a delay at Exeter or something.'

After an hour of catching up and eating Bet's fantastic mini-Cornish pasties, Ian called everyone to attention by tinging a glass with a spoon. 'And now we have a little entertainment for the birthday girl.'

'Oh *no*,' I said. I'd had a feeling that Anna had been up to something in the last few weeks.

Everyone turned to the stage and I prayed that Daniel would have something to do with it as well. Maybe he was going to pop out of a cake. I didn't care, as long as he was there with us, with me.

The pub suddenly exploded in laughter as Marie and Anna made their way to a piano at the front of the pub. They'd changed out of their goddess clothes and were now dressed as bag ladies, with patterned headscarves tied under their chins, round National Health glasses and, when Anna smiled over at me, I saw that she had in enormous buck teeth, the type you get from a joke shop. Marie took the seat at the piano.

'Dear Dee,' said Anna. 'We've written a little song for you for your fiftieth. We hope you like it.' She turned to Marie. 'OK, Marie, take it away.'

Marie began to play and I recognized the tune as 'Sixteen, Going On Seventeen' from *The Sound of Music*.

Marie sang first. 'I am forty-nine, going on fifty, My pubic hair's gone white. My hips have spread, I'm no good in bed. In fact my sex life is shite.'

Everyone burst out laughing as she continued, 'Totally unprepared am I, to face the next decade. Baggy and saggy and lined am I, With wrinkles that won't fade.'

Anna came in next: 'I am forty-nine, going on fifty, I'm into tantric sex. Up down and sideways, I do it most days, But first have to find my specs.'

She looked over at me and gave me an exaggerated wink. I glanced around again to see if Daniel had arrived. *He'd love this*, I thought. *He'd have creased up laughing. Oh, where is he?*

Marie sang: 'I am forty-nine, going on fifty, Baby, I've turned to drink, Gin, wine or brandy, whatever's handy . . .'

'And champagne, but make it pink,' Anna added.

They sang on with great gusto, clearly having a great old time.

'Gone is my sight and half my brain,
The memories they grow dim,'

I spotted Mrs Rowley from the corner shop at the bar. She looked like she was going to choke with laughter on her pint.

Anna and Marie hadn't finished: 'I am forty-nine, going on fifty, Everything's in decline. I lean on the Aga, Reading my *Saga*, And I drink far too much red wine.'

Marie: 'I am forty-nine, going on fifty, My hair is getting thin. I've turned out frumpy and I feel dumpy, Oh let's have another gin.'

Anna and Marie slowed their pace and scanned the audience slowly: 'You may think this kind of misfortune, Never may come to you. Darling forties going on fifty, Wait a year . . . Just wait a year . . . Just wait a year . . . Or two.'

Everyone clapped and stamped their feet, then Anna looked over at me. 'Speech, speech.'

Everyone joined in clamouring. 'Speech, speech.'

As I made my way to the front, I heard my phone beep that I had a text. I glanced down. Daniel. Maybe he'd arrived or was getting near and was letting me know. I knew it would be rude to check the message at that moment, so I tucked the phone into my gold bra and took the microphone. At the bar, I spotted Michael Harris again. He raised his glass. I looked around the room, so many faces smiling back at me, good friends, but I felt sad that there was no Daniel there to share it all with.

'Anna, Marie,' I said. 'How can I follow that? You're both clearly mad but I'm touched, genuinely. Turning fifty is a landmark, but a good one, so here's to the next fifty years. Thanks for coming, especially those who have travelled from far. Um. Enjoy the rest of the evening.' I held up my glass. 'Cheers.'

'Cheers,' everyone echoed then, led by Anna, sang 'Happy Birthday dear Dee'.

When they'd finished, at last, I could get away and read my text. I manoeuvred my way through the crowd and towards the Ladies, so I could read it in peace, but Michael Harris appeared at my side.

'Happy Birthday Dee,' he said.

'Thanks er . . . ' I was desperate to get away and read my text. I gestured to the room. 'Sorry not to talk much.'

'I won't take it personally,' he said with a smile. 'One can never get round everyone at an occasion like this. A great turn-out, wonderful testimony to you, the song, so many friends.'

'Yes, though a few couldn't make it.' *One couldn't make it*, I thought.

'I also . . . I wanted to say, about that letter from my brother, William, back in the New Year, I apologize. He has no patience. It was against my wishes. I wanted you to know that but I can't tell him what to do.'

He was being kind and, though every part of me wanted to rush off, I didn't want to appear rude. 'Don't worry. I won't hold you responsible. I have sisters and learnt long ago to distance myself from some of their comments and actions.'

He seemed relieved. 'I'm not sorry for the way things are working out, though. You belong here. Anyone can see that. Not just in Summer Lane, but the area.'

'I hear that you've been here a bit yourself.'

'I'm drawn to the place.' Was I imagining it, or was that sentence loaded with meaning? Did he mean drawn to me? *I can't deal with this now*, I thought. 'I've been looking at houses down here for my retirement—'

'And you need funds from the sale of Summer Lane?'

'No, not immediately, it isn't that. William's circumstances however are different to my own. Truth be told, that's why he's been putting the pressure on but I've managed to get him to back off. He can wait—'

'Good, that's great,' I interrupted. 'Let's catch up another time. Got to go, there's someone I have to talk to before they leave.'

He looked disappointed. 'OK. Course. I shouldn't monopolize the hostess. You go. Enjoy the rest of your evening.'

'Thanks. I will.' I turned and made my way through the crowd to the Ladies cloakroom, into an empty cubicle and, at last, checked my messages.

Darling Dee, Happy Birthday. So very sorry I can't be with you. Something came up. Will explain when we talk. Forgive me. Love you, Daniel. X

My heart sank and I sat on the loo seat for a few minutes while I tried to take in the disappointment. Daniel wouldn't be coming after all. All week I had been looking forward to having him here with me, my new partner, my soul mate. *It doesn't matter, it doesn't matter*, I told myself. *Eighty of my friends are out there. Good friends. It's my night. I can't let this spoil things. I won't*. But too late. I felt like crying and cry I did.

22

Fleur

Saturday 12 March

It was only sex. Up against the wall, didn't make it to the bed or manage to get our clothes off type sex, but still only sex. Purely for pleasure. And, truth be told, it was me who seduced him when he came over to collect a jacket he'd left at my place. I'd had a few drinks and was feeling reckless and alone. I wanted to see if I still had the touch and, though he resisted at first, it didn't take long to get him to change his mind. It had been a while for me and I thought I'd lost my sex drive, but he soon awakened the dead. *Queen of the Zombies, alive again and ready to limbo*, I thought as he bent me over the sofa.

I meant it to be just the one night but it turned into a few. Why not? Daniel was fit and a good lover and we both agreed, no strings attached, no ties. I did feel a pang of guilt. Of course I did. It had been obvious from the beginning that Dee liked him, and I asked about her before

Daniel and I laid a finger on each other. I do have some standards.

'Nothing has happened between us,' he said, 'and it never will. Dee has a crush on me, that's all. Apart from the fact that she's not my type and I don't fancy her, I can tell from the short time I've spent with her that I can't get involved with women like her. They want too much. Commitment, a relationship going into dotage. Not for me.'

I felt sad for Dee but reassured that I wouldn't be taking anything from her. I asked him never to let on to her that we'd met up. 'I won't,' he said. 'From what I can see, Dee's a sweet woman and I wouldn't want to hurt her or cause a loss of confidence or more sibling rivalry. Yes, best we keep quiet about it.'

I was glad about that. I wouldn't want to hurt her either, and we had just started to get on better. I know, I was a bit sulky in February. I put it down to PMT. It's plagued me all my life. One of my exes said I turn into Psycho Woman at that time of the month. 'And don't tell Rose about us either,' I asked. 'I don't want her knowing my business either.'

'No problem there,' Daniel replied. 'Our secret.'

Although we were both adults and I didn't need my sisters' permission, it made our liaisons feel forbidden and all the more pleasurable for that. It's not going to last. For one thing, Daniel's not a stayer, anyone could see that, and for another, I don't want anything from him apart from a bit of fun every now and again. It works for now. Naughty but nice.

23

Dee

Saturday 9 April, morning

Spring at last. March had been a hideous month, with day after day of relentless rain, but the clouds had finally blown away, the skies had cleared and there was lightness in the air heralding better weather. As I boarded the train in Plymouth to Exeter, a text from Mum came through. I felt a shiver of anticipation. I loved getting her messages, partly because they were from her, but also partly because it was Daniel who was sending them and it was contact with him as much as Mum. He'd more than made up for missing my birthday. Apparently the swami had been taken ill and he'd had to take him to hospital. He was so apologetic and had arrived the week after my birthday with flowers and a beautiful card but, best of all, he'd brought himself.

Mum's text read: 'A little thought and a little kindness are often worth more than a great deal of money,' John Ruskin (1819–1900).

Another quote about kindness. Most amusing, Mum, I thought. She'd have timed it to remind Rose, Fleur and me to be kind to each other on this, our fourth weekend of the programme. *OK*, I said to myself, *I will take heed and really put it into practice this time. I shall be kindness personified.*

A lot had happened since our last get-together in February when Fleur had flounced off in a strop. She'd clearly repented because, a few days after my birthday in March, she'd sent the most stunning bouquet of white roses and a card showing two little girls holding hands in the sunshine. The caption on the front said 'A sister is a little bit of childhood that can't be lost.' Inside was a message saying, 'Wishing you the very best of everything for the next year, Love Fleur XXX'. Schmaltzy for Fleur, but sweet, and I accepted her gesture with good grace. As much as anything, it meant she'd stopped sulking.

This weekend, I hoped to make further progress with her and Rose. So far, we'd met as Mum asked us to, every other month, with hardly any contact in between. I was sure that wasn't what Mum had intended.

I could understand her thinking in what she'd got us to do so far. Get us all to each other's homes. Give Rose a break from the city by coming to Cornwall. Give me a break from budgeting and scrabbling to make ends meet with the weekend of pampering and a stay at Fleur's luxurious flat. Send us quotes to try and inspire us to be nicer to each other. But I was starting to feel that – although the tasks were enjoyable enough and enlightening at times – the months in between were important too. What were Rose and Fleur up to? How do they feel about their lives? What was really going on in their heads?

On the weekends so far, there had been times when we were alone with each other in the evening or at lunch, but we'd managed to avoid each other at other times, or had tiptoed around, not wanting to be too intrusive or assume a closeness that was no longer there. I certainly didn't feel that I was much closer to either of them, for all of Mum's best intentions. I wondered what treats she had in store for us this time. I was surprised when I was asked to go to Exeter for this weekend because I was expecting to go to Rose's house – but no matter, whatever was planned, I intended to be bolder, more inquisitive and kinder.

Our meeting place was a hotel near the station. I was first to arrive to find a shabby-looking place with swirly carpets and a vague smell of boiled vegetables in reception. Rose and Fleur were coming from London and Daniel joining us from Bristol, where he'd been staying at one of the Heaven on Earth centres. In the last few months, we had only managed to see each other three times. He had work commitments and got away when his schedule allowed. I didn't press for more or complain. The last thing I wanted to be was a needy, clingy partner. I recognized that he was a free spirit and was happy to give him space and let him come to me when he could. In fact, the time apart only served to make our time together more precious and passionate.

*

Rose and Fleur looked out of place when they arrived in the downmarket hotel. Fleur was dressed in skin-tight white jeans, white cowboy boots and a pink silk shirt. Rose in a tailored black jacket, jeans and loafers. She looked tired, and for the first time I thought: Rose is ageing. I looked reasonably smart too, with teal linen trousers and a turquoise tunic over them. It had been sunny when I'd set off but the weather had changed and I was freezing. All in an effort not to look too shoddy next to my immaculately turned-out sisters. I studied them to see what it was that marked them out as people with money – Rose's Mulberry handbag? Fleur's Prada? The Chanel sunglasses that Rose wore? Whatever, they wafted in with the kind of London style that attracted stares from the staff and other customers in reception.

Fleur wrinkled her nose. 'I hope we're not staying here,' she said to Daniel who arrived moments after.

Daniel shook his head and, after talking to a lady with a bad perm on reception, led us to a small conference room at the back of the hotel. Rose went straight over to a framed painting of a river, straightened it, then took a seat at the plastic table. That was wonky too, so Rose took some paper from her bag and put it under the offending leg.

'How have you been since I last saw you, Rose?' I asked, once Fleur and I'd settled next to her and Daniel was busy at a second table in the corner setting up his computer.

'Good. Why?'

'I was thinking that I don't know much about your life any more and how you really are.'

For some odd reason, Rose glanced over at Daniel. 'I'm fine. Busy. Work. You know. How are you?'

'Good, thanks.'

'Still painting the birds?' asked Fleur.

'I am and I've almost got enough for an exhibition. I might have one in the summer. The place will be full of tourists eager to buy a memento from a local artist.'

'Don't they want seascapes, landscapes?' asked Rose.

'They do, but not always.'

'Big mistake to do birds then,' said Rose. 'Give your customers what they want. I know the market. Tourists visiting somewhere like Cornwall like a scene from the area as their memento. I've been to St Ives. The galleries there are full of seascapes.'

'So maybe they'd like something different.'

'I'm just saying that if you want to make money from something, you have to do your market research, then play to the crowd, give them what they want.'

I felt myself tense. What did she know? I was the one who lived in the area. I was the artist. 'I've spent years painting landscapes and yes, they sold—'

'See. So I was right. Stick to what you know.'

'Rose, you haven't even seen my new paintings.'

'Don't be prickly. I was trying to be helpful. Give you the benefit of my expertise.'

'Like I don't know anything?'

'I wasn't saying that. Oh, forget it. Do your birds. Send me some on email if you can. I'll tell you what I think.'

No way, I thought. *And have her apply her artistic expertise, of which she has none, and pick my work apart. No thanks*. It was so typical of her, trying to control my life – and we'd only been together for five minutes.

'Hey, come on. Kindness,' said Fleur. 'Mum sent us that text about it. Remember?'

'Oh shut up, Fleur,' Rose and I chorused.

Fleur huffed. 'OK. What about me then? Have you been thinking about how I am, Dee?'

'Of course. I was about to ask. How are you?'

Like Rose had earlier, Fleur glanced over at Daniel then back at me. 'I'll tell you later.'

What's he got to do with anything? I wondered. *Why are Rose and Fleur looking to him? Is there something I don't know?*

Daniel glanced up at Fleur. He could probably hear our conversation from where he was, and that she wanted to say something later that she didn't want him to hear. She was excluding him. I wondered how he felt about that.

Rose got up to move to the table where Daniel had set up his laptop. 'So, another recording?'

'It is,' replied Daniel. 'Fourth one, so you're over the halfway point. Then two more to go.'

I waited to hear Rose's reply, expecting her to say, 'I *can* add up', but no.

'Would you like something to eat and a coffee, Daniel?' she asked. 'A pastry? Croissant? Have you had breakfast? Fleur, Dee, can I get you anything?'

What was going on? Rose being nice to Daniel? And was I imagining it, but did Fleur just catch Daniel's eye and smile, like they were sharing some kind of private joke? I looked over at him questioningly but he didn't meet my eyes and, for a moment, I felt a lurch of panic. *Relax*, I told myself, *don't be paranoid. He's probably being friendly to them to put them off the scent about us.*

'Thanks, I've already had breakfast,' said Daniel. 'So. Are you all ready?'

Fleur and Rose nodded. 'As we'll ever be,' said Rose.

'Do your worst,' said Fleur. Again, she looked at Daniel. Was I imagining it, or had she loaded the words with innuendo? And the twinkle in her eye? I stared at Daniel to try and gauge his response but his expression gave nothing away.

I tried to focus on the screen but my mind had gone into overdrive. Fleur and Daniel? Rose and Daniel? I hadn't given a second thought to how they got along now we were well down Mum's list. We hadn't spoken about it since our first meeting with him back in October; we'd only ever talked about if I liked him, and I'd never discussed them with him apart from our agreement to keep our relationship secret. I felt a stab of jealousy that they might have their own connections with him, and made a mental note to ask him about them tomorrow when we met up after Rose and Fleur had left. Although he was going back to London this morning after our meeting, he had to be in Bristol on Monday, so had arranged to get a train back here on Sunday night to spend a few hours with me. *He'll be going out of his way travelling via Exeter, just to be with me for a short time. Surely that's proof I have nothing to worry about?* I told myself but, deep down, something niggled.

Fleur and I took our seats next to Rose. Daniel pressed Play and Mum appeared on the screen. She was in her kitchen, standing at the table with Jean behind an enormous canteen, from which she was doling out what looked like soup to a seated Martha. Mum and Martha were dressed as down-and-outs in fingerless gloves and old coats; Jean was wearing a fancy-dress dog hat with ears.

Fleur and I exchanged quizzical looks, Rose raised an eyebrow.

'Are we filming?' Mum asked. 'Hello again, my dollies. So, what's next? Well, we have something a bit different for you this weekend.'

'I'll say,' said Fleur. 'What does Jean think she looks like?'

'This time it's to give you a taste of the happiness that can be derived from giving something back,' said Mum.

'So today, you'll be helping out at an animal rescue centre,' said Martha, 'doing a soup run for the homeless this evening, then tomorrow a visit to an old people's home.'

'Oh for God's sake,' said Fleur.

'To do an act for someone else,' said Jean, 'for someone in need, can be the most rewarding thing of all. And, in case you're wondering, I'm supposed to be one of the dogs from the rescue centre.'

'Barking mad,' said Fleur, and laughed at her own joke. Daniel chuckled with her and I felt another surge of anxiety at their camaraderie.

'I know that you'll be doing this work for only two days, but we all felt we had to include something like this on the list,' said Mum. 'And Fleur, I also know that you donate generously to a number of charities—'

I glanced at Fleur. I didn't know that about her.

'But sometimes it's good to be hands on. Be with people or creatures less fortunate than yourself,' Martha added. 'One should always do one's bit. It can help one see one's own life from a better perspective.'

'As always, Daniel will have it worked out for you,' said Mum. 'OK, it won't be the most glamorous of the weekends, but try and do it with an open heart and spirit. Sometimes we all need a reminder that we share this planet with all sorts of people, and not everyone has had the opportunities and advantages that you have.'

'Hear hear,' said Martha.

'Woof woof,' said Jean, then grinned. I laughed to myself. How old was she? Eighty going on eight.

I glanced at Rose. She didn't appear any happier than Fleur about the arrangements and I hoped she wouldn't back out. She might not hesitate about letting Fleur or me down, but she'd think twice about disappointing Mum.

'Mum's text earlier wasn't so much about us being kind to one another as being kind to others,' I said.

Rose sighed and I knew she'd got the message.

'Bye for now, my dear girls, and I'll see you again in two months' time,' said Mum.

The screen went blank.

Rose turned to Daniel. 'Seriously?'

He nodded. 'I have a car coming to take you to the rescue centre in fifteen minutes,' he said as he put his jacket on, then handed us a sheet of paper each with times, places and car pick-up times. 'Any questions, you all have my number.'

'Hold on a minute there,' said Fleur. 'Look at me. I can't go working with animals in this.' She indicated her white jeans and pristine boots.

I could see that Daniel was having a hard time not laughing. 'I've had overalls delivered to the centre for you, and some old clothes for the soup run tonight. I thought you might not be dressed appropriately.'

Fleur held up a perfectly French polish manicured hand. 'What about my nails? They'll get ruined.'

'You'll find rubber gloves in the bags for you at the

centre,' said Daniel. He looked as though he was finding the prospect of us doing these tasks highly amusing.

'Rubber gloves? What are we going to be doing? Putting our arms up cows' arses?'

'I doubt it. It's cats and dogs only at the centre.'

'Where are we staying?' I asked.

Daniel grimaced. 'Ah yes, that. A hostel half a mile down the road. It's perfectly clean.' He handed me a second sheet with our booking details. 'It's all taken care of.'

Fleur let out a long sigh. I looked over at Rose.

She shrugged. 'Best get it over with then, hadn't we? Think of the money.'

Not what Mum had in mind, I thought as I got up.

*

After Daniel had left, Fleur got out her iPhone and started searching for something. 'Right,' she said a few minutes later. 'I'm booking into a boutique hotel for the night. Five star. I don't do hostels. Who's with me? I'll pay.'

'Count me in,' said Rose, 'and I can pay for myself, but thanks for the offer.'

'But what if Daniel finds out, or Mr Richardson?' I asked. 'We're all supposed to follow Mum's instructions and sign that we have done as asked, and if the programme says we stay at a hostel, then that's what I think we should do.'

'Rules are for breaking,' said Fleur. 'Anyway, how's Daniel going to find out? Or Mr Richardson? We won't tell them. And Mum's not going to know. Come on, let's be rebels.'

'She might be watching from somewhere,' I said.

Fleur burst out laughing. 'You always were such a scaredy-cat.'

'OK, but what about when the hostel tells Daniel that no one turned up,' I said. 'Don't forget, he settles the accounts.'

'OK. So here's the plan. We check in to the hostel. We go to our rooms, we leave our rooms, go to the nice hotel, have a decent meal and a good night's sleep. We go back the next morning. Hand in our keys. They'll never know.' She had such a mischievous look on her face. 'Come on, Dee. Bunk off with us.'

'I . . . ' I had my doubts but didn't want to be the killjoy.

'I totally agree with Fleur on this one. Choice. I do like to have one where I can. I think we should go to the good hotel, and you do know how I like a decent pillow, Dee.' She smiled at me as she said the part about the pillow.

'I do . . . OK. I'm in.' Actually it felt good and slightly wicked to be defying Mum's agenda, as if we were teenagers again.

While Fleur made the hotel booking, I turned to Rose. 'Er . . . how are you getting on with Daniel now?'

'Daniel? Fine. Why?'

'Oh, just I observed that you'd softened towards him.'

'Why do you say that?'

'Offering him coffee? Breakfast?'

'Just being polite, kind, that is what Mum asked this weekend. Mum appointed him to do this, so he must have some merits. He's OK. He's getting the job done.'

'What about you, Fleur?' I asked when she'd finished her call.

'What about me?'

'How are you getting on with Daniel these days?'

She shrugged and looked away. 'Don't really think about it. He's not on my radar. Why? Has anything happened between you?'

'No. No. And I won't, I mean . . . '

'But you do still like him?'

'Sure, though I wish you'd stop asking me about him every time we meet up.'

'You started it,' said Rose, 'just now, asking us.'

'I . . . He's . . . as you said, OK. This is getting boring.'

Fleur studied me for a moment and I prayed that I wasn't blushing. 'Just tread carefully with him,' she said.

'Why would you say that? And what was it you wouldn't say before? In front of him?'

She tapped her nose. 'Oh that. You and him . . . but you just told me to drop it.'

'Oh, for God's sake, Fleur, just tell me what you wanted to say.' I hated it when she'd announce she had a secret when we were little then refuse to tell us. Drove me mad.

'I wanted to say tread carefully, that's all,' said Fleur. 'My man antennae tells me that yeah, he's a nice guy and all that, but . . . I don't think he's the settling-down type and I reckon you'd want more from him than he would be prepared to give. He strikes me as a loner, the kind of man who values his freedom. But I don't want to start an argument again.'

'It was you who went off sulking last time,' I reminded her. 'And anyway, how would you know what he's like? Have you ever talked to him properly?'

'I know his type,' said Fleur.

'I have to agree,' said Rose. 'His kind aren't for settling.'

'How can either of you say that? You've only met him four times and only for a short while, and Fleur, with your history of men, you can't say you can trust your antennae.'

'That's *exactly* why I can, and my gut says Daniel is not a man for committed relationships. And anyway, why are you getting worked up when nothing has even happened between you?'

'I'm not getting worked up!' I protested, though I could feel that I was. 'And who says I want to settle? Anyway, nothing's going on, so this is all hypothetical.' But they'd got me thinking. In all the time we'd been together, Daniel and I had never talked about a future or the possibility of us living together at any point. Maybe Rose and Fleur were right. Maybe I'd been so delirious about finding him, enjoying our time, the good sex, that I'd missed the signals. He hadn't exactly made any promises.

*

The animal centre was about a mile out of town, a series of low buildings in the middle of open fields. Fleur huffed and puffed her objections all the way, while Rose looked sullen but resigned. I was looking forward to the day. As Mum had said, it would be something different, and I liked animals. I had often thought that when I retired, I would volunteer to work with them.

We got out of the car to hear a cacophony of dogs barking.

Rose shuddered, 'Mum knew I'm not a great animal lover.'

'Me neither,' said Fleur. 'It's OK for you Dee, you love cats.'

A frizzy-haired young woman in navy overalls and rubber boots came out to meet us. Her badge told us that she was called Sandra.

'We're really so grateful,' she said as she led us to an office at the back of the reception. 'Extra pairs of hands are always so welcome. Clothes have been sent for you so you can get changed in here, then I'll show you what to do.'

We did as we were told. Once dressed in what looked like prison overalls, Sandra led us to the area where the animals were kept. At the cattery, she stopped and pointed to a long drain that lined the side of the building.

'We've an inspection due shortly, so what would be most useful would be if you'd clear out the drains for us,' she said. 'I don't think it's been done for over a year. I'll get you buckets, plastic bags and a hose. Sorry it's a bit of an ucky job, but we're short staffed at the moment, and everyone else is busy inside admitting new arrivals. We've had seven new cats come in today, so have to get the cat pods ready for them, and three are going to new homes so we're rushed off our feet.'

'This has to be a joke,' said Fleur when Sandra had gone in search of our cleaning stuff. 'Do you honestly think Mum intended us to clean out drains?'

'First time for everything, Fleur,' I said.

'Believe me, it will be.'

Sandra came back with our equipment, demonstrated how the drain lid was divided into easy-to-lift-off sections, and reluctantly Fleur and I got on our knees and plunged elbow-deep into the gunge. Rose crawled along taking off the lids in front, while Fleur and I edged along after her emptying gloop into bin bags. The stench was over-whelming. Sandra was right. The drains hadn't been done for over a year and were oozing with the most disgusting slime.

It began to rain, a soft drizzle.

Fleur knelt back on her feet. 'I feel like I've landed in a scene from *Orange Is the New Black*. A prison sentence but no crime.'

Rose looked like she was going to be sick. 'And this is supposed to make us happy, how?' she said as she also knelt back and watched me immerse a rubber-gloved hand in the drain and scoop out a handful of gunk.

She stood up and looked up at the sky. 'Seriously Mum?' She took off her gloves and threw them on the ground. 'You two can stay, but not me. One thing I know, and that is, life is too short for this.'

'Are you OK, Rose?' I asked.

She looked very pale, as if she might faint. 'No. No, I'm not OK. I feel sick. That smell is foul, and God knows what bacteria is lurking in that stuff. What if I . . . I mean we . . . pick something up? Sorry, Mum. I've done the rest of what you asked but this is too much.'

'What are you going to do?' asked Fleur.

Rose supported herself against the wall. 'Go to that hotel of yours, Fleur. Have a peppermint tea and chill out. Either of you coming?'

'No. I'm staying,' I said. 'But are you OK? Do you need anyone to come with you?'

Fleur looked torn.

'What do we tell Mr Richardson and Daniel if you both go?' I said. 'Changing hotel I reckon we can get away with, but not if we don't do this. Please stay, Fleur. We can cover for Rose.'

'Oh for God's sake,' said Rose. 'Stuff them. I'm sure allowances can be made if one of us is off colour.'

'OK, you go Rose,' said Fleur, 'you really do look peaky. We'll explain.'

'Yes, go. I'm sure Mum wouldn't want you to do this if you're not well.'

Ten minutes later, we saw Rose drive off in a taxi, leaving Fleur and me to carry on. I was surprised that Fleur had stayed. I would have expected her to quit before Rose, but she continued, on her knees, slopping out.

'What was that word Mum said we had to experience?' she asked.

'The numinous.'

Fleur sat back and put her face up to the rain. 'That was it. An experience of elation? Of joy?'

I glanced at the plastic bag full of slime and laughed. 'I know. What on earth were they thinking? I'd have thought they'd have sent us to a cathedral or a National Trust garden if they'd wanted us to have experiences to make our souls soar.'

'Or a beach by the sea; somewhere in nature. But maybe they didn't realize we were going to be asked to clean out drains?'

'It is a horrible job, but when you think what the inheritance is going to be, it's actually a very well-paid job.'

'If Rose leaving doesn't disqualify us,' said Fleur.

'Anyone could see that she wasn't faking it. It'll be OK, but she wouldn't last five minutes on *I'm a Celebrity Get Me Out of Here*.'

'Me neither. I suppose we can be grateful for small mercies. At least we haven't been asked to eat a kangaroo's testicles.'

'The day's not over yet.'

*

Half an hour later, we were still only a quarter of the way along, my knees killing me, when we saw a taxi returning to the centre. Rose got out, paid the driver and came striding towards us.

She was carrying two brooms with stiff bristles and a carrier bag with facemasks. She looked a lot brighter. 'OK. Sorry about earlier. I'm back. I was heading for the hotel when I passed a hardware shop, so got us some proper equipment. But I can't kneel down and put my face anywhere near that stuff or I'll want to throw up again. So let's get a system going. Fleur, you go along and lift off the lids with the end of one broom, flick it up, that way you won't do your back in, and Dee, you can use the brush to sweep along the drain and get the goo into piles. Conserve energy.'

I stood up and saluted her. 'Yes sir.' This wasn't a time to object to Rose taking control. Her plan made sense. I took a brush and started sweeping along the drain. It was easy-peasy. 'You feeling better, Rose? You don't have to do this at all, you know.'

'Marginally better, thanks. You know me. I don't like to give in so easily, but if you don't mind, I'll delegate on the actual gloop scooping.'

'Absolutely. Glad to have you back.'

*

An hour later, the drains were empty, hosed and washed down with disinfectant. Job done. Even Rose looked pleased by what we'd accomplished.

'Do you think we can go now?' asked Fleur.

But no. Sandra reappeared, inspected our work and gave us the thumbs-up. 'Good idea, using brooms. I wish I'd thought of that. OK. Job number two. Clean all the cat pods of cobwebs. I'll get you some dusters.'

'You going to be OK to do this?' I asked Rose as we followed Sandra inside.

She nodded. 'I'll see how I go.' She was starting to look off colour again.

'OK,' I said, 'but feel free to leave if you want to.'

Sandra led us to a long corridor that was lined on both sides with raised cat kennels. Each kennel housed a cat and had a cat flap that led to a small outside caged area that looked out through mesh on to the rest of the centre. 'If you look on the side of the kennel, they are all colour coded,' said Sandra. 'Green means friendly, purple for nervous, yellow for mainly friendly but don't touch, red means the cat might go for you.'

I peered into the kennels. In each one, a furry face looked back out at us: black, tabby, white, ginger. Some of them looked so worried, and my heart went out to them. I knew how much cats liked to roam freely, and hated to think of one of mine in here, even if they were fed, safe and warm.

Sandra handed us a set of keys each for the kennels and feather dusters. She pointed at the ceilings in the outside enclosures. 'Those are the bits that need dusting. I hope none of you are worried by spiders.'

This time it was Fleur who went white. 'Yes, me. I hate spiders.'

'Use your face mask,' said Rose, and handed her one from her carrier bag. 'They can't hurt you.'

'I'll do it,' I said, as soon as Sandra had left us alone. 'Just look busy if anyone looks in.' I didn't want to risk Fleur doing a bunk as well, and Rose was complaining of feeling dizzy, so I found her a stool and told her to sit. For the next hour, I cleaned and dusted with gusto, while Fleur wandered up and down the corridor looking in on various cats and reading the records on the side of their kennel. I didn't mind as long as my sisters stayed, and luckily the staff were busy in the outer rooms and no one came to check on us.

Once I'd finished the dusting, Sandra reappeared with our last task. 'If you could spend the rest of your time with the cats, that would be great,' she said. 'Just be careful of the ones with red stickers. Pull up a stool, open the kennel and give them a bit of attention. Talk to them. Most of them are desperate for some contact and it helps if they have some human company every day at least.'

'And now I feel like I'm in frigging *Dr Doolittle*,' said Fleur once Sandra had disappeared again. 'Talk to the animals? What are we supposed to do with them?'

'Just give them some love,' I said. I walked up and down the corridor, looking in at all the faces staring back at me. Some looked so sad, others anxious, others bored, some asleep; others were pawing at the front of the kennel, desperate to get out.

Fleur had a wicked look on her face. 'Let's open all the pods and let them make a run for it. Like the Pied Piper, only with cats. Only joking, Dee. No need to look so horrified.'

'It says on the side if they've got a home already or not,' said Rose as she stopped at a kennel. 'Look, it tells you how old they are and how long they've been here.' She opened a kennel and an old ginger tom came forward and gently head-butted her hand. She looked at his chart. 'Clifford,' she said. 'Fourteen years old. His owner died so he had to be brought here.' She pulled out the stool from under the kennel and sat down and gave him a stroke. He was soon purring like an old bus.

I found a black and white cat called Bonnie and sat talking to her for a while. Fleur still seemed unsure and hovered behind me.

'What's one supposed to say to a cat? What language should I use?'

'Anything,' I told her. 'Just chat.'

'Chat? To a cat? What about? Politics?'

'Try the weather.'

'Seriously?'

'No, not seriously, Fleur, just chat. The human voice can be comforting.' I turned back to Bonnie. 'Hello puss, and how long have you been in here? I know, it's not nice, is it? But a beautiful girl like you will soon get picked so it won't be for long. You'll get a home and can run around again.' Bonnie curled on her side, purring and pawing the air.

Fleur watched me as I talked to Bonnie. Finally, she pulled out a stool and opened the kennel door to an adorable grey kitten. 'Well hello there, puss,' she said. 'I'm Fleur. I know I haven't got any fur, well, not any more, I have it all waxed off. I suppose that's pretty strange to you. Can't imagine you'd want to be waxed but maybe you could be a trendsetter. I can recommend a very good lady in Sloane Street.'

Hearing her chatting nonsense gave me the giggles.

'What's so funny?' she asked.

'You.'

'Don't be so rude. Me and Monty here are getting along just fine.' She turned back to the cat. 'Now then Monty, tell me all about yourself, how come you ended up in here?'

I watched the kitten approach Fleur, meow and gently head-butt her, then he nuzzled her neck. Fleur laughed with delight. 'OK. Major flirt here. Back off, kitty. I'm bad news. You don't want to get involved with me. I don't do commitment – or cat-mitment.'

*

When it was time to go, we'd visited most of the cats that were approachable and Fleur was almost in tears. 'But what will happen to Monty?' she asked Sandra.

'Don't worry about him. He has a reserve on him already,' she replied. 'The turnaround on the cats is pretty quick, particularly the pretty or friendly ones like him. We have people coming up every day looking for pets.'

'What about the ones with red stickers?' asked Rose.

'Yes, they can take a bit longer.'

'And the old ones?' I asked. I'd noticed a number of scrawny old cats that couldn't have much longer to live, including Clifford. It made me sad to think that they would end their days in such a restricted place, surrounded by strange cats.

'Sometimes they get the sympathy vote,' said Sandra. 'We do have some wonderful people who take them, especially because they know that they're old. Real cat lovers.'

'And the difficult, not-so-friendly ones?' asked Rose.

'Ah well, they can take time to rehome,' Sandra replied. 'But we have a no put-down policy. Some of them just take longer, that's all.'

'What about Clifford?' asked Rose. 'Has he got a home to go to?'

'He's a friendly old fellow but, sadly, no takers as yet. He's been in about six months.'

'Six months? Shame,' said Rose. 'He's a sweetie.'

Fleur and I did a double-take.

'That's not like Rose. The fumes have gone to her brain,' said Fleur as we left.

*

In the car going back to the lodge, I noticed that Rose still looked pale. We were all tired.

'We made a good team today,' I said.

'We did, but I'd still prefer to send them a donation and help out that way rather than clean drains,' said Fleur. 'That wee Monty, though – I think I might have had him if he hadn't already found a home.'

'See, you do have a heart, Fleur,' I said.

'I do. I might even get a pet. Less complicated than men.'

'And they love you unconditionally,' I said.

Fleur laughed. 'One mad old cat lady is enough in the family,' she said, but her tone was affectionate, not barbed as it had been when she'd voiced something similar at the beginning of the process.

*

After a light supper in a café near the first hotel, we went, as instructed, to a street in town, where a soup van had been set up and was already serving soup and bread to a short queue of homeless people.

There were three helpers already there. Two young women, Kat and Rachel, and a young man with a goatee called Ben. None of them seemed to know that we were coming and were not entirely pleased to see us.

'Is there anything we can help you with?' Rose asked Ben, who appeared to be in charge.

'Not really. We've got it covered,' he said. 'Who was it sent you again?'

'Our dead mother,' said Fleur.

Ben looked at her warily.

'She's joking,' I said.

'Was it an agency?'

'Not exactly,' I said. 'Er . . . we're doing a volunteer programme for the weekend.'

Ben sighed wearily. 'The agency is always sending people. Believe it or not, there's a waiting list to do the soup run.'

I got the feeling that we'd gate-crashed a party, which seemed odd considering the circumstances.

'I feel we're in the way,' I whispered to Fleur.

'Me too. Maybe we should ask if they have any drains they want cleaning?'

'You dare,' I said.

I noticed an old man sitting in the doorway opposite the van. He didn't appear to have any food. 'Shall I take him some?' I asked Ben.

'You could. He never says anything, ever, so don't expect him to speak to you.'

I doled out some soup, cut a big chunk of bread and took it over. The man took it without looking at me and started eating.

'Oi you,' called the old man as I went back to the van.

I turned. Ben had said that the man never spoke to anyone, but he was choosing to talk to me. I felt a warm glow at having been singled out as the one volunteer worthy of being talked to. I smiled and said, 'Yes?'

'Fuck off,' the man called.

Ben and Fleur in the van cracked up laughing.

'You thought he was going to say thank you, didn't you?' asked Fleur.

I nodded sheepishly. 'Where do these people sleep?' I asked Ben.

'There are a few hostels in town but, depending on the weather, some of them sleep on the streets,' Ben replied.

I glanced over at Fleur. I wondered if the hostel we were meant to stay in was one of the ones that housed the homeless.

'I'm not going to feel guilty,' she whispered, as if picking up on my thoughts. 'And neither should you. Let it go, Dee.'

After half an hour of hanging around, feeling that we

were no use to anyone, it appeared that no one else was going to come for soup.

'You may as well go,' said Ben. 'We'll clear up, but thanks anyway.'

'No problem,' said Fleur. 'Any time.'

We went straight into putting our plan into action and checked into the hostel.

'Love the minimal décor,' said Fleur when she saw the bare rooms with just a bed and bedside cabinet in them. We mussed up our beds a little so they'd look slept in. 'How about we put pillows under the blankets so it looks like someone's in there sleeping, like we used to do when we were little and sneaking out somewhere after lights-out.'

'Good plan,' I agreed, and stuffed a pillow under the thin blanket in my room.

We headed for Benwick's Boutique Hotel, where Rose went straight to her room because she was still feeling unwell. Fleur and I opted for room service, a bath and an early night too, but this time it didn't feel like we were deliberately avoiding each other, just that we were all bushed.

As I opened the door to my lovely spacious room, I remembered what Jean and Mum had said about happiness being contrast. How right they were. Cleaning filthy drains this morning to relaxing in a scented bath then slipping into clean sheets later. Bliss. Whatever Mum's intention had been for today, all I felt was gratitude that I had a roof over my head and a bed with comfy pillows.

24

Dee

Sunday 10 April, morning

'How are you feeling?' I asked when Rose appeared in reception after taking breakfast in her room; I'd noticed that the tray left outside her room was barely touched, apart from a cup of tea.

She brushed past me and headed to the exit doors. 'Good. Fine. It was nothing. Bit of stomach cramp. Anyone would have balked at the stink from those drains. So. One day down, one more to go. Let's see what delights Mum has in store today.'

We walked around to the hostel where the car that Daniel had arranged for us was waiting to take us to an old people's home. None of us was up for much conversation.

As Rose and Fleur got in the car, I went to hand in our keys at the reception.

'We err . . . went out for breakfast early,' I muttered to explain why I'd come from outside.

The pink-haired girl on reception didn't appear interested, took the keys and drawled, 'Have a nice day.'

'You too,' I said, and went back to join my sisters.

'Our secret,' said Fleur when I got into the car. 'No one must know.'

'Absolutely,' I agreed.

*

The old people's home was an overheated Victorian building in a residential part of town. Georgia, a pretty girl with a dark ponytail and wearing a blue uniform, welcomed us at the door.

'Have any of you any experience of working with elderly people?' she asked.

'Only our mother,' said Rose. 'And she didn't need care.'

'Well, we're delighted you're here. We have overalls for you and, if you don't mind, I'm going to give you cleaning tasks to do. If you want to interact with some of our residents, please do. Most of them like a new face to chat to.'

I was given the corridors to mop. As I set to, an old lady rushed forward, glad to see me.

'Mary,' she said. 'Mary.'

'No, I'm Dee. Hello.'

'Mary?'

'No, Dee.'

Her face flushed. 'You *are* Mary. Don't try and trick me.'

'No. I'm Dee.' I looked around to see if anyone could come to assist, but there was no one around. The woman looked as if she was about to slap me but changed her mind.

'Jesus, if you don't even know your own bloody name,'

she said as she stomped off down the corridor, 'you can go to hell.'

I continued mopping and saw a man in the sitting room where Rose was cleaning surfaces. He was walking around the room, picking articles up and collecting them in the corner. When Rose tried to coax him into sitting down, he began to scream. A lady in a chair who was holding a doll and rocking back and forward joined in with him. I was tempted to do the same. I found it distressing to watch them and not know what to do.

Rose came over to me. 'These people have dementia,' she said. 'I think we should leave interacting to the staff.'

I nodded. I felt inadequate, so turned back to my mopping. A lady had positioned herself outside the cloakroom. I mopped around her and smiled.

She smiled back. 'I'm waiting for the bus,' she said. 'The 107. It's late today.' She seemed a gentle soul, intent on her purpose.

'Hopefully won't be long,' I said.

Back in the sitting room, another man got up, walked over to the TV and started urinating on it.

Georgia appeared, guided him back to his seat, then cleaned up after him.

*

For the next few hours, we did what we could to help, took round hot drinks, then the meals, cleared up afterwards, made beds and helped clean the kitchens.

'Do they have visitors?' I asked Georgia when we took a break in the small staff kitchen.

'Some do, but many of them don't recognize them when they come. Others respond to the care and love that their relatives or friends have for them, as if some part of them recognizes their visitors as people who care, though there are also others who are too far gone even for that.'

I felt grateful that had never happened to Mum, sad for those it had happened to, and full of admiration for the staff who looked after them.

*

'Well, that was sobering,' I said as we drove off in our taxi late afternoon. 'Why do you think Mum wanted us to go there?' Rose and Fleur looked as subdued as I felt.

'No idea. I thought this was supposed to be about finding happiness,' said Fleur. 'I feel crap after that – and sad. To get in a car and drive away feels like a release, like we've got time off for good behaviour, but also I feel guilty. Those people are somebody's parents. God, Mum, this task has been hard.'

'Mum might have wanted to warn us what we might be in for,' said Rose. 'None of us knows what's around the next corner.'

'Not that, I hope. That was so depressing,' said Fleur. 'That place was like a hell of sorts. Death, dribbling and dementia, coming soon to a cinema near you.'

I smiled. Mum used to say things like that too. 'Just awful to lose your memories,' I said. 'It must be bewildering.'

'Mum said old age isn't for sissies,' Rose said. 'I'm just thankful she didn't have to go through that.'

'Me too. Makes me feel grateful for my health, for my life and my home,' I said.

'That's why Mum sent us there,' said Fleur. 'Obvious. She was always telling us to be grateful for what we had. Remember? She was rubbing it in this weekend.'

Rose nodded. 'Always told us about the starving children in Africa if we wouldn't finish what was on our plates.'

'I remember you used to wait until Mum was out of the room then put yours in the bin,' I said to Fleur.

'Only cabbage. I hated cabbage. Still do. And there are still starving children, and not just in Africa.' She looked out through the window. 'God, I feel so miserable after this weekend.'

'Do you think that she was saying she wants us to do some volunteering?' I asked.

'Maybe,' said Rose, 'or maybe she was trying to point out that we should seize the day. None of us knows what's coming, how our old age will present itself, and if we'll even get that far. I think she was saying make the most of it and cherish your loved ones while you can.' She was staring out of the window as she said this and I couldn't help but think how sad she looked. This weekend of Mum's had definitely made us all think.

'I'd like to think that I'd be there for you both,' I said. 'If it ever came to that.'

'No fucking way,' said Fleur. 'If either of you start pissing on TVs or end up remotely like that, I can tell you now, I'll arrange a mercy killing, have you suffocated in your sleep, then I'll take off to a Caribbean island where I'll end my days in decadence and debauchery.'

Rose smiled. 'Thanks Fleur. Always knew we could rely on you.'

'I'm not going down without a fight,' she said.

'Sadly, I bet that's how many of the people in that home felt,' I said.

Fleur put her hands up to her ears. 'Enough. Enough. But we did it. We got through the weekend. I'll send a donation and now we can go home to our self-indulgent self-obsessed lives.'

'Speak for yourself,' said Rose.

'I am doing,' said Fleur. 'Home, get out of these clothes, a long bath, a glass of fine wine. So I like nice things. Does that make me a bad person? I don't care. I'm a selfish cow and always will be.'

'No comment,' said Rose with a smile.

I noticed there had been a real change in how we got on this weekend. We were teasing each other but the sting had gone out of it. We'd always insulted each other as sisters when we were at home, said awful things, and most of it had been like water off a duck's back – it was just the way we related to each other. I felt like we were slowly getting back there, speaking more freely, being more our real selves around each other. That part of the weekend, at least, felt good.

*

When we reached the car park where Rose had left her car, she insisted on giving me a lift to the station.

'No, really, it's no bother. I can get a taxi.' I was meeting Daniel in an hour's time and we were going to have dinner. Then I was going to catch the last train back to Plymouth while he went back to Bristol where he had to be for a morning meeting.

'Get in,' Rose insisted. 'If today's taught us anything, it's to look after each other. What time is your train?'

'Oh . . . I have an open ticket,' I said.

'Well you don't want to be hanging about,' said Fleur, and got out her iPhone. 'I'll look up the times for you. If you have long to wait, we could get a cup of tea or a glass of wine somewhere.' *How am I going to get out of this?* I asked myself as she busied herself looking up timetables. All the other times, they'd taken off with not so much as a backward glance. Why oh why did they have to pick this evening to come over all caring sharing?

'There's a train in twenty minutes,' said Fleur. 'You should just make it.'

'Right. OK. Thanks.' I got in and Rose drove me to the station. As I sat in the back, I felt bad about lying to them. After seeing the old folk with dementia, it had hit home the fact that life could be so unpredictable and that family and friends were precious. *Maybe it's time to tell them about Daniel*, I thought. *Enough of the duplicity. It's time to open up and let them in and trust they will go easy on me. But not yet. I'll discuss it with Daniel tonight, then next time I'll tell them. Next time.*

*

'Are you out of your mind?' said Daniel after I'd told him of my intention to let Rose and Fleur know about us. We were in a wine bar in the centre of town, where I'd gone to meet him after I'd hung around the station long enough to be sure my sisters would be well on the road back to London.

'No, I'm not. I don't like lying to them,' I said.

'We haven't exactly been lying, just not telling the whole truth.'

'What if they ever found out? Slowly, slowly, we're beginning to bond again and, despite my earlier misgivings, I realize I'd like them back in my life. I don't want to jeopardize that.'

Daniel sighed. 'I think you'd be making a big mistake.'

'Why? Why should it be? We've only got two more weekends to go and then we will have completed Mum's list. I think I owe it to them to tell them honestly what has been happening in my life.'

'How are they going to react? It's too late, Dee. When they realize that you've been lying for months, how's that going to make you look? Or me?'

I hadn't considered that. 'I hope that they'll understand. I could explain that I felt vulnerable and also that you felt it best to keep it quiet so as not to interfere with Mum's programme.'

Daniel took a sharp intake of breath. 'Leave me out of it.'

'I can't. How can I leave you out of it? You did say to keep it quiet, our secret; well, I'm not sure I want it to be our secret any more.'

I remembered my paranoia yesterday about his connection with Fleur and Rose, the way Fleur had caught his eye, the way Rose had been sweet to him. I wondered whether to say anything.

Daniel took a sip of red wine. 'Look. Let's change the subject for a moment. We're both not thinking clearly. Tell me about your weekend. How did it go?' He chuckled. 'I did think of you having to sleep at the hostel. They notoriously have uncomfy beds.'

I felt myself blush. 'It was OK.' *Liar*, said a voice in my head.

'Did you get any sleep?'

'I thought we weren't supposed to discuss the programme.' I sounded curter than I'd intended. I also thought, *and now I'm lying to Daniel about where I spent the night. Too many secrets. How did this happen?*

Daniel looked surprised by my tone. 'I'm not supposed to comment or advise, and we won't talk about it at all, not if you don't want to.'

'Sorry. I didn't mean to sound sharp, just . . . '

We sat in an awkward silence, sipping our wine, though it tasted sour to me. *This is what happens when things aren't out in the open*, I thought, *and a good relationship should be honest.*

'I really don't see why we can't tell Fleur and Rose about us,' I said eventually. 'Go public. It would make things a lot easier. I didn't like lying earlier and sneaking around the train station. I think it's always better in the end, to tell the truth.' *Hypocrite*, I thought, as I remembered my lovely hotel bed last night.

Daniel sighed. 'Can we leave that for now? Sleep on it?'

I didn't feel happy about his reaction, crossed my arms and looked away.

Daniel took my hand. 'What's got into you this evening? You're not your usual self.'

'Maybe this is my usual self. I value honesty. I always have, and yet now I've found myself in a position where I'm lying. And maybe I've been wondering about us and if there's a reason you need to keep us a secret.'

Daniel looked shocked at my outburst. 'Now you're

getting paranoid. We agreed not to involve your sisters. *We*. Not just me.'

'In the beginning we agreed. Things change. Relationships evolve.'

I could see Daniel didn't like being confronted, and I was feeling uncomfortable too. *Shut up*, I told myself. *Sleep on it, as Daniel said*. But he had clammed up and I couldn't think of anything to say to break the atmosphere. I took a good long look at him. He was a very attractive man. Of course women would be interested in him. *I wonder if he has other lovers besides me?*

'OK. Come on, out with it,' said Daniel. 'I can see something else is bothering you.'

'OK. How do you feel about my sisters?'

Daniel looked puzzled. 'How do I feel about them? I don't know them very well, but from what I do know, they're very different women, interesting. Strong women.'

'How interesting? I mean, do you fancy either of them?'

Daniel let out a long sigh. 'Ah, so that's what's been bugging you? Why didn't you just come out and say it?'

'It hadn't occurred to me until this weekend. Well, do you?'

'No. Neither of them are my type.'

'So what is your type?'

'You, you idiot. Why would I go out of my way to come and see you if you weren't. What's brought this on?'

'Something Fleur said; it was as if she knew you better than I did.'

I studied his reaction but there wasn't even a flicker to suggest that anything had happened with Fleur. 'And what did Fleur say?'

'That you're not the kind of man to commit. Rose agreed. They both think that you're a loner.'

I waited for Daniel to contradict me but he didn't. He didn't say anything.

'I guess we've never really talked about our future,' I said.

Daniel didn't look at all happy. 'No, we haven't. Look Dee, whatever your sisters said or think, you know that we have something on another level to them, a connection. How can you doubt that? Is this a pattern you've fallen into before – imagining things? Sabotaging things when they're going well?'

I was taken aback by his accusation and felt defensive. 'I didn't imagine it with John. He was cheating on me. That's why I value honesty.'

'I'm not John.'

'I wasn't imagining anything with Nick either. Not that he cheated, he just didn't want to commit.'

'Look, we're having a good time, aren't we? Isn't that enough? What is it you want?'

I didn't say anything and the silence between us felt wrong. I wished I hadn't said anything. The conversation was not going as I'd hoped. But what had I hoped for? Reassurance? A commitment? Neither of which were forthcoming. In fact, I felt like I'd created a wall between us. 'Look, forget it, forget I said anything. I don't want us to fall out over my sisters.'

He reached out and took my hand. 'Me neither.'

I leant into him but cursed myself for having spoken before I'd had time to think it through, maybe talked it over with Anna. Daniel didn't deserve my distrust. Or did he? For the first time since we'd got together, I felt unsure of him. 'So when will I see you again?'

'Soon. I'll email you or call as soon as I know my commitments for the next month. Maybe we should go away somewhere? Somewhere nice?'

'That would be lovely, but Daniel . . . where are we going? Where is this going? What's going to happen after we finish Mum's tasks?' It was out before I could check myself. *Shut up*, an inner voice said, *you're being needy woman.*

'I don't understand why you have to ask, Dee. We don't have to put a label on what we have.'

'No, of course we don't.' I checked my watch. My train left in half an hour. 'Look, I have to go.'

'Me too.'

*

'You worry too much,' said Daniel as we stood outside the station. He wrapped me in his arms. 'I know it's not ideal, always saying goodbye, but what we have is special. You have to know that. Don't worry.'

I kissed him and it did feel special. For a moment, I felt reassured by his touch, his look of affection, then it was time to go.

'Just give me some time to catch up with you about telling your sisters,' he said. 'Your idea to tell them came out of the blue.' He smiled. 'I'm a bloke, remember? We can be a bit slow sometimes.'

'Course,' I replied. 'Sorry if I ruined our evening.'

'You could never do that. But don't worry, OK? We'll talk about it.'

*

When I got on the train, I went over what he'd said in my mind, what Rose and Fleur had said too, and I felt a niggling doubt that wouldn't go away. Where was he when he wasn't with me? He couldn't be working the whole time. Did he have other lovers, and amongst them one of my sisters? Rose could keep a secret better than anyone, but surely she wouldn't do that to Hugh or her children? Then Fleur? I dismissed that idea too. Fleur would have come out with it. She could never keep making a conquest to herself. Maybe other women I knew nothing of? Daniel hadn't ever made any promises, but then neither had I. *Was I expecting too much now, wanting too much?* We'll talk about it, he'd said. I must give him time. I stared out through the window as the lights of towns, houses flashed by, and felt that – somehow – I'd been fobbed off.

*

At Plymouth Station, I bumped into Michael Harris on the platform. I wasn't in the mood for seeing him but, too late, he'd seen me and waved.

'Been somewhere nice?' he asked.

'Exeter. Family event,' I replied. 'You?'

'I'm just heading back to London.'

'Why train? Where's your car?'

'I've left it on the peninsula.'

'Why?'

'I have to make a quick trip back to the city, work to

catch up on, and that's easy on the train. Then I'll be back down. I've been looking at houses down here so it's useful to have the car.'

I remembered he'd mentioned it at my party just before I'd dashed off to the Ladies. So he was serious.

'Seen anything?'

'A couple, one in particular. The Old Vicarage out towards Cawsand.'

'I know it. That's a lovely place, out on the coast road?'

'That's it, overlooks the bay.'

'You must hate me. You'd have Summer Lane if it wasn't for me.'

'I don't hate you, Dee. Far from it. Don't think that. No, I want something more rural than where you are; a few trees around me to look out on. You don't get that in the village.' He chuckled. 'Might even get a dog.' He glanced at his watch and the departure board. 'Better dash. You take care.'

'Will do. You too.'

As I headed out of the station, I felt sad. Michael appeared to be a kind man. From the beginning, he'd been reasonable about the house and it was his brother who'd been the driving force to get me out and sell. I thought about Daniel. *Is he a kind man?* I asked myself. Maybe picking the wrong men was a family trait and, like Fleur, I'd picked the wrong one in him; but too late, he had my heart, and there was no going back on that.

25

Fleur

Thursday 19 May

So long, Daniel. Time to call it a day with our *liaison dangereuse*.

It was never serious, and we only met up once a month, if that, but I'm bored already. What's the point? We're not going anywhere. And I think Dee still likes him. She says she doesn't, she's, like, la la la, I'm not interested, but she forgets, I grew up with her and remember how she was when she had a crush. She'd close down, put the walls up, as if protecting how she felt. She goes quiet when Daniel's around and I can see her visibly relax when he leaves. She'd be heading for heartbreak if she ever pursued him, but I don't want to add to it by continuing a relationship with him that means nothing to me. For me, he was like a cupcake that was going spare at a party. No one having this? Might as well not waste it then. Not exactly the grand passion. So I'm letting him go. She can pursue him if she wants, but I hope she won't. I don't want her to get hurt or rejected. He swears that nothing will ever happen between them but, all the same, that's not enough of a reason for me to continue with him.

I feel that Dee and I are getting close again, so I don't want any complications. It was always her I went to when we were growing up. After puberty, Rose was usually off with her own friends. Maybe that's why Mum devised the list. Rose has her family and her all-consuming work. Dee and I are both single. Maybe Mum wanted us to find one another again.

I hope we'll stay friends after we finish the tasks. Men, they come and go. Who needs them? And sex? I'm losing interest. I might have it all filled in and a gas fire fitted. Friends and sisters are always there, part of life, and I don't want a meaningless affair – for that's all it was – with Daniel to ever come between us. So it's going to be '*Ciao* baby.' It was good while it lasted. Don't call me, I'll call you. Only I won't. He'll soon get the message that comes with the unspoken word.

26

Dee

Friday 10 June

Weekend five.

'So what's the plan?' asked Anna.

'I'm meeting Fleur and Rose at a hotel in Reading.'

'Great, not too far, and you can get the train.'

'I know. Mum really had thought out every detail and has organized places that were reachable for all of us, even me down in the southwest. I get the train up this evening. Fleur and Rose are arriving tomorrow.'

'And Daniel?'

'Meeting him tonight, and we're going to stay the night in the hotel where the next part of the kicking the bucket list is to take place.'

'You wanton woman.'

'I am. Wanton woman with a secret sex life, only not for much longer – the secret part, that is. I hope the sex life part will go on for quite a while yet, though I've felt a distinct cooling off in the last months.'

'Your side or his?'

'Not sure. It's been ever since I broached the subject of telling Rose and Fleur, but I hope our evening together will clarify things.'

'And you're going to tell Fleur and Rose about Daniel?'

'I am. I don't care what he says. It feels wrong now that my relationship with my sisters has got better.'

'Maintain radio contact. Report back if and when you need.'

'Will do.'

*

As I sat on the train, I played and replayed in my mind what I was going to say to Rose and Fleur. It's not too late. I'll explain everything, from the start, totally come clean and hope that they understand why I didn't tell them in the beginning. All of us were prickly in the first few months, but I felt there had been a breakthrough on our last weekend together in April. I'd also begun to suspect their lives weren't as picture perfect as I'd imagined; that Fleur was lonely in her beautiful flat, and Rose worn out with her busy life – and by just being Rose. I wanted to get closer to both of them, be there for both of them. Nothing must jeopardize that, not even Daniel. *I will do it*, I told myself, *Saturday night, when we're all together.*

I arrived at the boutique hotel, which was on the main road near the station. Inside was painted Farrow and Ball French Grey and stone colours. *Very tasteful*, I thought as

I went to my room to find that someone had left a message at reception. I called down. It was from Daniel. He couldn't make it this evening. Would call me later. *Why didn't he call my mobile?* I wondered as I flung my overnight bag on the bed. *He has the number and usually calls or texts.* I felt a niggle. What was going on? We'd met up a couple of weeks ago when I'd gone up to London and we'd had a pleasant day mooching around Camden Market. We'd bought lots of goodies from a local deli and gone back to his flat for supper. I purposely hadn't mentioned our conversation about any future together. I'd been light and bright but it had felt hollow somehow, as though I couldn't completely be myself with him. He'd seemed distracted too, but I didn't question him about it. I'd sensed he was a man who didn't like to be pinned down about anything.

I ordered room service and watched TV and kept my phone on for Daniel's call. It didn't come. *A watched phone never rings*, I told myself. I thought about calling him but was determined not to turn into a Miss Whining, where are you? *Is this the beginning of the end for us?* I wondered. My gut was telling me that something wasn't right with us any more.

Saturday 11 June

After breakfast, I went to the meeting room, hoping to catch Daniel before Fleur and Rose arrived, but they were already there, having driven together from London. Daniel was also early and was setting up.

He smiled, said, 'Hi.' I nodded back at him. He was so

good at acting as if nothing was happening. *Today is about Mum*, I told myself. *I'm not going to let whatever is or isn't happening with Daniel ruin the time I have with her on these recordings.*

When we were settled, Daniel pressed Play, and there was my dear mother. Even after all the months, it was still a shock to see her on screen, looking so alive. A bitter-sweet experience: a joy to see her there with more to say; a sorrow to know she was no longer alive at the other end of the recording. Seated beside her on her sofa, Jean and Martha had their eyes closed, their hands in their laps, palms up. They were all dressed in white and wearing Perspex triangular hats.

Fleur laughed. 'Is she sending us to Ascot?'

'Afraid not,' Daniel replied.

'Hello, darling girls. Like the hats? We're wearing them because this weekend is about the power of the mind,' said Mum. 'You could say it's the mental approach to happiness.'

Martha and Jean opened their eyes.

'How one can change one's life by changing one's attitude,' said Martha.

Jean nodded. 'Create the life you want by changing your thoughts.'

Rose groaned. 'Oh Christ. Not this.'

'Yes,' said Martha. 'The mind is a powerful force. One's thoughts are potent. It can take some people a lifetime to discover just how much, but that's what we're going to address this weekend.'

'All the great thinkers from way back in time say the same thing,' said Jean. 'Your life is a manifestation of your thoughts, of what you have chosen.'

'Tell that to the people in war-torn countries,' said Rose, 'or the terminally ill.'

I glanced at Fleur. She discreetly raised an eyebrow. Rose was in one of her contrary moods.

'Successful people are not successful because of luck,' said Martha. 'They work at it, yes, have goals, yes, but most of all believe in the power of thought. They believe they will succeed.'

'Thoughts are like magnets. What you think, you attract to you,' said Mum.

Rose sighed with exasperation.

'So you have to be careful what you think over and over again,' said Jean.

I glanced at Daniel. *Am I creating a distance between us by my thoughts? Sabotaging what we have because I believe men let you down*, I wondered. *I mustn't think like that then. Get out negative thoughts. Get out now.*

'I thought this weekend might appeal to you in particular, Rose,' said Mum, 'it being a more cerebral approach.'

Clearly not, I thought as Rose rolled her eyes. 'Wrong,' she said.

'Today is about taking charge of one's mind,' said Martha. 'You're going to look at what you are thinking, what thoughts are predominant and, thus, shaping your life. Then you'll spend a bit of time identifying what it is that you truly want and making positive affirmations to make it happen.'

'I must, I must, I must improve my bust,' said Fleur. 'Remember that one? We all used to do it in front of the mirror. Didn't bloody work.'

'Probably not what Mum was alluding to,' I said as I

noticed Daniel's fleeting glance at Fleur's chest and felt a stab of jealousy.

'Today will also be about how to eliminate worry, guilt and blame. You must each take responsibility for your life as it is now, the choices you have made, and not blame anyone else,' said Mum. 'I know you all have your worries so, as part of the programme, you will make worry boxes and put all your cares and concerns in there. And when that's done, you'll work on visualizing what you truly want. Dee, as an artist, you must see this daily. You visualize something in your mind and make it real on the canvas. Today will be about learning to do that in life, not just art. You will learn how to create the destiny you want.'

Rose scoffed again. This time Daniel glanced at her and she met his eyes, acknowledging something between them. A thought? A shared response to what Mum was saying? What? Another spear of jealousy hit its mark inside me. 'Create your destiny? *Pff*,' said Rose.

What is her problem? I wondered. I liked the idea of getting my thoughts under control and reshaping my destiny. By the way I was feeling this morning, I clearly needed to.

'Shh,' said Fleur.

'You shh,' said Rose.

'Aim to be the person you want to be, were meant to be,' said Jean. 'See it in your mind.'

'As always, Daniel will tell you what to do,' said Mum. 'You won't have to go far and can do most of it right here or in your hotel room.'

'We know a lot of what you work on today may be private,' said Jean, 'so, like with the writing exercise you did on weekend two, don't feel you have to read anything out, but share it if you want to. It's for you to assess where you are in life, if that's where you want to be and where you want to go next.'

'On Sunday,' said Martha, 'we want you to try out some mindfulness techniques. It's like meditation, and aims to bring you into the present moment. We spend so much time thinking about the future, having regrets about the past, that it's easy to miss the present.'

'Which is the only time that's real, and where true happiness lies,' said Mum. 'We think, oh, I was happy in the past at such and such a time, but that time is gone, never to return. We think oh, I'll be happy in the future when I've done this, achieved that, got this, gone on holiday, met the One, etc., and so on, wishing away our lives, but the future is a closed curtain. The present is the only time that's real. So there will be exercises to help you to live mindfully in the moment, to be present in the present, to taste what you eat, hear the sounds around you, see the changing seasons and the skies. When did you last look at a sky – I mean, *really* look? Or at a flower? Or a tree?'

'OK, I am telling you right now I am not going tree-hugging,' said Fleur.

'So, my darling girls, be present,' Mum continued. 'Be in the here and now, live your lives fully and consciously and choose thoughts to be happy.'

'And abundant,' added Martha.

All three of them closed their eyes and smiled beatifically. With their strange hats, they looked like three very weird and wrinkly aliens.

Then they were gone.

'Horseshit,' said Rose.

'Don't hold back Rose,' said Fleur. 'Why is it horseshit?'

'I've heard all this stuff before. It's idealistic fluff. You've heard of *The Secret*? All that waffle about manifesting what you want. Think you're going to be a millionaire and you will be.'

'Worked for me,' said Fleur.

'Sounds good to me,' I said.

'Then you've both got your heads in the clouds. The only people who make money out of this way of thinking are the people who write the books and make the CDs about it,' said Rose. 'There are a lot of gullible people out there, suckers who don't know how to do a day's proper work.'

'Why so negative, Rose?' asked Fleur. 'We can at least give it a go. I like the idea of a worry box.'

'Like that will help anything.'

'Why not?' I asked.

Rose sighed. 'Because real life is more complicated than these positive-thinking gurus make it sound.'

I glanced over at Daniel. He was looking at Rose again. His eyes were soft with an expression of tenderness. It took me by surprise. *Why is he looking at her like that?* I wondered. He noticed me staring at him and looked away from Rose, who hadn't noticed, nor had Fleur. *I didn't imagine that*, I thought. *But Rose and Daniel? That doesn't make sense. Hugh and Rose are rock solid. Always have been. Has he got a crush on her? Drawn to the unattainable, whereas I've been too submissive, a pushover. He knows he can have me so there's no challenge left?*

'OK, Daniel,' said Fleur. 'Tell us what to do, then we shall change the world by the power of our minds. We will bring about world peace, erase poverty and rid ourselves of cellulite.'

I could see it was going to be an interesting two days.

*

Daniel left us with a CD player, CDs, a schedule of instructions and paper and pens to do exercises.

'Call me if you need to,' he said, 'but I think it's straightforward.'

He seemed in a hurry to get out and, also, a bit glum. I debated whether to text him later and ask what was going on. Where he was last night? Why didn't he come to see me? Would we meet up on Sunday? Why was he looking at Rose in that way? And why did he seem fed up towards the end? I decided not to. I could hear myself asking the questions and knew that I would sound anxious and needy. I didn't want to come across as a nag, keeping tabs on him, especially if I was right about him being a man who liked a challenge when it came to women. I'd been there before with Nick and John and I wasn't going to do it again. Men like them could turn things around so suddenly and make out that it was me that was the problem. I didn't want to be told that I was being demanding or paranoid. *No. Been there, done that*, I thought.

Just after he left, three mobile phones beeped. 'More messages from beyond the grave,' said Fleur as we reached into our bags.

Mum's message read: 'Ask, and it will be given to you; seek, and you will find; knock, and it will be opened to you,' Matthew 7:7.

'OK. I'm putting in my order then,' said Fleur. 'Ask, and it will be given to you. I'll have a café latte and an almond croissant. Dee? Rose? What do you want?'

Saturday 11 June, 11 a.m.

The first item on the schedule was to listen to a CD. *Creating Your Dreams*. We sat in comfy chairs and listened. It lasted almost an hour and the narrator was an Australian man called Jack Marcuson. He talked about the power of positive thought. I think Fleur nodded off at one point. I almost did. Rose sat, stiff backed, eyes opened. Occasionally she'd huff or puff her objection to something that was being said.

'What do you really want? Think about it, then put your prayer out in the same way that you'd put in an order in a catalogue. Then let the universe do its magic. Ask. Trust it will happen. Accept. Ask clearly and precisely. Believe that it will happen. Visualize yourself enjoying what it is that you want as if it is already happening in the present. Don't say I *will* have: no, say I *have*; always use the present tense. The universe will resonate with you on this and deliver.'

'Like a pizza delivery man,' said Fleur, suddenly coming round. 'Make mine a Quattro Formaggi.'

Jack continued: 'Like attracts like. Your thoughts send out a magnetic signal. If you don't like what you're seeing manifest in your life, tune into a different frequency. If you want to change your life, change channels by changing your thoughts. See yourself living in abundance.'

'Already do matey,' said Fleur.

It was true. Fleur had always believed she was destined to be successful. I wondered how much of my life I had brought on myself. I definitely didn't live in abundance. I struggled and had done for years. Had I brought this on myself by my way of thinking?

Jack hadn't finished. 'The mind doesn't hear negatives, so never phrase anything like, I don't want to live in poverty, or I don't want to lose my job, because the universe hears I *do* want this or I *do* want that. Your life is a manifestation of your thoughts and you will attract those that are predominant. So think affirmative thoughts. Never negatives. Your feelings are the feedback. Ask. Trust it will happen. Accept as if you already have it.'

'Bollocks,' said Rose in a loud voice.

'Have you suddenly developed Tourette's?' asked Fleur.

'Shh, I'm listening,' I said.

'When visualizing,' Jack continued, 'remember moving pictures are easier to imagine than static ones. For example, imagine a garden. Now imagine yourself out there, mowing the lawn, planting plants and bulbs. Get it? It's easier to imagine yourself as if in the scene, living the life that you choose. You can choose whatever you like. The universe is endlessly creative and abundant. You make what you want to happen with your mind. Expect the things you want. See yourself enjoying these things. The law of attraction makes it happen. Good luck my friends. Remember you are the genie and you are the lamp.'

When the CD finished, Fleur stood up. 'I am the genie, I am the lamp. Oh fuck, I'm on fire.'

I laughed. Rose didn't.

'You OK, Rose?'

'Yes. Why wouldn't I be?'

'Because you're in a stinking mood, that's why,' said Fleur. 'What's the matter? Work? Hugh? Menopause? Vaginal dryness?'

Rose sighed. 'Don't be gross, Fleur. I'm a bit tired, that's all, and just wait until you hit the menopause.'

'Ah, so it is that,' said Fleur.

'None of your business,' said Rose. 'Listen, Laura and Simon are home from university this weekend. It's close enough to London to drive back, so do you mind if I work on whatever exercises there are to do in the lunch break so I can finish early? Then I'm going to head home to see Simon and Laura and to my own bed. You don't mind, do you?'

Fleur looked at me. 'I don't mind. Dee?'

'I . . . no go ahead. Course.' I wanted to tell them about Daniel and me, but I couldn't do it if Rose was rushing off. *Tomorrow*, I thought, *I can tell them about Daniel tomorrow.*

*

We worked on through the rest of the day, with sandwiches brought in for lunch. I enjoyed doing the exercises. I thought about what I wanted to do, who I wanted to be, and let my imagination run riot. 'Don't put limits on yourself and what you can achieve,' Jack had said. So I didn't, and I visualized myself having a successful art exhibition, being there in the room, meeting and greeting people. I saw myself completing the purchase of No. 3, Summer Lane, as if it was really happening: signing the documents, getting the deeds to the house in my hands. It felt good.

'You could manifest yourself a man,' Fleur said to me. 'Write down exactly what you want. I'm going to do the same.'

Not a bad idea, I thought, and started to describe Daniel, then I crossed out what I'd written and wrote, kind. I want a kind man. I have a kind man. And then I was off. He is honest, generous, has nice hands . . .

Fleur was writing pages too. 'Mr Positivity there on the CD said be as specific as you can be.'

'So what have you written Fleur?'

'I want a Buddha with balls and a Bentley,' she replied.

I was surprised. 'Buddha? You want a spiritual master?' I laughed. She really had taken the 'no boundaries' part of the CD seriously.

'I mean a spiritual man but one who isn't a wimp. I don't go for the open-toed sandals and grows alfalfa sprouts brigade. I want one with testosterone, hence the balls part, so a manly man who has some respect for life and relationships. No oafs, Casanovas, rats or two-timers.'

'And the Bentley?' asked Rose.

'Meaning he'd have his own income. I'm not having anyone sponging off me. Oops, just used negatives. How can I rephrase that? He will be financially independent. He is financially independent. See, I'm getting the hang of the lingo.'

'So basically you want Mr Perfect. Well, good luck with that Fleur,' said Rose.

'Ask, trust it will happen, accept,' she said in a perfect take-off of Jack's Australian accent. 'I'm giving it a try. I have money and all that, but maybe I could do with a partner, and that CD said I can make one up, so that's what I'm doing.'

'What about you, Rose?' I asked. 'You don't have to say if you don't want.'

'Mainly stuff about my kids and Hugh, though you know I don't believe in this stuff.'

'But what about you?' asked Fleur. 'What do *you* want?'

For a moment, Rose looked tearful, but she shook it off. 'You to butt out of my business, Fleur Parker.'

On to the next exercise. *How is your time divided?* I read on the sheet of paper. Make a circle and divide it into pie-size slices that relate to how much time you give each of the following: spirit, exercise, play, work, friends, romance, adventure.

Work got a huge slice. Friends medium. Exercise: a thin sliver. I've neglected that of late. Romance a thin slice, since Daniel and I see each other so rarely now. Adventure medium slice due to Mum's kicking the bucket list. Play, nonexistent at the moment. I've been too busy painting. *But I enjoy that*, I thought, so made that slice bigger.

Now look at your circle. Is there an imbalance? Take note of the pie slices that are too small and try and address that. *OK,* I thought. *Must meditate more. Pray and play.*

Next was an instruction to write affirmations about what we wanted. I did them as if I was doing lines in detention.

I, Dee McDonald, am a successful artist. I, Dee McDonald, am a successful artist. I, Dee McDonald, am a successful artist.

'These exercises are frigging endless,' said Fleur as she glanced over the pages we were supposed to fill. 'I don't know. Five adventures I'd like to have? Ten things I'd like in my life? Name my goals/dreams for five years' time. Actions I can take to achieve that. Plan a perfect day. What exactly is the point of all this?'

'To identify goals and how you can achieve them,' I said.

'Of all the tasks, this is the most boring,' said Fleur. 'Apart from the make a man bit. I liked doing that.'

'I agree,' said Rose. 'Very boring.'

I decided to ignore the two of them and their complaining and continued with my papers, thinking about goals and what I'd like to achieve. For things to be clearer with Daniel. My exhibition to be a success. My sisters and I finishing this kicking the bucket list and staying in contact. The completion of my house sale.

'And, lastly, the worry box,' said Fleur.

'And what is the point of that exactly?' asked Rose.

'To give your cares to God and let him take care of them,' I replied.

'What if you're an atheist like me?' asked Rose.

'I don't know,' I replied. 'Write them to Santa Claus.'

'Like I believe in him,' said Rose.

'The tooth fairy,' said Fleur. 'You used to believe in her.'

'How about we save ourselves some time?' said Rose.

'How?' I asked.

'Write – All my worries on every level for the rest of time, Amen, and put that in the box,' said Rose.

'I don't think that's taking it very seriously,' I said.

'Oh, I think it is and it covers everything.'

'Agreed,' said Fleur.

Rose scribbled her line, folded her piece of paper and stuck it in the leather worry box that had been provided.

'So I'll be off then. See you both tomorrow.' Minutes later, she was gone.

'Looks like it's up to you and me to create a cure for cancer and bring about world peace then,' said Fleur as she wrote a few more lines and put them in the box. 'Do you think Rose is OK?'

'I . . . what makes you ask?'

'Dunno. She looks tired and prickly if you ask her anything about her life.'

'What? More than normal?'

'Maybe not. Maybe it is the menopause.' She chewed on the end of her pen for a few moments. 'This list of Mum's, do you think it's bringing us closer?'

'Sometimes yes, sometimes no.'

'Me too, though I feel like I've hardly reached Rose and she's just doing it for the inheritance. I was thinking, she could have driven us all back to London. It's been ages since I saw Simon and Laura and Hugh. Not since Mum's funeral, in fact. It didn't even occur to her to ask if we'd like to go back, all together, like family.'

'I know what you mean. Have we created the situation with our thoughts?'

Fleur shrugged. 'No way. Rose is just being Rose but . . . Dee, would you mind terribly if I went back to London too? It's only a short drive away and I've got some work I should finish. I'll be back first thing in the morning and I just don't fancy another night in a strange bed in a strange hotel hanging about till morning.' I must have looked disappointed because she added, 'Nothing personal, honestly. I really do have some calls to make, emails to send.'

'Course I don't mind,' I said. An idea popped into my

mind. Daniel was only a short drive away too, and could easily come to join me if I let him know I'd be alone.

After Fleur had left, I was about to send a text, then hesitated. Daniel'd know that Fleur and Rose weren't with me. Our time spent together was surely as much of Mum's list as the tasks she'd set us; in fact, sometimes I wondered if the tasks were just an excuse to get us together in the hope that we'd have cosy suppers together. If I let Daniel know that Rose and Fleur had gone, that might disqualify us from having completed the condition of Mum's will properly. We were too close to completing it, so I went to my room, got room service, watched a movie, and wished I'd been able to drive home like my sisters.

Sunday 12 June

In the morning, a text came from Mum. It said: 'Make every day your favourite day.'

I smiled to see the old, familiar line. Mum always said it when my sisters and I were little and one of us went to her crying or with some complaint about the other. *Well, let's see about that*, I thought, as I got ready to go down and meet Fleur and Rose. There had been no contact from Daniel, and I was finding it hard to remain detached. I felt hurt by his lack of communication.

Sunday 12 June, 11 a.m.

Our mindfulness teacher was waiting for us in a small conference room on the ground floor of the hotel. He looked in his fifties, tall with white hair and a beard. He looked serious but serene, and I noted that he had several thread bracelets on his wrist similar to the ones that Daniel wore. I noticed Fleur checking him out. Although he was attractive, I didn't think he was her type. He looked the kind of man who spent time outdoors, cutting down trees, gardening or sailing. I always imagined that Fleur would go for a more sophisticated man with all the appearance of wealth. This man had a checked lumberjack shirt on and a pair of jeans.

'Good morning ladies,' he said when we were seated in comfortable chairs in a conference room. 'I'm Andrew and am your teacher for the day. Are you ready to begin?'

We nodded.

'Today I want to introduce you to the concept of mindfulness.'

'How does it differ from meditation?' asked Rose.

'It has many similarities. Often meditation is something people do in silence, going within to find stillness, and I believe, from talking to Daniel, that you have already had a session doing that, so today will be more about living mindfully. Mindfulness is a way of carrying that stillness from inside into our external world so we live consciously. For example, often people eat and don't taste what they're eating as their mind is elsewhere. They don't notice their surroundings because of what they have to do next, and they're already thinking about that so miss the moment they're in. Mindfulness is a way of living consciously, using all the senses to experience the present moment.'

Sounds good, I thought.

'What if you don't want to be present?' asked Fleur. 'Like you're having your legs waxed? Or you're at the dentist? In fact, you want to be anywhere but where you are?'

'Excellent question, Fleur,' said Rose. 'Andrew?'

Andrew smiled and appraised Fleur for a moment. 'Yes, good question. In those situations, I'd suggest that you should use meditation to go within,' he replied, 'to find a place inside of yourself that is still and calm, or you could use a visualization to help remind you of a different environment. But, as I said, today is about living mindfully – where you can and where you choose to.'

'Maybe you could teach me that other stuff too: visualizations,' said Fleur. 'I hate the dentist.'

Andrew smiled again. 'Me too. OK. So sit comfortably, relaxed but alert, then we will go through a series of everyday experiences to demonstrate. Just take a few breaths to bring yourselves into your bodies. Be aware of how the chair feels beneath you, feel the weight of your feet on the floor. Good.' He cut up apples and handed them to us. 'First we're going to eat mindfully. I want you to hold the apple in your hand. How heavy does it feel? What's the texture like? Smooth? Hard? Soft? Now lift it to your face. How does it smell?' We lifted and inhaled the soft, sweet scent. 'Good. Now take a bite. How does it feel on your tongue? In your mouth. Crunch. Chew. How does that feel?'

We swallowed and I got what he was saying. So often I ate something and was so immersed in my thoughts or anxieties I wasn't even aware of what it was I'd eaten.

'See? Easy? You can apply this simple method to all walks of your life,' Andrew continued. 'When you see someone, a friend, a family member, really look at them.'

'We don't have to smell them, do we?' asked Fleur.

'No Fleur, we don't – nor eat them.'

So Mr Serious does have a sense of humour, I thought.

'Can you use these techniques for sex?' asked Fleur. I could tell that she was determined to wrong-foot him.

'I would say they would enhance sex greatly, wouldn't you?' Andrew replied and raised an eyebrow at her.

'Are you going to demonstrate?' Fleur persisted. I had to laugh. Fleur had been the same when at school – always the one asking awkward questions just for the fun of it.

'Not today,' said Andrew, 'but if you'd like to come to one of my workshops on sex and mindfulness, you'd be most welcome.'

'Is that a date?' asked Fleur.

'Fleur, leave the man alone,' said Rose. 'He's just doing his job.'

'I don't mind,' said Andrew. 'It's not the first time I've been asked.'

Fleur looked peeved that her question wasn't original.

'Whatever the activity,' Andrew continued, 'focus on your breath to bring you into the present moment. Be aware of the rise and fall of the diaphragm, and those simple tools will slow you down, make you more aware. So much of our lives, sex included, people often act out on autopilot. When you practise being mindful, you become more alert to where you are, what you're doing, how it feels and – in relation to sex, Fleur, that can only be a good thing.'

Fleur studied him. 'I agree. Too many men rush it.'

'I believe one should enjoy the journey as well as the destination.'

Fleur gave him a slow smile. 'Do you now?'

Andrew smiled back at her. 'I do.'

We spent the rest of the session sampling different tastes and smells – the sweetness of honey, the bitter taste of dark chocolate, a selection of herbs Andrew had brought along. It was enjoyable and it did make me feel in the present moment.

At midday, Andrew took us out into the hotel grounds.

'I want you to walk mindfully,' said Andrew. 'Not to get the exercise over and get back inside. No. I want you to be aware of all your surroundings. Look at the trees, the textures – really look at them: the roughness of the bark, the smooth feel of the leaves. Look at the colours, the shades of green. Really notice them. Feel the sun on your skin. Feel the ground beneath you, the hardness of the path, the softness of the grass.'

'This bit is dead boring,' Fleur whispered after five minutes.

Andrew heard her. 'Be aware of your boredom, Fleur. Don't repress it. Feel it.'

'Seriously?'

His eyes twinkled with amusement as he looked back at her. 'Seriously. Feel your boredom, embrace it.'

We walked on. I was enjoying this part too. Focusing on my breath and really trying to be in the moment. Rose was quiet throughout, but when she finished, she said, 'This makes sense. Be here now. It's not new.'

'True, the idea is not new,' said Andrew, 'but every situation is new, especially if you take the time to experience it.'

'Smarmy git,' Fleur whispered again.

'Heard that, Fleur,' said Andrew.

Fleur's eyes twinkled this time, and I got the feeling that some major flirting was going on under my nose.

We walked mindfully, returned to the hotel and drank tea mindfully, sat in our chairs mindfully, breathed mindfully, felt every sensation possible in the location we were in – sounds, tastes, sights, smells, feelings – mindfully.

At the end of our session, I felt as if someone had put the brakes on me. I felt slowed down. It felt good, peaceful. My cares and worries lay in the future, in the past.

Just before Andrew left, Fleur asked him for his card.

'Feel free to get in touch, and you're welcome to attend any of my workshops,' he said as he handed his contact details over.

'Are you driving back to London now?' asked Fleur.

'No. Getting the train,' said Andrew. 'My car's having its MOT today.'

'I'll give you a lift,' said Fleur. 'Let me just grab my stuff.'

*

I caught Fleur in reception as she was checking out. 'Are you going to take up mindfulness then?'

'Maybe, but after the exercises yesterday of putting out your order into the universe, I think I might have just manifested my perfect man.'

'Andrew? Good for you.'

I felt happy for her as I watched her walk out to join him in the car park. From the short time I'd spent with him, he seemed like a man who might be able to handle her. I also realized I'd lost another opportunity to tell Fleur about Daniel. *Perhaps I could still get some time with*

Rose, I thought as I turned to see her coming down the stairs.

She breezed past. 'I'm off too. See you next time.'

Next time, I thought. *I'll tell them both next time.*

27

Dee

Friday 15 July, evening

The roses and wild geraniums were out, the sun was shining, my exhibition was ready to go. I was happy with it. I'd worked hard over the months, as if possessed, and I'd completed forty works since the New Year, though I was only going to display twenty. Some had taken weeks to complete, like the one of a peacock inspired by my ex, John, which I'd done in oils in Picasso style, in slashes of bright greens and blues, the head and wings distorted; others, charcoal and pastel ones, I'd done in a day, though working late into the night. I'd also put into practice what I'd learnt on the 'be positive' weekend. I'd visualized a good outcome. I'd written out affirmations over and over again. I, Dee McDonald, am a successful artist. I, Dee McDonald, am a successful artist. I, Dee McDonald, am a successful artist.

'Test the water with these,' said Anna as she helped me

with last-minute preparations in the gallery area upstairs in the village hall where my work had been hung. 'You can always swap some later.'

Wine had been delivered, my friend Marie had come to stay and had been busy baking breads and preparing dips, and I was dressed and ready in the outfit that I'd bought in Harrods back in February.

'You feeling nervous?' Anna asked.

'A bit, but looking forward to it too.'

'Well, you look great. I'm sure it's going to be a success.'

'Thanks and . . . please don't make a slip and mention Daniel to Fleur when she gets here,' I said to Anna and Marie.

Fleur had announced that she was going to come down for the opening. 'Wouldn't miss it,' she'd said when I'd told her about it. We'd spoken a few times on the phone since June, even Skyped once, and it was good to be getting on with her again. As well as my sister, she was a connection and reminder of Mum, and I was grateful for that. I'd told Rose about the exhibition too, but as always she was busy busy, but she had asked me to take photos of the evening and send them.

My heart had sunk at first when I'd heard that Fleur wanted to come to the exhibition, because Daniel had promised that he'd be there and I couldn't think how I would explain that to Fleur. At the same time I felt sad that they couldn't both be there on such a big occasion. It had been years since I'd had an exhibition, and the last one had been a resounding failure, partly due to gale-force winds keeping people away, but also partly because my paintings were safe and unoriginal. This time, I felt more confident that what I had to display showed more of what I was capable of.

Anna zipped her lips. 'I won't say a word, though I do think you've got to tell her and Rose soon.'

'I will, but I need to pick my moment. As I told you, I did try when we met up in June. I've got enough to think about this evening, though, and Daniel still thinks I should wait.'

'For what?'

'Until we've finished Mum's kicking the bucket list. We've only got one more weekend to go.'

Anna shrugged. She didn't like lies any more than I did. 'OK. But . . . Dee, are you sure about this man? I know I've only met him once and he seemed nice and fond of you, but is he making you happy?'

I sighed. 'When we're together, I'd say yes, most definitely, but lately, I do wonder where is it going? At first, it felt wonderful, the anticipation of seeing him, even the secrecy, but as the months have gone on, I do think I'd like him to share my life. As you know, I want our relationship to be public. I want to be able to introduce him as my partner to everyone, not just Fleur and Rose.'

'But you don't think he's one for commitment?'

'Rose and Fleur both think not, but thankfully they've both got off my case about him. I will tell them about Daniel the next weekend we are together in August, most definitely. I'm not going to let anything stand in the way. Also, it will be our last time together so, after that, Daniel can't object. We will have completed Mum's list, so the fact that we have a relationship can't, as he put it, cause any undercurrents.'

'Good,' said Anna, 'because at our age, we're too old not to know where we stand in love. But for now, tonight is going to be your night. Let's put any thoughts of Daniel out of both of our minds and enjoy your success.'

I grinned. 'Yes, because I, Dee McDonald, am a successful artist.'

Anna gestured to the room filled with my work. 'Indeed you are.'

*

The gallery opened at six and the hall filled up quickly with holidaymakers and villagers. Kingsand was usually a quiet place, with not a lot happening in the evening, so an art exhibition and chance for a gathering would be the highlight of the month. After half an hour, there were red dots on three of the paintings – one of them, a winter landscape in pastel with a red-breasted robin as the only splash of colour against the snow, sold to Michael Harris, though I couldn't see him in the hall. I felt touched that he'd bought one of my paintings after all the trouble I'd caused him.

Fleur wafted in half an hour after the opening and drew the usual stares from people. She was dressed in a white dress with gold sandals and looked, as she always did, as though she'd stepped from the pages of a glossy magazine.

'Dee, these are fabulous,' she said after she'd had a good look around. 'I definitely want to buy a few for the flat.' She pointed at my painting of the eagle. Even though it had already sold (to Daniel), I'd still wanted to show it because I thought it was my best work. 'I love that one. Has it definitely sold?'

'Yes.'

'To someone here?'

'No. A private buyer.'

'From the village?'

'No. Er, from London. They were down here in the area.'

'They? A couple?'

'No. A man.'

'Man? A friend?'

'Sort of.'

'Because how else would he see your work if this is the first showing of it?' I was squirming inside. Why couldn't I tell her that Daniel had bought it? *This is exactly why I have to come clean about him soon. I can't bear situations like this.* Luckily Fleur didn't pursue the matter. 'Anyway, it's fabulous, like the bird is ripping out of the canvas; it's almost violent. I'd have loved the original. Will you do prints?'

'I will.'

'Maybe I could have one of those, though it won't be the same as owning the original.'

'I'll do another for you,' I said, though I doubted I could revisit the state of mind I was in back in January when I'd painted it.

Fleur wandered over to the food table, and Michael Harris appeared through the doors and approached me. Despite our strange relationship over my house, I was glad he'd come to see my work.

'Well done Dee,' he said. 'I'm very impressed.'

'Thanks. And I see you've bought one for yourself.'

'I have. I'd maybe like to buy more for my new place. Ian tells me there are some that aren't on display.'

'That's right, there are. So did you put an offer in on the Vicarage?'

'I did, it's all going through, so I'll need things to furnish it, art to make it home. Maybe I could see the other paintings sometime?'

'Of course.'

'Great. I'd love that.' He indicated the full room. 'A good turn-out.'

'Not a lot happens in the evenings down this way, so it gives people a chance to get out.'

'And your partner? Is he not here?'

How does he know I have a partner? I wondered, then realized Ian must have told him. I quickly glanced around to see where Fleur was, to make sure she couldn't hear, and saw that she was at a nearby table, helping herself to a glass of wine. She didn't appear to be listening.

'Partner?' I asked.

'Oh. Sorry. None of my business.'

'No. It's OK, but I haven't got a partner, not exactly.' *Or have I? I don't know*, I thought.

'Oh, I thought . . . Sorry, my mistake.'

We were interrupted by a young woman who wanted to ask about a charcoal drawing of starlings. It was the one inspired by my meditation when I felt my head was full of birds; it was black and menacing. As I answered the woman's question, Michael moved on. When she'd gone, Fleur shot over.

'So dish the dirt. Who's the man you were talking to a moment ago?'

'That's my landlady's son.'

She glanced over at him. 'Ah. The famous Mr Harris.'

I nodded.

'And who was he asking about? I heard him ask about a partner? Did he mean the man from London who bought the painting I wanted? Have you been holding out on me, Dee Mcdonald?'

'No! Not at all,' I blustered. 'Michael probably saw me with Ian or someone. Ian is Anna's boyfriend. He's over there, the bald guy stuffing hummus and pita bread into his face.' I pointed to the other side of the room and Fleur turned to look. Inside, I felt sick. I was digging myself deeper in the lie. If and when I did finally tell Fleur and Rose about Daniel, Fleur would remember this time and ask why I hadn't come out with it. I cursed Michael Harris and I cursed Daniel. Why couldn't he be here? And why couldn't we be like a normal couple? Supporting each other at important times? All out in the open? I wished he could have been here to see my paintings, to see the public response, but no, I'd got wrapped up in protecting our secret. It felt underhand and wrong and had to stop. Soon. Very soon. But not yet. Not yet. Not today.

Anna appeared by my side. 'Don't look now but look who's just arrived.'

I turned and my heart sank. *Oh no, not him, not now*, I thought as I saw my ex, John, at the far end of the gallery. He was dressed in a cream linen suit and Panama hat. He was always a pretentious schmuck. Fleur had seen him too. 'Isn't that John?' she asked.

'It is. Probably here to give his professional critique.' I noticed he was looking at the painting of the peacock which he had inspired. I had enjoyed working on it, distorting it until it looked like a kind of bright-feathered monster.

John turned, caught my eye, bowed in greeting, then beckoned me over with a curl of his index finger.

'Look at him! He's summoning you,' said Fleur. 'Don't go.'

I nodded politely at him then turned away. 'I'm not going to. The days went I went running to him are long over.'

'Want me to go and spill wine over him?' Anna asked.

Fleur laughed. 'I always liked you, Anna. Let's both do it.'

I shook my head. 'No, *no*. They say the best revenge is to live well. I'm doing that.'

'Good for you Dee,' said Fleur, and looked at me with admiration.

John appeared at my side a few moments later. 'So, young Dee,' he said. I bristled. I hated when he used to call me that.

'Fifty now, hardly young,' I said.

'Well, you're looking splendid, if I may say.'

I searched my mind for an excuse to move away but he pointed at the wall of my work. 'A new direction for you. Birds. Hmm . . . '

I knew him well. Hint that he was about to say something and get you to draw it out of him. It was one of his methods of control.

'So John, what do you think?' Fleur asked.

John considered her question. 'A progression . . . of sorts. Yes, I see something, the seeds of . . . '

'Progression? Seeds of? You know what, John, you always did talk bollocks when it came to art,' said Fleur. 'There are no seeds here, just a full-blown talent in flower. What are you even doing here?'

John's expression soured. 'I read about the exhibition in the local paper. I like to see what other local artists are doing, and I couldn't miss seeing what my little Dee has been getting up to.'

Little Dee? His little Dee? How did I ever survive so long with this man? It was so clear now, everything he said had been belittling, though delivered with a smile; comments to keep me in my place, insecure, unsure. I must have been out of my mind.

'Well, she's doing just fine as you can see by the red dots, so I suggest you either buy something or bugger off,' said Fleur.

'Well. There's no need to be rude!' said John. He turned and walked away.

'Never liked him,' said Fleur, loud enough for him to hear. 'Or his paintings.'

*

The rest of the evening was a resounding success. I sold four paintings and five drawings.

Once the last of the people had gone, Fleur and I went to the pub and got a table with Anna, Ian and Marie, who were already there ensconced in the corner. I prayed that Anna had warned Ian not to say anything about Daniel. *I can't go on like this*, I thought. Daniel and I had been seen in the pub when he came to visit. I knew that tongues would have been wagging. I glanced around to see who was in and felt my stomach tense. Anyone could have seen me with him. At this rate, I'd have to go around asking everyone in the pub to keep quiet. *Lying is definitely not for me*, I thought. *It always leads to complications*.

'He likes you,' said Fleur, when we saw Michael Harris come in and go over to the bar.

'Why do you say that?'

'He was watching you in the gallery. Never took his eyes off you.'

'Not interested.'

'You should be. I like the look of him. He has a kind face.'

'Then you have him.'

'Not my type. Anyway, I have my own fish to fry.' For an awful moment, I thought she might be about to confess that she'd been seeing Daniel.

'You do? Who?'

'Andrew, of course.'

'The mindfulness teacher?'

Fleur nodded and her eyes softened. 'Early days, but I like him a lot.'

I felt so relieved that she hadn't been talking about Daniel, and that any niggles of suspicion I'd felt about them having a secret affair over the last months were just my paranoia. I also wished I could have told her about Daniel as easily as she had just told me about Andrew. I was glad for her. I'd sensed that she had been lonely for some time and liked to think that she wouldn't be any more. She obviously had the same concerns about me and, as I watched Michael chatting to Bet behind the bar, I thought I probably would have been interested if it hadn't been for Daniel.

Fleur stood up. 'Drinks anyone? I think a bottle of champagne is in order to celebrate your success, Dee. On me.'

'Excellent idea,' said Anna. When Fleur got up and went over to the bar, she moved closer to me. 'Listen, Dee, Fleur asked me about you and Daniel,' she whispered.

'Asked you what about him?'

'How you felt about him. If you liked him.'

'Oh no. I thought she'd dropped all that. What did you say?'

'I was vague. Acted ignorant, but I don't like this Dee. Now I'm having to lie too.'

'God, I'm sorry, Anna. But you didn't say we'd been seeing each other?'

'No. No. Course not, but you know you have to tell her – and soon.'

'I will. I will. When we're with Rose next.'

'Why not tell Fleur this weekend? One down and all that.'

'Shh,' I said as Fleur turned to look at us from the bar. 'Want crisps?'

We shook our heads, but eagle eyes Fleur never missed anything, and I could see that she'd clocked something was going on. When she brought the drinks back, she asked, 'So what were you two whispering about?'

'Nothing,' I said.

'Nothing is always something.'

'Dee has something to tell you,' said Anna.

'I . . . '

Michael appeared at our table. 'Mind if I join you?'

'No, course not. Sit,' said Fleur, and she moved so that Michael had to sit next to me. As she did, she gave me a wink. *Oh no*, I thought, *this is turning into some kind of farce.*

Fleur spent the next ten minutes doing a PR job, talking about how marvellous I was, how talented. I felt very embarrassed. Michael listened and was very charming. *The way Fleur is going on, he must think I'm desperate*, I thought, As I knocked back a slug of wine, I prayed that he wouldn't ask me about my partner again. Or Ian did. Or Anna.

'You're drinking a lot,' Anna commented as I started on a third glass.

'Celebrating,' I said, though that was a lie. This evening should have been a great night. I was a success, but I felt full of anxiety and unease about who was going to say what to whom and when.

Fleur, on the other hand, seemed to be having a great time. She was completely at home with my friends and the locals. As I watched her in between Anna and Marie, being one of the girls, making them laugh, I felt a pang of tenderness towards her. She was clearly relishing being with people, part of something, and not sitting on her own in her soulless perfect flat back in London.

*

After half an hour, I felt rather drunk and very tired. I stood up and wobbled on my feet. Michael got up to support me. 'No, no,' I waved him away. 'Don't need help.'

'It's no trouble,' he said.

'Wrong there – men are always trouble,' I said, and staggered towards the door, doing my best to walk in a straight line and not knock anything over.

Anna was beside me in an instant and helped me out of the pub.

'Tell Fleur,' she said.

'Bossy boots. Too pissed. Need clear head.'

Anna laughed, and when Fleur joined us, they pretty well carried me home where I went straight up to bed. However, despite the wine, I couldn't sleep, and I tossed and turned, thinking: how can I tell Fleur about Daniel? Must tell her. But when? I didn't want to ruin things just as we'd got closer. And Michael Harris. I seemed to remember waving him out of my way. I groaned into my pillow. *I just don't seem to know how to behave around men*, I thought. Needy and paranoid with Daniel, rude to Michael.

Saturday 16 July, morning

I woke early and went downstairs, resolute that today was the day. I'd tell Fleur everything.

'How's the head?' she asked when she came down to join me.

'Not great. I'm never going to drink again.'

Fleur laughed. 'You're so lucky to have such good friends down here. Who needs men when you have good girl-friends?'

I took a deep breath. 'Listen Fleur, I wanted to talk to you about Daniel.'

'Daniel. Oh. OK.' She opened the fridge door, not meeting my eye.

'I . . . I know I should have told you earlier but well—'

Fleur turned back and looked at me. 'You don't have to say anything. I already know.'

'You *know*?'

'Dee, it's been obvious from the start.'

'Has it?'

'Course it has. I knew from the beginning that you had a crush on him.'

'More than a crush.'

Fleur sighed. 'Look Dee, we had a great time last night. Let's not talk about him now. It only leads to upset. It will only ruin things.'

'Why would it ruin things?'

Fleur shrugged. 'Just . . . I don't think he's the one for you.'

'Why not?'

'I don't want you to get hurt. That's all. Come on, let's not talk about him. Let's put into practice what we learnt about mindfulness – live in the present.'

Why doesn't she want to talk about it? I wondered. *Why not? She was always the one who was asking if I was interested in Daniel, trying to set me up?*

'Yes but—'

'Yoo-hoo. You up?' called Anna as she came in the front door with Ian who was carrying a bag of croissants.

Anna looked at my face, then Fleur's, and clocked the situation straight away. 'Bad timing? Were you having a private chat?'

'Absolutely not,' said Fleur, taking the croissants from Ian. 'Oo, still warm. Yum. So. Who's for coffee to go with these?'

All the insecurities from my teen years threatened to

emerge as I watched Fleur busy herself getting coffee and plates. Our conversation had felt weird and I remembered the same feeling of doubt from many years ago when my intuition had told me that Fleur was not to be trusted about something. Nine times out of ten I was right back then, so what could it be that she was trying to avoid? Something to do with Daniel? She'd just started seeing Andrew and had appeared genuine about liking him, so what could it be? Could it be that she knows something about Daniel? Maybe not to do with her but Rose? I felt sick at the thought. Maybe he had been seeing Rose, Fleur knew about it and was trying to protect me.

After breakfast, Fleur went into busy mode, insisting that she had to be back in London for the afternoon. She set off before Anna and Ian left and I could question her more. It was as if she knew I was going to confront her and was getting out as fast as she could, also putting an end to my attempt to tell her about my affair with Daniel.

I had my exhibition to go to and, as I walked up the lane to the village hall after Fleur had gone, Rose's words from months ago played over and over in my head. *Mañana, mañana*, it's always *mañana* with you, Dee.

28

Dee

Saturday 13 August

A text from Mum came through just before I knocked on Rose's front door in London. 'Do not judge, or you too will be judged,' Matthew 7:1.

Very timely, as always, I thought as I heard someone approaching from within. *I hope my sisters take heed of this when I tell them about Daniel*. I had my speech planned. This time, nothing was going to stop me. No more *mañana mañana*. I'd put into practice the visualization techniques that I'd learnt on our last weekend together and pictured us, a cosy trio over a cup of tea in the evening, Fleur and Rose with understanding expressions having heard my confession, and both of them wishing Daniel and me well.

Rose had lived in the same house in Highgate for over ten years so I was familiar with the road and place. A four-bedroomed semi-detached Edwardian build on a quiet, leafy street. It wasn't an exceptional-looking house from the outside, though, due to the location and it being London, probably worth a few million, maybe more. *That much would buy a stunning detached manor house with acres of land down where I lived*, I thought as Rose opened the door and beckoned me inside.

I couldn't see that much had changed since my last visit over three years ago, though the hall looked tidier than when Simon and Laura had been at home. When they were at school, there were always coats, shoes and bags, where now there was an elegant console table with a crystal vase of white peonies. From what I could see in the other rooms as we passed through the hall, they were just as I remembered. Rose favoured a traditional style of décor with comfy chairs and books everywhere, on shelves, on coffee tables, even piled up on the floor by armchairs.

Through the open door to the back room, I saw family photos in silver frames: Simon, Laura, Mum and Dad and, surprisingly, I saw one of Rose, Fleur and me when we were very young, sitting on a bench on a sunny day by the tennis courts where Mum used to play.

'Hugh's out playing cricket, so it's just us,' said Rose as we got to the kitchen diner at the back of the house. This room had been changed and a large conservatory built on to the back, a wonderful light space that was also full of books, piled on the floor amongst rattan chairs and palm plants in massive grey pots.

'Looks fabulous in here, Rose,' I said.

'Thanks.' Rose was dressed more casually than usual, in leggings and an oversized shirt, perhaps because she was at home. She looked pale and tired and her hair looked thinner and not as glossy as normal. Perhaps a symptom of the menopause? I made a note to ask her if she was OK later.

'I don't believe it!' I exclaimed when I spotted who was curled up on a chair basking in the sun. It was Clifford, the ginger cat from the rescue home. 'You went and got him?'

Rose smiled. 'I did. They said he didn't have long to live and, I don't know, something about him touched me. I wanted him to end his days in comfort. He's a lovely old boy.'

'Rose is growing soft in her old age,' said Fleur.

I turned to see Fleur and Daniel, mugs of coffee in front of them, at the long, wooden kitchen table. Daniel nodded hello then went back to fiddling with his laptop. I went to the French windows and looked out over the garden. An easy-to-maintain level garden that looked picture perfect in the August sunshine. Beds with small plants at the front, tall at the back, a riot of pink, lavender, blue and purples. No doubt Rose had someone come in to do it. She wasn't a gardener, but I could see that her beds had been professionally planted.

'I feel sad that this will be the last recording,' I said to no one in particular.

'Me too,' said Fleur. 'I've looked forward to seeing Mum. As long as we've had these times with her, it's been as if she hasn't really gone – but after this, what will we have of her but memories?'

'Exactly.' I felt an emptiness about this weekend that I hadn't on others. We'd had a visit from Mum every other month, even if it had been from cyberspace. 'But we have each other now don't we? Mum lives on through us all, and personally I feel that she has achieved what she wanted. Look at us, we're talking again, we've spent time in each other's houses.'

'But what about after this? Will we still meet up when we don't have to?' asked Fleur.

I took a seat at the table. 'I hope so.'

Rose didn't comment. 'So what's in store for us this time, Daniel?'

Daniel didn't waste any time and switched on his laptop. 'Let's find out.' He didn't meet my eyes at any point, apart from when he said hello, his expression neutral as it always was on these occasions. I felt annoyed by his lack of response to me, or to anything that any of us said; it was as though he was being oh-so-careful to be invisible. At first I'd admired his cool, now it irritated me.

On the screen of his laptop, Martha, Jean and Mum were seated in armchairs and appeared to be dressed normally. Martha in a lavender twinset, Mum wearing her favourite green cardigan, Jean in a blue one.

'Hello dollies,' said Mum from the screen. 'So . . . this is our last weekend. I hope you're all there and soon you can sign Mr Richardson's form saying you've all done what I asked and you can get your inheritance. Hurrah. Don't spend it all on sweets. Seriously, I wanted to say something about that today. Yes, the money will help. It does that, but don't any of you get caught up in it. Money doesn't bring lasting happiness. It can give you some security and a few more options here and there, but my happiest times have always been with family and friends; with people I loved – nothing to do with what was in the bank. Sometimes we had more money, sometimes we were struggling, but my friends were always there for me, in good times and in bad.'

'So, this weekend, we want you to enjoy some simple pleasures. A bit of home-baking to start with,' said Martha. 'There's nothing like the smell of a cake or baking in the oven to make one feel more cheerful and to make people around feel cared for.'

'Daniel will have got all the ingredients for you and I've given him my old recipes for scones and my famous Victoria sponge,' said Mum. 'And I asked you all to bring your photo albums this time, so I hope you got the message from Daniel to do so. I know from my visits to you that you all have photos from different eras. Take a trip down memory lane. Remember when you were little, growing up together. Fill each other in on lost years. You don't have to go further than the sofa with a cup of tea and a freshly baked scone.'

'Tomorrow, we want you to take a trip to a local garden. I do hope it's summer when you reach this part of the list, so that gardens are in bloom and you can take time to look at the flowers,' said Jean. 'Making a garden, seeing things grow, is one of the most life-affirming things you can do, and then to stand back and think, I planted that from a seed. Magic.'

'Today, though, you can just enjoy being at home together,' said Martha. 'Tonight, you'll watch a DVD. We picked one from David Attenborough's *Life* series. His programmes show the glory of creation and can be a splendid alternative to the focus on the news of all the sadness and disasters that are happening. It is a wonderful world, despite all the fighting and madness they show us at six and ten o'clock.'

'So that's it,' said Mum. 'The end of the kicking the bucket list. We do hope that you've enjoyed it and that it's brought you closer. And yes, I'm sure that you can say, and Rose you probably have, that many of the things you've done have been transient pleasures, like the massages or the shopping trip, the visit to the garden tomorrow, but all the things on the list were to help add up to a happy life. I'm sure there are many other things we could have included but there just wasn't time.'

'Like sex,' said Martha. 'I wanted to include a tantric sex workshop. Good sex can make you very happy.'

Mum laughed. 'We vetoed that one. Sitting cross-legged in the nudie talking to your vaginas might have been a tad too far, even for you liberated girls.'

'Well, thank God for that,' said Fleur. 'I don't mind looking at my lady parts I'm but not sure I'd have wanted to look at yours.'

'Shh,' said Rose as Mum continued. 'In the end, it's state of mind that determines happiness, but all the things you have done on the list can contribute to that.'

'Not sure I agree about cleaning out cat poo,' said Fleur.

'Our last message is really about simple pleasures, time spent with people you love. Love one another, love the people you love, show them love, be kind to one another, choose happiness,' said Jean.

'And don't judge,' said Mum. 'No one ever knows the whole story of someone else's life.'

Martha and Jean nodded at this.

'If you have days when you're feeling blue and aren't in a happy state of mind, try one of the things on the kicking the bucket list,' said Martha. 'Take a walk, go to a dance class, meditate. You can shift states of mind. Remember, whatever is happening, you always have a choice as to how you're going to react to it.'

'So much of what you think matters,' said Jean, 'you will find doesn't matter at all. What lasts is love. Sometimes it comes from the most unexpected places, but it is the most potent force of all. If you can find love, you will find happiness lies there.'

'And it needn't be a nebulous thing, love – an idea, a feeling. No, put it into practice. Practise love in action. Do things for the ones you love, show them you care—'

'With acts of kindness,' Mum added.

'And cake,' said Jean. Martha laughed and nodded.

'And so this really is goodbye now,' said Mum. Her eyes were glistening. She knew it would be the last time we would see her and I felt my throat constrict at the thought of it. 'I'll have been gone a year by the time you see this last recording.'

Martha, Jean and Mum stood up and, from behind their backs, they produced three small silver hearts about the size of a hand, which they held towards the camera and indicated from left to right as though pointing out at Rose, Fleur and me.

Mum brushed away tears. 'So this is it,' she said.

Martha bowed. 'Au revoir,' she said then left the room.

Jean took her bow. 'Arrivederci,' she said and also made her exit.

'Auf Wiedersehen. Adios. Goodbye,' Mum said. She bowed, gave such a tender look of love into the screen that I gasped at the sweet, sharp pain it evoked. She blew a kiss and walked off.

We were left staring at empty chairs and an empty room. I felt such an ache of loss at the finality of it. I suddenly remembered when we were little, when Mum and Jean used to hide if one of us had left the room to fetch something, then they'd spring out from behind a curtain or sofa.

'That's it,' said Daniel and he went to turn the laptop off.

'No! Wait,' I said. 'She hides sometimes. Remember? Her and Jean? They might come back.'

I longed for her to come back. For five more minutes, for one more minute. We waited and I prayed to see her appear from somewhere, playing her familiar prank, but all was silent and, after a few minutes, I realized it wasn't going to happen.

'I think she's gone,' said Rose.

'Yes. I'm afraid that really is it,' said Daniel.

Fleur burst into tears and I was close to doing the same. I got up to put my arm around her. 'It's like she's gone all over again,' she said. 'I can't bear it. This last year was supposed to give us some hints about how to be happy but, seeing that empty room, Mum well and truly gone now, I don't think I've ever felt more unhappy in my whole life.'

'But at least we're together this time, that part is different,' I said as I thought back to the day that I'd had the phone call from Hugh telling me that Mum had passed, when the three of us had hardly been talking.

Rose fetched a box of tissues and put them in front of Fleur.

'Is that really really it, Daniel?' I asked. 'Any more texts? Anything?'

He shook his head. 'And . . . I suppose this is where I must take my leave too.' He stood and began to collect up his things.

'Mum didn't give you any more instructions for this last day?' asked Fleur.

He shook his head again. 'It had to end somewhere.'

And I'm supposed to reveal my secret, I thought as I looked at Rose and Fleur. How I wished I'd done it earlier, not on a day like this with all of us experiencing such a fresh wave of grief.

'Thanks Daniel,' said Rose, then turned to Fleur and me. 'Actually, I have something to tell you and ask you. I wonder if we could make a small change to this afternoon. I want to go somewhere. Just for an hour. We can come straight back here afterwards, that is, if you all agree to it. If not, I'll just pop out.'

'Where to?' asked Fleur.

'Remember the swami?'

We both nodded.

'Well, he's going back to India and there's a farewell for him this afternoon, not far from here. I'd really like to go.'

'You? But why now?' I asked.

Rose glanced at Daniel then back at us. 'I got a lot out of the meditation. I . . . actually, I've been going and having some sessions in between times when we met up for our weekends.'

'You have? Why didn't you say?' I asked as my mind went into overdrive. Rose going to do meditation of her own free will? I really didn't know her at all. Daniel. Rose. Having some sessions? Sessions of what?

'It was just something I . . . I needed to do on my own.'

'Did you know about this, Daniel?' I asked.

Daniel looked at Rose who nodded at him. 'Er . . . yes, I did,' he said. 'It was nothing to do with your mum's list.'

Nothing to do with the list? The possible implications knocked me into silence.

'Why? And why on your own and keep it secret?' asked Fleur. 'You could have told us.'

Rose sighed. 'A lot of what the swami said resonated, that's all. I felt I needed to find some peace in my life. The other stuff, as Mum said, so much of it is transient – fleeting pleasures. I needed to find some inner peace. Find the peace that never changes.' She gave Daniel a brief smile, which he returned.

I felt sick. All the time I'd been seeing Daniel, he'd been seeing Rose too and hadn't mentioned it once. Why not? If it was innocent, just meditation, why not say something? Had they got close? Had they been having a relationship? How long had Rose been going to see the swami?

'And did you find it? This peace?' asked Fleur.

'Some days. I'm getting there,' Rose replied.

'Rose, is there something going on that we don't know about?' I asked.

Daniel looked at Rose again. There definitely was. 'I'm going to go,' he said. 'I think you have some things you need to discuss with each other.' He picked up his bag. 'I'll see you this afternoon.' He said this last to Rose, not to me. I felt bewildered at the exclusion.

'Discuss what? What's he talking about, Rose?' I asked as soon as the front door had closed.

'Yes,' said Fleur. 'Has something been going on with you and Daniel?'

'Yes. Yes and no. No, not like that. Look. I do have something to tell you but I'd like to wait until later. Can we get on with this morning's tasks? Hugh will be here later. I want to wait until he's here.'

Oh God, I thought. *Could it be that she's been having an affair with Daniel and is leaving Hugh and is going to tell him?*

'Christ, Rose,' said Fleur. 'You and Daniel?'

Rose got up. 'It's not what you think.'

'Never is,' said Fleur.

'I don't want to talk about it yet,' said Rose. 'And no, it's not me and Daniel. Not exactly.'

I felt a surge of rage. She was still doing it! Controlling us. Choosing to tell us what she wanted when she wanted, with no consideration for what we might be feeling. *But then, she doesn't know I've been having a relationship too*, I thought. *Oh God, how did this get so complicated?*

'And you expect us to sit here all morning, bake cakes, look at all our old family albums, be nostalgic and remember a sometimes-happy childhood?' I said, and I knew I sounded angry. 'Well, Mum could never have seen this coming.'

'It's not what you think, Dee,' said Rose again. She had shut down. 'Later. I promise that I'll tell you later.'

*

I had an agonizing morning trying to carry on as normal. Fleur was in a strange mood and Rose was measuring out ingredients as though on automatic pilot. I felt panic. I texted Daniel. *What the hell is going on?* He texted back. *Talk to Rose.*

I knew there was no point in trying to get Rose to talk. She'd do it in her own good time. And so we baked scones. It felt surreal and far from the homely atmosphere that I was sure Mum had intended.

Whilst the scones were in the oven, we sat and looked at albums in silence. Fleur had brought the one she had, I'd brought a couple and Rose had one plus a couple of Mum's that she would have had in the retirement home. I could see that – under different circumstances – today could have been a good day, full of laughter at old haircuts and styles, reminiscing, but the hours dragged on.

As I watched Rose flicking through pages of an album, I tried to gauge what she was feeling or keeping from us. Her face betrayed little apart from possible sleepless nights.

'Are you OK, Rose?' I asked. 'You look tired.'

'I'm fine.'

'Are you sure, Rose?' Fleur asked. 'You do look a bit out of sorts.'

Rose ignored her, stood and looked at her watch. 'Time to go. Are you coming or do you want to wait for me here?'

'Coming,' Fleur and I chorused.

Saturday 13 August, 1 p.m.

The meeting was to be held in a smart hotel near Kensington. When we arrived, Daniel was waiting in a reception area with honey-coloured marble pillars and floor. He looked anxious as he waved hello to us. Rose went over to him. I was now convinced that they'd been having an affair. I could see an intimacy between them as they talked, then Daniel glanced over at Fleur and me. I was about to go over and confront them but Fleur pulled me back. 'Dee, I have something to tell you.'

'Can't it wait? What?'

She pulled me into an alcove from where we could still see Rose and Daniel. I didn't want to lose sight of them and wanted to study their faces further for clues as to what their relationship was. 'No, it can't wait. It's about Rose – or rather about Daniel.'

'Oh. OK. What?' I was itching to go over to Daniel and Rose.

'He's a fake, a phony. If Rose has been having an affair with him, I can be pretty sure she doesn't know that I was too.'

At first I thought I'd heard her wrong. 'You were *what?*'

'Having an affair, though I'd hardly call it that. It wasn't serious, just sex.'

She had my full attention now. '*You?* Having an affair with Daniel?'

'Yes, but as I said, it was just for fun, for sex.'

I felt like I'd been punched. A body blow. I gasped for air, finding it hard to breathe. Felt sick. I'd been right in my suspicions but . . . if Fleur had been with Daniel and I had too, surely *surely* he couldn't have been with Rose as well? 'Just *sex?* For fun? Fleur, what are you saying?'

'I'm sorry. It's over now.'

'I . . . ' I could hardly take in what she'd said and felt a need to sit down before my knees gave way. 'Why didn't you tell me before?'

'Daniel and I agreed to keep it secret.' *That sounds familiar*, I thought. 'And I didn't want to hurt your feelings. I knew you liked him.'

'I did. Do. Did. I . . . ' The nausea inside turned into a red-hot anger. I didn't know what to do with myself. Kick something. Fleur? Daniel? Rose? Myself for being such an idiot, for not seeing the signs, not trusting my intuition about Fleur – but now Rose too. I looked over at Daniel. 'I thought I knew him—'

'I wouldn't have done it if anything had been going on between you,' Fleur continued, 'but he assured me that it wasn't and . . . sorry to say this, but never would. That's why I tried to warn you off him.'

I wanted to tell her to shut up but I also wanted to know more. 'But how do you know that?'

'I asked him.'

'You *asked* him?'

'Yes. Of course! I'm not that much of a shit. I wouldn't have gone near him if anything had been going on with you and him. I'm so sorry about that, Dee. I wouldn't have said anything, but now Rose is in the equation, I don't want her to do something stupid over a man who isn't to be trusted.'

'But . . . but I *was* having an affair with him.'

'No you weren't.'

'I think I'd know.'

'But I asked him. He said it was never going to happen.'

The rage inside was growing. 'We agreed to keep it secret. Sound familiar?'

The penny dropped for Fleur. 'Oh.'

'Yes. Oh. I asked him about you too, Fleur. He said that was never going to happen either.'

Fleur looked shocked and I could see Daniel staring at us. He looked worried.

'Seriously, Dee? Since when?' asked Fleur.

'Since last December. You?'

'Since March, but it's over now.'

'Did he end it or did you?'

'I did. There was no point. It didn't mean anything. What about you?'

I felt like I was going to throw up. Telling Fleur about Daniel, it wasn't supposed to happen like this. 'I . . . I don't know any more. It's cooled off but I think we are – or thought we were – still a couple. We've been seeing each other whenever we could . . . ' What I said rang false in my ears. A couple? We weren't. Not really. And I'd only seen him once in the last month. We'd met halfway, in Bristol, and had both been distracted. We'd had dinner, made love, but it had felt flat. I'd convinced myself that it was just a phase all lovers went through after the first flush and excitement of having found each other.

Fleur put her hand on my arm. I shrugged her off. I felt confused, angry, stunned, hurt and sick. *So much for my positive visualization about telling Fleur and Rose over tea and sympathy*, I thought as I took a deep breath and tried to calm the avalanche of emotions that were threatening to engulf me.

Fleur looked over at Rose and Daniel. 'He's duped us all. We have to tell Rose. Now.'

'Now? Do we? Why?' Part of me still wanted to wait, to

tell Rose later, when we got home, not in such a public place; another part wanted to march over and punch Daniel's lights out. *No wonder Rose is looking pale*, I thought, *she's been carrying all this and has a family. At least Fleur and I don't have that to deal with.*

'Look, I know it's a lot to take in. Actually, it is for me too,' said Fleur. She looked flushed with anger too. 'The complete bastard. He honestly *honestly* said that nothing was going on with him and me?'

'He did. I asked if he fancied you. Too high maintenance, he said one time, not his type.'

'And he said that you would want too much from him, and also that you weren't his type. The shit. He's been lying to all of us. I wonder what he's said to Rose. Let's find out.'

Daniel turned his back when he saw that we were going over.

'Rose, there's something you have to know,' said Fleur in a loud voice, which caused a few people in reception to turn to look at her.

Daniel took a few steps in retreat. 'I'll leave you ladies—' he started.

'Oh no you don't,' said Fleur. 'You stay right where you are.'

Daniel stopped in his tracks.

'What's going on?' asked Rose.

Daniel sighed. 'I should go. I think you three need to talk to each other.'

'No! You stay put,' said Fleur.

'Yes, I think you have some explaining to do,' I added.

Rose looked mystified. 'Is someone going to tell me what this is about?'

'This lying bastard here has been conning all of us,' said Fleur, still in a loud voice so that anyone in reception could hear. A few people were already staring. 'Did you know that this creep has been sleeping with me and Dee?'

Rose looked shocked. 'Both of you? You're kidding. Seriously?' She turned to Daniel, studied his face. 'Is this true?'

'And he told me that he didn't fancy Fleur,' I said as I watched Daniel to see his reaction. The phrase 'rabbit caught in the headlights' came to mind.

'And me that he didn't fancy Dee,' said Fleur.

I continued to stare directly at Daniel. 'Our secret.'

Fleur did the same. '*Our* secret.'

He looked as if he wanted the ground to open up and swallow him.

'But you told me that you weren't interested in either of my sisters,' said Rose. She looked at me and, when she saw my face, bit her lip. 'Sorry Dee,' she said and turned back to Daniel, 'but . . . Fleur as well?'

'So join the club, Rose. We're just a list of sexual conquests.'

'No.' She shook her head. 'It wasn't sexual with me, it was—'

'But you were seeing Daniel?' asked Fleur.

'I was . . . I was going to explain later. I *will* explain later. Not here.' She was red in the face, flushed. She looked at Daniel. 'Why the lies? I expected more from you.'

Daniel squirmed and took a few steps back towards a pillar, as if he wanted to hide behind it. 'Me a liar? What about you, Rose? And you, Dee? And you, Fleur? All of you have been lying too.'

Rose clenched her fists and shook her head. 'I trusted you, you asshole.'

'And so did I,' I said. This was the man I had shared my bed with for eight months, had experienced intimate moments with, had loved. Where was that man now? Why didn't he step forward and explain?

Behind us, people were still looking in our direction, nudging each other, trying to work out what was happening.

'Since when Dee?' asked Rose.

'December.'

'Fleur?'

'March, but it's over—'

Rose's face flushed even redder. She looked as if she was about to explode. She moved forward and shoved Daniel's chest so that he had to step back to keep his balance. 'Screwing my sisters while acting Mr Nice Guy and telling me I had to find my peace? How could you?'

Daniel bristled. 'I . . . Screwing is a very cold word, Rose. And I never made out I was anything I wasn't. Not to you.'

'But you did to my sisters, so that affects me too. To think that my mother put her trust in you. What would she make of what you've done? She employed you to organize the events of the last months, a list of *her* wishes, intended to bring us closer, but you took advantage of your position. You've destroyed anything Mum might have hoped to achieve with your lies and deception. You've made a fool of her too, and *that* makes me madder than anything. Christ, I could kill you for what you've done. You, you're a . . . a devil in saint's clothing. You . . . you . . . ' Rose lost it and pushed him again, this time with such force that he lost his balance and fell back. He tried to correct himself but toppled towards the pillar, hit his head and fell backwards on to the marble floor. In a second, a line of blood pooled out behind him.

'Oh Christ!' I cried as I knelt down beside him. I looked up. 'Somebody call an ambulance.'

Several people in reception came running over and stood over Daniel. Rose looked as though she was going to faint and a man stepped towards her to catch her.

'And the police,' a women called.

Fleur already had her phone out. She made the call then also knelt over Daniel. 'Oh shit,' she said. 'Shit, shit, shit.'

29

Dee

Sunday 14 August

I reached into my bag and took out a bottle of Rescue Remedy. I unscrewed the top, tilted my head back, squeezed four drops on to my tongue and swallowed. It was my second dose since I'd arrived at the police station an hour earlier. I always kept some on me in case of emergencies – good for stress, panic and fear, though I'd rarely used it before the events of the last twenty-four hours.

I glanced out of the window in the waiting room of the police station and could see Fleur, on her way in. I wasn't happy to see her. I was still reeling from yesterday's revelations. So many lies had been told, my own included, and now this nightmare situation with the police. *How had it come to this?* I asked myself. *Things like this don't happen to people like us.*

'Morning,' said Fleur when she reached the area where

I was sitting on a bench. 'Have you seen this?' She handed me a newspaper. The man behind the desk glanced up then stared, as men always did when Fleur made an entrance. I felt like a bag lady in comparison; my clothes were crumpled and my hair uncombed. I groaned and shook my head as I scanned the headings in the paper. 'No.'

'Not on the front page. Third. I marked it for you.'

'Do they mention Rose by name?'

'I'm afraid so.'

I sighed. 'What about us?'

'No and, thankfully, no photos. I bought all the papers first thing and have been through them. The story's only made this one. Have a read and I'll go and get us some coffees. Any sign of Rose's solicitor yet?'

I was surprised that Fleur was even speaking to me, never mind offering to buy drinks. I was torn. Part of me wanted to refuse coffee; I wanted Fleur to know she couldn't get round me that easily. I felt so hurt; I wanted to turn away and never speak to or see her again, and had expected her to feel the same – both of us in a sulky silence like when we were teenagers and angry with each other. But we were in this together. Fleur, Rose and me. Plus I was gasping for a drink, and a caffeine hit might make me feel more ready to face the day. 'No to any sign of the solicitor yet, and the police won't tell me anything. They just said to wait,' I replied. 'Yes to coffee.'

'Back in a jiffy,' said Fleur. She turned around and headed back out through the station door, leaving me to read the article in *The Chronicle*.

ASSAULT AT PEACE CONFERENCE

Swami Muktanand (87) spiritual leader, announced his retirement from public life and teaching at a press conference held by the Heaven on Earth cult yesterday. He later boarded a flight back to India where he intends to retire to a remote part of the Himalayas.

Two of his followers were involved in a fracas at the London hotel where the conference was held. Daniel Scott (50) was assaulted by attendee and publishing executive, Rose Edwards (52), in the hotel grounds. A witness claimed to hear her threaten to kill him. He was later taken to Rathbone Hospital where his condition is said to be critical. Mrs Edwards was seen to be distraught when arrested. She is currently being held pending enquiries.

I put the paper aside. What a joke. If the situation had been different, I might have laughed. Heaven on Earth wasn't a cult, it was a centre where people went to meditate, and Rose was not one to assault anyone – not normally.

'So what now?' asked Fleur when she returned ten minutes later with cappuccinos.

I crossed my arms and legs in the hope that my body language might convey the fact that I wasn't letting her back in and was still angry with her. 'We wait,' I said. 'Any news on how Daniel's doing?'

'Still out for the count,' said Fleur. 'I've a mind to go to the hospital and put a pillow over his face if he wakes up.'

I shushed her and glanced at the policeman behind the desk, who was still checking Fleur out when he could.

'Remember where you are, you idiot. *I* know you're not serious, but *they* might not.'

'Who says I'm not serious?' said Fleur. 'I should have trusted my first instinct and had nothing to do with the creep. I'm so—'

The conversation was cut short by the appearance of Rose's solicitor.

'I blame Mum,' I said as I got up to greet him. 'If it wasn't for that stupid condition in her will, none of us would be in this mess.'

'Have you seen her? Is she OK? What's happening?' asked Fleur.

'She's not here,' he said. 'Her husband asked me to give you these.' He produced two envelopes which he handed to Fleur and me.

'But is she all right?' I asked.

'Mr Edwards just instructed me to give you the letters,' he said, 'and to say you can call him when you've read them.'

He didn't hang around so I sat down, ripped open my envelope and began to read.

'Dearest Dee,

'So many secrets, so many lies, and you must still be wondering what I was holding back from you. Truth is, I have cancer.' I heard Fleur gasp beside me as she read her copy.

I found out the day of the reading of Mum's will. That's why I had to dash off. I didn't tell you then because I didn't know then what the prognosis was. It wasn't good. A grade IV cancer. Incurable. How did I manage to keep it a secret, you might be thinking? Cancer's a peculiar thing. You can feel well for a long time before you go downhill, but it has caught up with me and I will no longer be able to carry on as I did.

I had hormone treatment for three months, then when that failed to work, three months of chemotherapy, which did seem to work, then a further three months, which didn't.

Then came my options. To go back to a hormone treatment, which has fewer side effects than the chemotherapy, or to continue with a different kind of chemo. I feel like King Canute, trying to stop the ocean, and have grown tired. For the last few months, I have been on hormone therapy again, but with my prognosis, it is limited in what it can do. So I have made my decision and have stopped all treatment.

I want my last days to be at home. The Macmillan nurses can do that for me. I've had enough of being prodded, scanned and poked. I want to be at home with my loved ones, in my own bed with my own pillows. You know what I'm like Dee . . .

And Daniel? What was he in all of this? Not so bad. Not what you thought. I bumped into him one afternoon at the solicitors. I found him easy to talk to. Someone independent of friends and family. He helped me accept what was happening. With his swami, he has helped me find some peace of mind, and for that I am grateful. I honestly had no idea that he was seeing both of you and had formed relationships with you. When I heard that, I felt rage, because love is a precious and delicate thing and I felt he abused his position and Mum's trust as well as ours. I didn't mean to hurt him, though, and pray he makes a recovery.

I am sorry I lied to you – or not so much lied as didn't tell the truth. I hope you understand. When I first heard about my illness, I chose not to tell you because what could you say? What could you do? Nothing. It was hard enough telling Hugh, Simon and Laura and dealing with their reactions. I wanted the time with you and Mum to be as normal as it could be. Ha! That's a joke. Mum's kicking the bucket list was mad from the start, but hey, we did have some good times, didn't we? I pray you'll forgive me for not having told you. Despite our differences, I do care for you both. As Mum did, I want you to be happy. I was going to tell you both yesterday, but when I realized what Daniel had been doing, I felt so helpless and hopeless and angry with him and that took over.

Yes, there's a part of me that's afraid, of course there is, but another part that now has this heightened sense of appreciation. It has made me more mindful, which is why I liked that session with Andrew. Ever since I had my diagnosis, perhaps because I know I will be leaving soon, I see so much beauty in the world: children playing, a careworn face in a queue at a supermarket, a flower, a sky, an expression in Hugh's eyes. This world is beautiful. At times, I have been filled with love, inexplicable and dazzling. We live on earth, this jewel in deep space, it's incredible. The human body is amazing, and before I was always rushing so fast, I never saw it. I never experienced my life, not really; I was always thinking what I had to do next.

At other times, my fears overwhelm me, but the meditation has helped. Inside all of us – yes, even me – there is a place of peace that is always there, always still, regard-less of the circumstances, and the swami helped me to find it. I have also learnt that the most important thing in this world is love. Love of friends or family.

I wish you both the very best, take time to stop and appreciate what you have and where you are, like that poet, W.H.Davies said, "A poor life this if, full of care, We have no time to stand and stare." So make sure you do.

Hugh will fill you in on the rest later,

With love, your sister,

Rose X

I looked over at Fleur. She was pale, her expression so sad. 'I . . . ' I was speechless, numb with shock and distress.

'How could I have got it so wrong?' Fleur asked.

'*We* got it so wrong, not just you.'

'I had no idea.'

'Me neither.'

'Christ. Poor Rose.' Fleur moved over, put her arm around me and I turned and hugged her. We were both in tears.

'And her poor family,' I said.

We sat for a few minutes in silence, both trying to take in the enormity of what was happening.

It was Fleur who spoke first. 'Dee, I am so *so* sorry about everything.'

'Me too, but I can't bear to think what she's been going through and I never knew. I just thought the worst, that she was just being Rose – secretive, manipulative—'

'We think we know, don't we? We think we know about other people's lives, what's going on with them, but we don't.'

I got out my phone and called Rose's number. Hugh picked up.

'What can we do?' I asked.

'You've read the letters then?'

'We have. I'm so sorry, Hugh. How is she?'

'Not doing great today. Yesterday was too much for her. An ambulance took her from the station early morning, took her to a hospice. Simon's with her. We're doing everything we can to get her home.'

'Can we go to her?'

'Not yet. We need to get her settled, ask what she wants. She wanted you to have the letters in case . . . ' He took a sharp intake of breath. 'We don't know how long she will have now. Weeks? Months? I'll be in touch. I promise.'

30

Dee

Sunday 14 August, 10 a.m.

I called the hospital as soon as we got out of the police station.

'I'm calling about Daniel Scott,' I said as Fleur and I headed towards a taxi rank on the main road. 'He was admitted yesterday with head injuries. Is there news?'

'What's your relationship to the patient?' asked a male voice at the other end of the phone.

What could I say? Lover? Not any more. Sister of the woman who put him in there? Probably not. 'Friend.'

'I'm sorry, but we can only disclose information to close relatives.'

'We could lie,' said Fleur, when she saw me shut off my phone then shake my head.

'I think we've had enough of lies, haven't we?'

'Yes, course.' She looked as fed up as I was. 'What shall we do now?'

I had no idea. We were standing at the taxi rank and it was a grey, damp morning. I didn't know where to go. The thought of returning to Cornwall felt wrong. I wanted to be on hand in case there was any news.

A taxi drove up and the driver wound down his window. 'Where to, ladies?'

Fleur looked at me. 'Sloane Street,' she said, and opened the back door for me. I climbed in.

'Come home with me,' said Fleur. 'We'll take it from there.'

I hadn't the energy to argue with her. I felt empty, stunned, sad and bewildered. I didn't know who to be worried about most: Daniel, in case his injuries were life threatening, or Rose, whose illness was. Rose. Of course Rose. There had been too many emotions, too many revelations in the space of hours, I couldn't think straight. Daniel and his lies. I'd thought he was the love of my life. Or had I really? Lately I'd felt duplicitous, lying to my sisters and not able to properly communicate with him. That was no real ground for a lasting relationship, and now I knew that I couldn't trust him either – though to his credit, he had kept Rose's secret for her. Now he was lying somewhere in a hospital and I couldn't go to him, didn't even know if he'd want me there. Fleur and Daniel. Although I'd had my suspicions, it came as a shock all the same, and though Fleur kept telling me it meant nothing, to me it did. It belittled what I thought I'd had with him. But it all faded into insignificance now that I knew about Rose. Incurable, she'd said in her letter. I kept repeating the facts in my head but still couldn't take it all in.

Fleur leant over and put her hand on mine. 'Dee, I'm so sorry about everything. I know, too much at the moment, but we'll talk, when you're ready.'

Rose is her sister too, I thought. *And she was lied to by Daniel as well as lied to by me*. 'Do not judge or you too will be judged': that was Mum's last text. I moved my hand so I was holding hers. She squeezed it and we rode the rest of the way in silence.

*

Back at Fleur's flat, she made coffee, ran me a bath, added scented oil, put heated towels on the rail and steered me towards the bed as though I was a sick patient.

'Rest,' she said. 'I'll let you know if there's any news.'

'And you? Are you OK?' I asked.

She shrugged. 'I'll be fine.'

After a bath, I called Anna and told her all that had happened.

'Jesus Dee,' she said, 'I'm so sorry about Rose.'

'Me too, it's too sad.'

'And that bastard Daniel – but, like you, I wouldn't wish him permanent damage. What a lot to go through. Are you going to be all right?'

'What I feel is unimportant next to what Rose must be going through. I'll survive. You know me.'

'What can I do to help? Shall I come up?'

'Thanks, but Fleur's here. Just keep looking after my cats and that will be enough. I'll call you when there's more news.'

'OK, but just don't close up again. Daniel's just one man. Not all men are like him. Let me know how he is, will you?'

When I'd finished the call, I knelt by the bed and joined

my palms together to pray. 'Dear God, please help. I know I've talked to you before but this time, I'm serious, and not just doing it because my mother asked. This prayer is from me. Please let Rose be OK and please let Daniel make a recovery. Thank you.'

I sat on the bed and eventually lay back and fell into a fitful sleep. I'd hardly slept last night because I'd booked into a noisy and uncomfortable hotel near the police station in Kensington so that I could be near for the morning.

*

After a few hours, I woke to the sound of a phone ringing in the flat. I scrambled into a dressing gown and strained to hear Fleur's muffled voice as I went to find her. I felt adrenalin flood through me when I found her in the living room and listened as she took the call.

'Daniel?' I asked when she'd finished.

She nodded. 'That was Hugh. He called the police and they've heard that Daniel is sitting up and is fine. They're keeping him in the hospital in case of concussion. He told the police that he won't be pressing charges.'

I sat heavily on the nearby sofa. 'Oh thank God. Thank God for him and thank God for Rose. She didn't need to be dealing with a prosecution on top of everything else.'

'And Daniel knew that,' said Fleur.

'What about Rose?'

'Hughie said that she'd like to see us. Not today. They're still getting her settled at home. He gave us a message from her. She said, "Go to the garden."'

'Garden?'

'Go to the garden, finish the list.'

For a moment, I didn't know what she was talking about, then it clicked – the kicking the bucket list. Today's task was to go and look at flowers in a garden, the last thing I felt like doing. I felt like curling up under the duvet and never coming out. I looked at my watch. It was only two o'clock. We had time.

'She's still telling us what to do, so that can only be a good sign,' said Fleur. 'So come on. Let's go and hug a tree.'

*

The clouds had cleared and, outside, the sky was blue. Fleur and I spent the afternoon at Kew Gardens sitting in the sunshine, looking at flowerbeds and talking. And boy, did we talk. I told her all about Daniel, when and how it had started, what I'd felt, how it had been, and she held me at one point when I broke down. She didn't expand on her relationship with him.

'Not because I'm holding back, but because it was just supposed to be a bit of fun, and when it wasn't that any more, I ended it. There didn't seem to be any point in continuing. Even though I didn't think it was going to come to anything with you and him, I still knew you liked him, and I didn't want anything to get in the way of you and me becoming friends again. My relationship with you matters much more.'

It hurt to hear her say her piece, but I understood. She hadn't known about Daniel and me and that was my fault as much as his. 'I'm sorry too,' I said as we headed back to the car park. 'I should have told you and Rose about

Daniel. If I had, none of this would have happened.'

'You mustn't blame yourself and it's not over yet,' said Fleur. 'Nothing's ever over till it's over.'

My love affair with Daniel is over and it's over for Rose, I thought. 'I feel as though I'm floating in a dream where anything could happen.'

'I know what you mean,' said Fleur as she started up the engine. 'Eat your heart out, Alice in Wonderland.'

'Not quite turned out as Mum intended I don't think, do you?'

'Nothing ever does,' Fleur replied as she headed the car out of the car park and towards the main road. 'At least we're all together in our own dysfunctional way. I think she intended that.'

*

In the evening, Fleur found us a bottle of wine and we sat together on the sofa and watched the DVD that Mum had chosen for us. It was about courting rituals in nature, and I watched in awe as a puffer fish made a crop circle, a hundred times its size, resembling a sun mandala, thirteen metres under the seas in Southern Japan. It had perfect dimensions and symmetry and was to lure the female in and provide a place with soft sand for her to lay her eggs.

'Least we don't have to try that hard,' said Fleur.

'Speak for yourself,' I replied.

A male spider came on screen next, doing a tango-style dance to catch his mate. He blew out a huge bubble of stunning beauty, colour and pattern above him.

'Mardi Gras insect style,' said Fleur.

'Pure art,' I commented.

'Except that when they've mated, the female spider eats him,' said Fleur.

'Part of the plan. His body provides food for her young.'

'Least we don't have to do that either,' said Fleur. 'Having seen this, I reckon we've got off lightly.'

I laughed. 'Maybe that's why Mum picked this DVD – to stop us moaning about relationships and count our blessings.'

'Either that or she was saying we need to wear exotic hats.'

'Probably that, knowing Mum,' I said.

*

When the programme had finished, Fleur and I went to our rooms.

'Hello God. Me again. First of all, thanks for Daniel's recovery, if that was you. But please don't forget Rose. She needs your help too.

'I've just watched a DVD with my sister and I have to hand it to you. I know I doubt your existence from time to time, but the DVD made me want to believe. There was creativity that, as an artist, I can only dream of, and yet there it is in nature – endless varieties of colour, pattern and beauty. All hail. Churches, preachers, temples and theology leave me cold, but one David Attenborough programme and I'm a believer. But then I switch to the news or think about Rose and my faith deflates. Such horrors on our planet caused by war, anger and hatred, so many people suffering illnesses and in pain. I have so many questions, God, so much doubt, but that wee fish and his perfect sand mandala make me want to believe that there's something wonderful behind it all. You can't have a painting without a painter, a piece of art without an artist, so surely not a creation without a creator? But where are you? And where's Mum now? The evidence all around us in nature indicates that the hand behind it is one of endless creativity and renewal, so why so much pain and sorrow in our human world? No pressure, just get back to me when you can. Thank you.'

My prayer done, I fell into bed and, this time, slept deeply.

31

Dee

Tuesday 16 August

Rose was sitting up in bed when we arrived at the house in Highgate on Tuesday morning. She looked pale but not unwell. It was hard to believe by looking at her that she had an incurable disease. Tucked up on the end of the bed, fast asleep at her feet, was Clifford.

'You look great,' said Fleur as we took a seat on either side of the bed.

Rose pulled a face. 'I've felt better. You were always such a liar, Fleur . . . Talking of which, I guess you've heard that Daniel is going to be OK.'

'Hugh told us,' said Fleur.

'And what about you two? Are you going to be OK?' asked Rose.

'I'm fine,' said Fleur and looked over at me. 'I'm not so sure about Dee.'

371

'Hit you hard?' asked Rose. 'I'm sorry, Dee. I should have realized that you'd got involved.'

'You both did your best to warn me off.'

'We did.'

'I feel such a fool—'

'Me too. I feel crap. Off shagging Daniel when you were going through this ordeal and we never knew,' Fleur blurted.

'Me too,' I said. 'But forget about us. What about you? Are you in pain?'

She shook her head. 'There have been some side effects from the drugs but it's been manageable. I'll have morphine for when it gets bad.'

'Is there really nothing more they can do?'

'There are other options. More chemotherapy. We've given up on the hormone treatment as that wasn't working.'

'So why don't you try more chemotherapy?' asked Fleur.

Rose sighed. 'I'm done, Fleur. I want some time without it. I know it must be hard to understand, but I knew from the beginning that what I had was incurable. I've discussed it at length with my doctors and Hugh and I really don't want to talk about it any more or defend my position to you or anyone else. I just want some time, even if it's a short time, when I have some quality of life. Drug free, treatment free, even if it's just for a few weeks. For this last year, I've felt like I've been trying to hold back the inevitable and it's beginning to catch up with me. I'm tired. I've done my raging at the dying of the light and all that. I don't like feeling like this, and it isn't going to get any better. I'm ready. I want to go now, slip away quietly when the time comes.' She saw that Fleur was crying. 'Come on, we all have to die of something sooner or later.'

Fleur sniffed. 'Well that's cheered me right up.'

'I'm tired of fighting, of being strong. I would never have chosen this thing but it is happening. I know, hard to understand, but I've had a year of it, time to come to terms – as far as anyone ever can. It's new to you, you've barely had time to take it in, but I want to give in to it, to let go. Let me go.'

I reached out and took her hand. 'What can we do, Rose?'

'We want to be here for you,' said Fleur.

Rose grimaced. 'I was thinking about that. What can you do? The nurses are wonderful. They can do a lot but it's afterwards that I worry about. Could you, would you stay in touch with Hugh and Simon and Laura?' Her voice cracked and she grew tearful when she said their names. 'They're the hardest part. Knowing that I will miss so much. I won't be there on their big days, their graduations, their weddings, the birth of their children, my grandchildren,' she took a sharp intake of breath, 'so would you be? Be there for me, my sisters, their aunts to represent me. Keep an eye on them. Invite them to your houses. Be family.'

'Of course. I'd be glad to,' I said.

'Me too,' said Fleur. 'Anything. But what about you? What can we do for you?'

'The nurses will be here to take care of me when I need it, and Hugh is taking leave from work.'

'But surely we can do something?' said Fleur.

'I know what we could do,' I said. 'Mum's list.'

'The kicking the bucket list?' said Rose. 'What are you suggesting? We get Beverly over? Another colonic? No thanks.'

'No, not those parts, but other parts. We could take care

373

of your food, maybe not Ottolenghi every night but I can cook. We could get you whatever you want.'

Fleur got the idea immediately. 'And I know some of the best masseurs in London. If you felt like it, I could book them to come over. Reflexology, head massage, whatever you want. I'm sure it would be nice to have a different kind of touch to—'

'I know what you mean Fleur.' She looked thoughtful. 'Maybe that would be nice. I feel tired, more and more every day, but what I dread sometimes is in my mind. It might be nice to have distractions so it's not all about this thing that is taking over and slowly destroying my body.'

'We could take you out if you can manage it, a visit to a garden, somewhere lovely. You tell us and we'll do it.'

Rose gazed out at the garden. 'Maybe.'

'Or we could bring a garden to you if you're not up to it,' said Fleur. 'We'll bring flowers.'

'Let us look after you, Rose,' I said. 'Let us do whatever we can to ease things for Hugh, Simon and Lucy and the nurses. We can cook and care for them too.'

'"Love in action," as Martha said,' Fleur added.

Rose sank back in her cushions and looked out of the window. After a while, she turned back to look at us. 'Do you know, I think I'd like that.'

*

And so we did. We cooked for her and her family. We fed Clifford the cat, who spent most of his time close to Rose, her constant companion. We organized relaxing treatments.

We burnt healing oils on a burner so the room smelt clean and not of sickness. We played her music. Fleur even had the idea to send her quotes from time to time, like Mum had, but Rose threatened to shoot her if she continued, so we gave up on that one.

Some days, she was bright and bossy as ever. Other days, she slept. As the weeks went on, she slept more and more and her appetite was like a bird's.

Tuesday 30 August

A letter came from Mr Richardson addressed to Rose, Fleur and me. I ripped it open to find a note from the solicitor saying that Daniel had left for the States to run the Heaven on Earth centres over there. He had asked that a letter be passed on to us. I called Fleur and we took it up to Rose's room.

'A letter from Daniel,' I told her. 'Apparently he's gone to live in the States.'

'And no doubt conquer another bunch of gullible women over there,' said Fleur.

'Can you read it out?' Rose asked.

'Of course,' I said and began.

Good day Rose, Dee, Fleur.

I've had four attempts at writing my side of the story but I don't seem to possess the skills to express the depth of emotions that have floated through me this year.

Each flower has its own beauty: remember your mother

wrote that to you? I saw that. Each of you, individual, beautiful in your own way. Am I to be blamed because I saw that beauty and couldn't resist?

I was not who you thought I was and regret if that caused you pain. I reflected back to you your needs and desires at the time and became what each one of you wanted.

I have long been fascinated by the mystery of the feminine, the goddess within each woman. I have always thought that women have more to offer the world than the male linear solutions, and I can't help but stand at the altar and worship that goddess in her many shapes and forms. And you were three such goddesses, each so vibrant in her own way.

I know Dee and Fleur may say, no, Daniel was just a horny fellow with no self-control – and who could blame you? Maybe there's some truth in that, but you chose me as much as I chose you. Women are and continue to be a mystery to me and I wanted to find out more about you all, to consume all I could and be consumed, to be what you wanted me to be.

By the time you get this letter, I will have gone, and you will probably think good riddance. But let me say this: you all have influenced me greatly and for that I am grateful. To have met you and spent time with you was a gift, and in that I include your mother, Iris. I hope, in time, you can forgive me and go some way to understanding that, in different ways, I loved you all. You are amazing strong women I am grateful to have known. Rose, so cerebral, a thinking, strong woman. Fleur, visually so beautiful and fun to be with. And Dee, gentle soul with such a big heart and so much love to give. I felt honoured to have spent time with you.

As you probably noticed, words were never my strong point, and I have no more to say except goodbye, thank you, and may you each find your peace, especially you Rose.

With love
Daniel

Fleur, Rose and I looked at each other.

'What a load of complete and utter bollocks,' said Rose.

We all cracked up laughing and it felt really good. As I watched them, I realized that I'd never felt closer to either of them, or loved them both more. *And there it was, at last, the moment that Mum had wanted us to have*, I thought.

Fleur took the letter and looked it over. 'And can you believe it? He's put an email address on it.' She turned to me. 'Dee, you mustn't contact him. Understood?'

I saluted her. 'I'll put it in the bin.'

I got up and went down to the kitchen where I put the letter in my bag. I wanted to read it again. Maybe I would reply. To have heard his side wasn't enough. I wanted closure.

September

Rose's decline accelerated. Most of her days and nights, she spent sleeping, rarely talking, and it got to a point where she was so weak that she could barely leave her bed. Fleur and I tended her as well as we could in between visits from the Macmillan nurses, washing her, preparing simple meals, just being there holding her hand as she slept.

'What's it like in there?' I asked her one day when she was doped from the morphine.

'Quite nice,' she slurred and squeezed my hand.

'Floats them out with the fairies sometimes,' said the nurse when I spoke to her later.

*

Rose died peacefully on 28 September at three in the morning, with Hugh by her side.

32

Dee

Saturday 1 October

On the train back to Cornwall, I gazed out of the window.

I thought about Rose. How she'd finally let Fleur and me into her life and the three of us had grown close. It was sad that it took her having cancer to bring that about, but at least we'd been there to say goodbye, tell her that we loved her and mean it.

I thought about my daughter Lucy. So far away. In her last text, she'd said she was sorry I'd had to go through so much on my own but, in the end, it hadn't been like that. I'd had Fleur. Lucy had no sisters, but she did have me, and although our relationship hadn't been close, that could change. When she was growing up, Andy had always let her do what she wanted when she had visited him, whereas I was the one she'd lived with day to day. I told her to get up for school, do her homework, be in by eleven. No wonder she rebelled against me. But we were older now. I had enough money now to visit her more often, and also to pay for her to come back to the UK whenever she wanted. Mum's list and legacy had shown how deeply she cared. I wanted to show Lucy the same, let her know she was cherished, always had been. That thought gave me comfort.

I thought about Mum. Her loss still felt as raw as the day it happened. I was coming to accept that it always would. In some cases, time does not heal, it's too deep a wound, but perhaps I would get used to living with it.

And then Daniel. There had been no goodbye, so all I was left with were memories that were tainted in the light of his lies. What happened with him felt unfinished. I thought about what I'd have liked to say to him if I'd had the chance, so got out a scrap of paper and started writing. When I was satisfied with what I'd written, I got out my laptop and transferred my words on to an email.

> I summon you to the highest court
> The court unseen
> Where the law is unspoken
> Love reigns supreme.
> This court for you
> No divorce or alimony
> From our liberated age, twenty-first century
> For your damage is not apparent
> Your weapon was not seen
> Yet it broke a spirit
> And maimed a trust
> So an innocence lost
> Only a fleeting sadness in the eye

Symptom of a deeper sorrow
To show we'd ever touched.
I summon you to this highest court
I pray that it will grant me healing
I pray that it will show you its law.
PS: Please don't reply. Dee.

I took a deep breath and pressed Send.

I walked through the ticket barriers at Plymouth and out into the grey, damp afternoon. Returning home felt bleak. I would buy my house but it was a hollow victory. I felt sad there would be no one to share it with.

There on the pavement outside the station was Michael Harris. He stepped forward when he saw me.

'Are you waiting for someone?' I asked.

'Yes. You. I hope you don't mind. Anna was going to come but something came up so I said I'd meet you. Car's this way.'

Despite my mood, I was glad he was there, a decisive presence to take over and get me home. I followed him to the car and he held open the door for me.

'I . . . Anna and Ian filled me in on recent events,' he said as we drove away from the station. 'Some of them anyway.'

'Don't lie. I know Anna. She'll have filled you in on everything.'

'She's a good friend and cares about you very much.'

'I know.'

'First let me say how sorry I am about your sister Rose. That's why I wanted to be here, for someone to be here.

Anna was going to come but her car was in being serviced and wasn't ready. I asked if I could take her place.'

'That's very kind of you.'

'Have you eaten?'

'Not much of an appetite lately.'

'Anna's cooking something for when you get back. She's missed you.'

'And I her.'

Soon we were on the road heading for the Torpoint ferry and back to Kingsand.

'I had a thought when I was driving to meet you,' said Michael. 'I wondered if you'd like to go up to Rame Head on the way back. I remember you telling me what peace you find up there.'

I thought about it for a moment then nodded. 'I think I would. Thank you.'

We drove on in silence the rest of the way and, when we got to Rame, he parked the car and we made our way up to the top. Michael helped me up the last steps, then we went and sat at the front of the church and gazed out to the horizon. Like the first time we'd been up here, we didn't say anything, and I was grateful for that. So much had happened. So much loss in a year: Mum, Rose, Daniel. Mum's sweet and kind plan to set me up on the road to happiness. Mum and Rose both gone to that place where I cannot follow.

Out in the distance, a peregrine falcon flew into sight, hovered, then soared in front of us. After a minute, it was joined by another. They swooped, rose, floated on the air currents, swooped again – an aerial ballet on an astral plane, Mum and Rose, dancing in space.

Then they were gone and there was just sky and sea, sky and sea, sky and sea. Tears came, brimmed over, fell. *Dear God*, I prayed quietly, *wherever they are, wherever you are, look after them.*

After twenty minutes, I looked over at Michael. 'Hey, I'm freezing.'

He turned and smiled. 'Me too. Let's go.'

I got up and he came over to stand beside me.

'Thank you for this,' I said.

'You're welcome Dee. You've had a tough time of late. Just let me know if I can do anything.'

I took his hand. It felt warm and reassuring. After a few moments, he let go of my hand and put his arm around me. I leaned into him and we stayed that way for a further few moments. In the distance, storm clouds were clearing, a ferry blew its horn. We turned and walked back down the hill.

ACKNOWLEDGEMENTS

With many thanks to:

My agents, Christopher Little and Emma Schlesinger, for their continued support, encouragement and invaluable guidance.

My editor, Kate Bradley, for her passion for the book and for making the process so enjoyable.

All the team at HarperFiction for their warm welcome and for getting behind the book with such enthusiasm.

Elliott Brenman for his professional input. Much appreciated.

Claire Ward, for her original and inspired cover.

And lastly, my husband Steve, for his endless patience in listening to me talk out plot points and characters at every opportunity, especially in the car when he couldn't escape.

Iris had her own ideas about what could make a person happy, so instead of the usual Q&A, we're only going to ask you one question, Cathy Hopkins – what would your Ten Steps to Happiness be?

Warghhh. Oh God. No idea. That's the million dollar question isn't it? It's so random. For example, you can be on a beach on a paradise island and feel miserable. You can be in the middle of a crowded city on a rainy day and feel fantastic for no reason at all – so I guess it's down to state of mind as much as anything. As Iris says in the book, you've got to do all you can to help that – eat right, exercise, be creative, meditate etc., but ultimately you have to accept that happiness comes and goes.

Some years, external forces are the cause and tough times can be thrown at you – enforced change, illness, stress, death of loved ones, redundancy, heartbreak. It can be hard to maintain any level of real happiness. Other years, the rollercoaster ride of life starts to go up again and good things happen; you feel happy and hopeful again.

So many factors can influence how you feel. A lot of it is to do with contrast too – for example, you feel happy to get home when you've been away. You may feel happy to be going away when you've had a long period at home. Happy to be cool when you've been hot, happy to be warm after you've been cold. A quiet time after a busy time, a busy time after too much quiet. Contrast.

I also think that happiness comes from having something to do – a project and reason to live, whether that be a family, a home, a career; I think having a purpose can be a major contributing factor to happiness.

But if I was pushed to give an answer, I'd say letting go of a lot of stuff can help too – all of which I don't necessarily do but know I should.

So, my Ten Steps to Happiness. Here goes:

1) Let go of worry. Easy to say, hard to do. You can do what you can about a situation but worrying about it is a waste of time and energy because it isn't going to help or change things, not one little bit except to make you feel miserable. So do what you can to help the person or situation but don't worry about it. I've spent weeks/months/years worrying, mostly about things that never happened. So step number one, stop worrying. (And now I will worry if this is good way to start my ten steps . . .)

2) Let go of blame – whether it be your parents, your upbringing, your family, your partner, your job or whatever it is that you think is making you unhappy.

If you're unhappy with something or someone, take steps to change the situation. We always have choice in life so take responsibility for your own happiness and don't blame someone else for the lack of it. OK, so you might have had a difficult start, unsupportive family or difficult work colleagues but it's too easy to blame that. Better to consider your options and move on. Choose to be happy. Ultimately, whether you're happy or not is down to you. You have to create your own happiness.

3) Let go of people you've outgrown or bring you down. Nurture your real friends and the people whose company uplifts or inspires you. Good friends means many happy times so plan times with people whose company you enjoy and look forward to and let go of the ones who offload on you or moan all the time, and the one-way-streeters where you do all the running. If people don't make an effort to be in your life, don't try so hard to be in theirs, it's not worth it. Your real friends will seek you out, keep up with what's happening with you and be there when the times are tough. There's that saying – if you want a friend, be a friend – so if you feel you haven't got any, get out there and make some, join a book club, a choir, whatever your interests are, then invite the people you meet and like over. Be a friend.

4) Let go of the need to always be right. Try to see the other person's point of view, learn to listen, be kind. Makes you feel a darn sight better than being angry.

5) Let go of the need to be in control. You can't control everything and if things don't go according to plan, it

can make you feel bad. So learn to let go and go with the flow. Though I do find that always having a book in my bag helps enormously; when appointments are running late, I can read, if the train is diverted, I can read, if the hairdresser is backed up and I have to wait, I can read.

6) Let go of self-criticism and feeling you have to be perfect. Sometimes we don't need anyone or anything to make us unhappy, we can do it to ourselves – you're too fat, too old, too young, too immature, your bum's too big, your breasts are too small, you're too tall, too small, not talented enough, too old, too young, not this or not that. I am ace at this, like there is a demon in my head that loves to find fault. Learn to accept yourself as you are. There's only one of you, one mould, you're unique, magnificent, perfect as you are. And while you're at it, let go of criticizing or judging others too. Everyone has their story. Maybe they're different or don't think like you do. Let them be. Maybe they were rude or short with you – so maybe they just had some bad news. Who knows? Not you or me.

(This doesn't apply when watching *Strictly Come Dancing* or *The X Factor*, when part of the fun is shouting insults at the TV.)

7) Let go of anger and complaining. It's boring to listen to and it's draining to dwell on negativity. Yes, so much is sometimes not right in the world, from the public news to more personal issues. But ever spent a day with a grumpy person? One of those glass-half-empty people? Exactly. Take time to look at the beauty in the world and focus on that. Smell a flower, look at the

sky, the stars, a bird in a tree, read about the many amazing and inspiring people who are being creative and generous and working so hard for the good of the world and the people in it. Other stuff is happening all around us besides what's on the news. I wish they'd have a good news section so we'd get more of a balance. It's not *all* bad out there and focusing on the negative only creates fear and worry. I'm not saying don't listen to the news as it's important to be aware of what's happening and it's true that there is some anger and hatred from people whose aim is to cause suffering, but there are millions and millions and millions more people who want a peaceful world and believe in kindness, love and helping others.

8) Let go of needing to impress anyone. It's liberating. The best become the best by being themselves so don't try and copy anyone or be anything you're not. No matter what you do or how you act, some people will never get you or where you're coming from, so relax, be yourself and you'll find the ones who do get you. Let go of worrying what people think of you – they'll either like you or they won't.

9) Let go of working too hard – make time every week to go somewhere and do something that lifts your soul. That might be a visit to an exhibition or a garden, a trek in the mountains, time with a friend or time alone with a book or a piece of music. Make it happen. Make time for yourself and what you enjoy. As the saying goes, life isn't a rehearsal. We only get one crack at it so don't waste it all working to create a lifestyle that you never get to enjoy. Time-manage playtime into

your schedule. (I should really take note of this. I can spend days glued to my desk, especially when writing a first draft.)

10) Let go of believing that happiness lies in the past or future. The past is a closed book, no going back there, the future is an unopened curtain and the show hasn't started yet. The only time that's real is the here and now, so try and spend your time in it, looking, listening, feeling, touching, being.

Finally, I'd like to include a piece of writing I saw when I was sitting in the osteopath's waiting room and wondering what I should write for the 'Ten Steps to Happiness'. I glanced up and saw it pinned to the wall. Curiously, I used to have it on my wall back in the 1970's when I was a student. I think it says it all.

Desiderata by Max Ehrmann

Go placidly amid the noise and haste, and remember
    what peace there may be in silence.
As far as possible, without surrender, be on good terms
    with all persons.
Speak your truth quietly and clearly; and listen to others,
even to the dull and ignorant; they too have their story.

Avoid loud and aggressive persons, they are vexations to
    the spirit.
If you compare yourself with others, you may become
    vain and bitter,

for always there will be greater and lesser persons than
     yourself.
Enjoy your achievements as well as your plans.

Keep interested in your own career, however humble;
it is a real possession in the changing fortunes of time.
Exercise caution in your business affairs, for the world
     is full of trickery.
But let this not blind you to what virtue there is;
many persons strive for high ideals,
and everywhere life is full of heroism.

Be yourself. Especially do not feign affection. Neither be
     cynical about love;
for in the face of all aridity and disenchantment it is as
     perennial as the grass.
Take kindly the counsel of the years, gracefully
     surrendering the things of youth.
Nurture strength of spirit to shield you in sudden
     misfortune.
But do not distress yourself with dark imaginings.
Many fears are born of fatigue and loneliness.

Beyond a wholesome discipline, be gentle with yourself.
You are a child of the universe no less than the trees
     and the stars;
you have a right to be here. And whether or not it is
     clear to you,
no doubt the universe is unfolding as it should.

Therefore be at peace with God, whatever you conceive
    Him to be.
And whatever your labors and aspirations, in the noisy
    confusion of life,
keep peace with your soul. With all its sham, drudgery
    and broken dreams,
it is still a beautiful world. Be cheerful. Strive to be happy.